RACERS

FAST TO THE FINISH!

Also by Deanna Kent and Neil Hooson

Glam Prix Racers
Glam Prix Racers: Back on Track!

Snazzy Cat Capers
Snazzy Cat Capers: The Fast and the Furriest
Snazzy Cat Capers: Meow or Never

For Sam, Max, Zach, Jake, Jackson, Ethan, Ella, Anna, Colton, Charlotte,
Claire, Dean, Mackenzie, Parker, Tanner, Finn, Kristie, Mike, Rich,
Kerri, Kim, Rob, Ophelia, Oscar, our parents & parental types, friends,
librarians, and everyone who believes that sparkle and
teamwork make the world more wonderful.

Feiwel & Friends
An imprint of Macmillan Publishing Group, LLC
120 Broadway, New York, NY 10271
mackids.com

Library of Congress Control Number: 2022900624

First edition, 2022
Book design by Neil Hooson and Elynn Cohen
Illustrations by Neil Hooson
Feiwel and Friends logo designed by Filomena Tuosto
Printed in China by 1010 Printing International Limited, Kwun Tong, Hong Kong

ISBN 978-1-250-26542-5 (hardcover) / ISBN 978-1-250-26543-2 (ebook)

1 3 5 7 9 10 8 6 4 2

Attention, Glittergear Island racers and fans!
Zombies with zambonis are not usually terse,
But Zyah says stealing books will result in a curse.
Your sparkle will vanish without a trace,
And you will never (ever, ever) win a Glam Prix race.

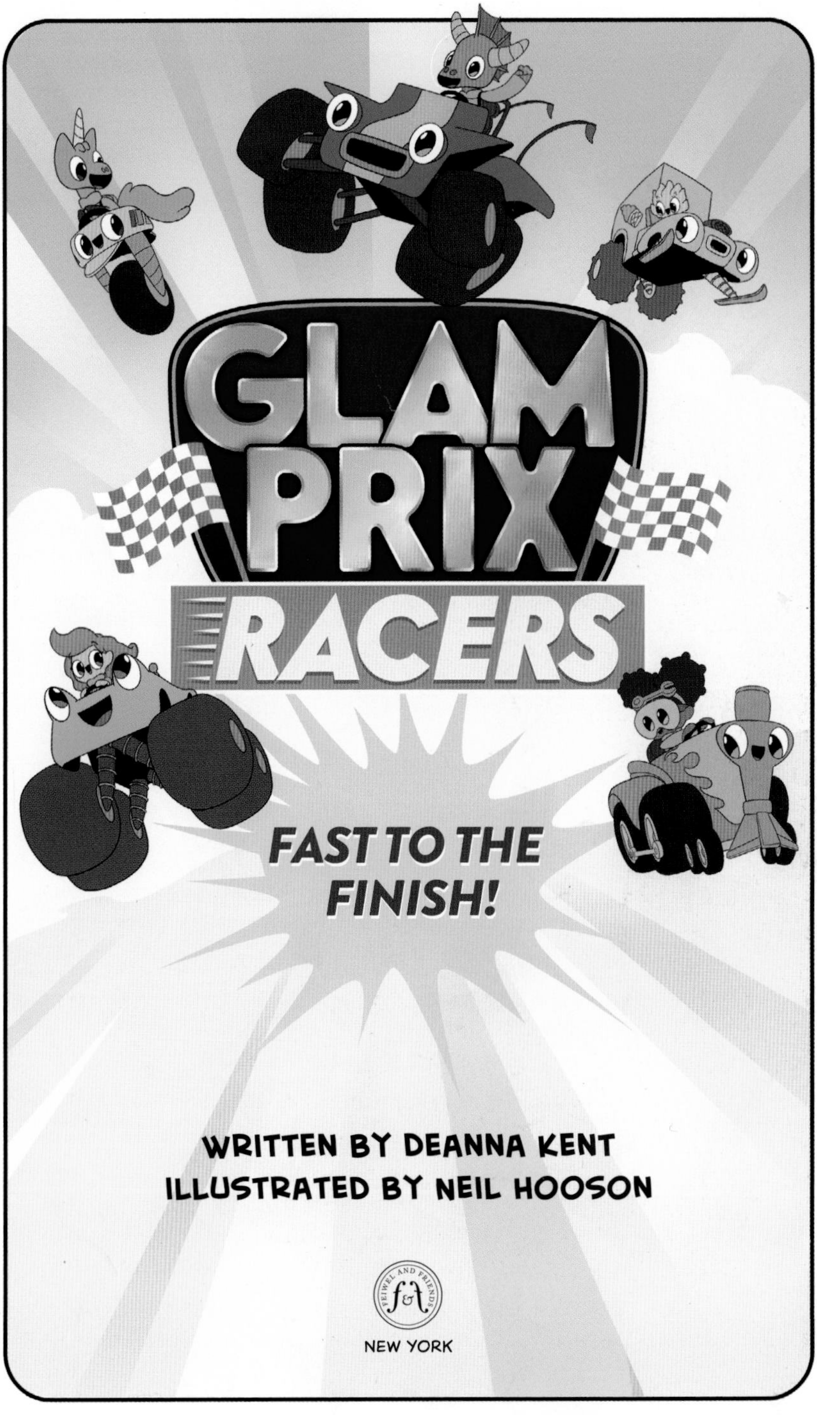

GLAM PRIX RACERS

FAST TO THE FINISH!

WRITTEN BY DEANNA KENT
ILLUSTRATED BY NEIL HOOSON

FEIWEL AND FRIENDS
NEW YORK

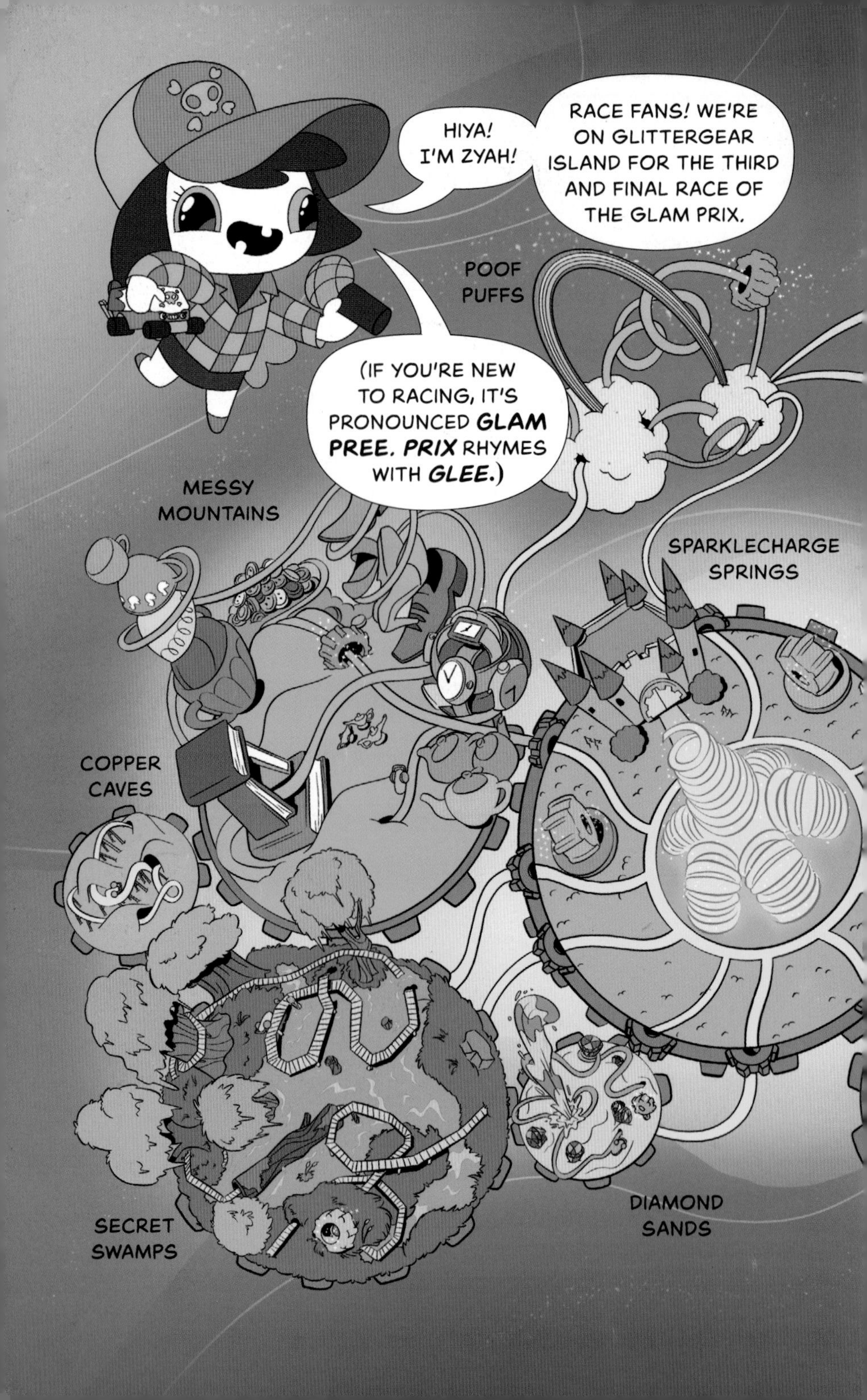
HIYA! I'M ZYAH!
RACE FANS! WE'RE ON GLITTERGEAR ISLAND FOR THE THIRD AND FINAL RACE OF THE GLAM PRIX.
(IF YOU'RE NEW TO RACING, IT'S PRONOUNCED **GLAM PREE. PRIX** RHYMES WITH **GLEE.**)
POOF PUFFS
MESSY MOUNTAINS
SPARKLECHARGE SPRINGS
COPPER CAVES
SECRET SWAMPS
DIAMOND SANDS

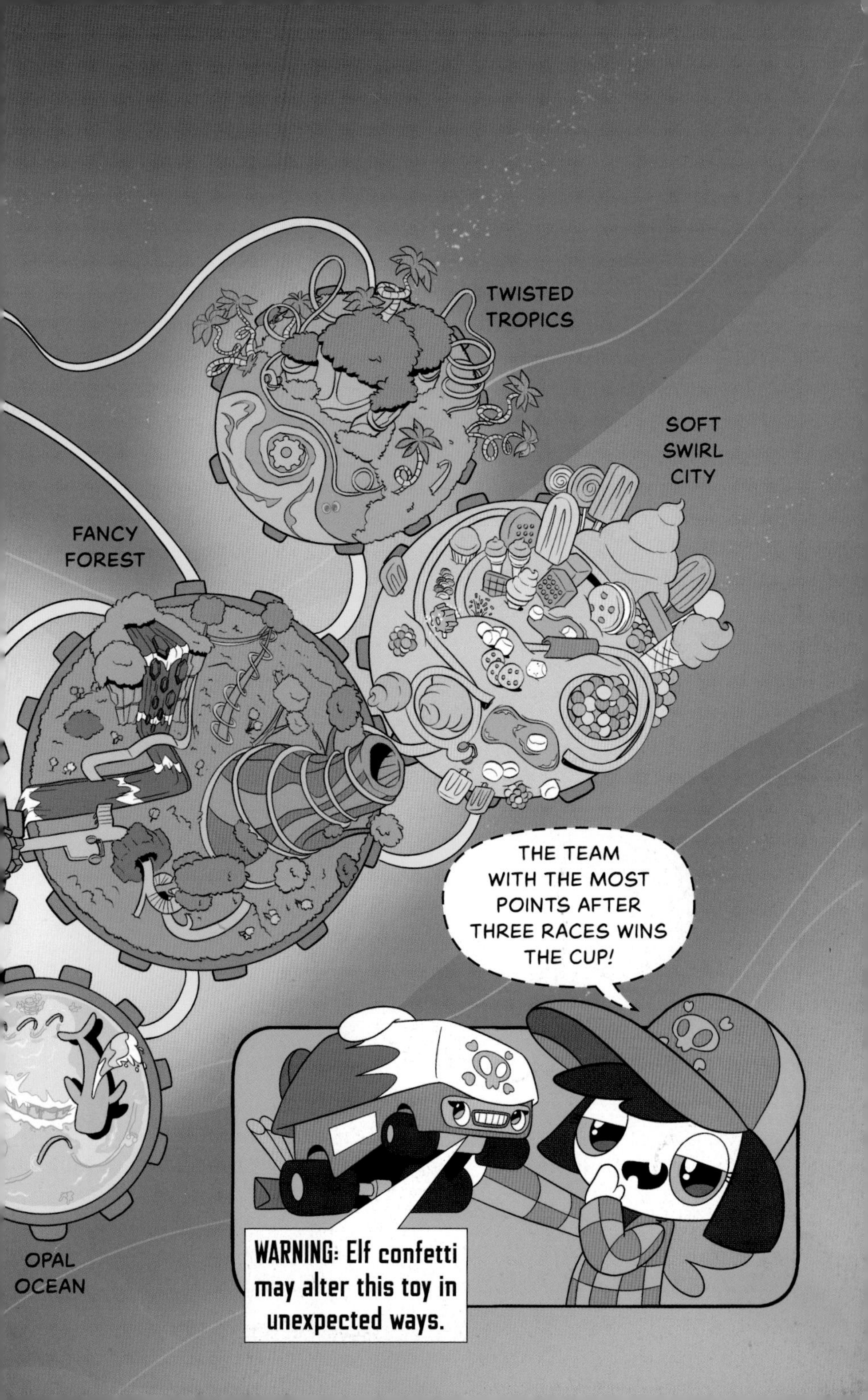
TWISTED TROPICS
SOFT SWIRL CITY
FANCY FOREST
THE TEAM WITH THE MOST POINTS AFTER THREE RACES WINS THE CUP!
OPAL OCEAN
WARNING: Elf confetti may alter this toy in unexpected ways.

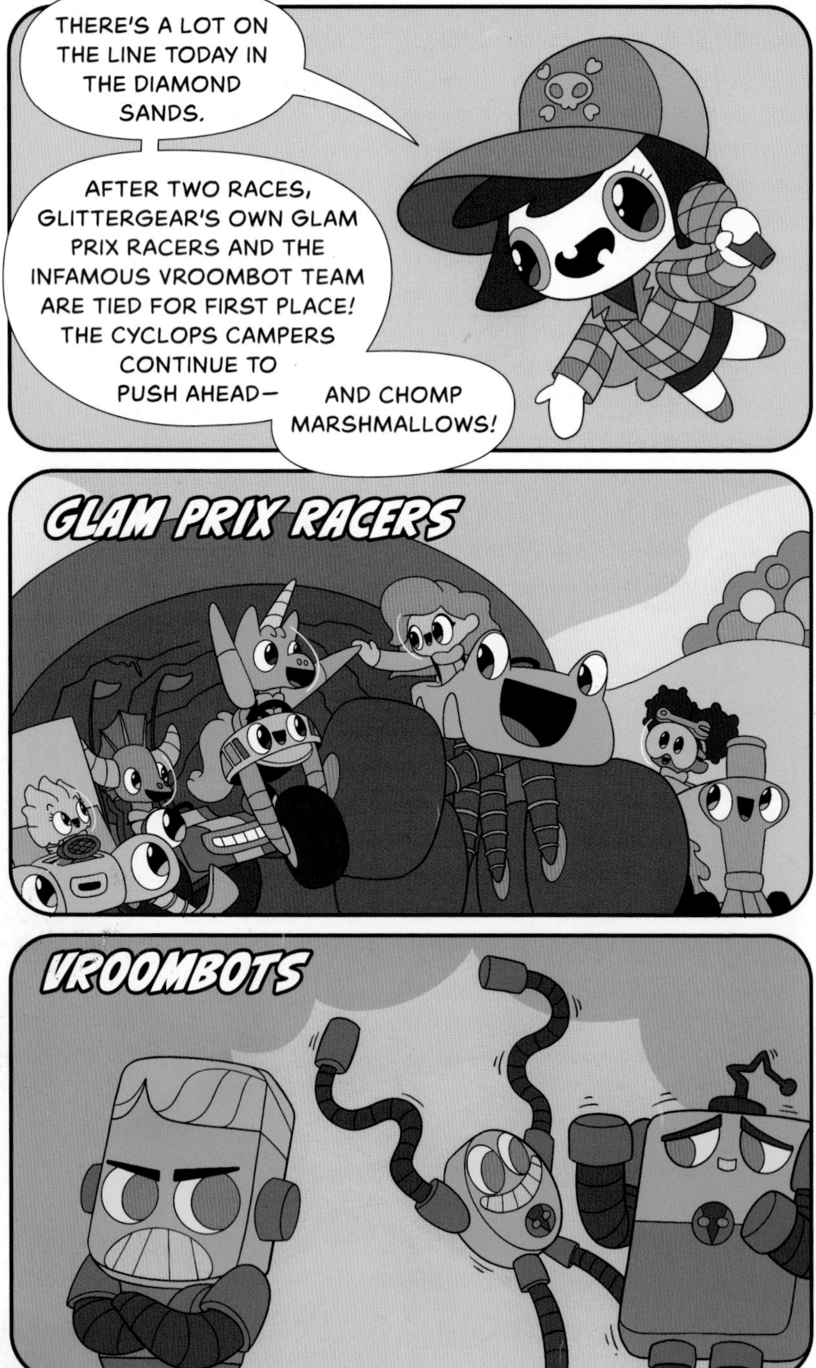
THERE'S A LOT ON THE LINE TODAY IN THE DIAMOND SANDS.
AFTER TWO RACES, GLITTERGEAR'S OWN GLAM PRIX RACERS AND THE INFAMOUS VROOMBOT TEAM ARE TIED FOR FIRST PLACE! THE CYCLOPS CAMPERS CONTINUE TO PUSH AHEAD—
AND CHOMP MARSHMALLOWS!
GLAM PRIX RACERS
VROOMBOTS

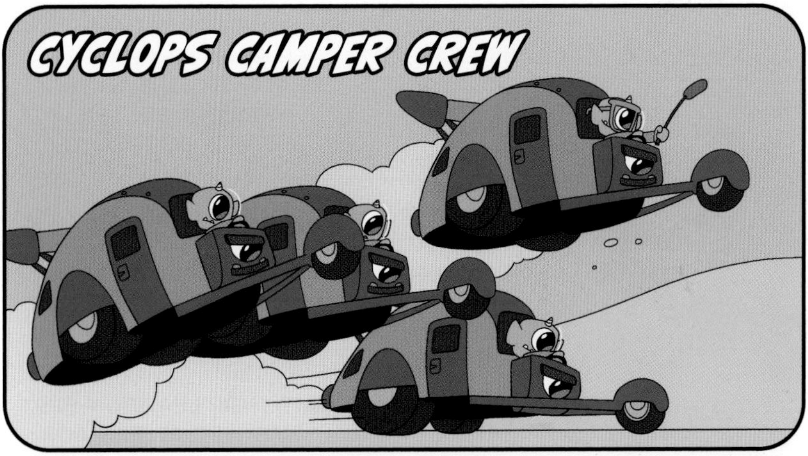
CYCLOPS CAMPER CREW

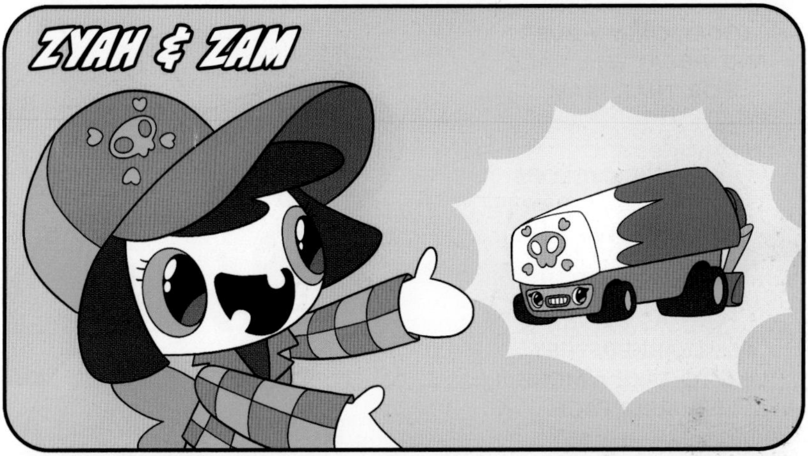
ZYAH & ZAM

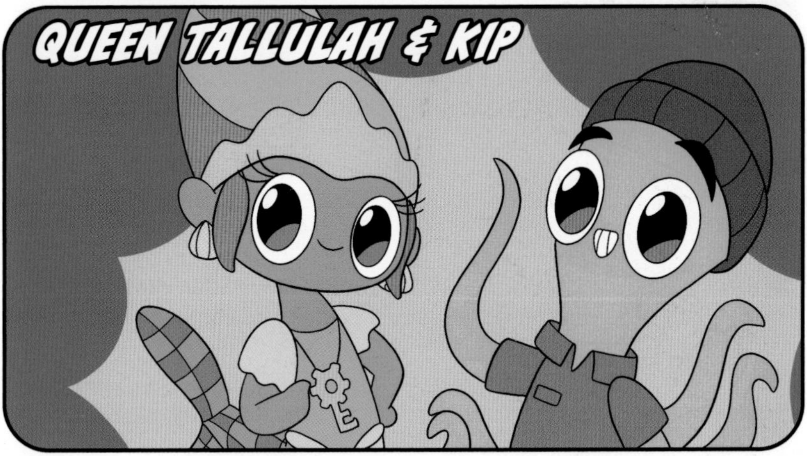
QUEEN TALLULAH & KIP

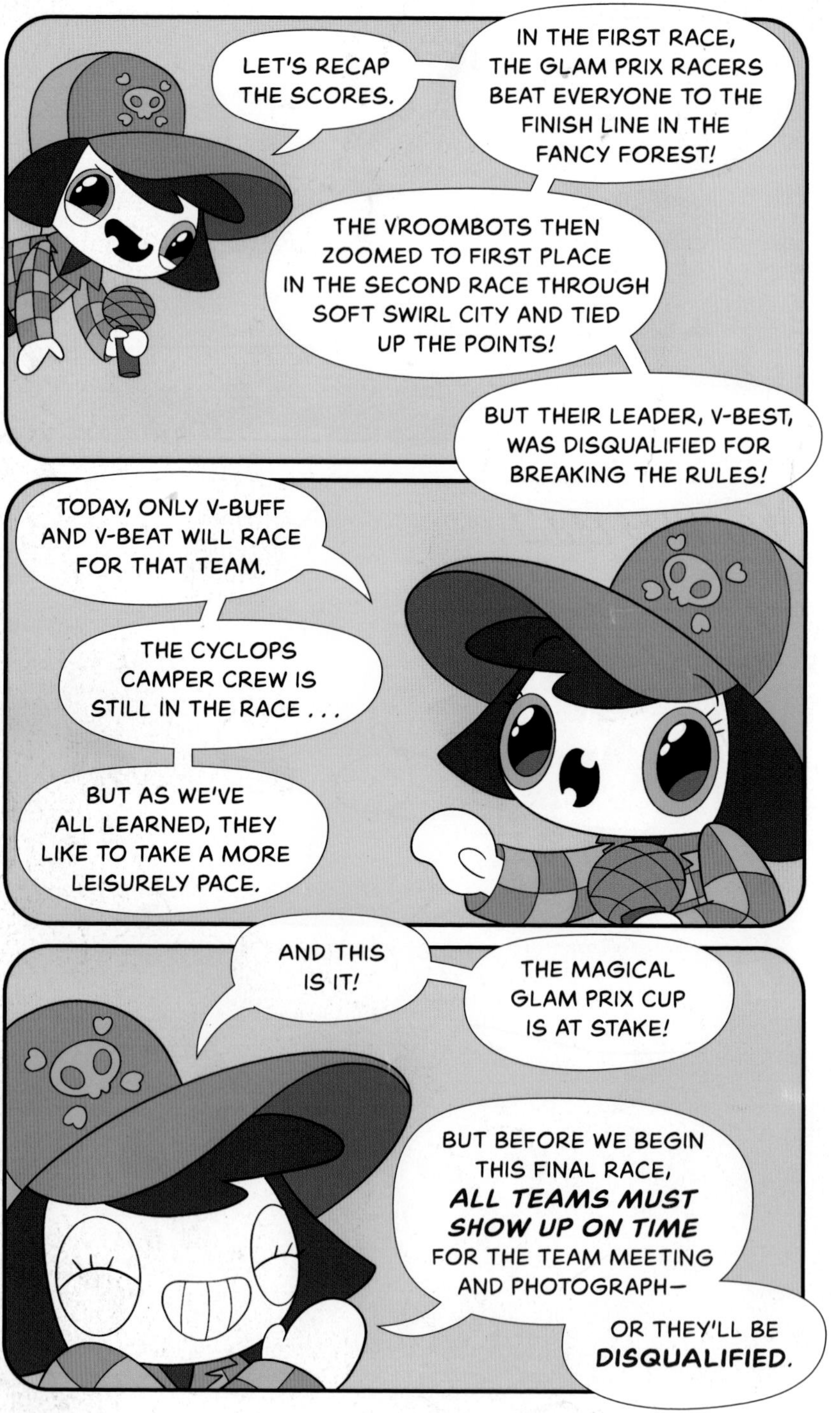
LET'S RECAP THE SCORES.
IN THE FIRST RACE, THE GLAM PRIX RACERS BEAT EVERYONE TO THE FINISH LINE IN THE FANCY FOREST!
THE VROOMBOTS THEN ZOOMED TO FIRST PLACE IN THE SECOND RACE THROUGH SOFT SWIRL CITY AND TIED UP THE POINTS!
BUT THEIR LEADER, V-BEST, WAS DISQUALIFIED FOR BREAKING THE RULES!
TODAY, ONLY V-BUFF AND V-BEAT WILL RACE FOR THAT TEAM.
THE CYCLOPS CAMPER CREW IS STILL IN THE RACE . . .
BUT AS WE'VE ALL LEARNED, THEY LIKE TO TAKE A MORE LEISURELY PACE.
AND THIS IS IT!
THE MAGICAL GLAM PRIX CUP IS AT STAKE!
BUT BEFORE WE BEGIN THIS FINAL RACE, ***ALL TEAMS MUST SHOW UP ON TIME*** FOR THE TEAM MEETING AND PHOTOGRAPH—
OR THEY'LL BE **DISQUALIFIED**.

CHAPTER 1:
DOUBLE TROUBLE

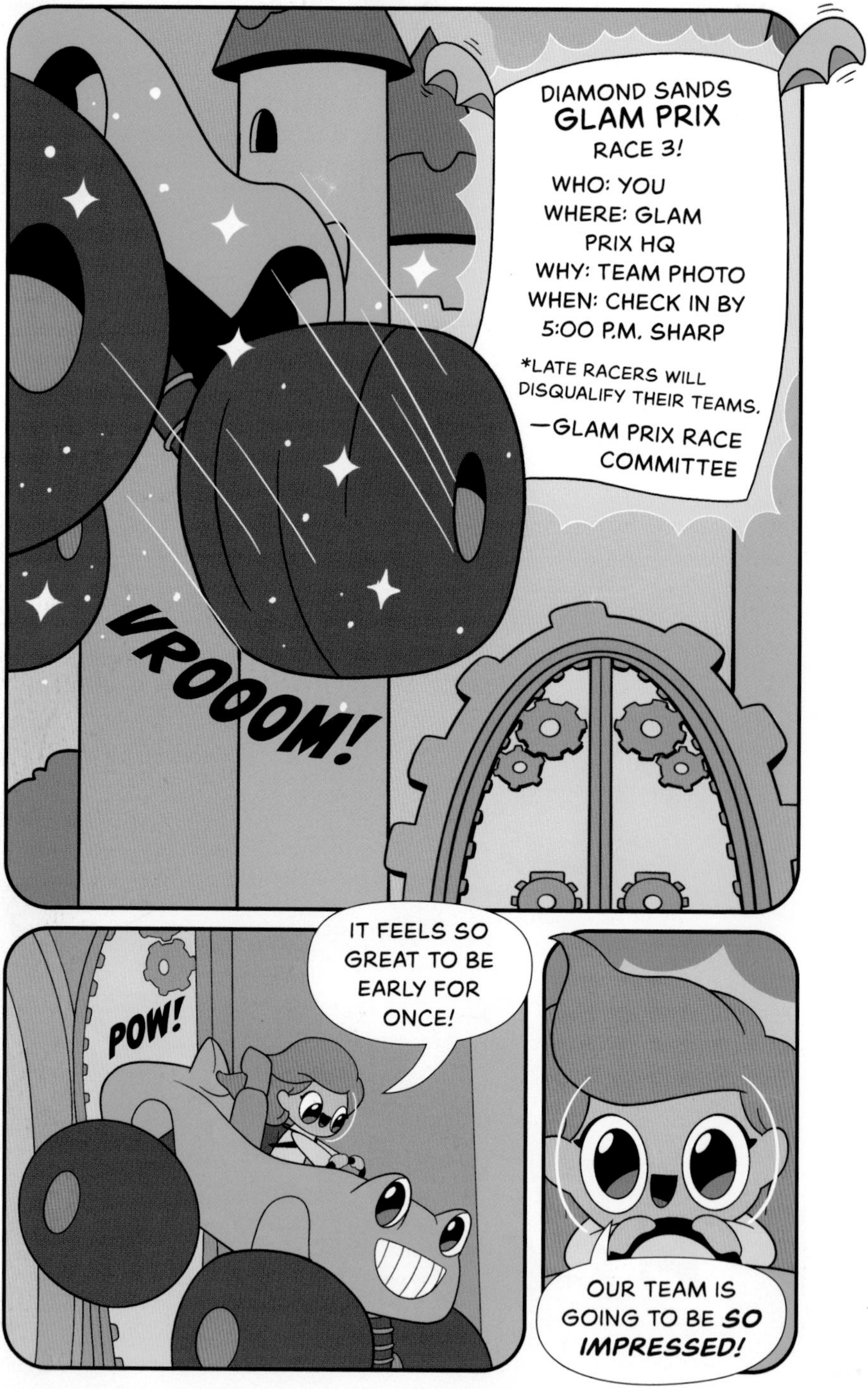
DIAMOND SANDS
GLAM PRIX
RACE 3!
WHO: YOU
WHERE: GLAM PRIX HQ
WHY: TEAM PHOTO
WHEN: CHECK IN BY 5:00 P.M. SHARP
*LATE RACERS WILL DISQUALIFY THEIR TEAMS.
—GLAM PRIX RACE COMMITTEE
VROOOM!
POW!
IT FEELS SO GREAT TO BE EARLY FOR ONCE!
OUR TEAM IS GOING TO BE *SO IMPRESSED!*

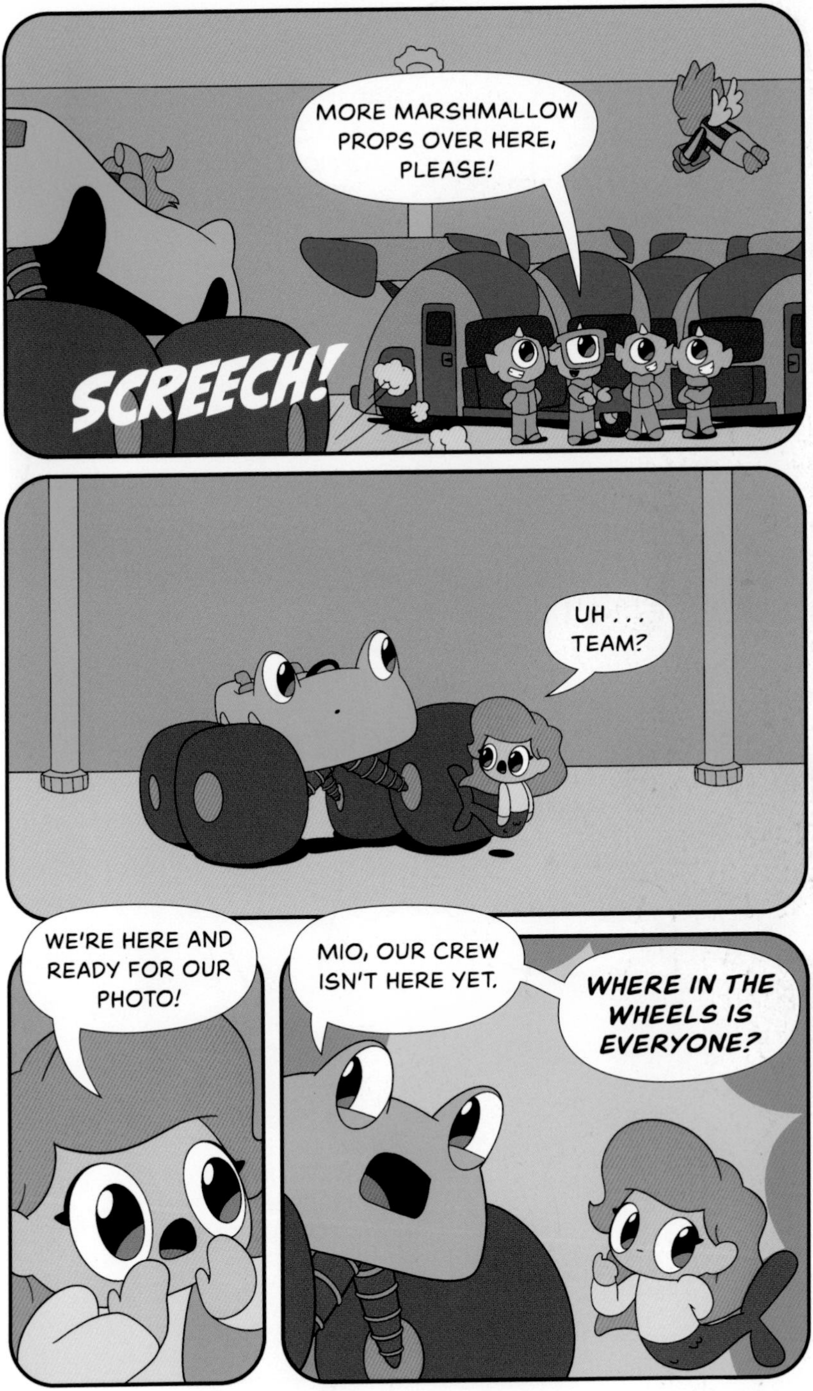
MORE MARSHMALLOW PROPS OVER HERE, PLEASE!
SCREECH!
UH . . . TEAM?
WE'RE HERE AND READY FOR OUR PHOTO!
MIO, OUR CREW ISN'T HERE YET.
WHERE IN THE WHEELS IS EVERYONE?

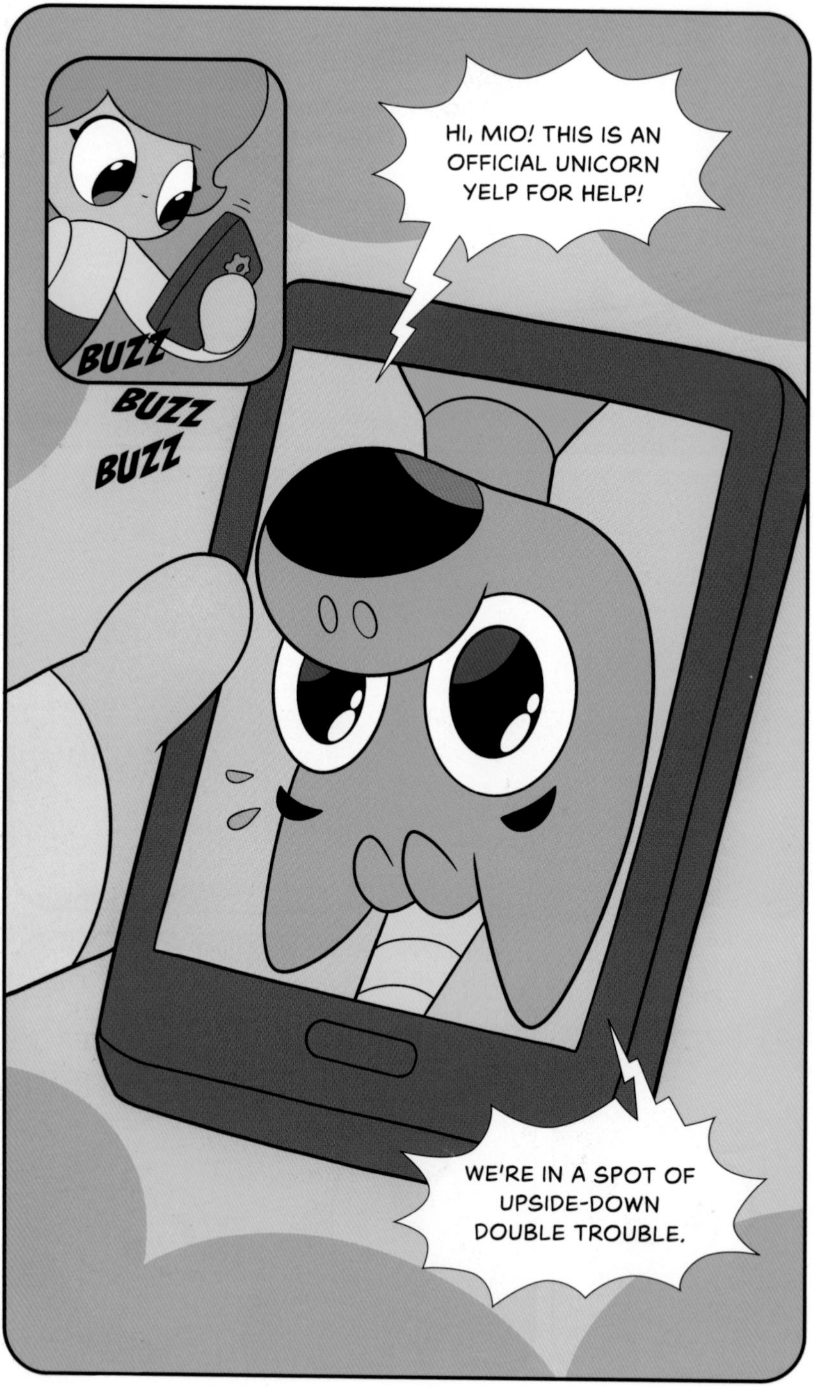
BUZZ
BUZZ
BUZZ
HI, MIO! THIS IS AN OFFICIAL UNICORN YELP FOR HELP!
WE'RE IN A SPOT OF UPSIDE-DOWN DOUBLE TROUBLE.

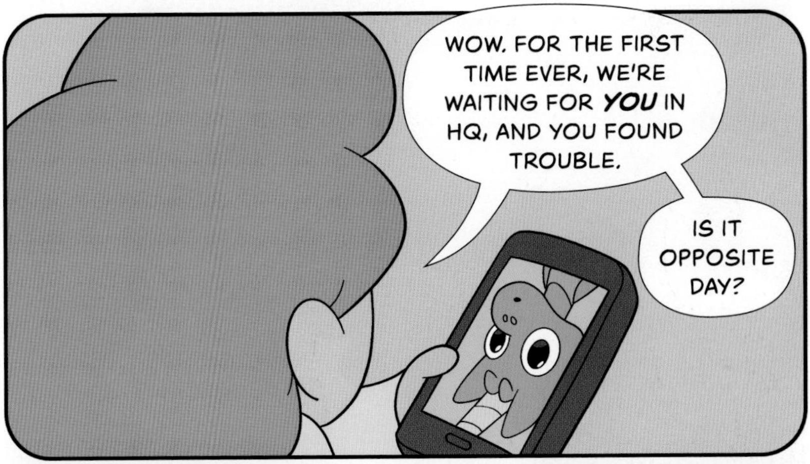
WOW. FOR THE FIRST TIME EVER, WE'RE WAITING FOR *YOU* IN HQ, AND YOU FOUND TROUBLE.
IS IT OPPOSITE DAY?

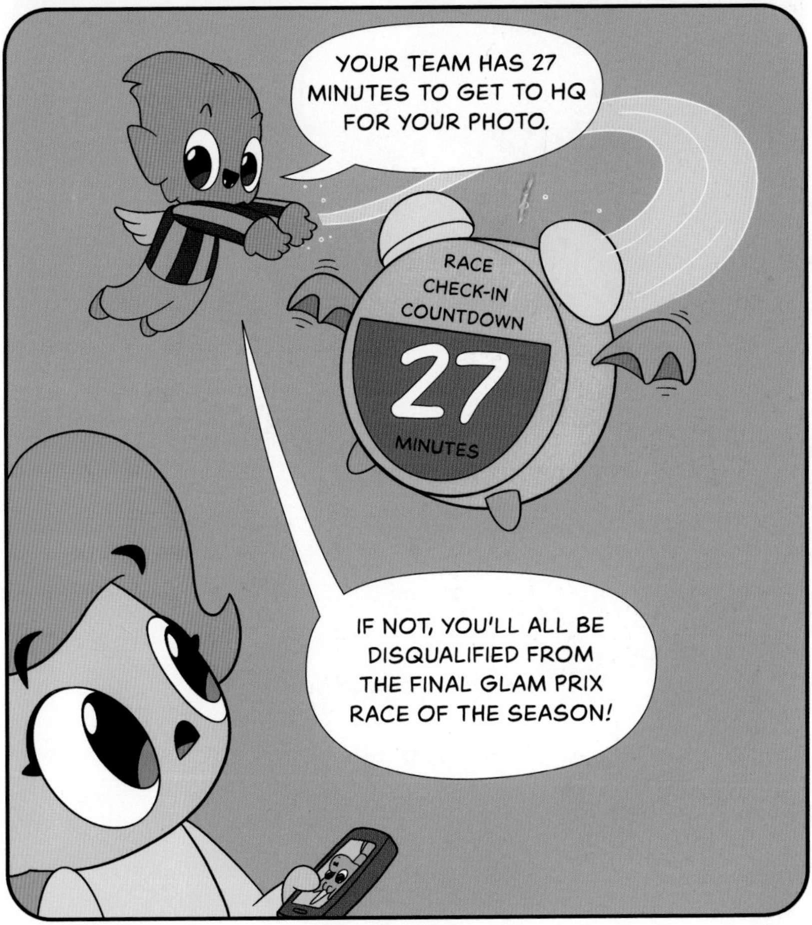
YOUR TEAM HAS 27 MINUTES TO GET TO HQ FOR YOUR PHOTO.
RACE CHECK-IN COUNTDOWN
27
MINUTES
IF NOT, YOU'LL ALL BE DISQUALIFIED FROM THE FINAL GLAM PRIX RACE OF THE SEASON!

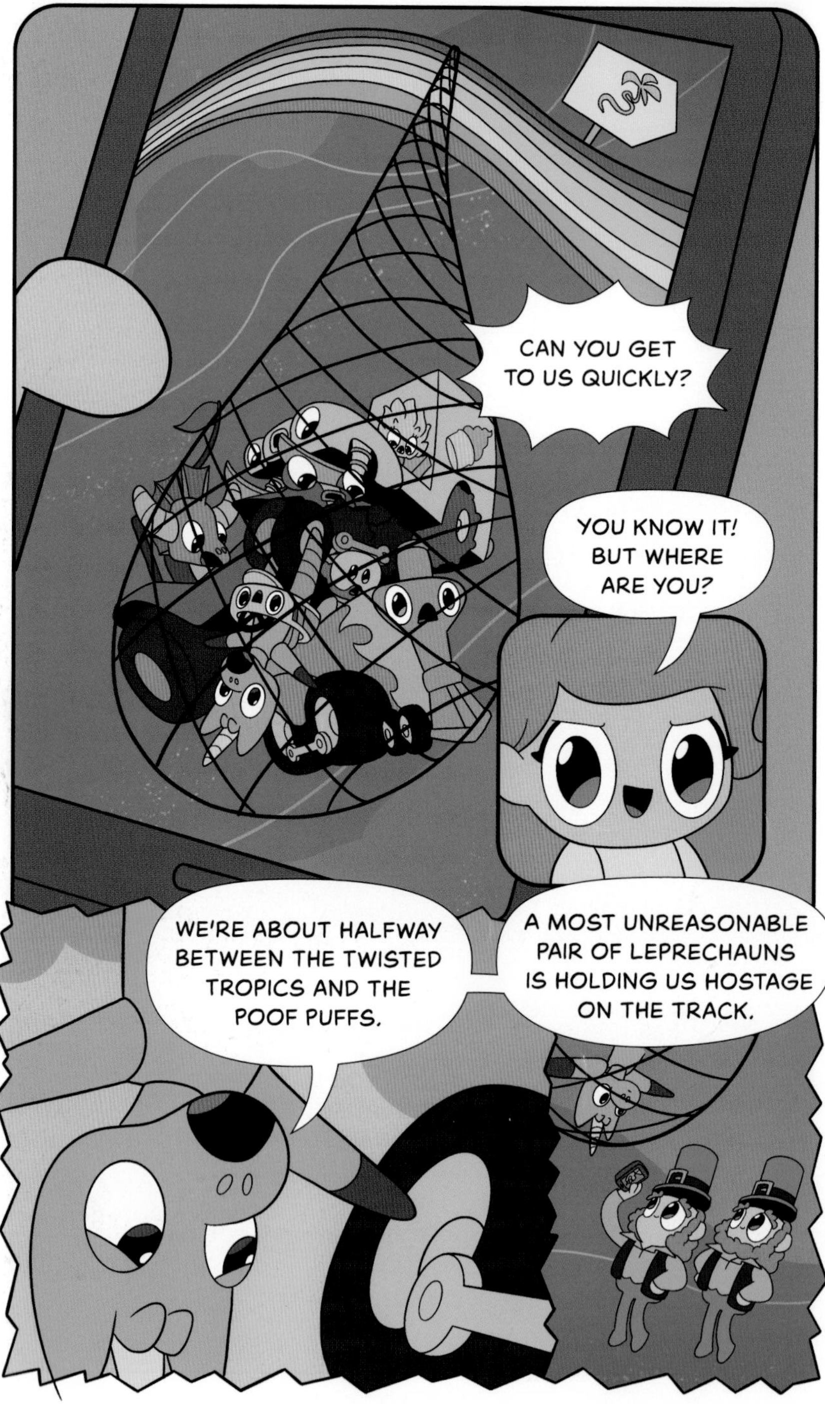
CAN YOU GET TO US QUICKLY?
YOU KNOW IT! BUT WHERE ARE YOU?
WE'RE ABOUT HALFWAY BETWEEN THE TWISTED TROPICS AND THE POOF PUFFS.
A MOST UNREASONABLE PAIR OF LEPRECHAUNS IS HOLDING US HOSTAGE ON THE TRACK.

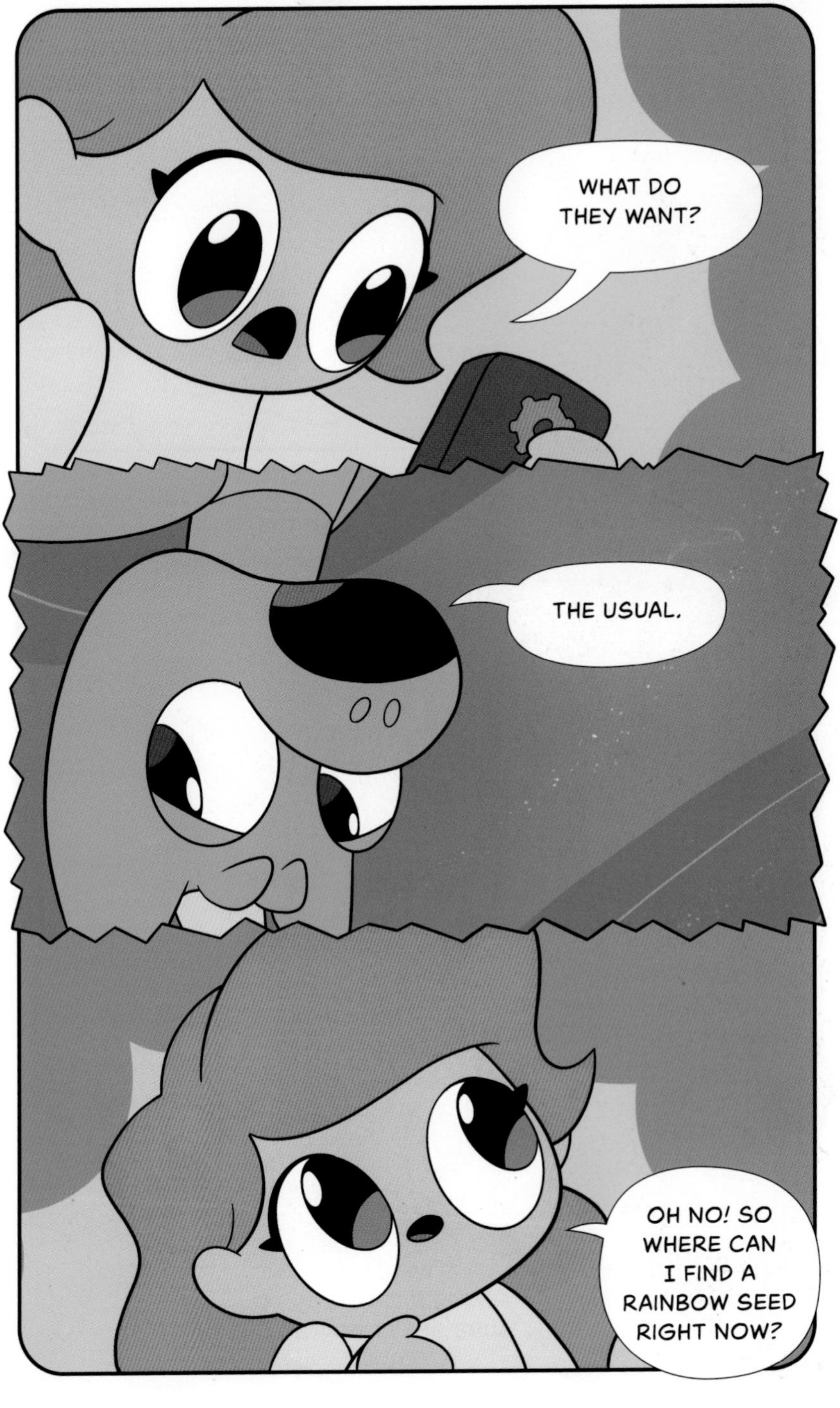
WHAT DO THEY WANT?
THE USUAL.
OH NO! SO WHERE CAN I FIND A RAINBOW SEED RIGHT NOW?

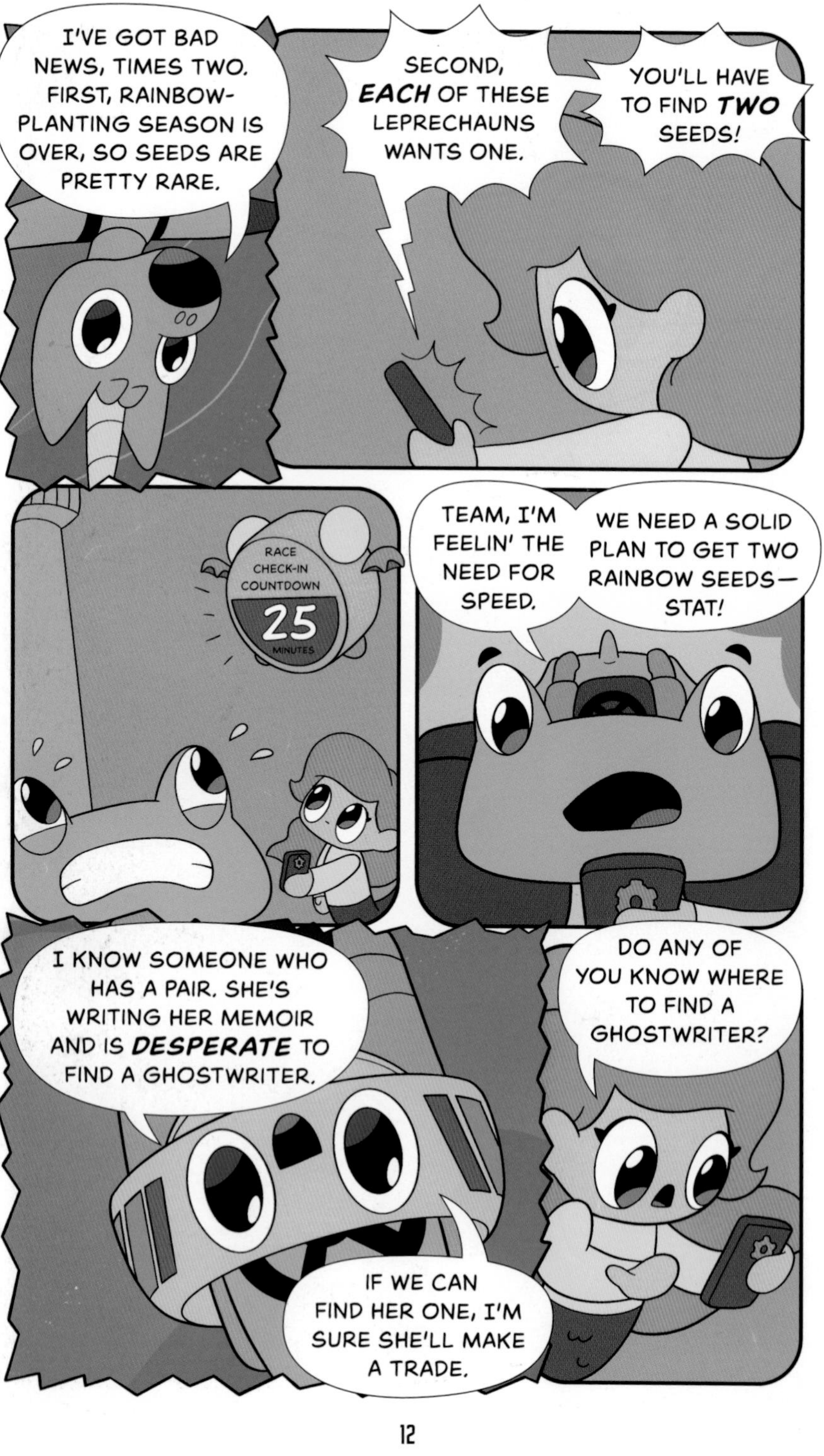
I'VE GOT BAD NEWS, TIMES TWO. FIRST, RAINBOW-PLANTING SEASON IS OVER, SO SEEDS ARE PRETTY RARE.
SECOND, **EACH** OF THESE LEPRECHAUNS WANTS ONE.
YOU'LL HAVE TO FIND **TWO** SEEDS!
RACE CHECK-IN COUNTDOWN 25 MINUTES
TEAM, I'M FEELIN' THE NEED FOR SPEED.
WE NEED A SOLID PLAN TO GET TWO RAINBOW SEEDS—STAT!
I KNOW SOMEONE WHO HAS A PAIR. SHE'S WRITING HER MEMOIR AND IS **DESPERATE** TO FIND A GHOSTWRITER.
IF WE CAN FIND HER ONE, I'M SURE SHE'LL MAKE A TRADE.
DO ANY OF YOU KNOW WHERE TO FIND A GHOSTWRITER?

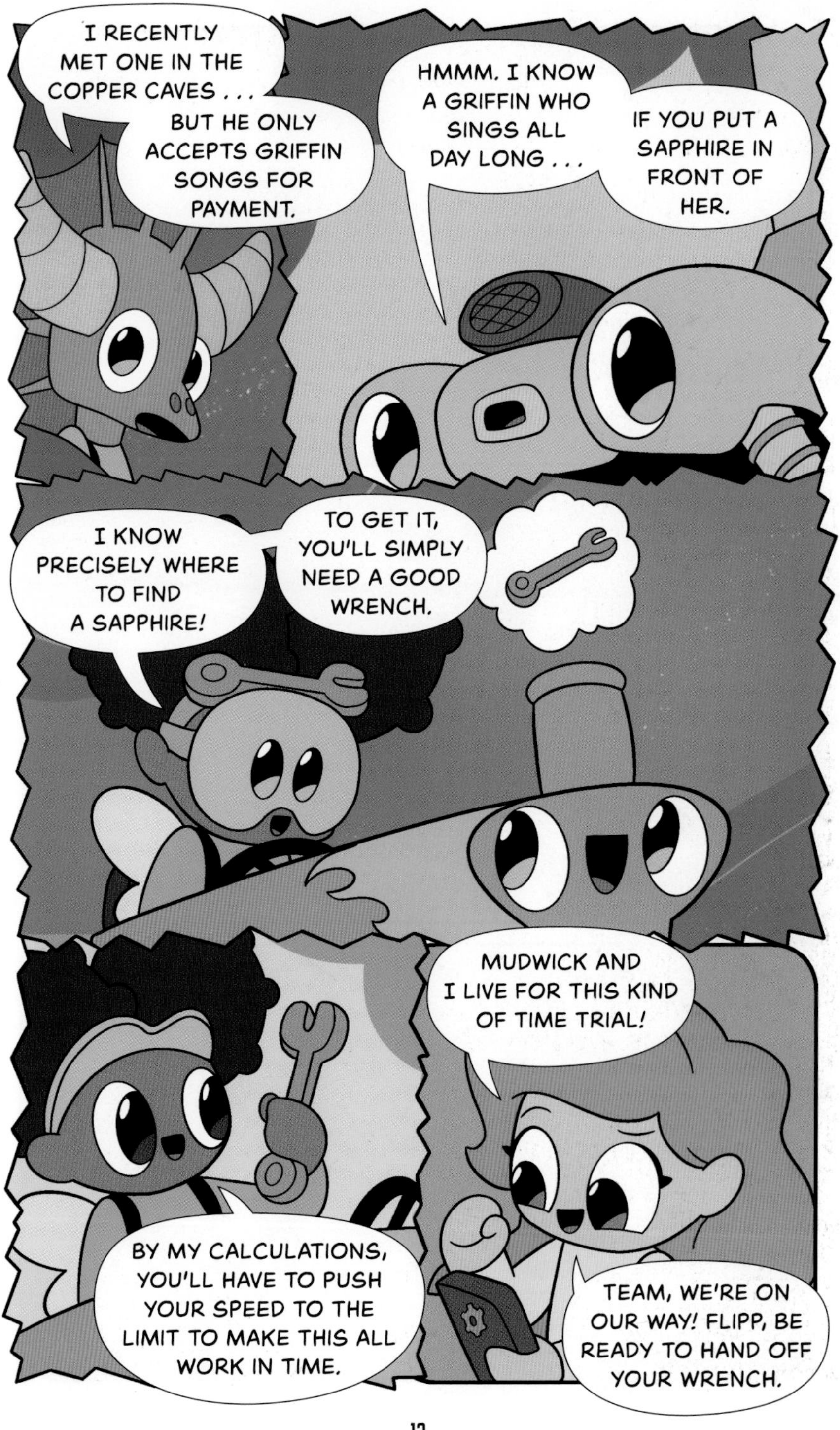
I RECENTLY MET ONE IN THE COPPER CAVES . . .
BUT HE ONLY ACCEPTS GRIFFIN SONGS FOR PAYMENT.
HMMM. I KNOW A GRIFFIN WHO SINGS ALL DAY LONG . . .
IF YOU PUT A SAPPHIRE IN FRONT OF HER.
I KNOW PRECISELY WHERE TO FIND A SAPPHIRE!
TO GET IT, YOU'LL SIMPLY NEED A GOOD WRENCH.
MUDWICK AND I LIVE FOR THIS KIND OF TIME TRIAL!
BY MY CALCULATIONS, YOU'LL HAVE TO PUSH YOUR SPEED TO THE LIMIT TO MAKE THIS ALL WORK IN TIME.
TEAM, WE'RE ON OUR WAY! FLIPP, BE READY TO HAND OFF YOUR WRENCH.

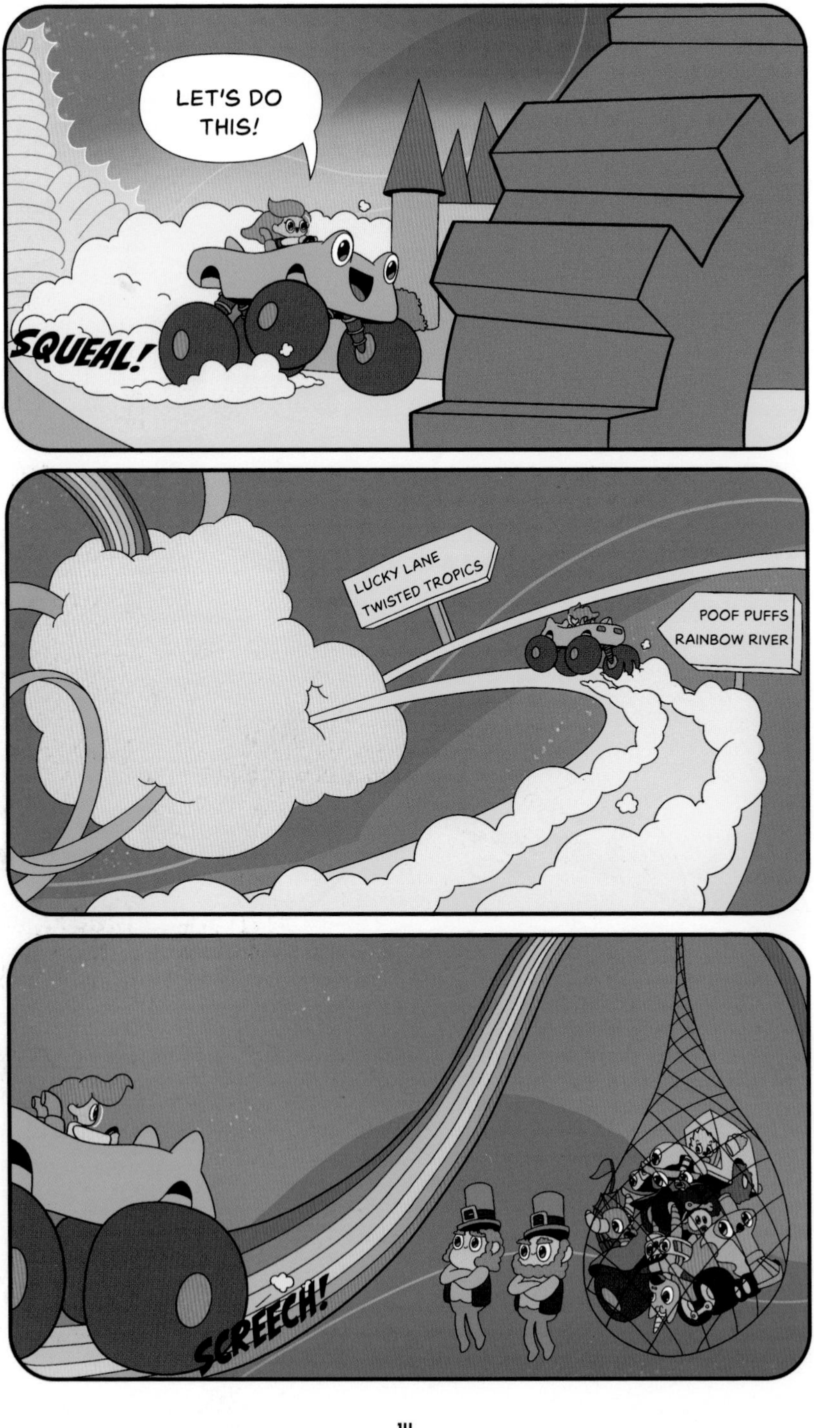
LET'S DO THIS!
SQUEAL!
LUCKY LANE
TWISTED TROPICS
POOF PUFFS
RAINBOW RIVER
SCREECH!

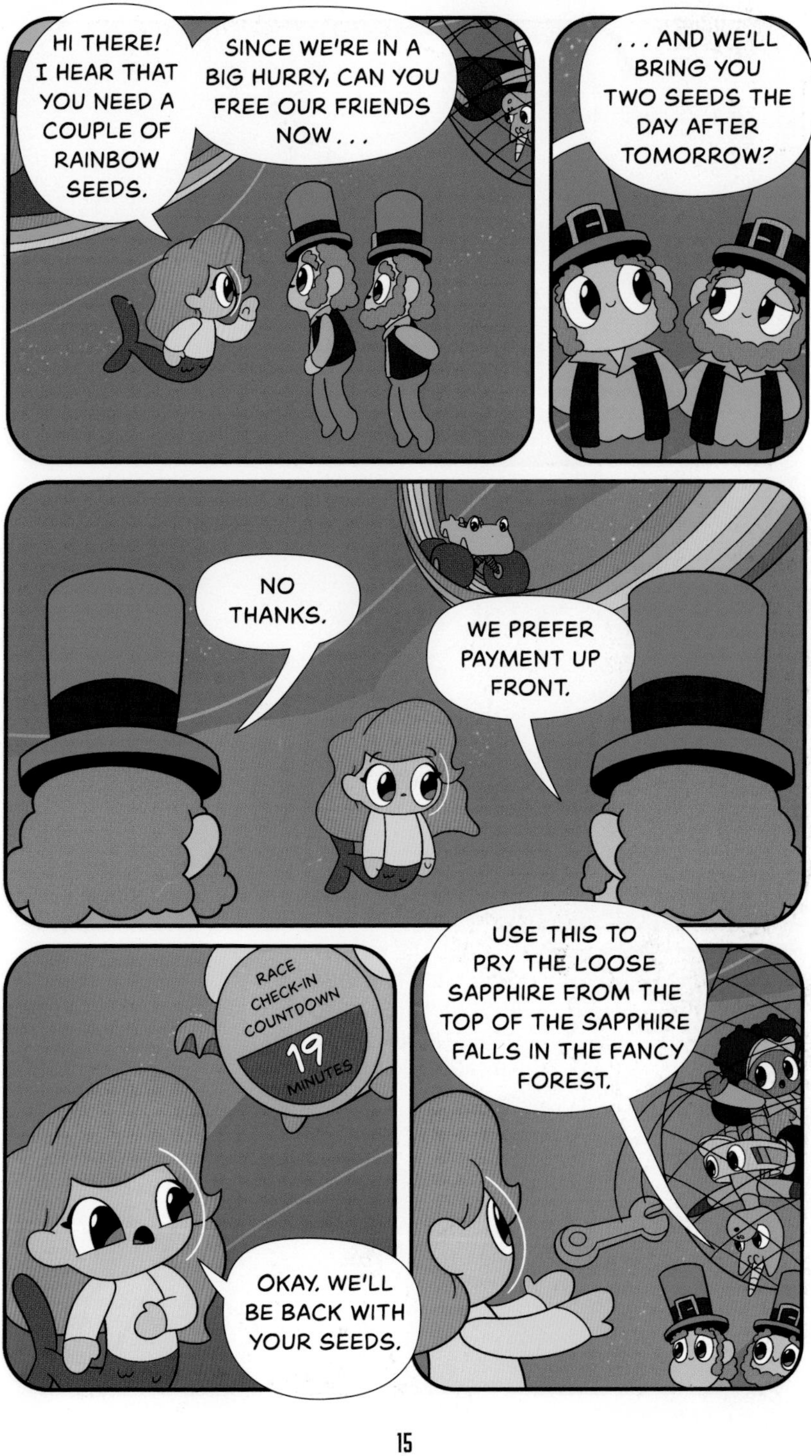
HI THERE! I HEAR THAT YOU NEED A COUPLE OF RAINBOW SEEDS.
SINCE WE'RE IN A BIG HURRY, CAN YOU FREE OUR FRIENDS NOW . . .
. . . AND WE'LL BRING YOU TWO SEEDS THE DAY AFTER TOMORROW?
NO THANKS.
WE PREFER PAYMENT UP FRONT.
RACE CHECK-IN COUNTDOWN
19 MINUTES
OKAY. WE'LL BE BACK WITH YOUR SEEDS.
USE THIS TO PRY THE LOOSE SAPPHIRE FROM THE TOP OF THE SAPPHIRE FALLS IN THE FANCY FOREST.

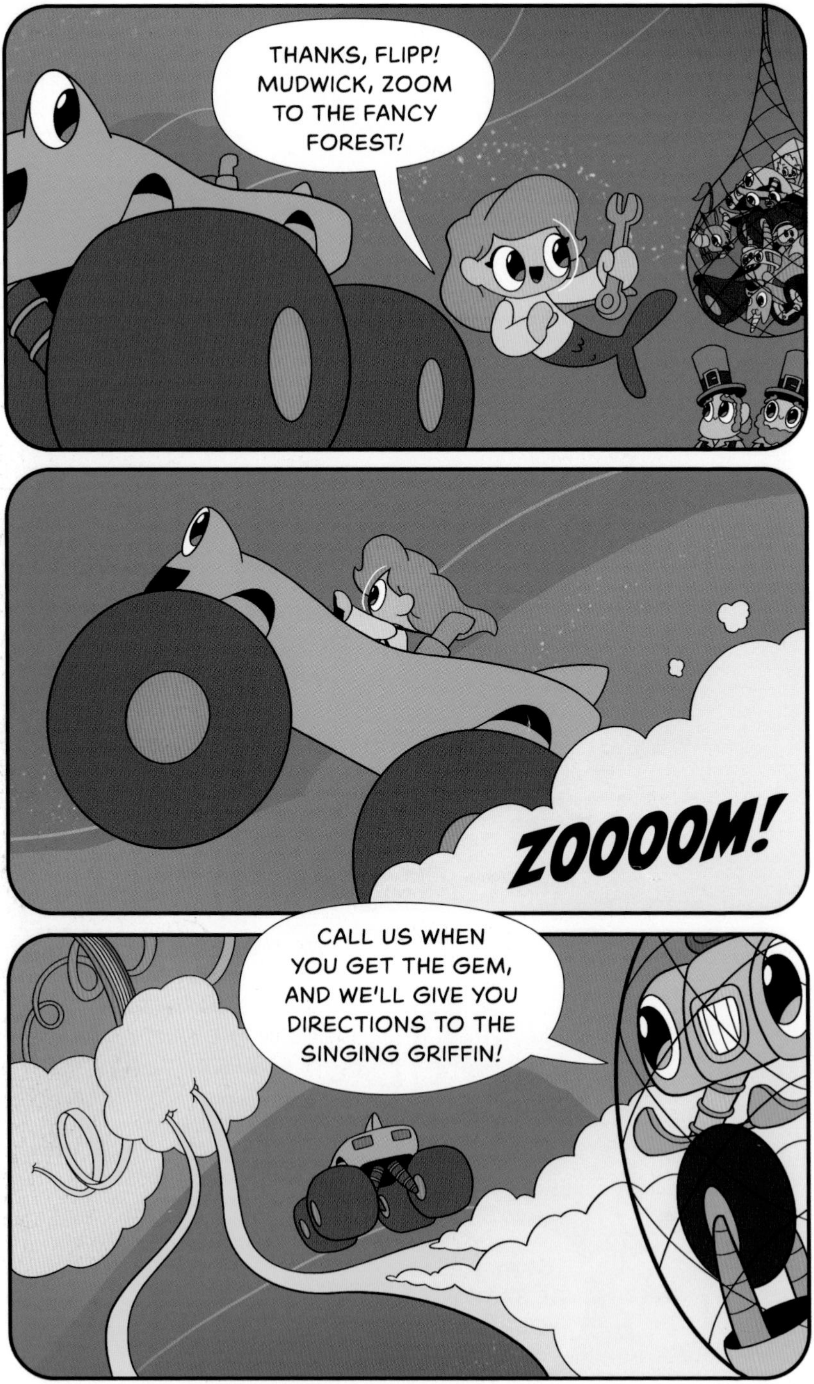
THANKS, FLIPP! MUDWICK, ZOOM TO THE FANCY FOREST!
ZOOOOM!
CALL US WHEN YOU GET THE GEM, AND WE'LL GIVE YOU DIRECTIONS TO THE SINGING GRIFFIN!

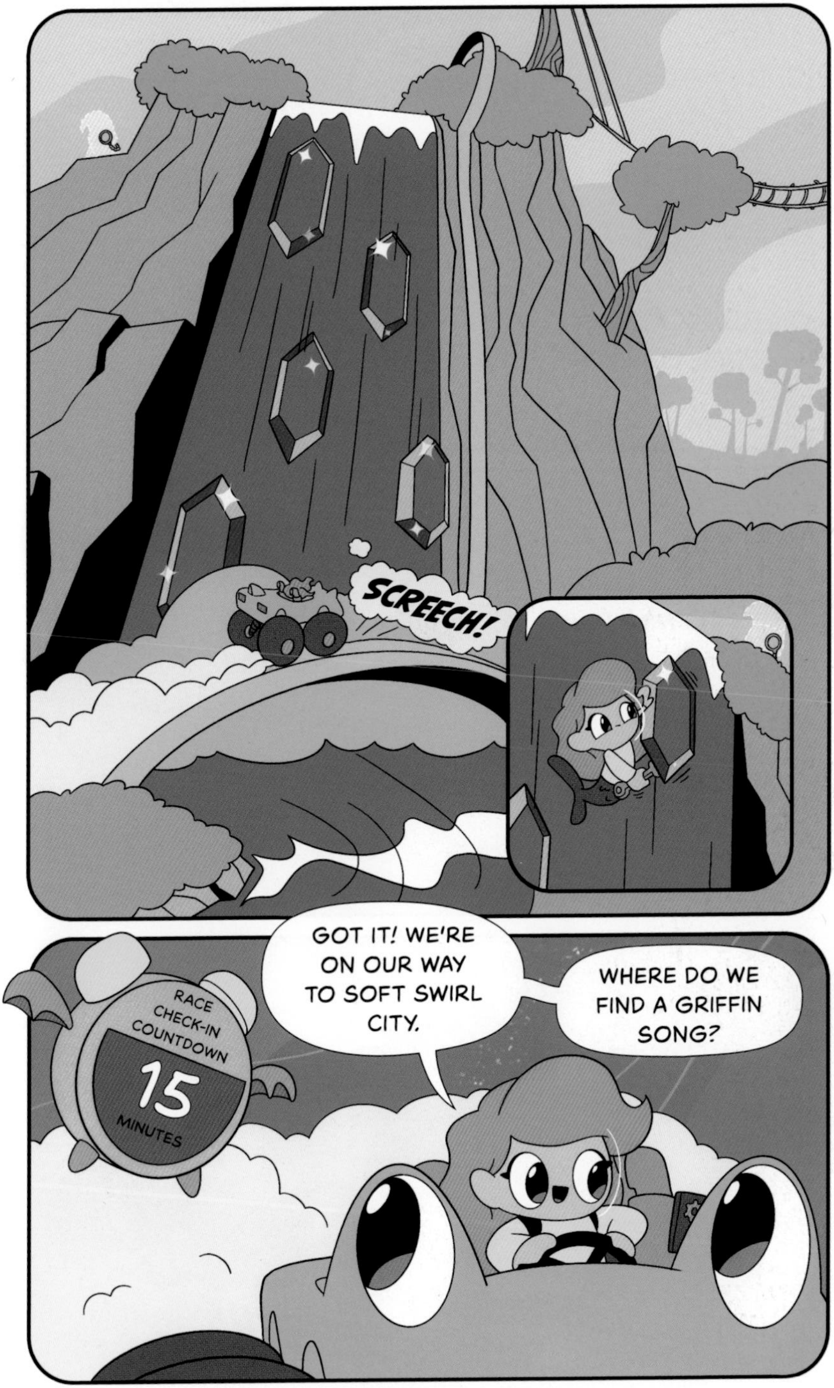
SCREECH!
RACE CHECK-IN COUNTDOWN 15 MINUTES
GOT IT! WE'RE ON OUR WAY TO SOFT SWIRL CITY.
WHERE DO WE FIND A GRIFFIN SONG?

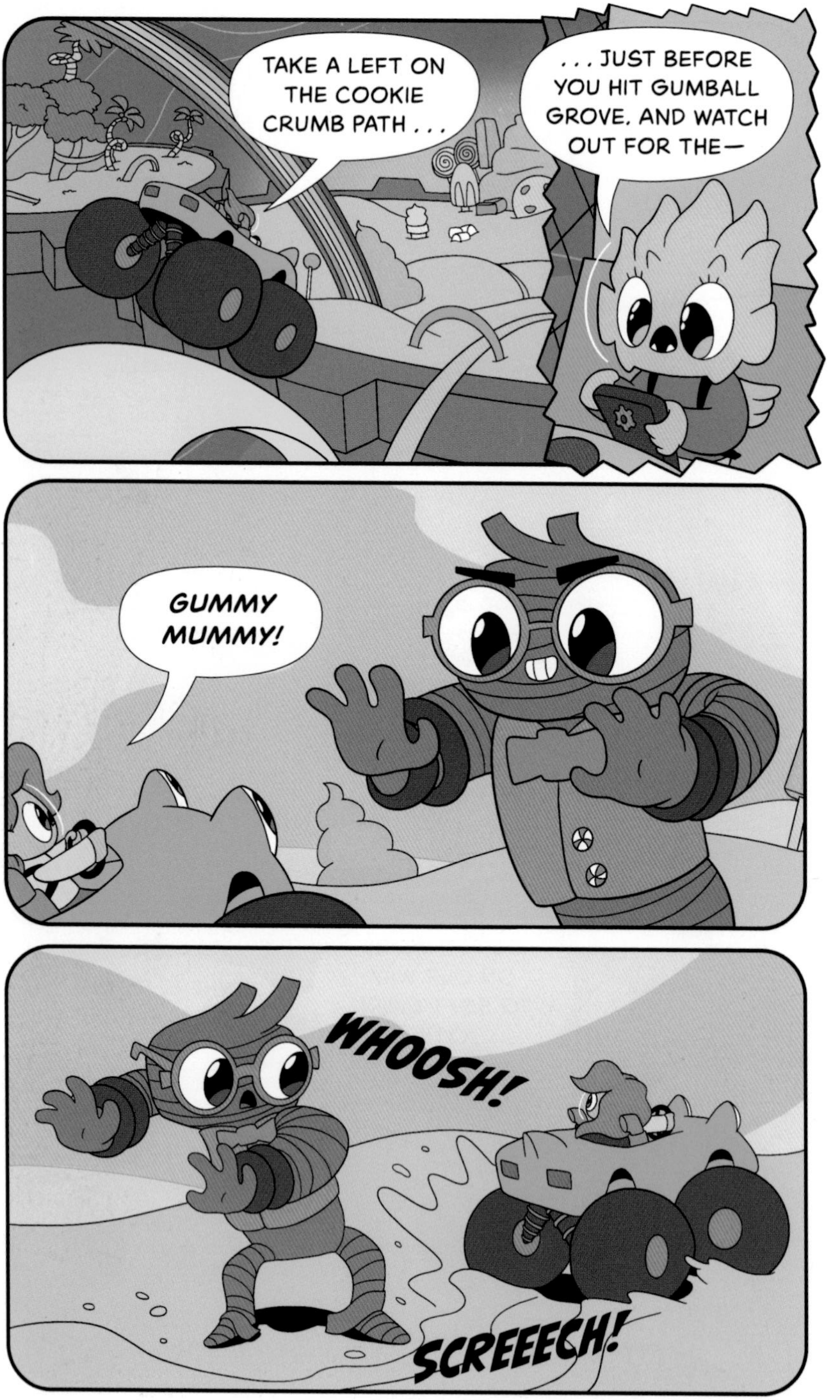
TAKE A LEFT ON THE COOKIE CRUMB PATH . . .
. . . JUST BEFORE YOU HIT GUMBALL GROVE, AND WATCH OUT FOR THE—
GUMMY MUMMY!
WHOOSH!
SCREEECH!

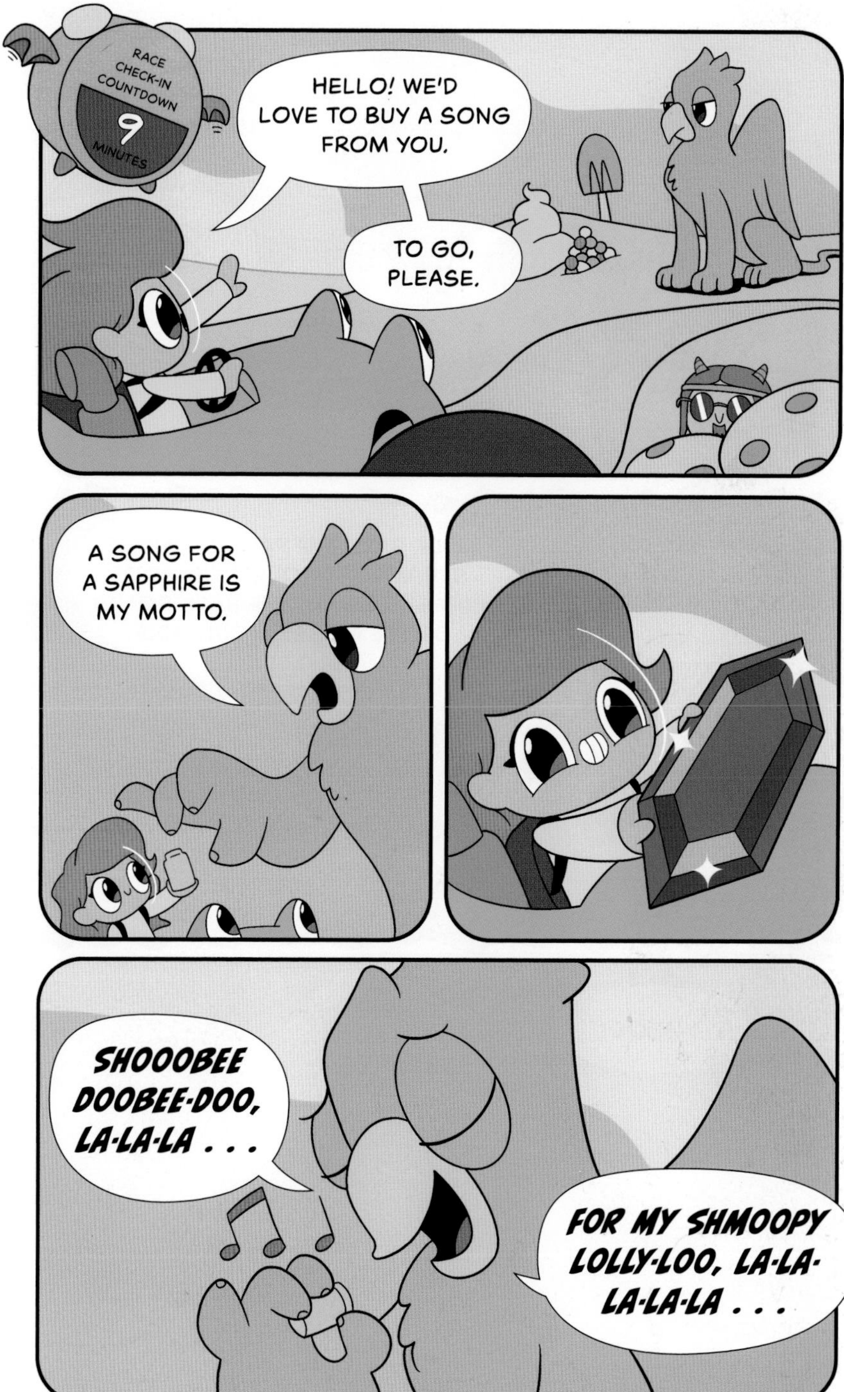
RACE CHECK-IN COUNTDOWN 9 MINUTES
HELLO! WE'D LOVE TO BUY A SONG FROM YOU.
TO GO, PLEASE.
A SONG FOR A SAPPHIRE IS MY MOTTO.
SHOOOBEE DOOBEE-DOO, LA-LA-LA . . .
FOR MY SHMOOPY LOLLY-LOO, LA-LA-LA-LA-LA . . .

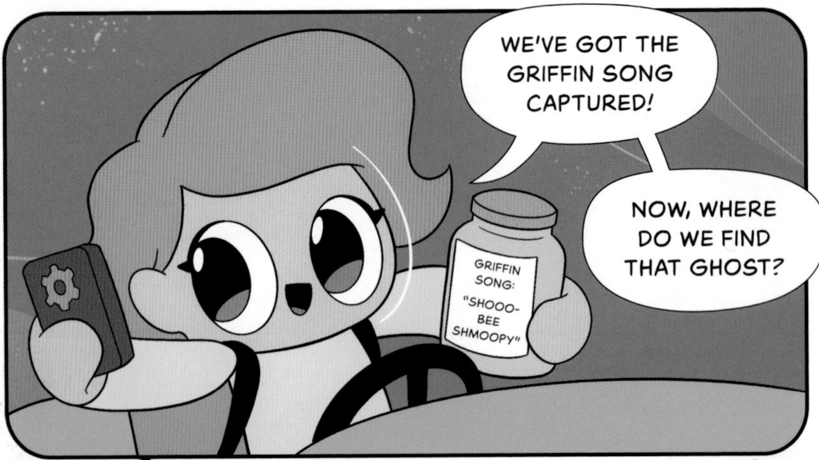
WE'VE GOT THE GRIFFIN SONG CAPTURED!
NOW, WHERE DO WE FIND THAT GHOST?
GRIFFIN SONG: "SHOOO-BEE SHMOOPY"

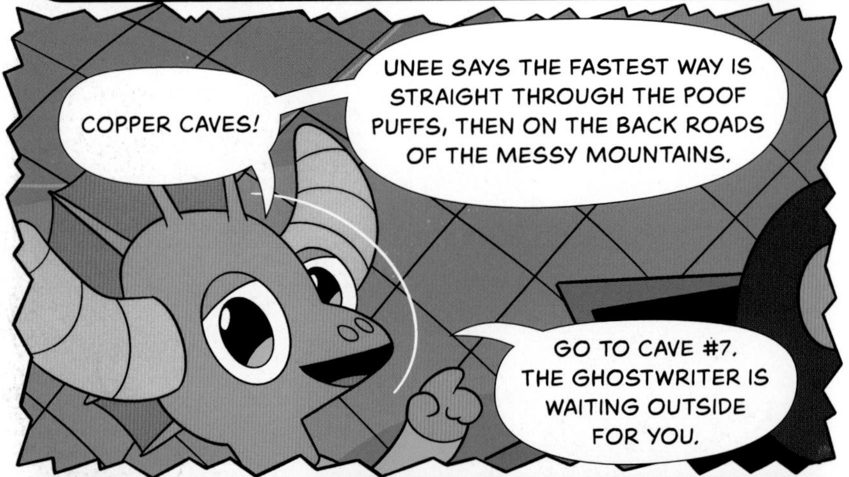
COPPER CAVES!
UNEE SAYS THE FASTEST WAY IS STRAIGHT THROUGH THE POOF PUFFS, THEN ON THE BACK ROADS OF THE MESSY MOUNTAINS.
GO TO CAVE #7. THE GHOSTWRITER IS WAITING OUTSIDE FOR YOU.

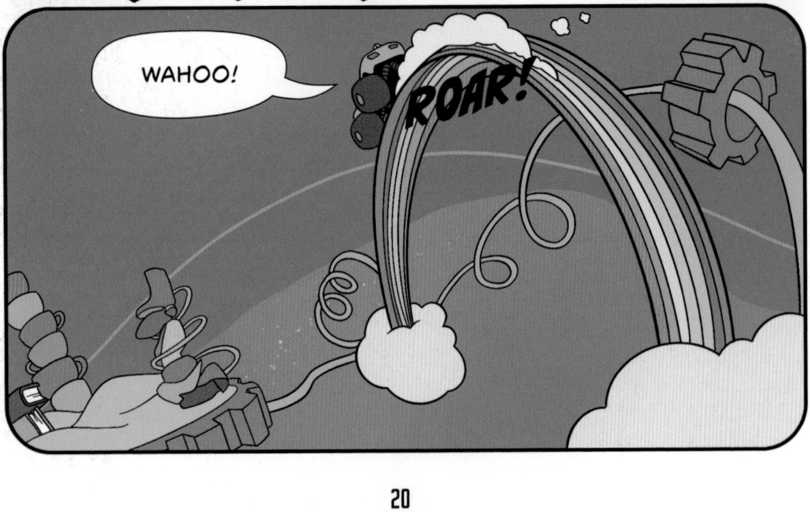
WAHOO!
ROAR!

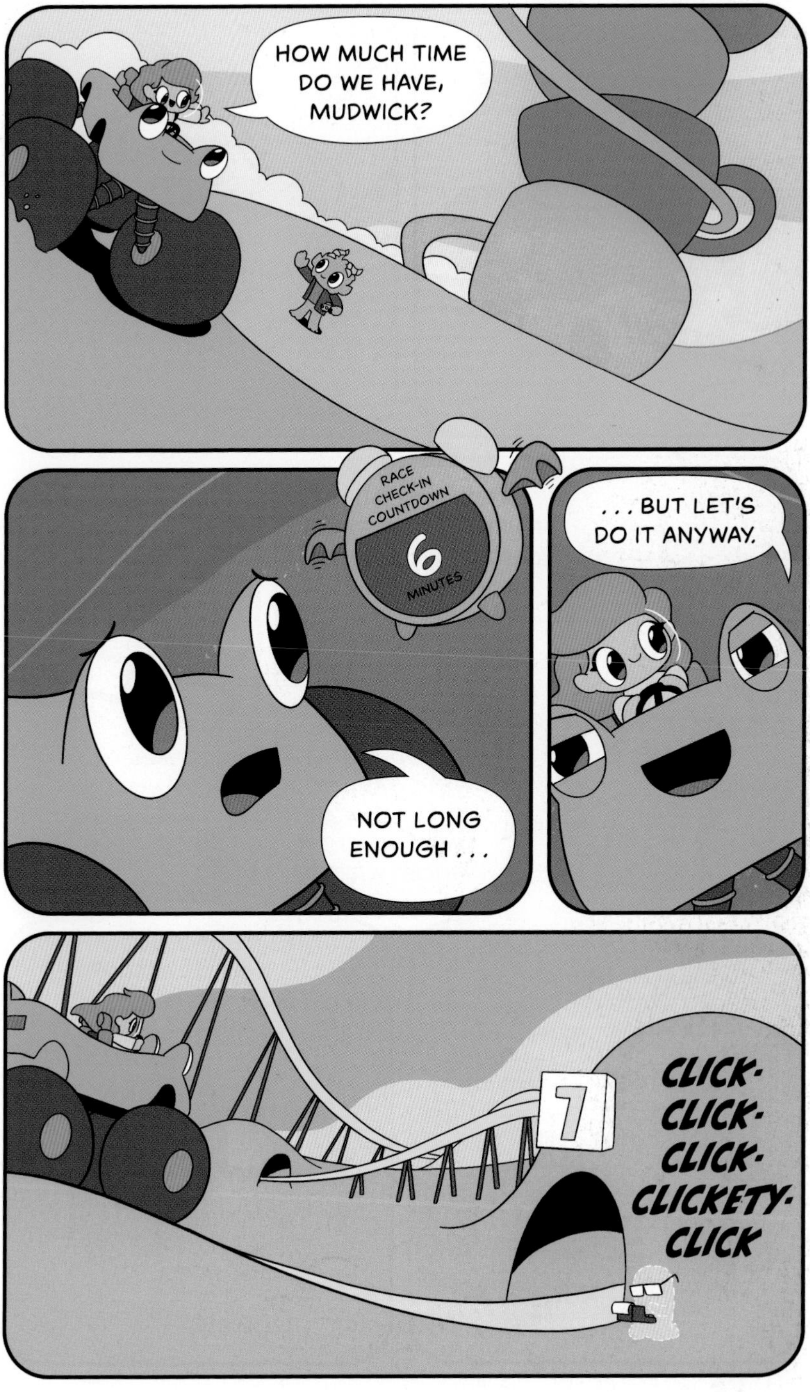
HOW MUCH TIME DO WE HAVE, MUDWICK?
RACE CHECK-IN COUNTDOWN
6
MINUTES
NOT LONG ENOUGH . . .
. . . BUT LET'S DO IT ANYWAY.
7
CLICK-
CLICK-
CLICK-
CLICKETY-
CLICK

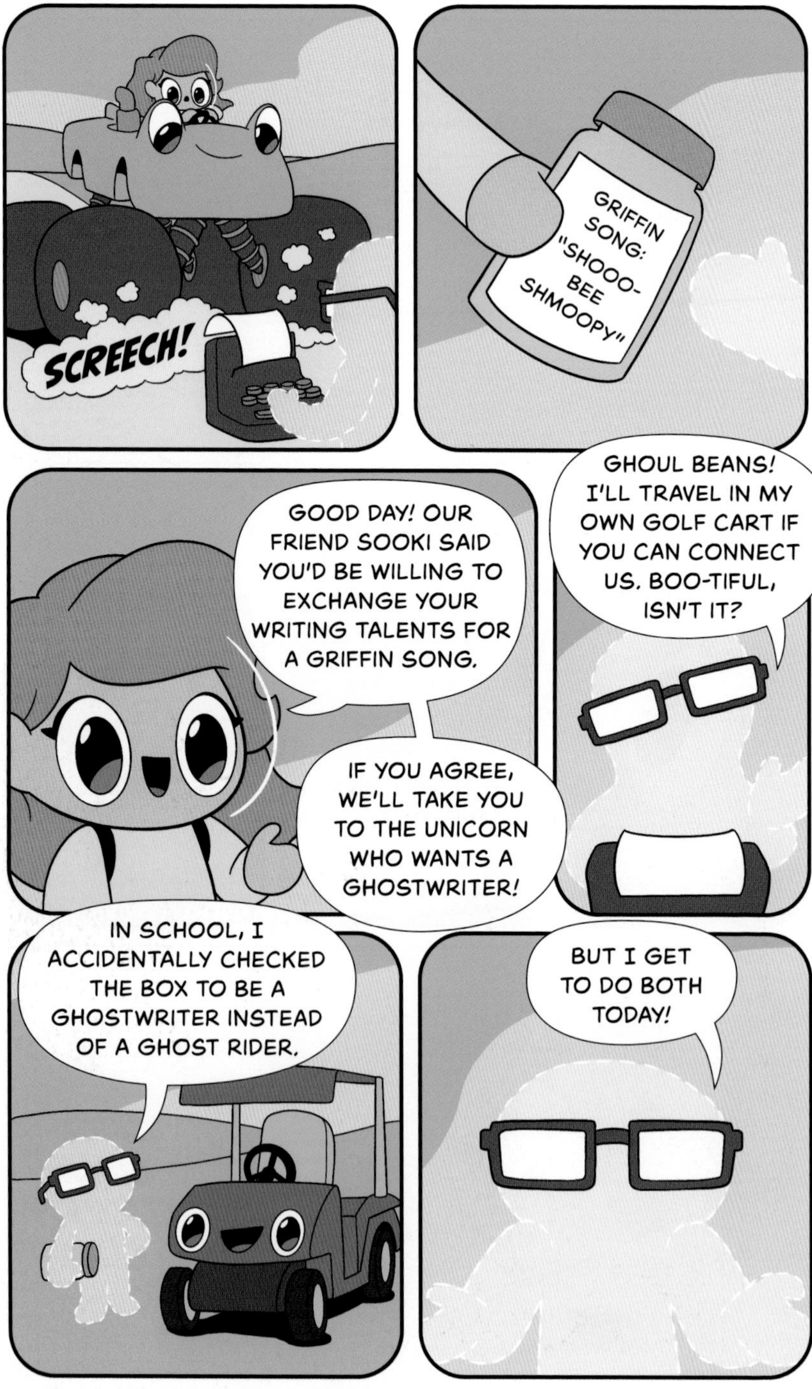
SCREECH!
GRIFFIN SONG: "SHOOO-BEE SHMOOPY"
GOOD DAY! OUR FRIEND SOOKI SAID YOU'D BE WILLING TO EXCHANGE YOUR WRITING TALENTS FOR A GRIFFIN SONG.
IF YOU AGREE, WE'LL TAKE YOU TO THE UNICORN WHO WANTS A GHOSTWRITER!
GHOUL BEANS! I'LL TRAVEL IN MY OWN GOLF CART IF YOU CAN CONNECT US. BOO-TIFUL, ISN'T IT?
IN SCHOOL, I ACCIDENTALLY CHECKED THE BOX TO BE A GHOSTWRITER INSTEAD OF A GHOST RIDER.
BUT I GET TO DO BOTH TODAY!

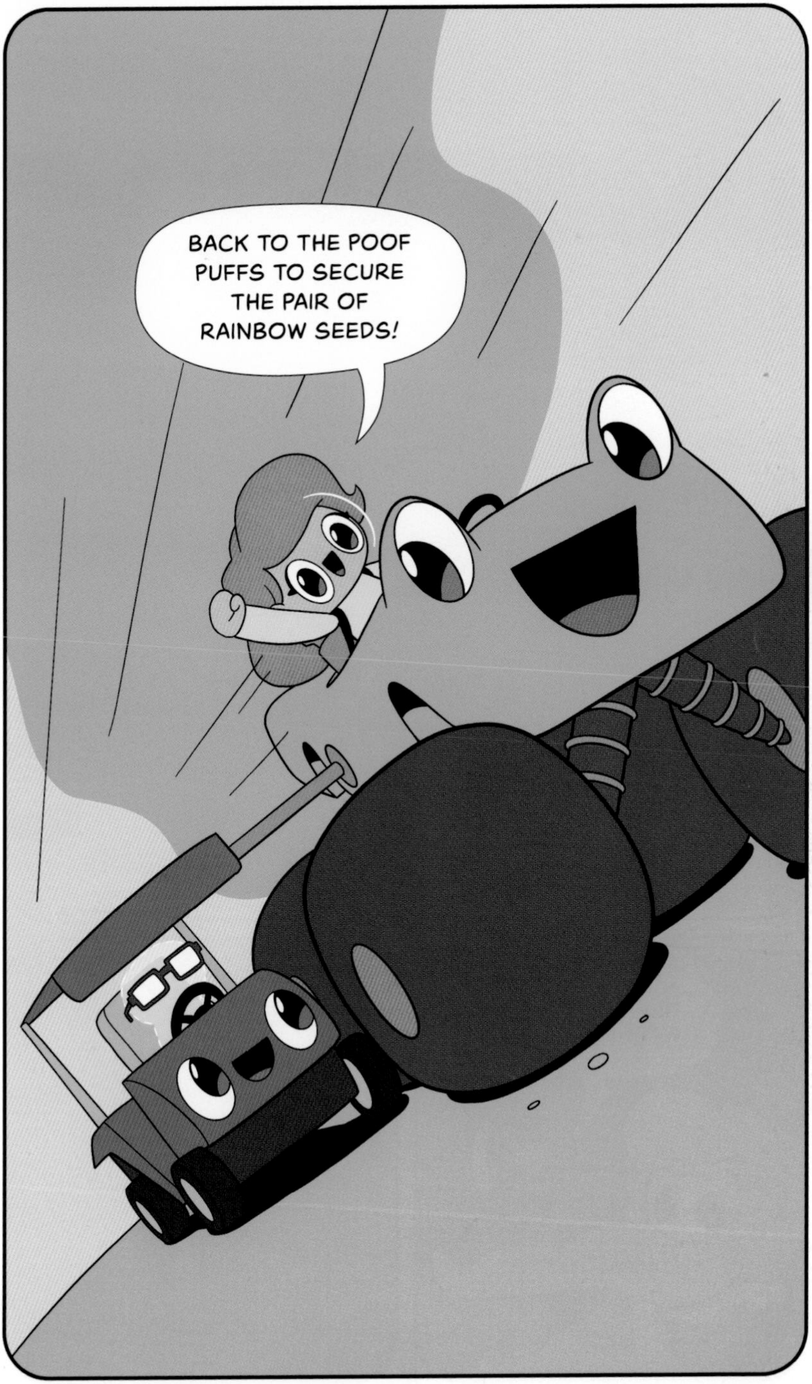
BACK TO THE POOF PUFFS TO SECURE THE PAIR OF RAINBOW SEEDS!

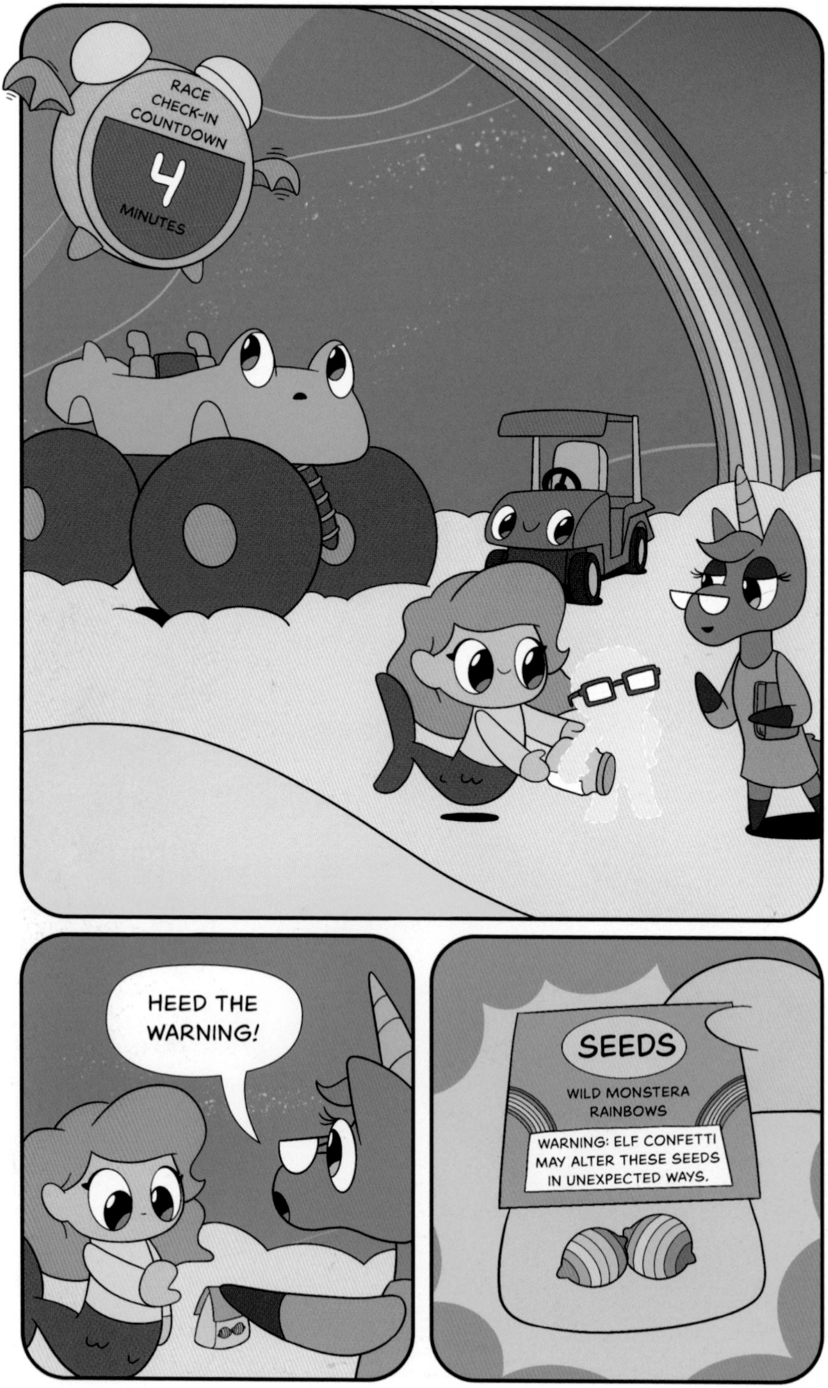
RACE CHECK-IN COUNTDOWN
4
MINUTES
HEED THE WARNING!
SEEDS
WILD MONSTERA RAINBOWS
WARNING: ELF CONFETTI MAY ALTER THESE SEEDS IN UNEXPECTED WAYS.

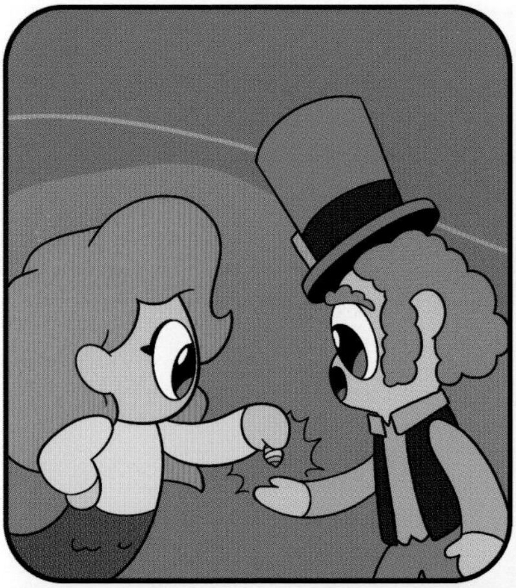

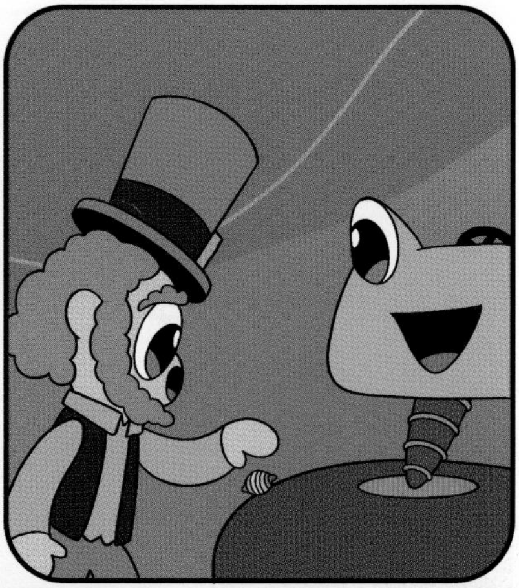

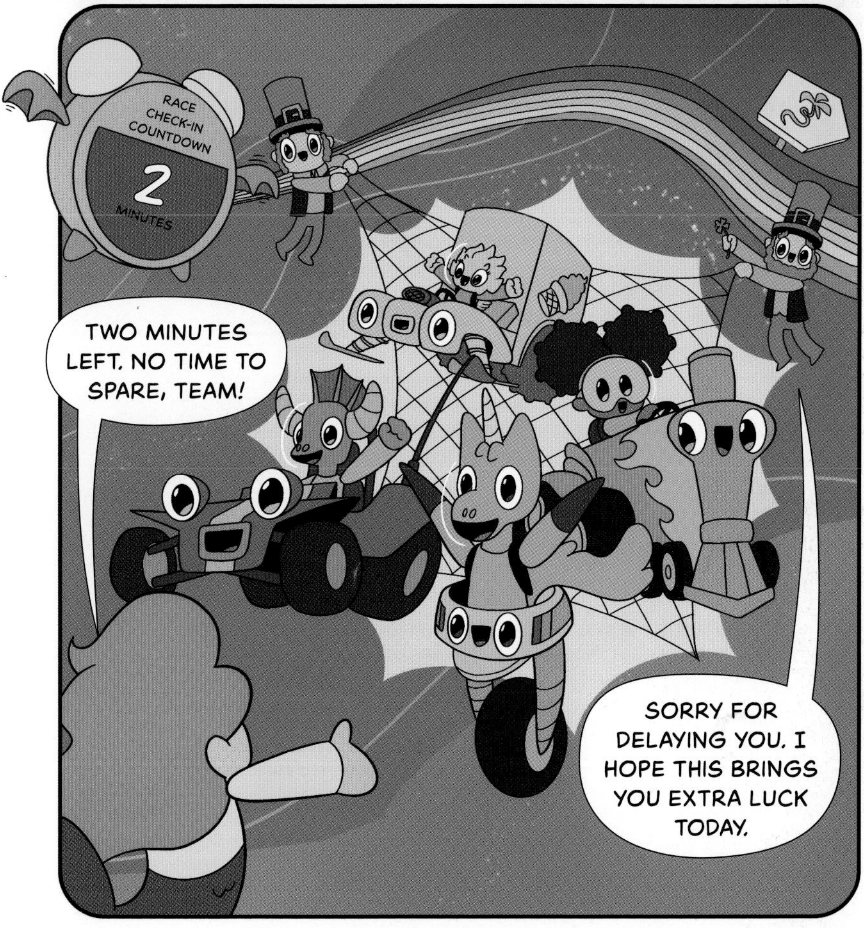
RACE CHECK-IN COUNTDOWN
2
MINUTES
TWO MINUTES LEFT. NO TIME TO SPARE, TEAM!
SORRY FOR DELAYING YOU. I HOPE THIS BRINGS YOU EXTRA LUCK TODAY.

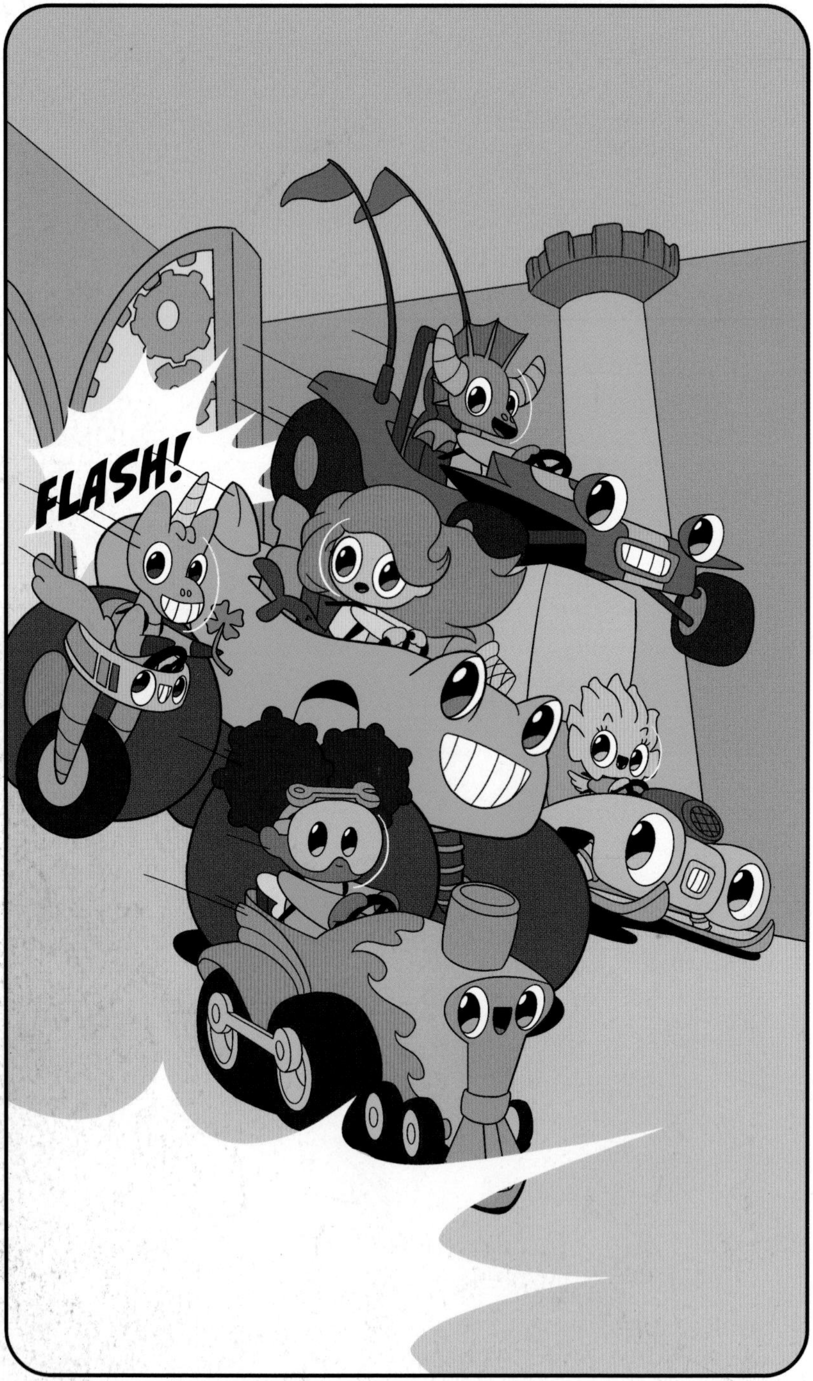
FLASH!

CHAPTER 2:
RACE 3 READY!

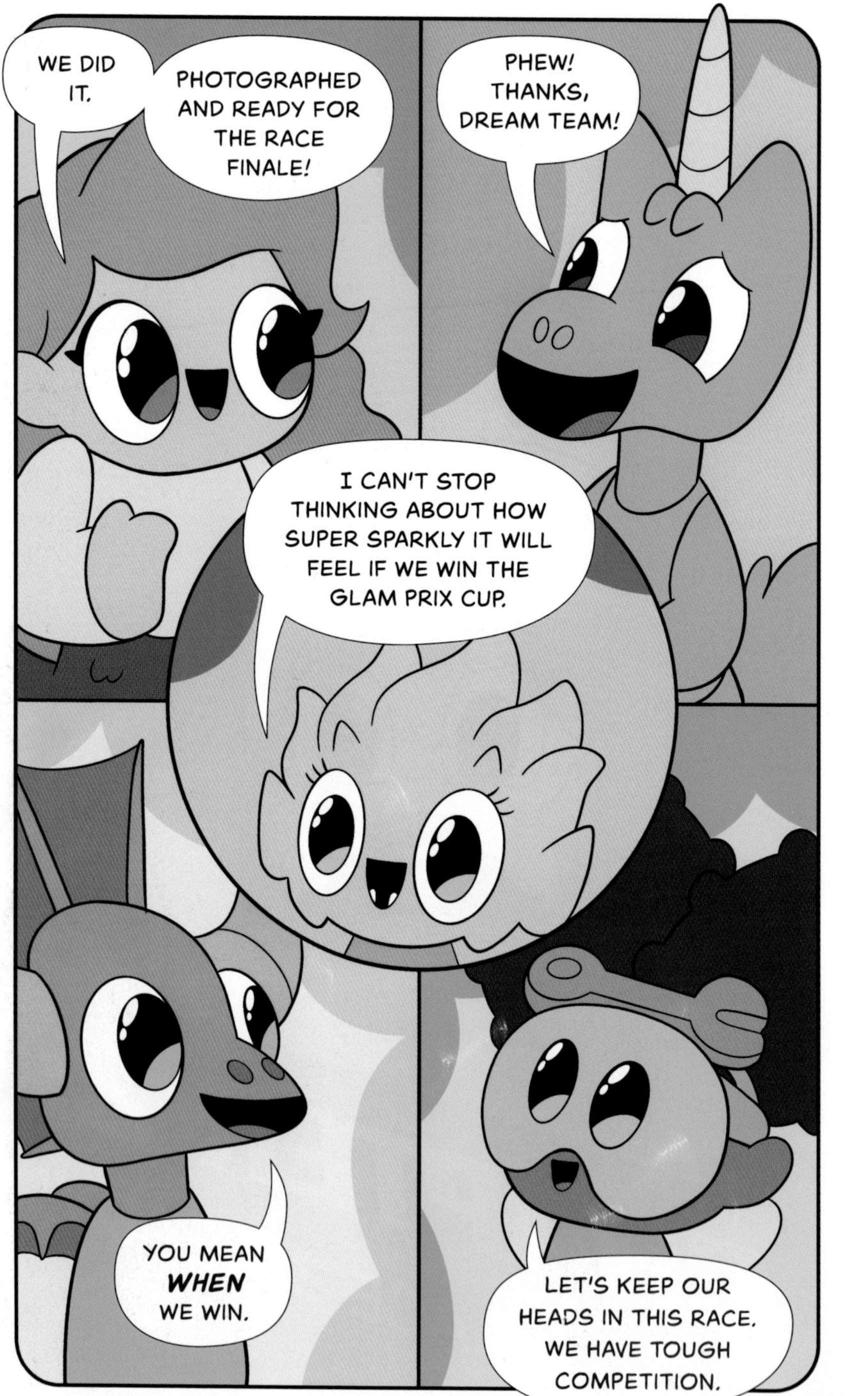

WE DID IT.
PHOTOGRAPHED AND READY FOR THE RACE FINALE!
PHEW! THANKS, DREAM TEAM!
I CAN'T STOP THINKING ABOUT HOW SUPER SPARKLY IT WILL FEEL IF WE WIN THE GLAM PRIX CUP.
YOU MEAN **WHEN** WE WIN.
LET'S KEEP OUR HEADS IN THIS RACE. WE HAVE TOUGH COMPETITION.

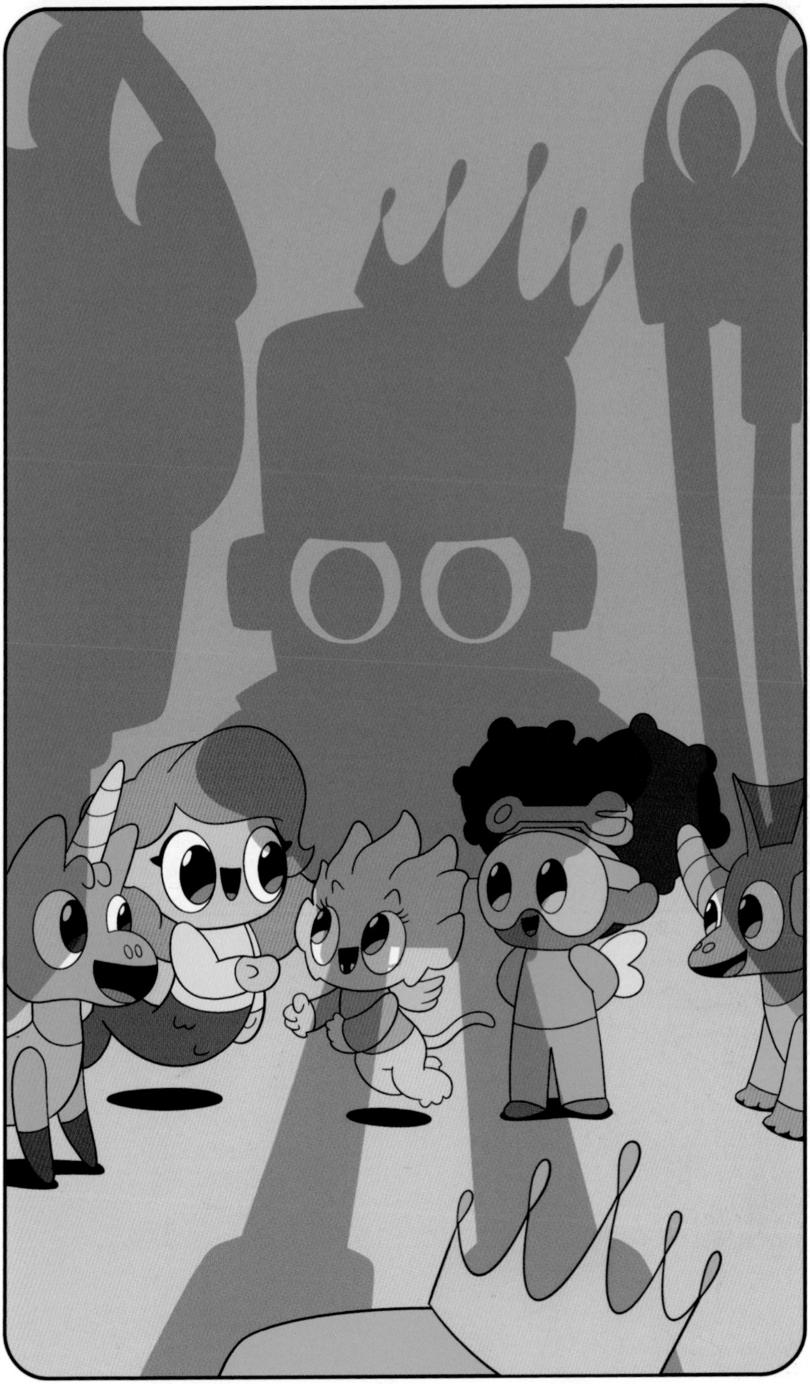

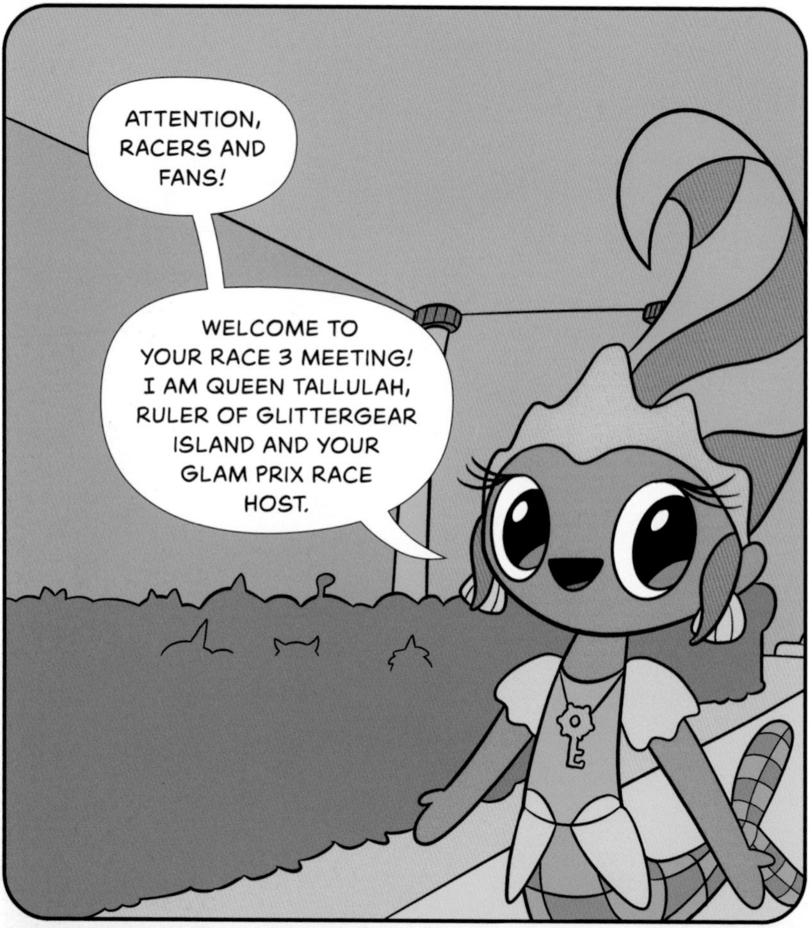
ATTENTION, RACERS AND FANS!
WELCOME TO YOUR RACE 3 MEETING! I AM QUEEN TALLULAH, RULER OF GLITTERGEAR ISLAND AND YOUR GLAM PRIX RACE HOST.

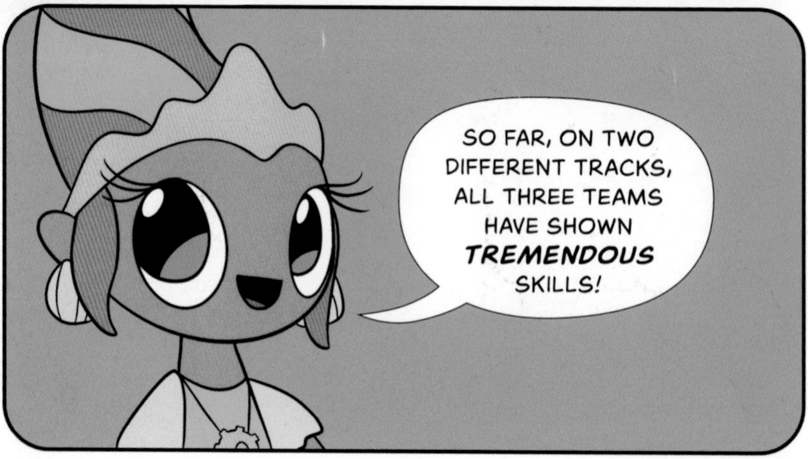
SO FAR, ON TWO DIFFERENT TRACKS, ALL THREE TEAMS HAVE SHOWN ***TREMENDOUS*** SKILLS!

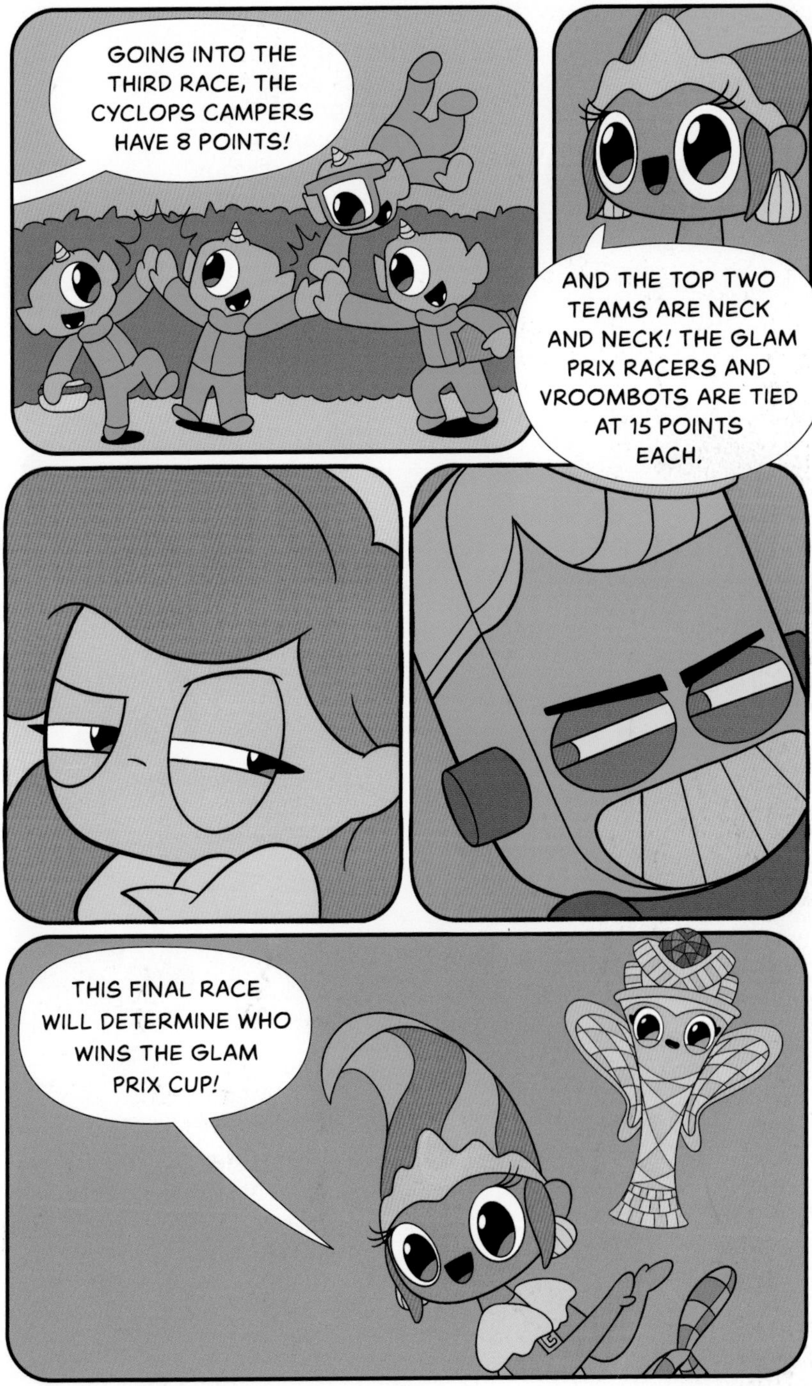
GOING INTO THE THIRD RACE, THE CYCLOPS CAMPERS HAVE 8 POINTS!
AND THE TOP TWO TEAMS ARE NECK AND NECK! THE GLAM PRIX RACERS AND VROOMBOTS ARE TIED AT 15 POINTS EACH.
THIS FINAL RACE WILL DETERMINE WHO WINS THE GLAM PRIX CUP!

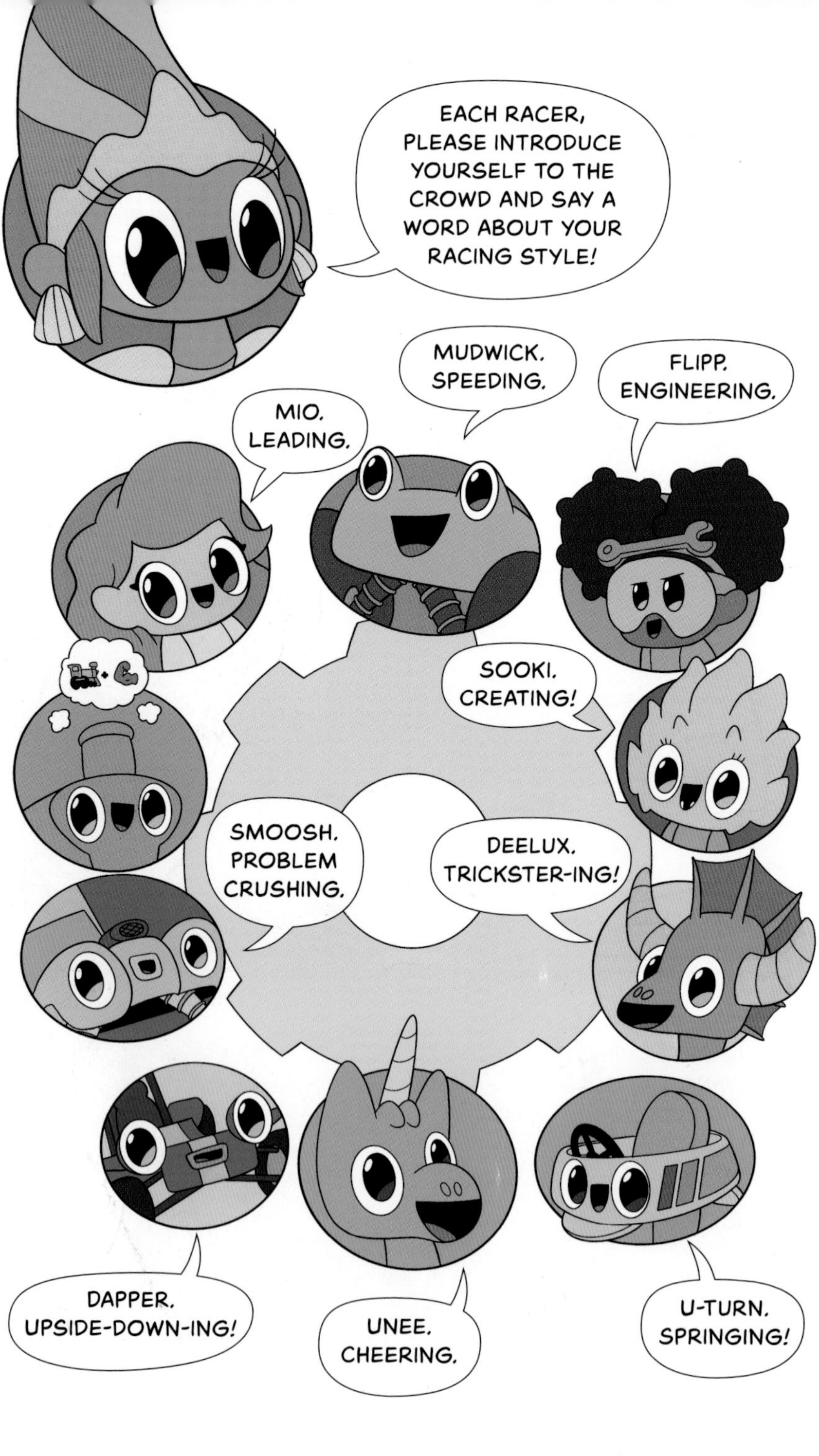
EACH RACER, PLEASE INTRODUCE YOURSELF TO THE CROWD AND SAY A WORD ABOUT YOUR RACING STYLE!
MUDWICK. SPEEDING.
FLIPP. ENGINEERING.
MIO. LEADING.
SOOKI. CREATING!
SMOOSH. PROBLEM CRUSHING.
DEELUX. TRICKSTER-ING!
DAPPER. UPSIDE-DOWN-ING!
UNEE. CHEERING.
U-TURN. SPRINGING!

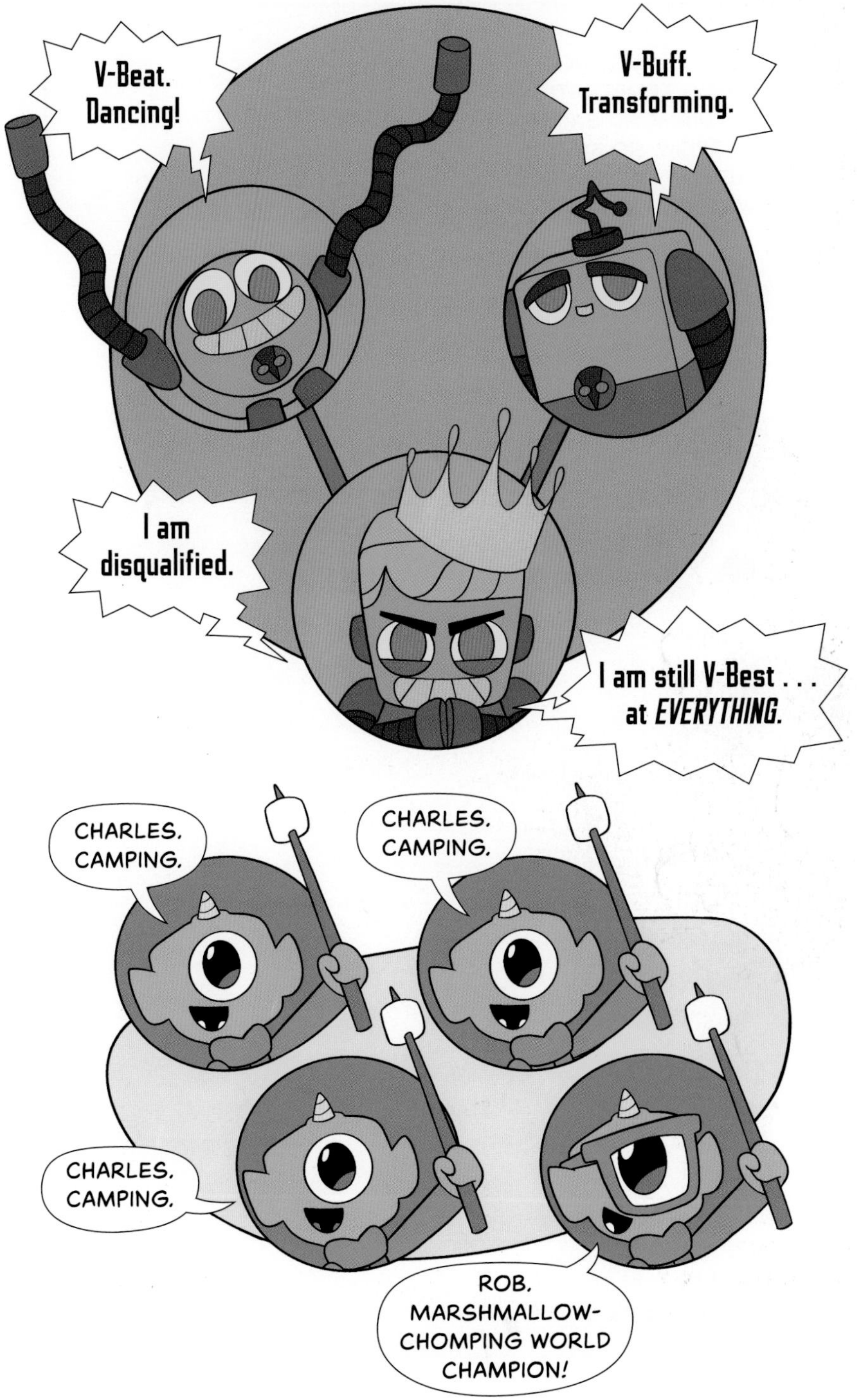
V-Beat.
Dancing!
V-Buff.
Transforming.
I am
disqualified.
I am still V-Best . . .
at *EVERYTHING.*
CHARLES.
CAMPING.
CHARLES.
CAMPING.
CHARLES.
CAMPING.
ROB.
MARSHMALLOW-
CHOMPING WORLD
CHAMPION!

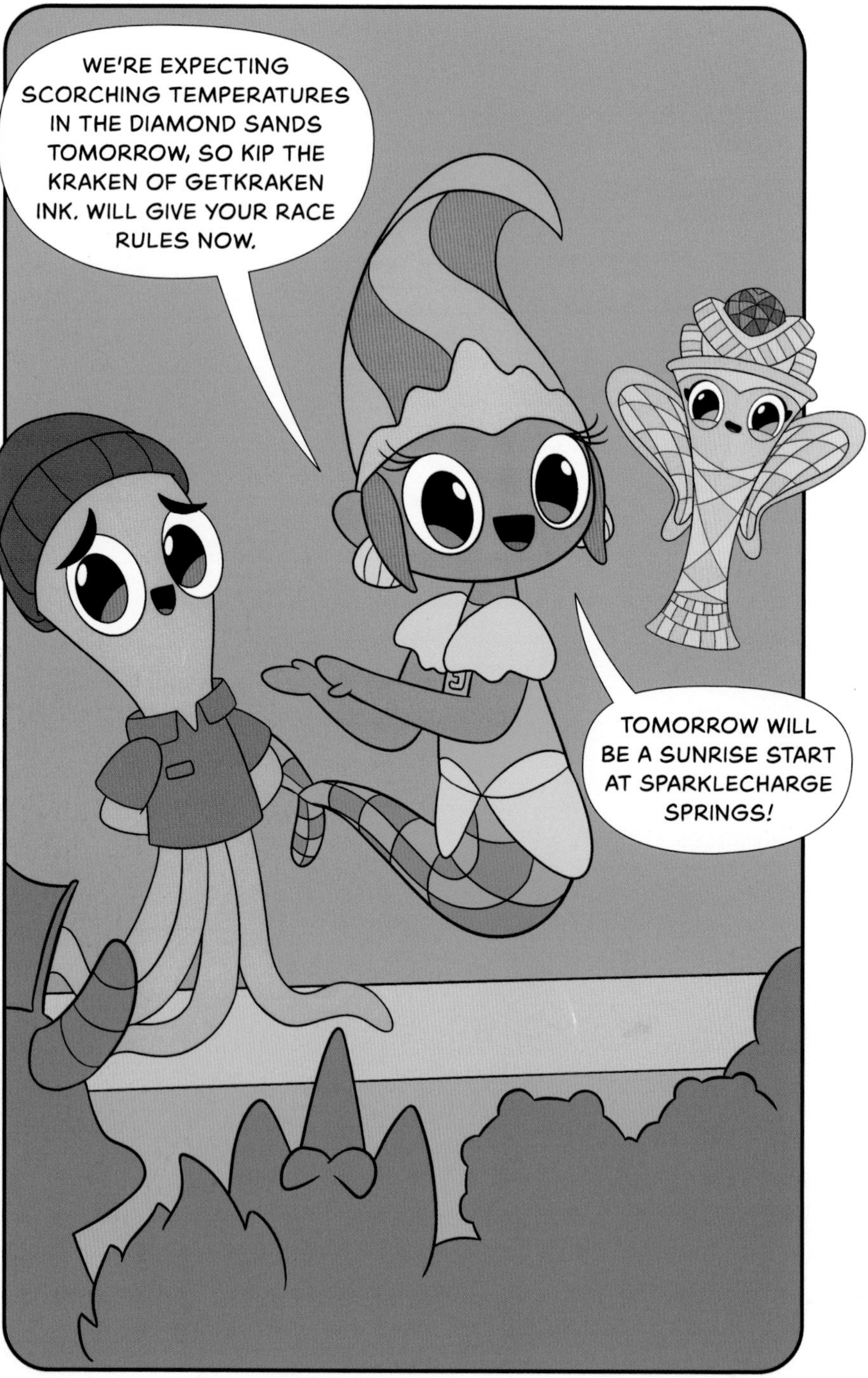
WE'RE EXPECTING SCORCHING TEMPERATURES IN THE DIAMOND SANDS TOMORROW, SO KIP THE KRAKEN OF GETKRAKEN INK. WILL GIVE YOUR RACE RULES NOW.
TOMORROW WILL BE A SUNRISE START AT SPARKLECHARGE SPRINGS!

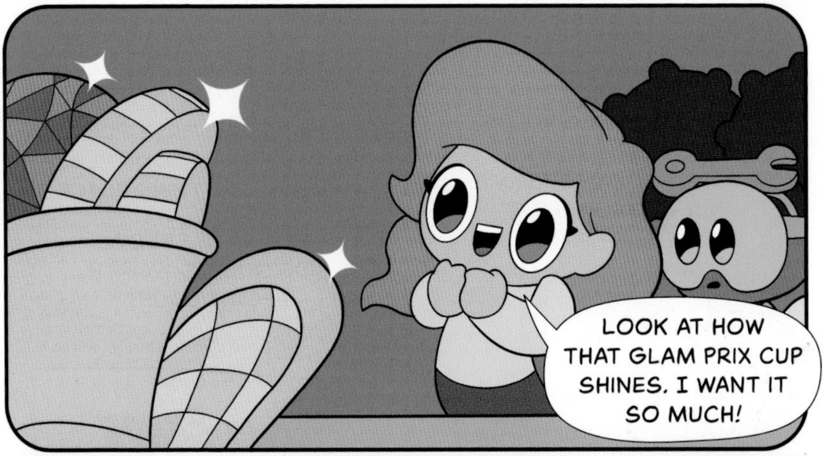
LOOK AT HOW THAT GLAM PRIX CUP SHINES. I WANT IT SO MUCH!

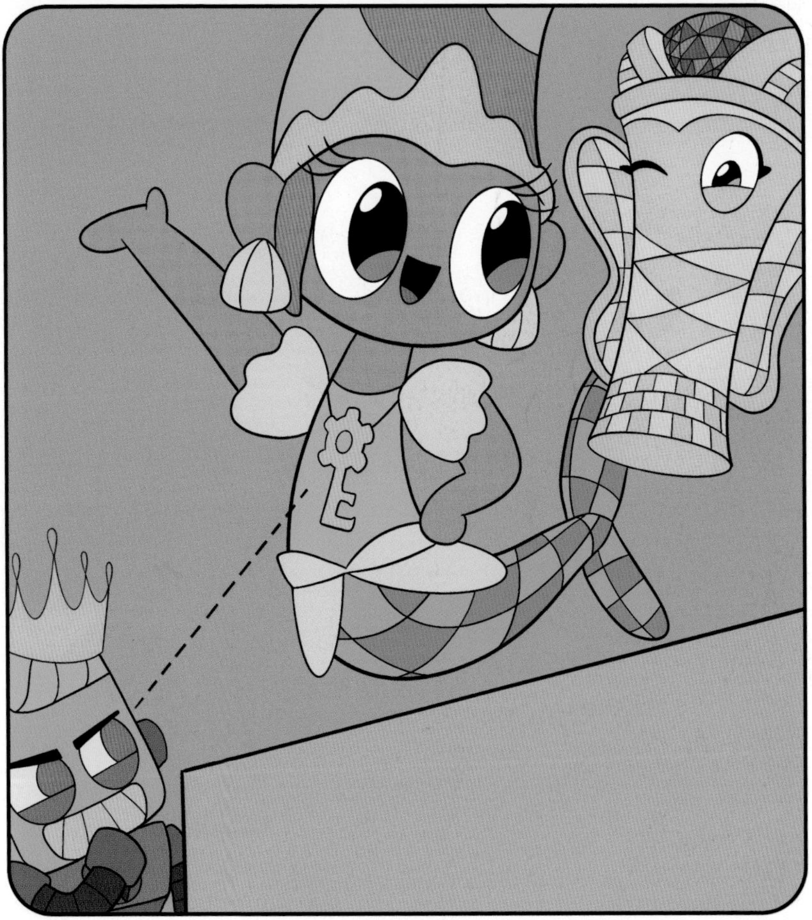

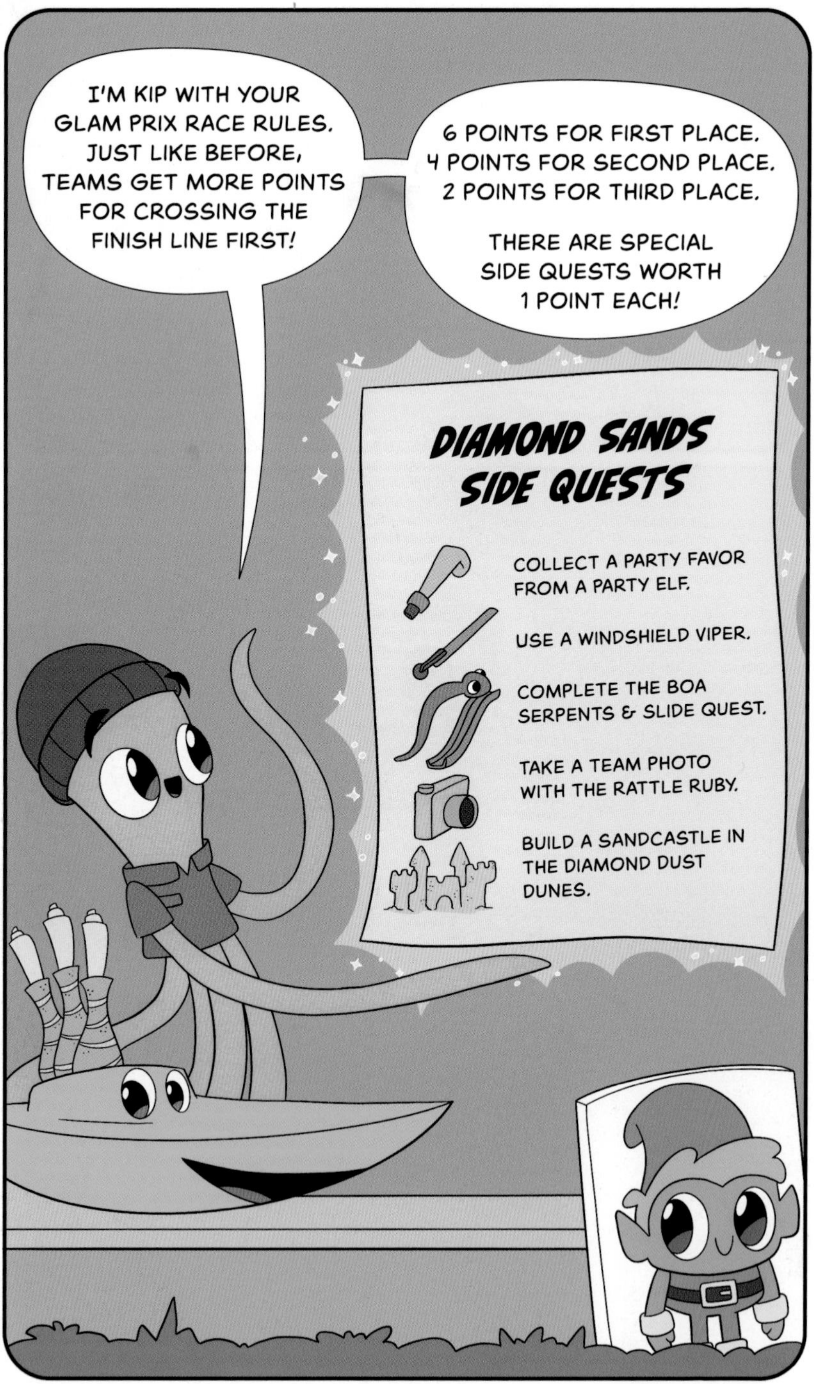
I'M KIP WITH YOUR GLAM PRIX RACE RULES. JUST LIKE BEFORE, TEAMS GET MORE POINTS FOR CROSSING THE FINISH LINE FIRST!
6 POINTS FOR FIRST PLACE. 4 POINTS FOR SECOND PLACE. 2 POINTS FOR THIRD PLACE.
THERE ARE SPECIAL SIDE QUESTS WORTH 1 POINT EACH!
DIAMOND SANDS SIDE QUESTS
COLLECT A PARTY FAVOR FROM A PARTY ELF.
USE A WINDSHIELD VIPER.
COMPLETE THE BOA SERPENTS & SLIDE QUEST.
TAKE A TEAM PHOTO WITH THE RATTLE RUBY.
BUILD A SANDCASTLE IN THE DIAMOND DUST DUNES.

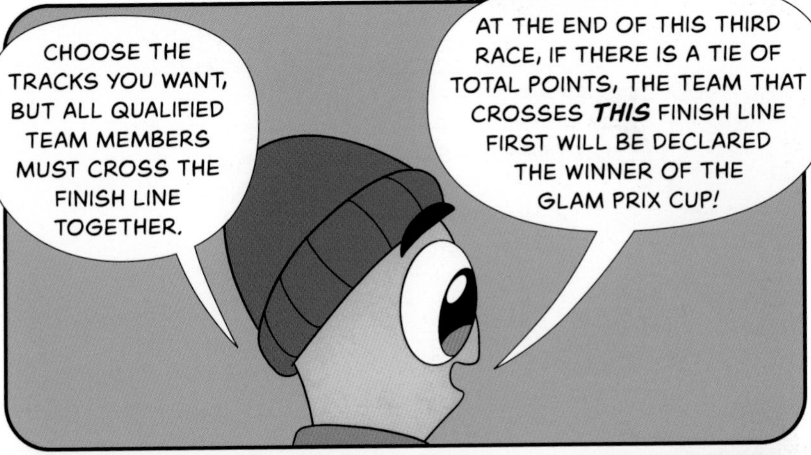
CHOOSE THE TRACKS YOU WANT, BUT ALL QUALIFIED TEAM MEMBERS MUST CROSS THE FINISH LINE TOGETHER.
AT THE END OF THIS THIRD RACE, IF THERE IS A TIE OF TOTAL POINTS, THE TEAM THAT CROSSES ***THIS*** FINISH LINE FIRST WILL BE DECLARED THE WINNER OF THE GLAM PRIX CUP!

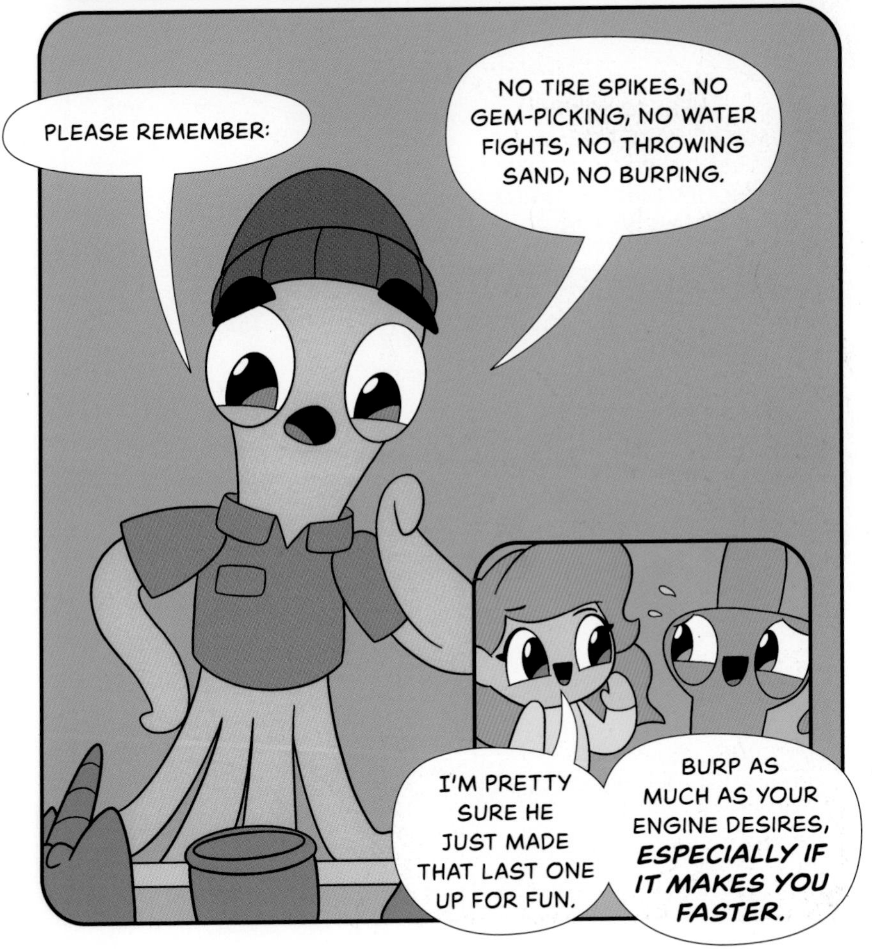
PLEASE REMEMBER:
NO TIRE SPIKES, NO GEM-PICKING, NO WATER FIGHTS, NO THROWING SAND, NO BURPING.
I'M PRETTY SURE HE JUST MADE THAT LAST ONE UP FOR FUN.
BURP AS MUCH AS YOUR ENGINE DESIRES, ***ESPECIALLY IF IT MAKES YOU FASTER.***

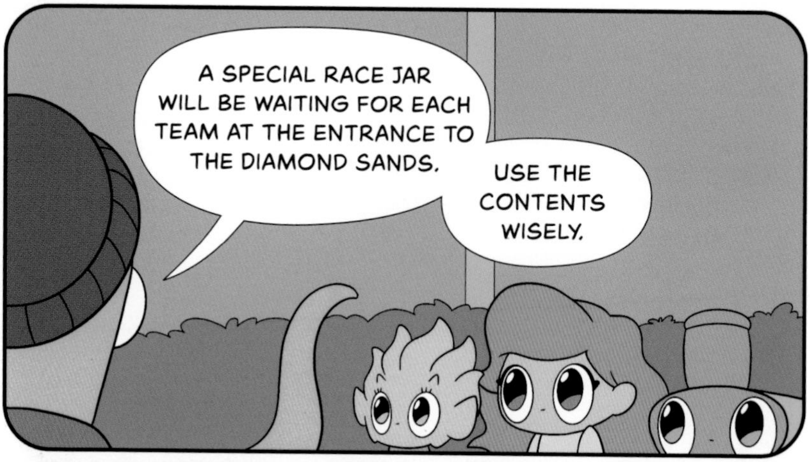
A SPECIAL RACE JAR WILL BE WAITING FOR EACH TEAM AT THE ENTRANCE TO THE DIAMOND SANDS.
USE THE CONTENTS WISELY.

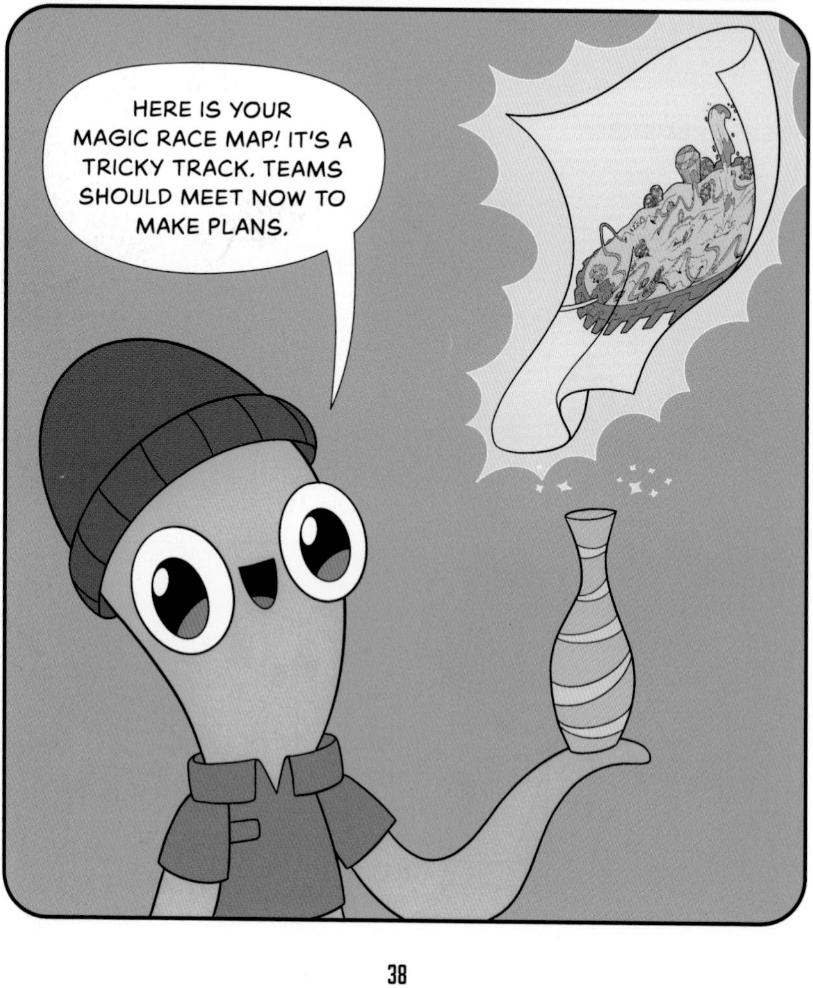
HERE IS YOUR MAGIC RACE MAP! IT'S A TRICKY TRACK. TEAMS SHOULD MEET NOW TO MAKE PLANS.

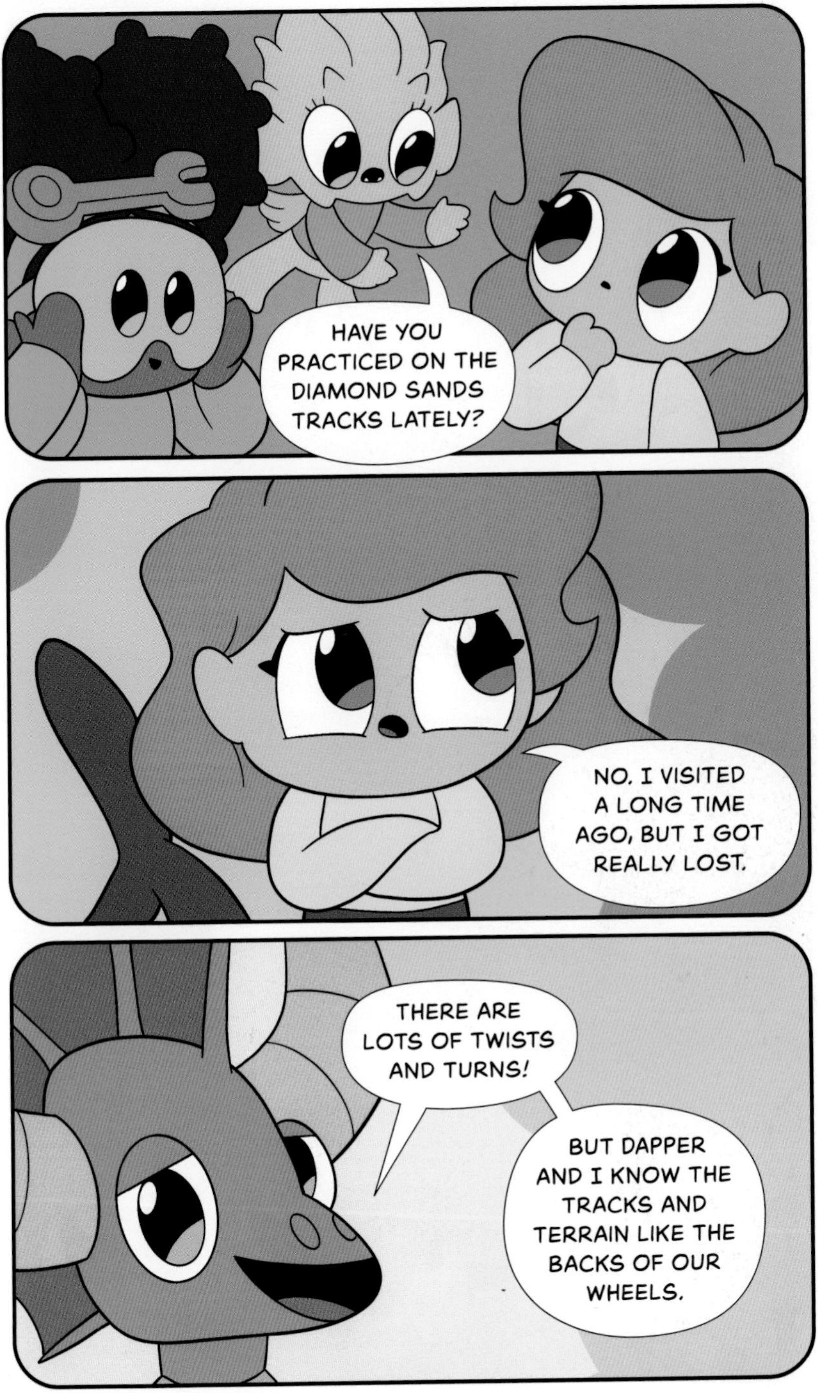
HAVE YOU PRACTICED ON THE DIAMOND SANDS TRACKS LATELY?
NO. I VISITED A LONG TIME AGO, BUT I GOT REALLY LOST.
THERE ARE LOTS OF TWISTS AND TURNS!
BUT DAPPER AND I KNOW THE TRACKS AND TERRAIN LIKE THE BACKS OF OUR WHEELS.

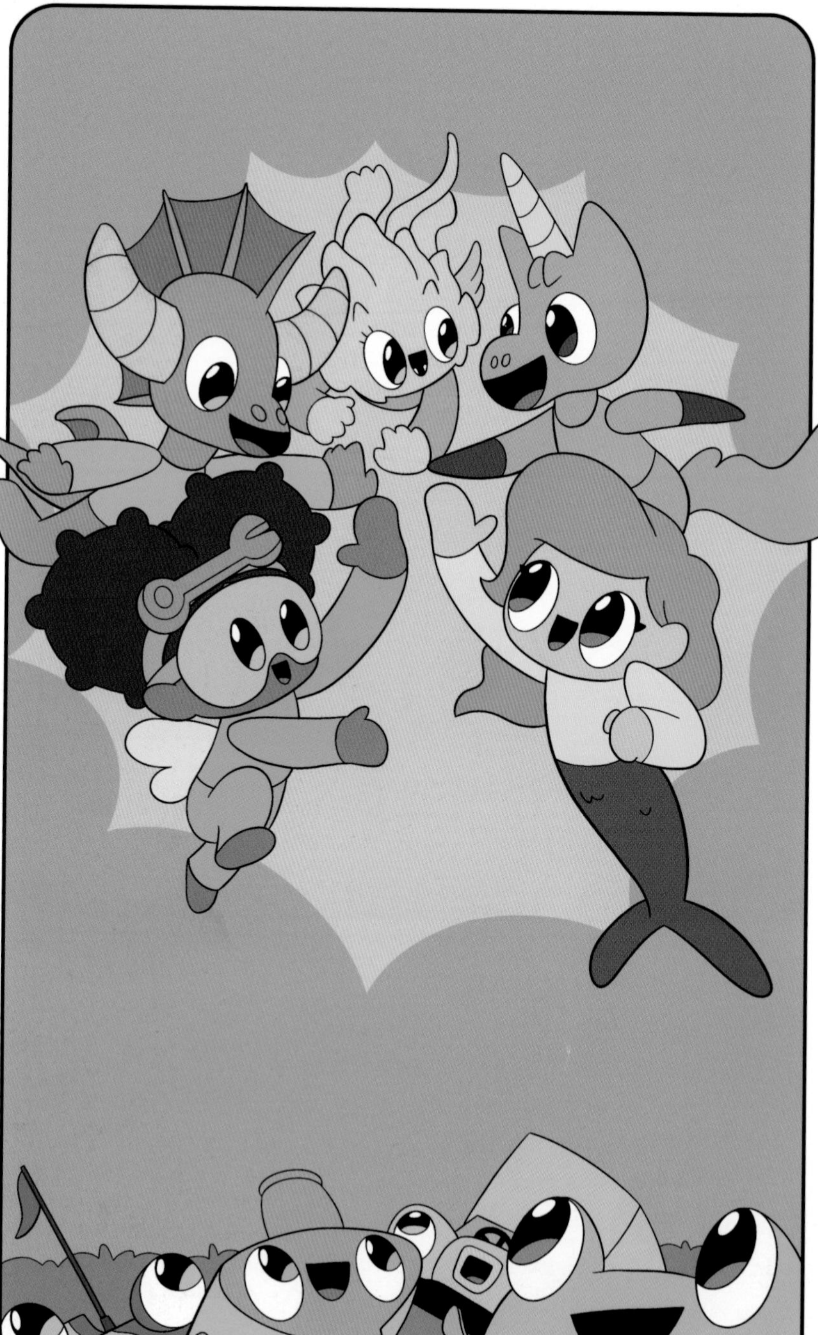

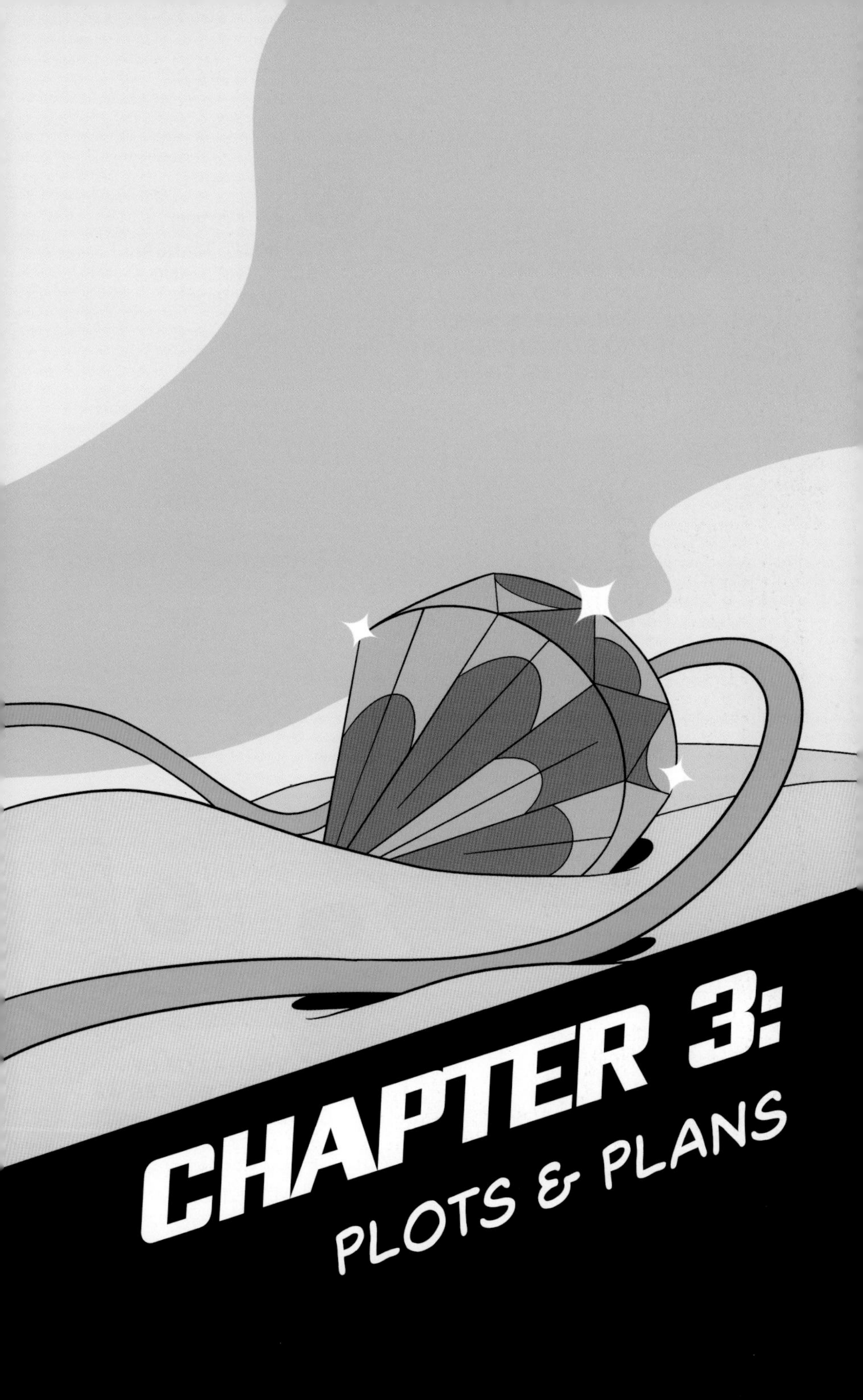

CHAPTER 3:
PLOTS & PLANS

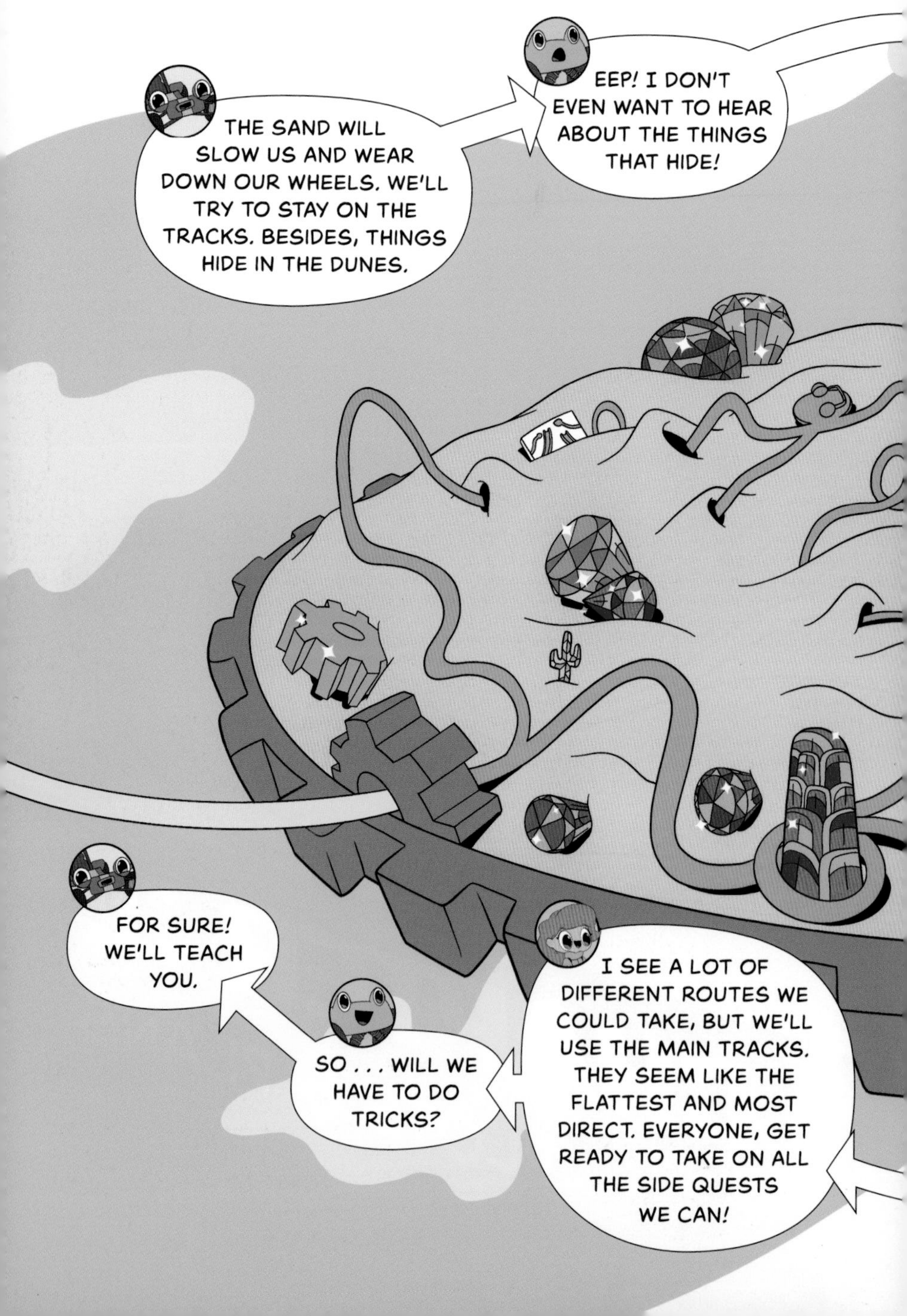
THE SAND WILL SLOW US AND WEAR DOWN OUR WHEELS. WE'LL TRY TO STAY ON THE TRACKS. BESIDES, THINGS HIDE IN THE DUNES.
EEP! I DON'T EVEN WANT TO HEAR ABOUT THE THINGS THAT HIDE!
I SEE A LOT OF DIFFERENT ROUTES WE COULD TAKE, BUT WE'LL USE THE MAIN TRACKS. THEY SEEM LIKE THE FLATTEST AND MOST DIRECT. EVERYONE, GET READY TO TAKE ON ALL THE SIDE QUESTS WE CAN!
SO . . . WILL WE HAVE TO DO TRICKS?
FOR SURE! WE'LL TEACH YOU.

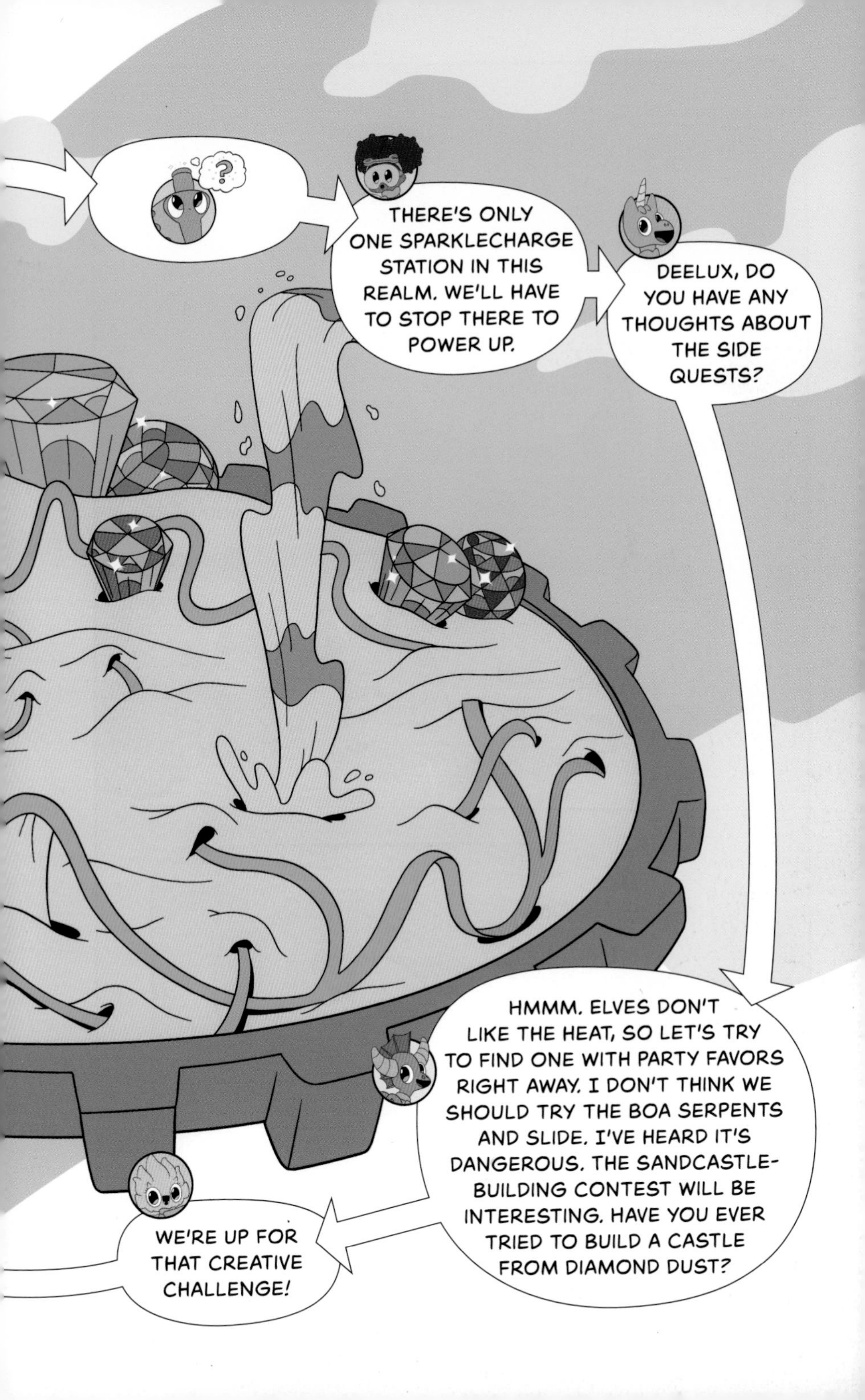
THERE'S ONLY ONE SPARKLECHARGE STATION IN THIS REALM. WE'LL HAVE TO STOP THERE TO POWER UP.
DEELUX, DO YOU HAVE ANY THOUGHTS ABOUT THE SIDE QUESTS?
HMMM. ELVES DON'T LIKE THE HEAT, SO LET'S TRY TO FIND ONE WITH PARTY FAVORS RIGHT AWAY. I DON'T THINK WE SHOULD TRY THE BOA SERPENTS AND SLIDE. I'VE HEARD IT'S DANGEROUS. THE SANDCASTLE-BUILDING CONTEST WILL BE INTERESTING. HAVE YOU EVER TRIED TO BUILD A CASTLE FROM DIAMOND DUST?
WE'RE UP FOR THAT CREATIVE CHALLENGE!

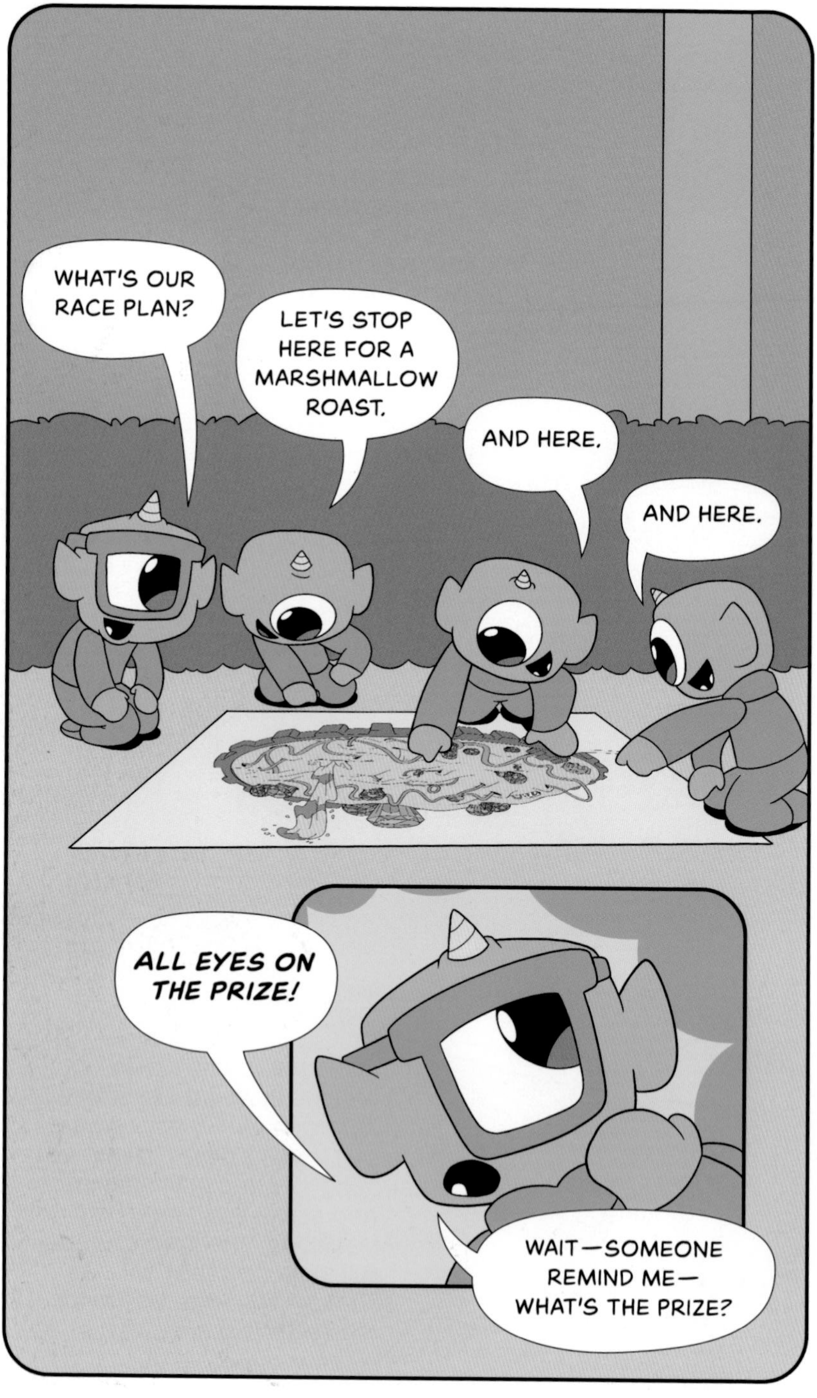
WHAT'S OUR RACE PLAN?
LET'S STOP HERE FOR A MARSHMALLOW ROAST.
AND HERE.
AND HERE.
ALL EYES ON THE PRIZE!
WAIT—SOMEONE REMIND ME—WHAT'S THE PRIZE?

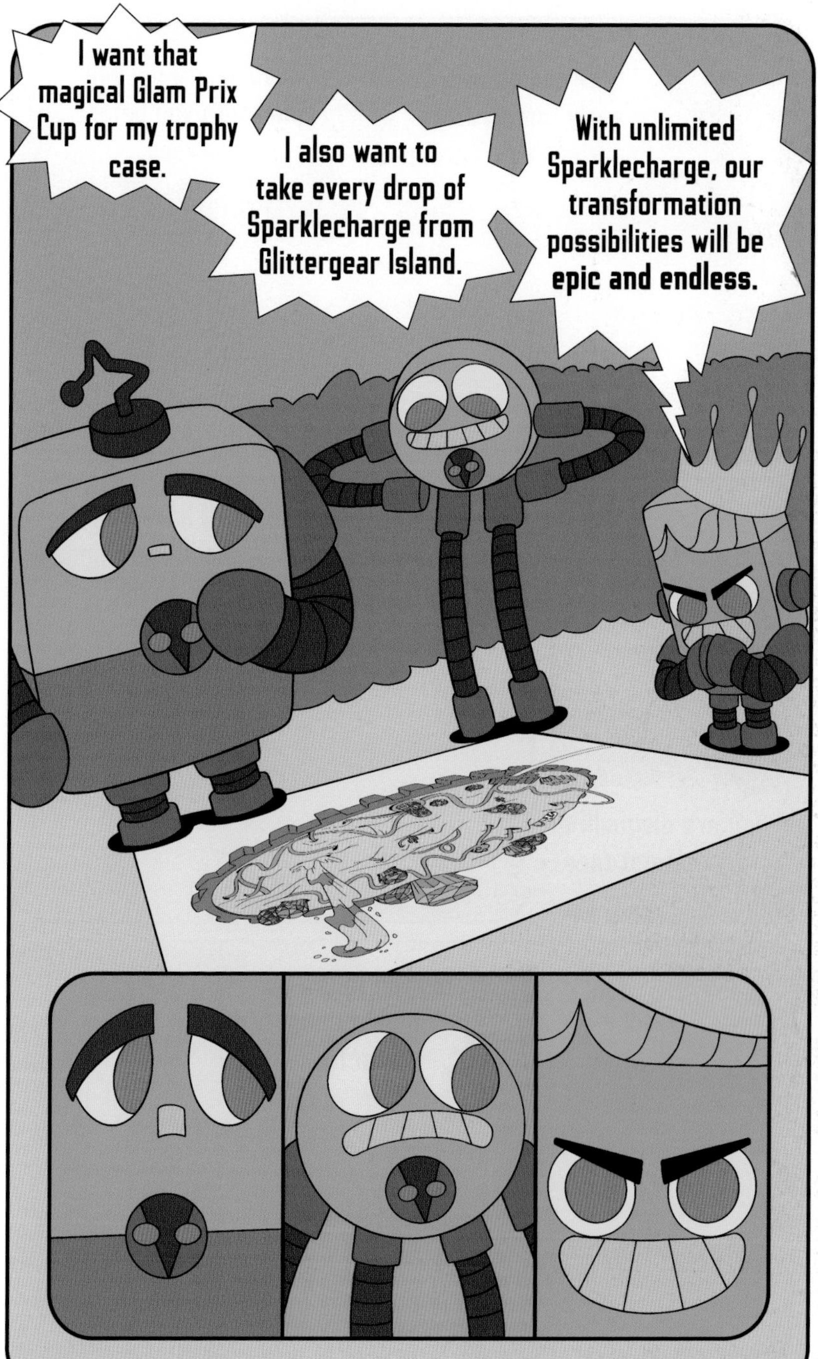
I want that magical Glam Prix Cup for my trophy case.
I also want to take every drop of Sparklecharge from Glittergear Island.
With unlimited Sparklecharge, our transformation possibilities will be epic and endless.

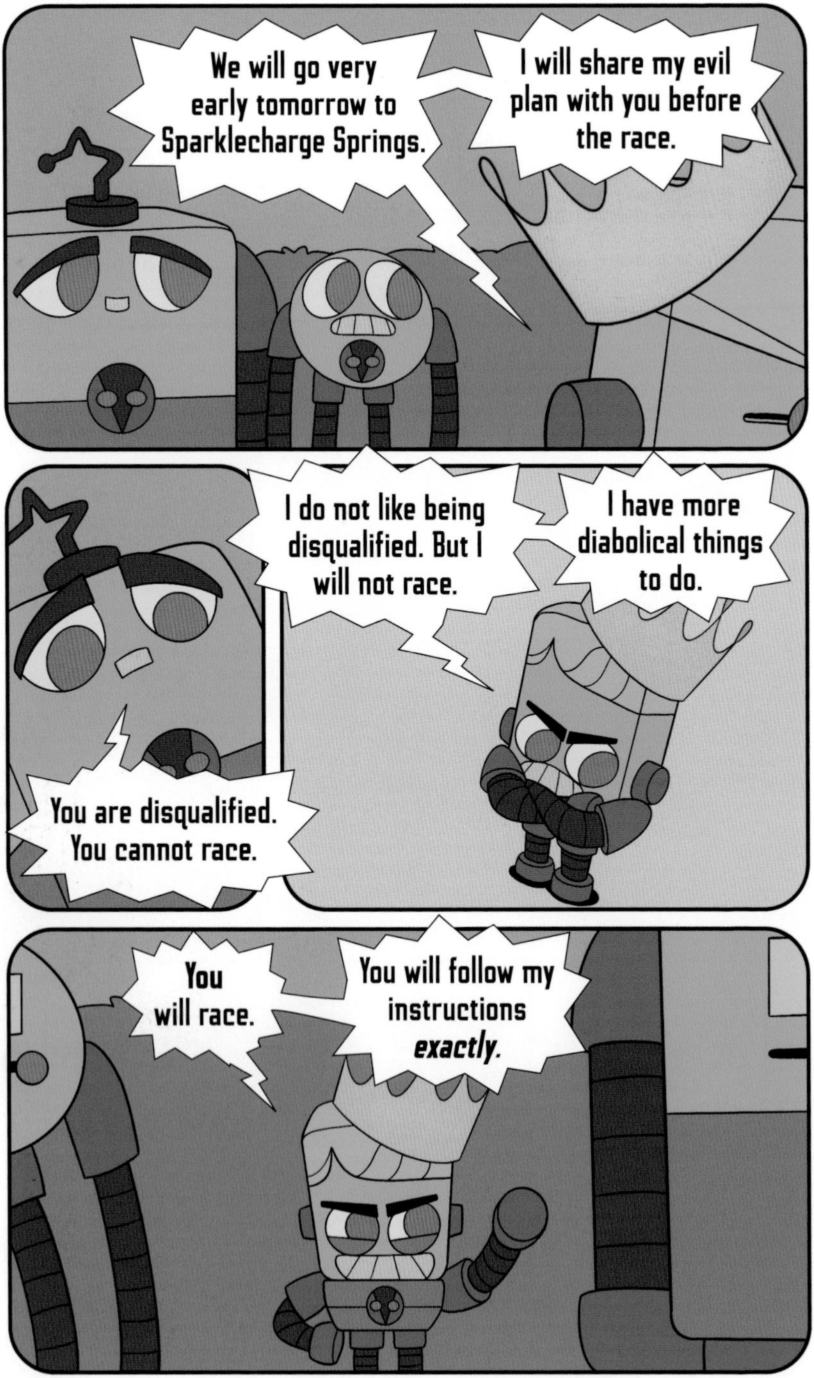
We will go very early tomorrow to Sparklecharge Springs.
I will share my evil plan with you before the race.
You are disqualified. You cannot race.
I do not like being disqualified. But I will not race.
I have more diabolical things to do.
You will race.
You will follow my instructions *exactly*.

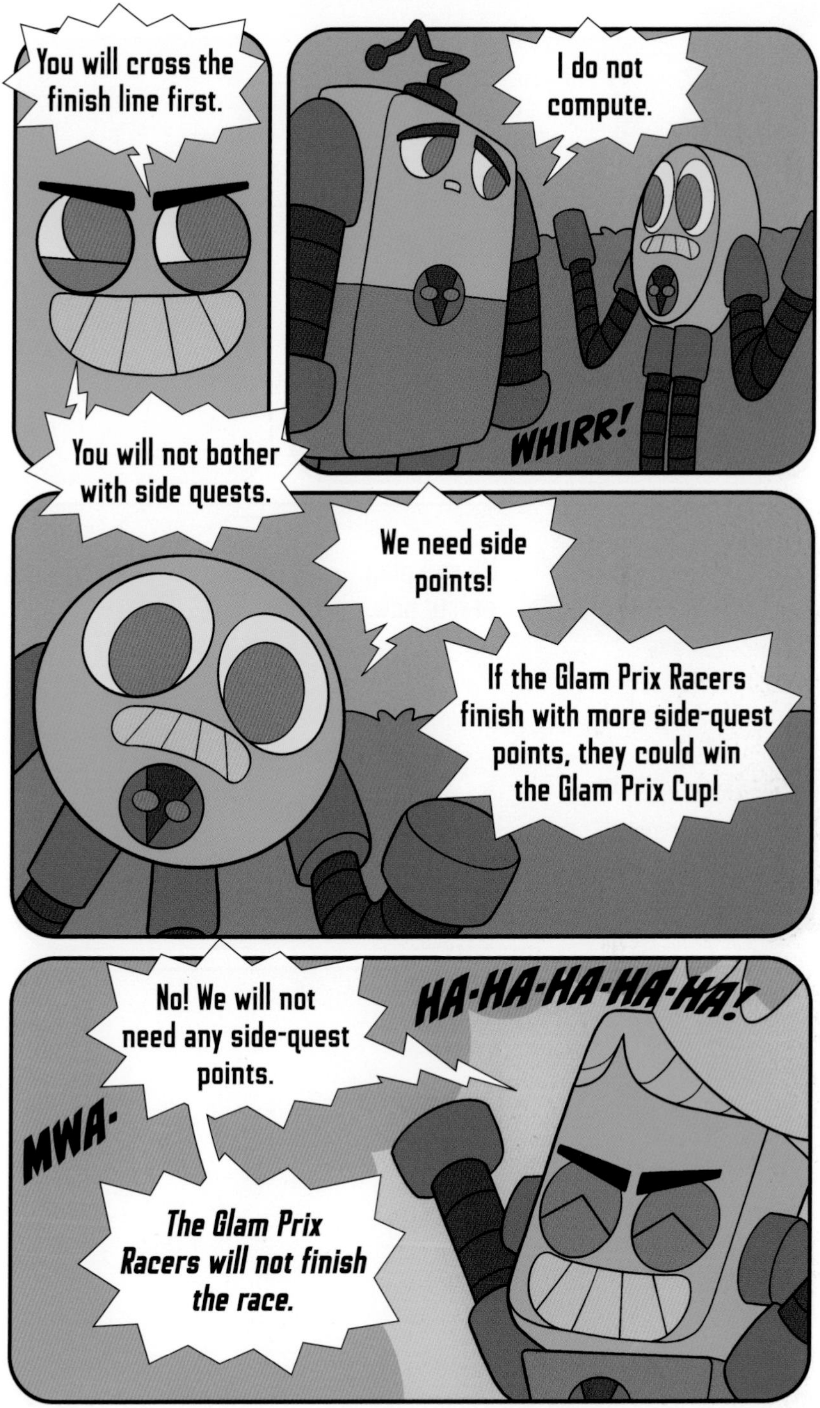
You will cross the finish line first.
I do not compute.
WHIRR!
You will not bother with side quests.
We need side points!
If the Glam Prix Racers finish with more side-quest points, they could win the Glam Prix Cup!
No! We will not need any side-quest points.
HA-HA-HA-HA-HA!
MWA-
The Glam Prix Racers will not finish the race.

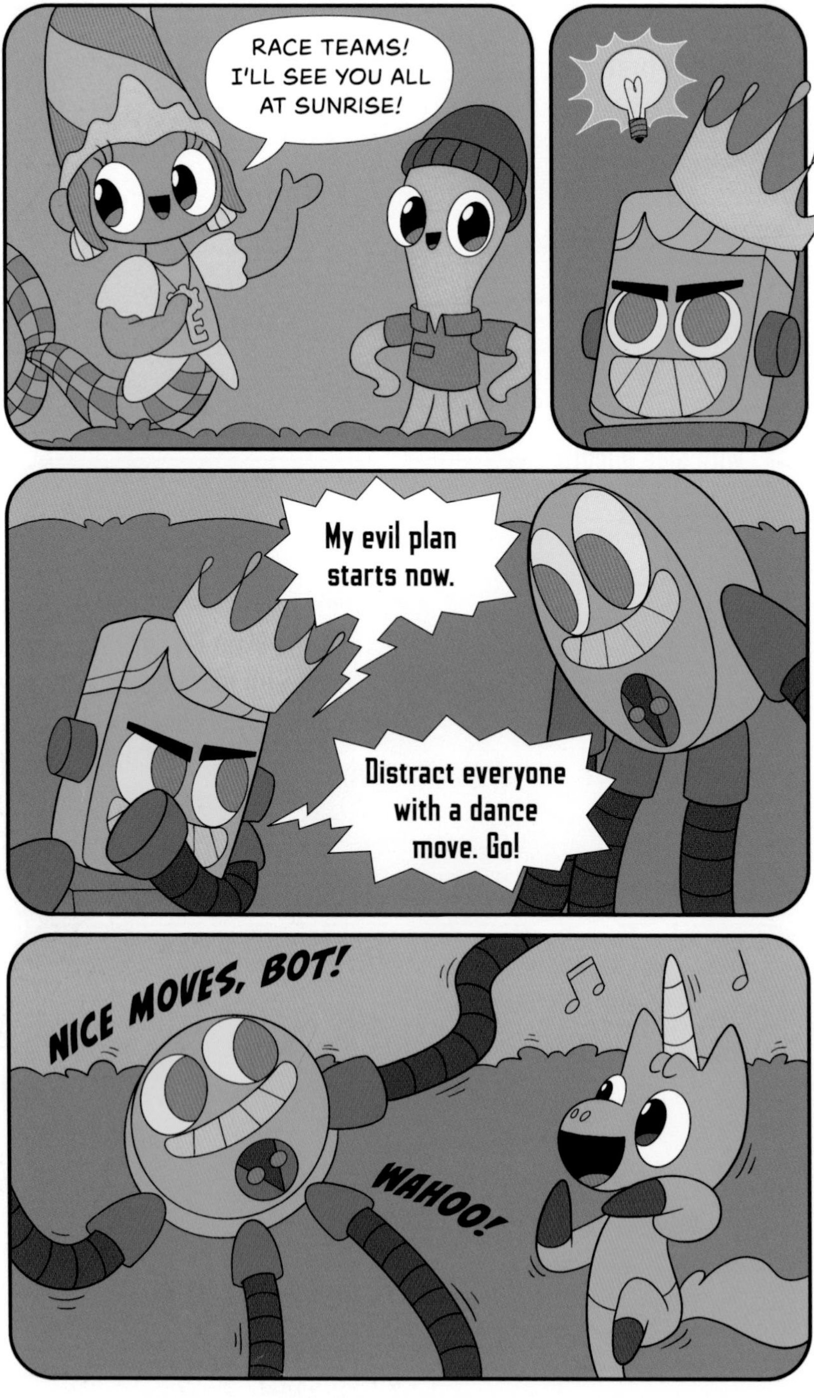
RACE TEAMS! I'LL SEE YOU ALL AT SUNRISE!
My evil plan starts now.
Distract everyone with a dance move. Go!
NICE MOVES, BOT!
WAHOO!

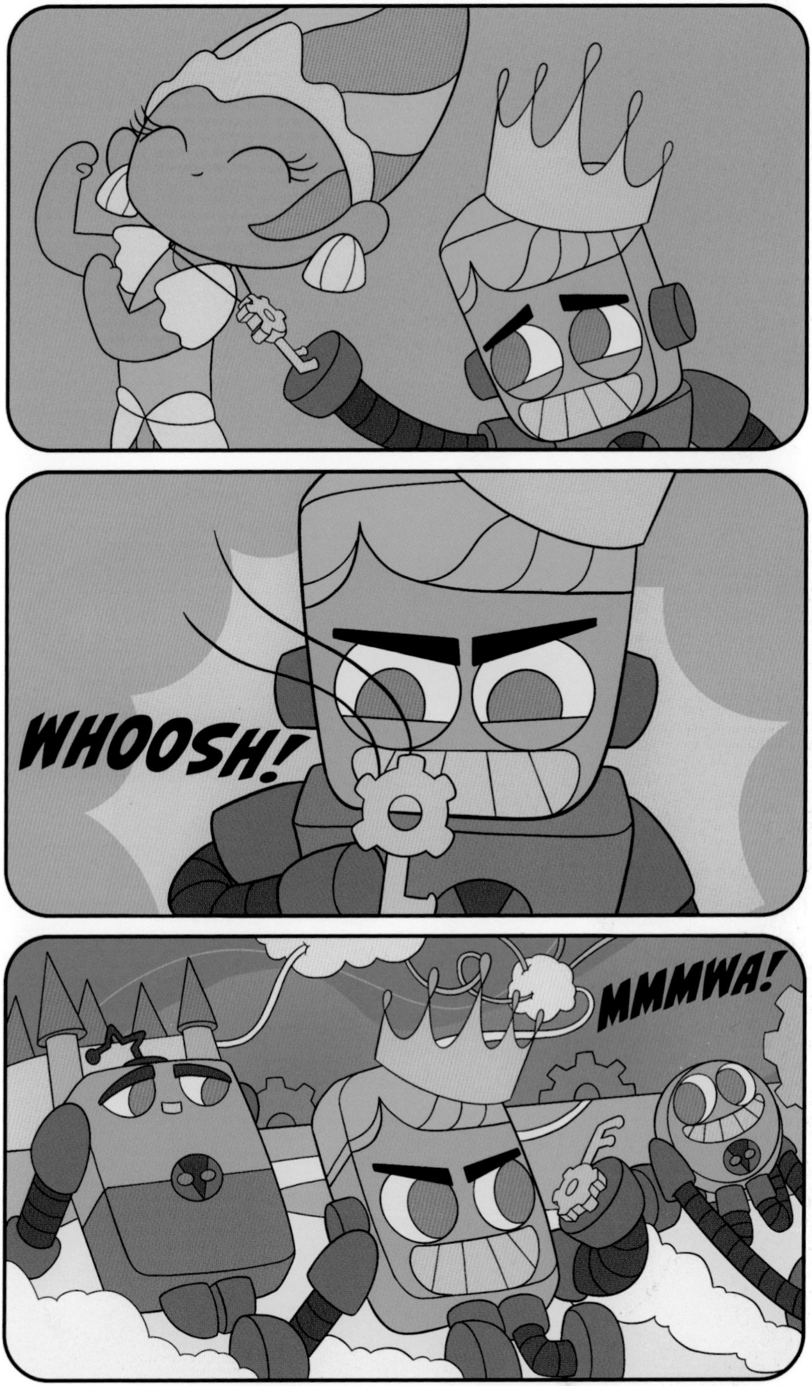
WHOOSH!
MMMWA!

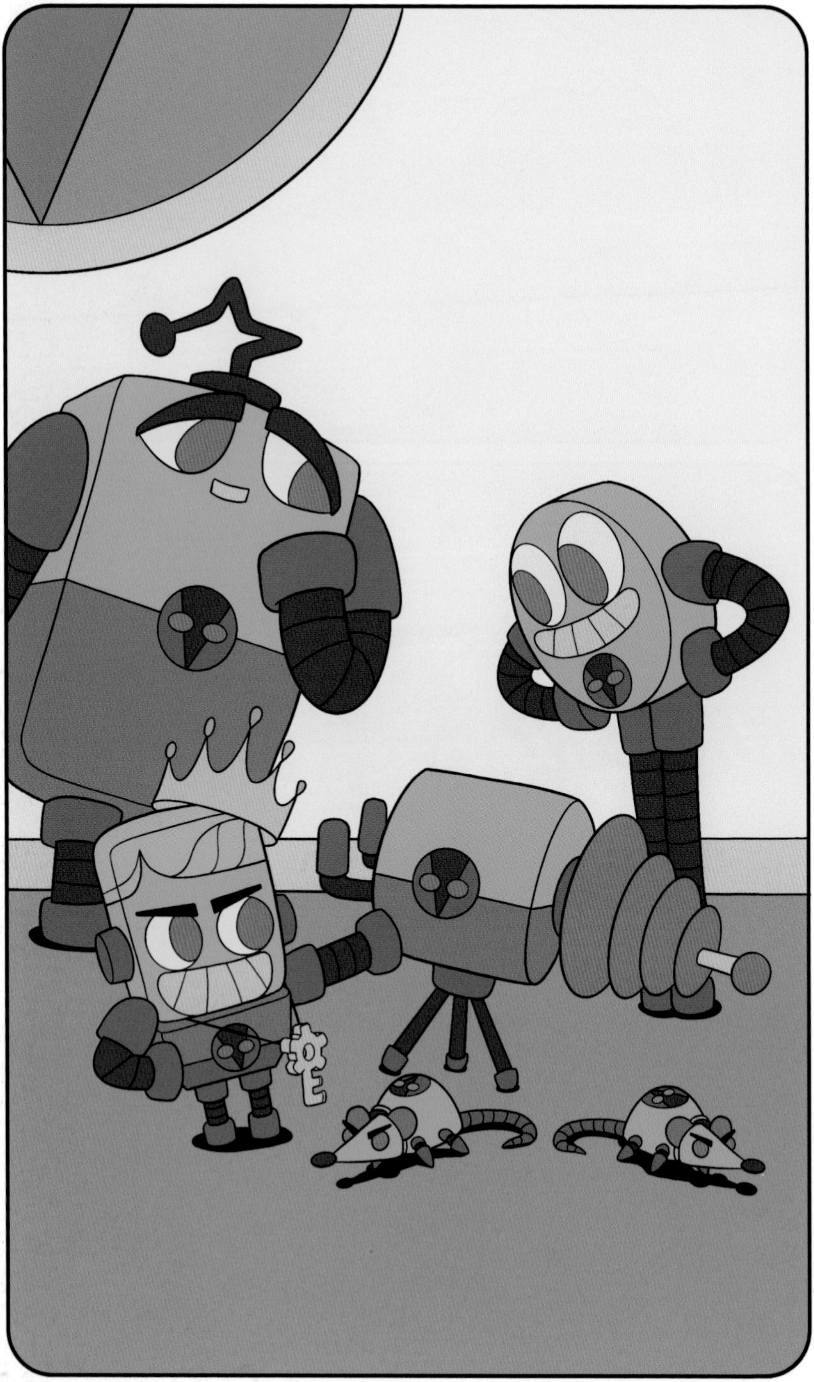

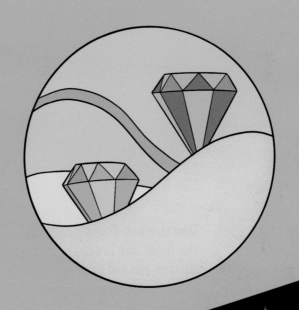

CHAPTER 4:
GET S-S-S-SET, GO!

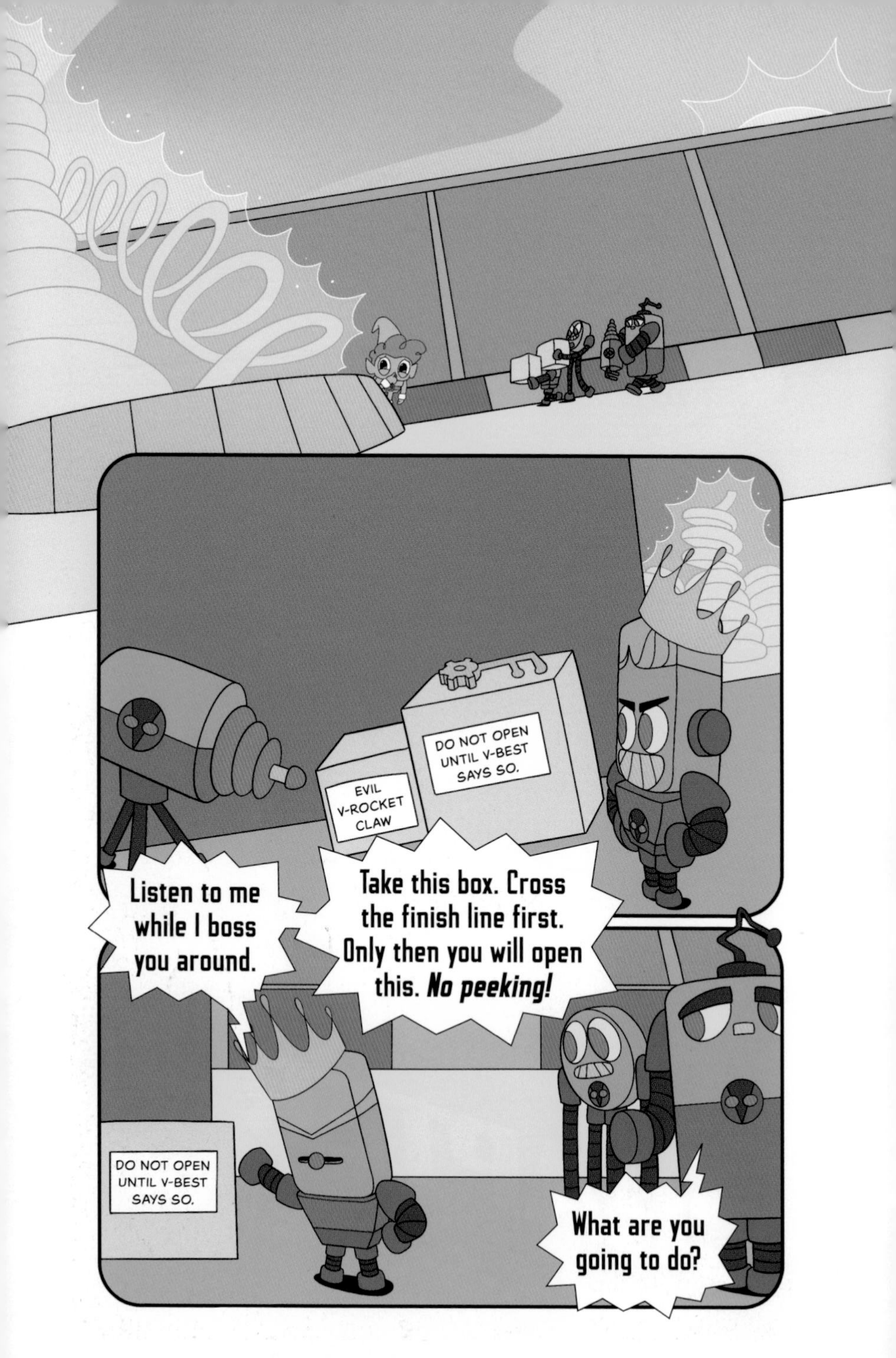
EVIL
V-ROCKET
CLAW
DO NOT OPEN
UNTIL V-BEST
SAYS SO.
Listen to me while I boss you around.
Take this box. Cross the finish line first. Only then you will open this. *No peeking!*
DO NOT OPEN
UNTIL V-BEST
SAYS SO.
What are you going to do?

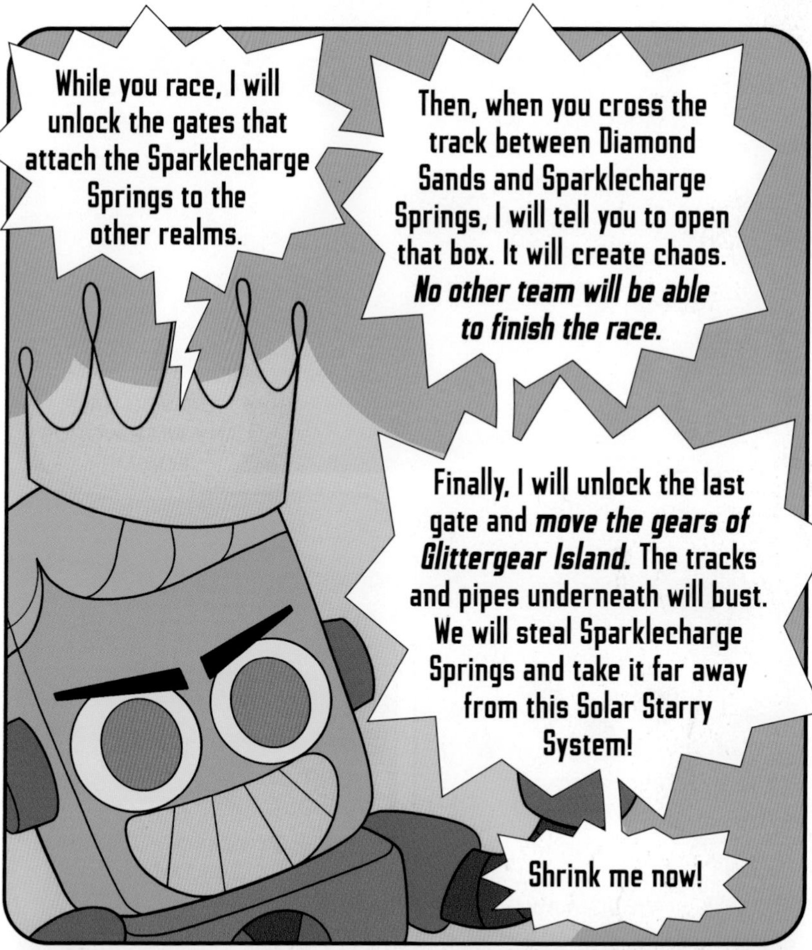
While you race, I will unlock the gates that attach the Sparklecharge Springs to the other realms.
Then, when you cross the track between Diamond Sands and Sparklecharge Springs, I will tell you to open that box. It will create chaos. *No other team will be able to finish the race.*
Finally, I will unlock the last gate and *move the gears of Glittergear Island.* The tracks and pipes underneath will bust. We will steal Sparklecharge Springs and take it far away from this Solar Starry System!
Shrink me now!

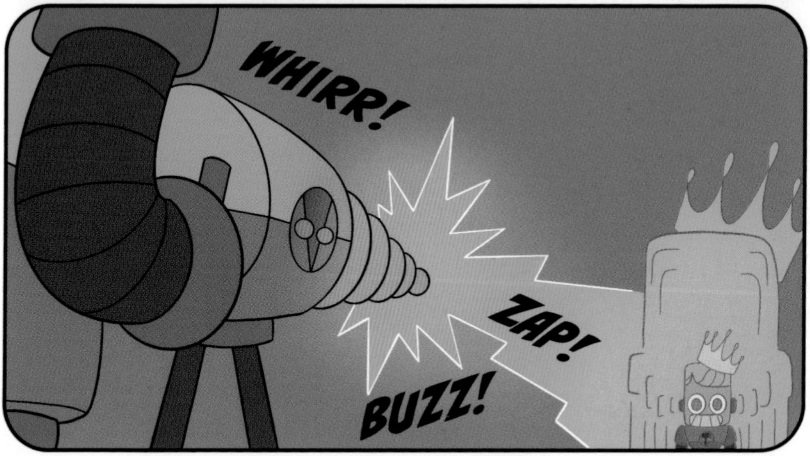
WHIRR!
ZAP!
BUZZ!

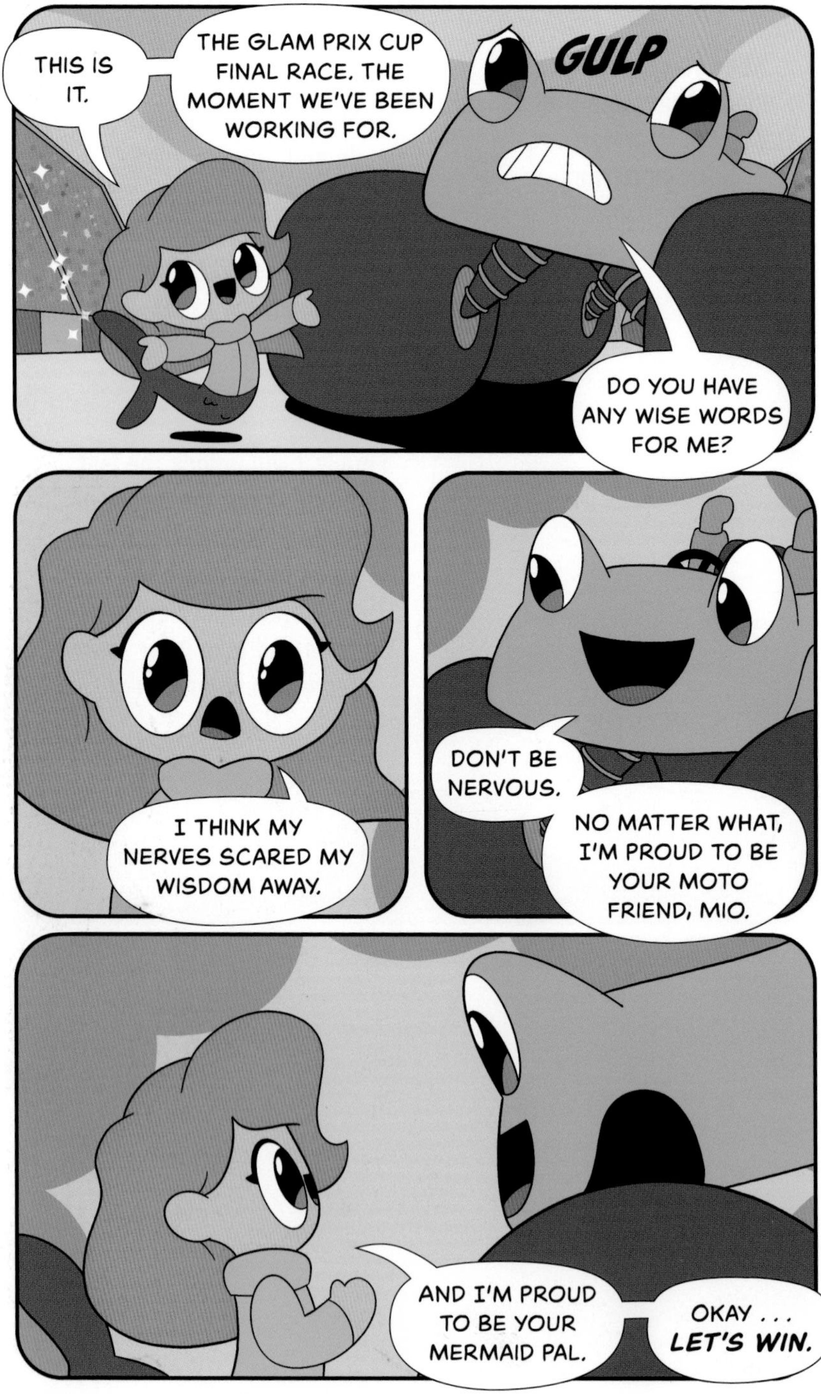
THIS IS IT.
THE GLAM PRIX CUP FINAL RACE. THE MOMENT WE'VE BEEN WORKING FOR.
GULP
DO YOU HAVE ANY WISE WORDS FOR ME?
I THINK MY NERVES SCARED MY WISDOM AWAY.
DON'T BE NERVOUS.
NO MATTER WHAT, I'M PROUD TO BE YOUR MOTO FRIEND, MIO.
AND I'M PROUD TO BE YOUR MERMAID PAL.
OKAY . . . LET'S WIN.

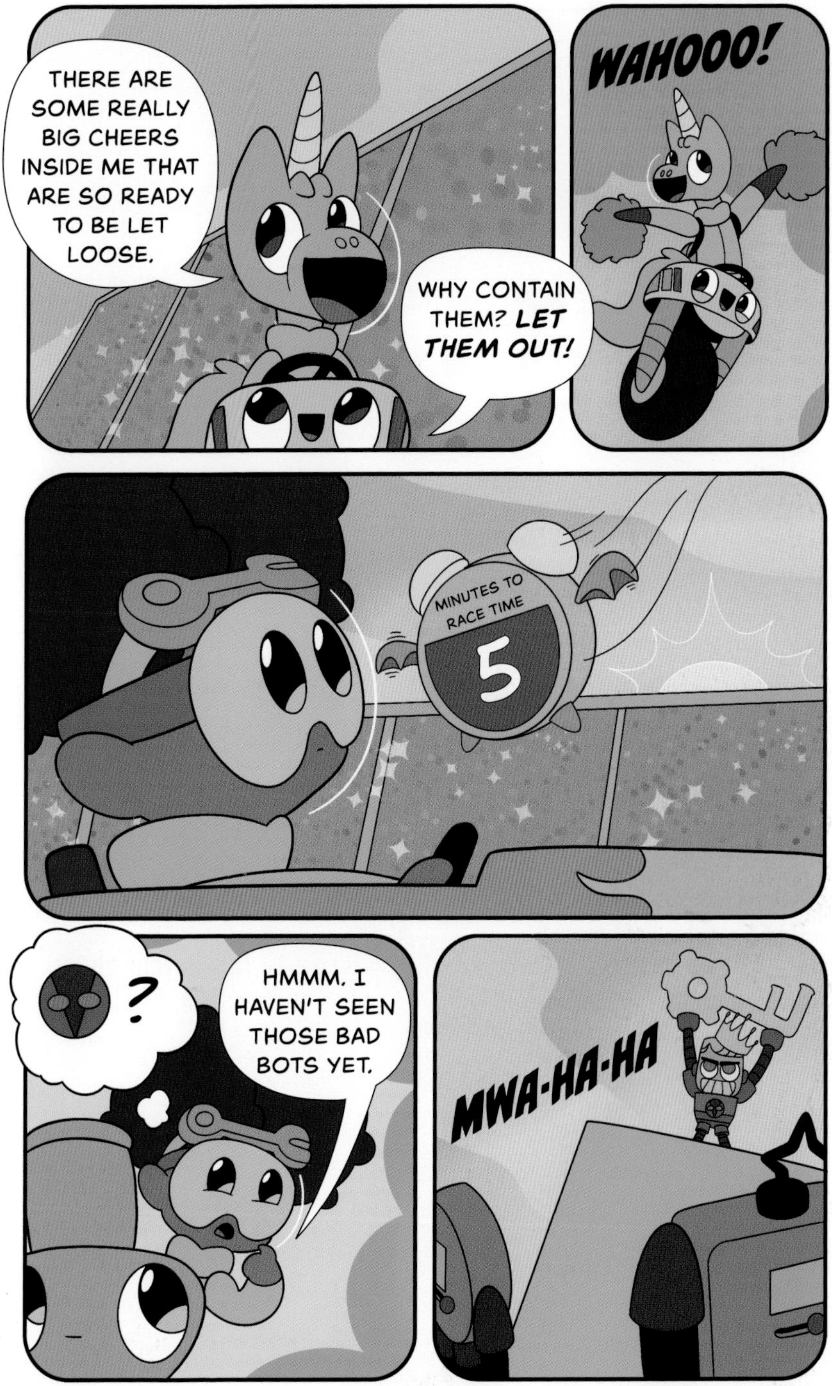
THERE ARE SOME REALLY BIG CHEERS INSIDE ME THAT ARE SO READY TO BE LET LOOSE.
WHY CONTAIN THEM? **LET THEM OUT!**
WAHOOO!
MINUTES TO RACE TIME
5
?
HMMM. I HAVEN'T SEEN THOSE BAD BOTS YET.
MWA-HA-HA

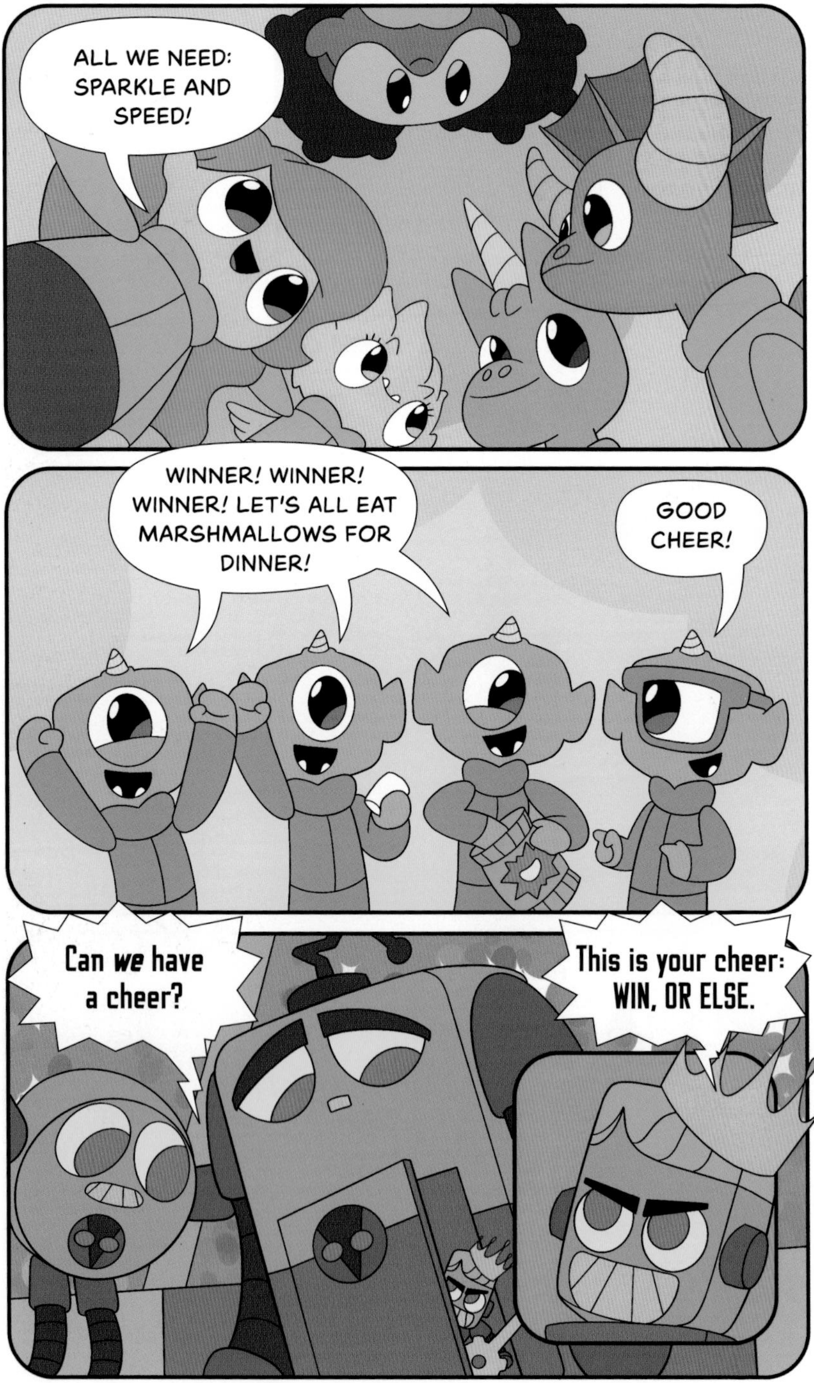
ALL WE NEED: SPARKLE AND SPEED!
WINNER! WINNER! WINNER! LET'S ALL EAT MARSHMALLOWS FOR DINNER!
GOOD CHEER!
Can *we* have a cheer?
This is your cheer: WIN, OR ELSE.

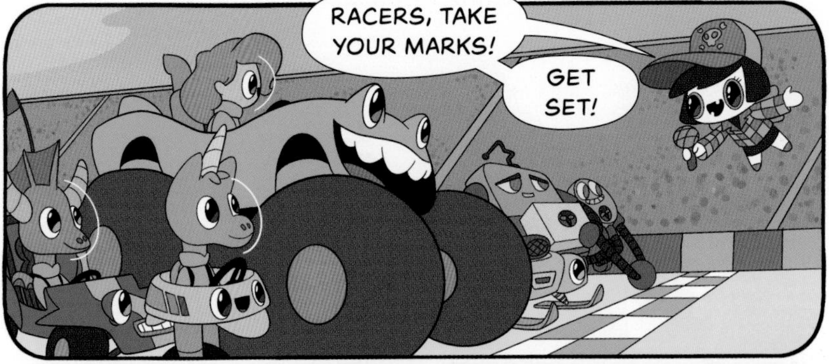
RACERS, TAKE YOUR MARKS!
GET SET!

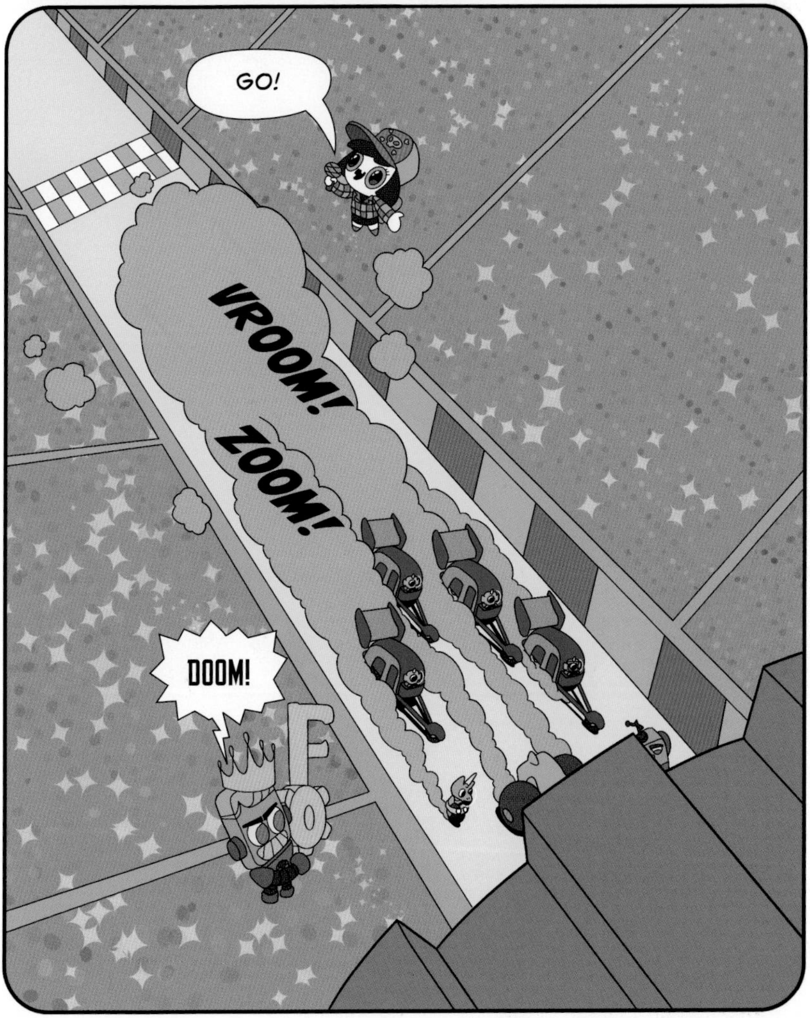
GO!
VROOM! ZOOM!
DOOM!

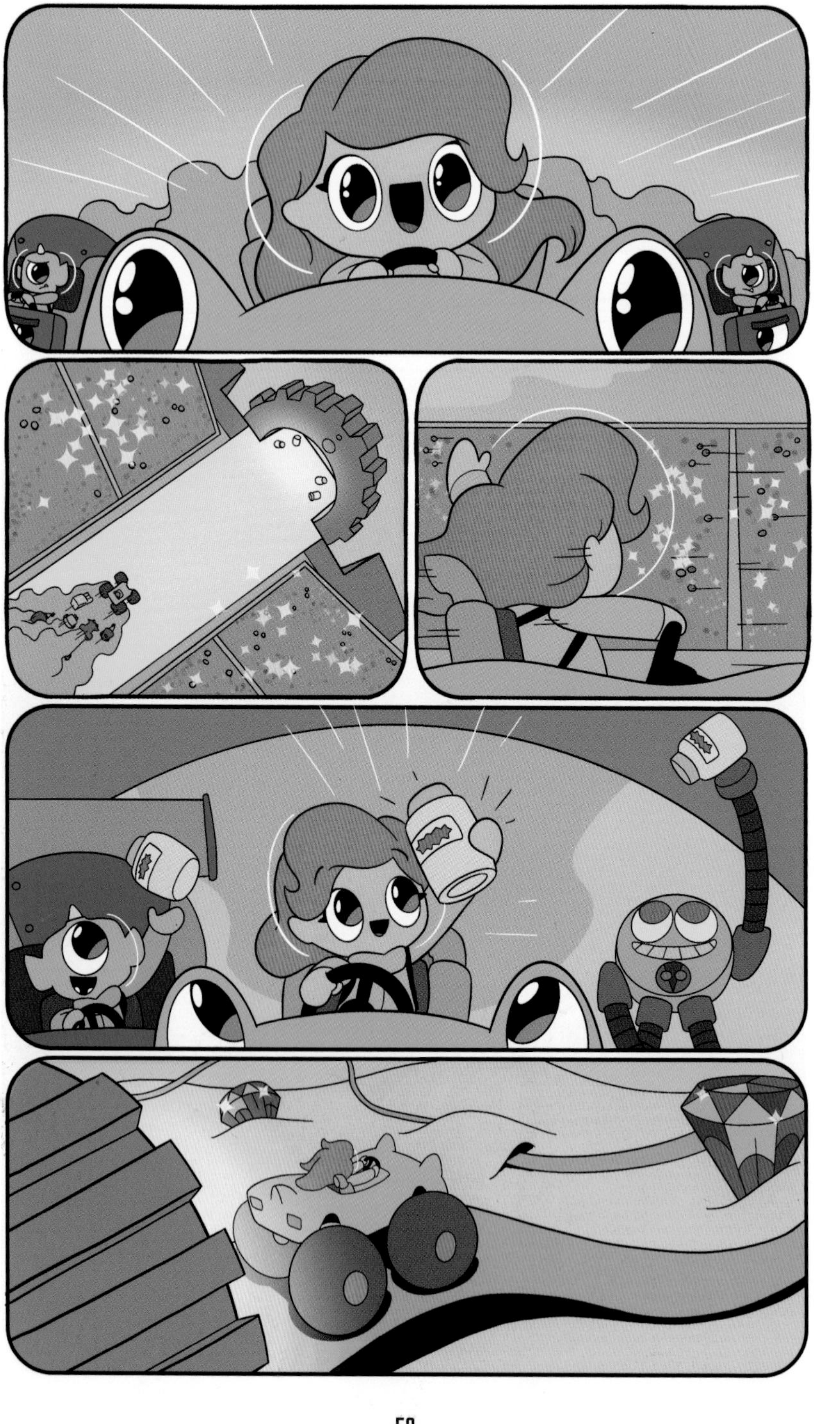

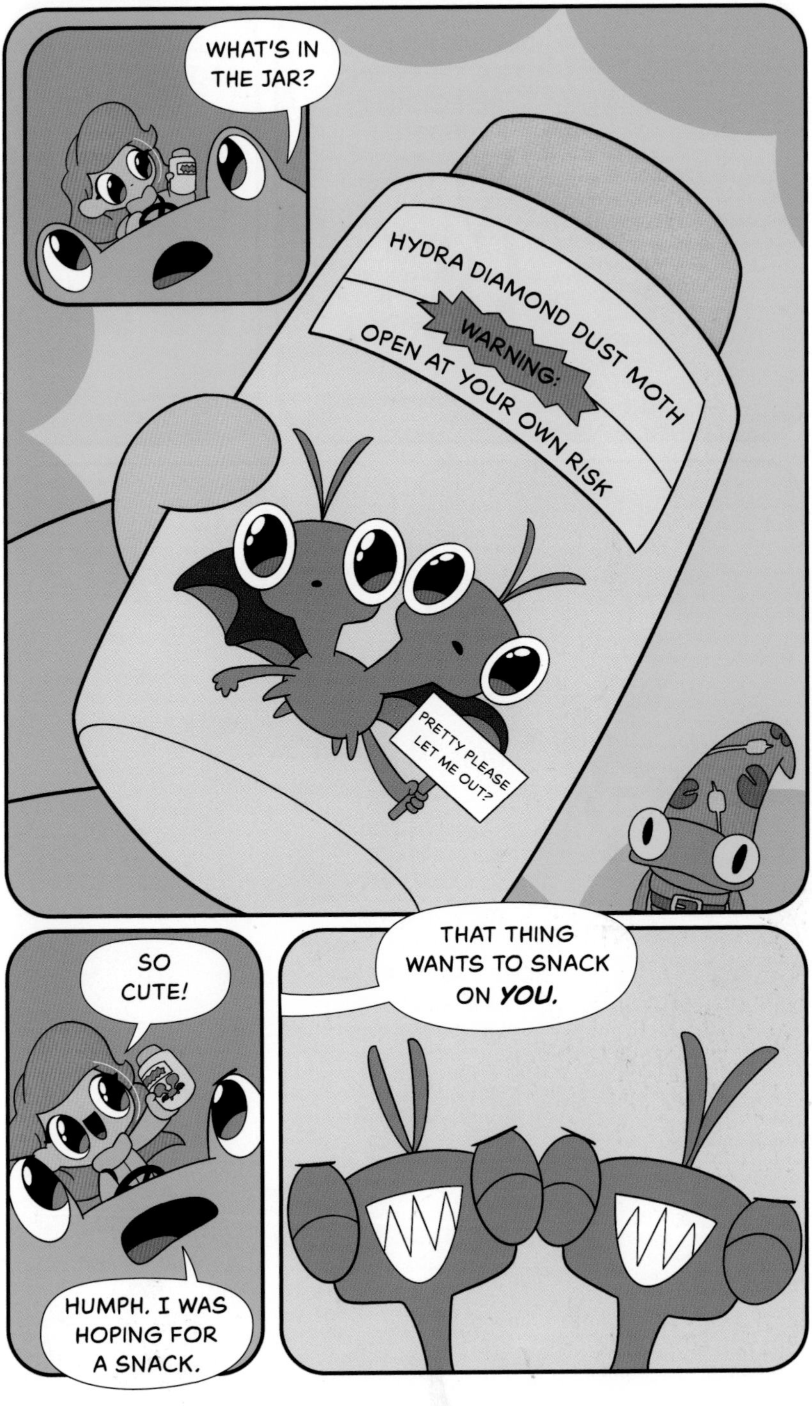
WHAT'S IN THE JAR?
HYDRA DIAMOND DUST MOTH
WARNING:
OPEN AT YOUR OWN RISK
PRETTY PLEASE LET ME OUT?
SO CUTE!
HUMPH. I WAS HOPING FOR A SNACK.
THAT THING WANTS TO SNACK ON *YOU.*

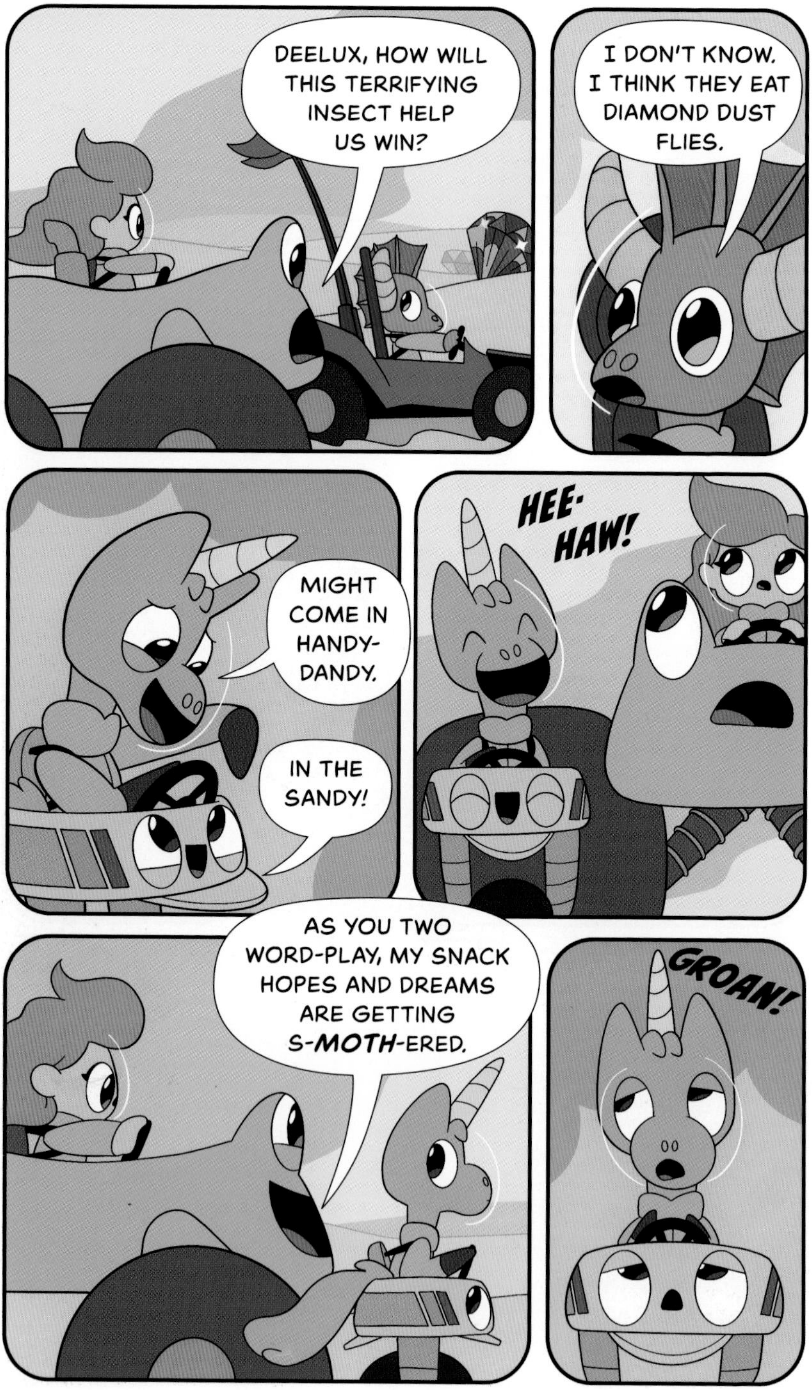
DEELUX, HOW WILL THIS TERRIFYING INSECT HELP US WIN?
I DON'T KNOW. I THINK THEY EAT DIAMOND DUST FLIES.
MIGHT COME IN HANDY-DANDY.
IN THE SANDY!
HEE-HAW!
AS YOU TWO WORD-PLAY, MY SNACK HOPES AND DREAMS ARE GETTING S-*MOTH*-ERED.
GROAN!

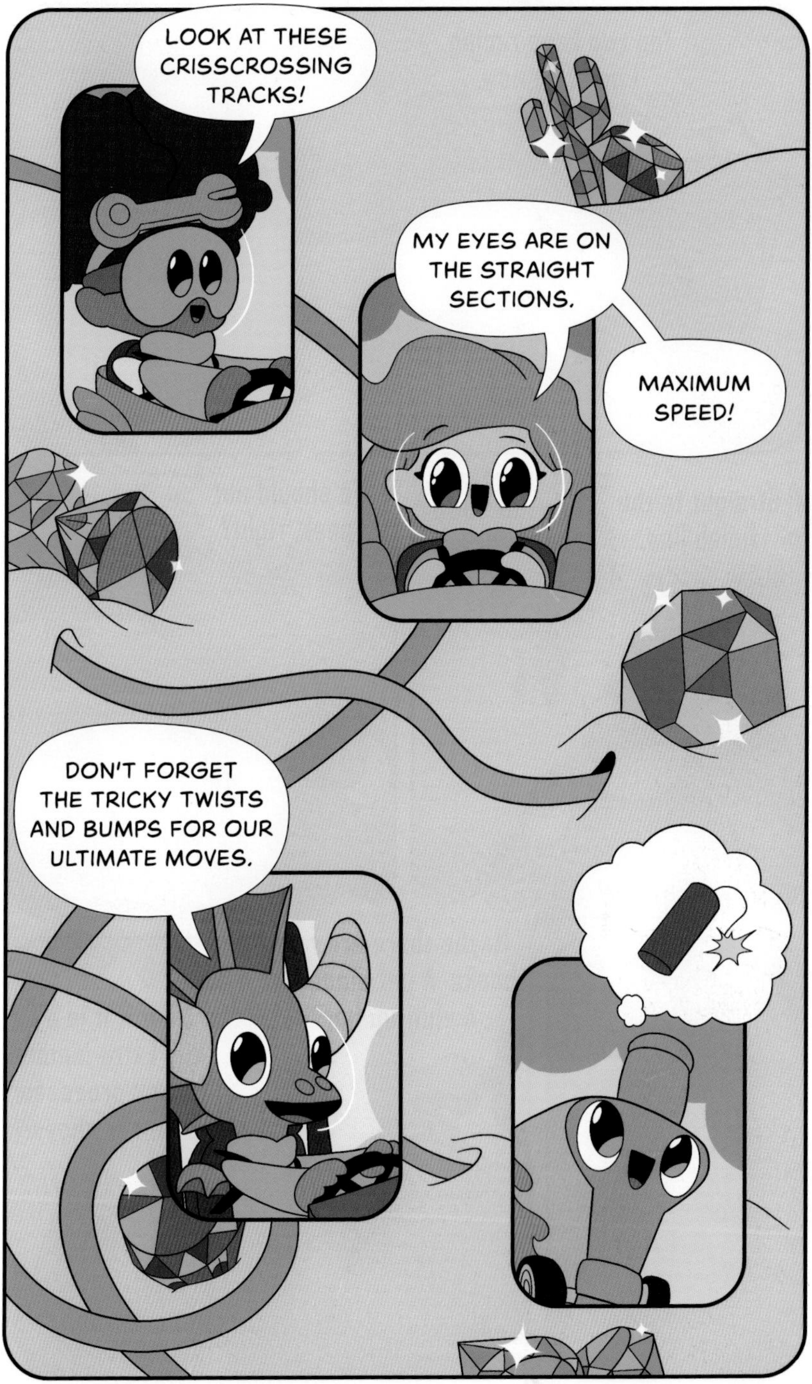
LOOK AT THESE CRISSCROSSING TRACKS!
MY EYES ARE ON THE STRAIGHT SECTIONS.
MAXIMUM SPEED!
DON'T FORGET THE TRICKY TWISTS AND BUMPS FOR OUR ULTIMATE MOVES.

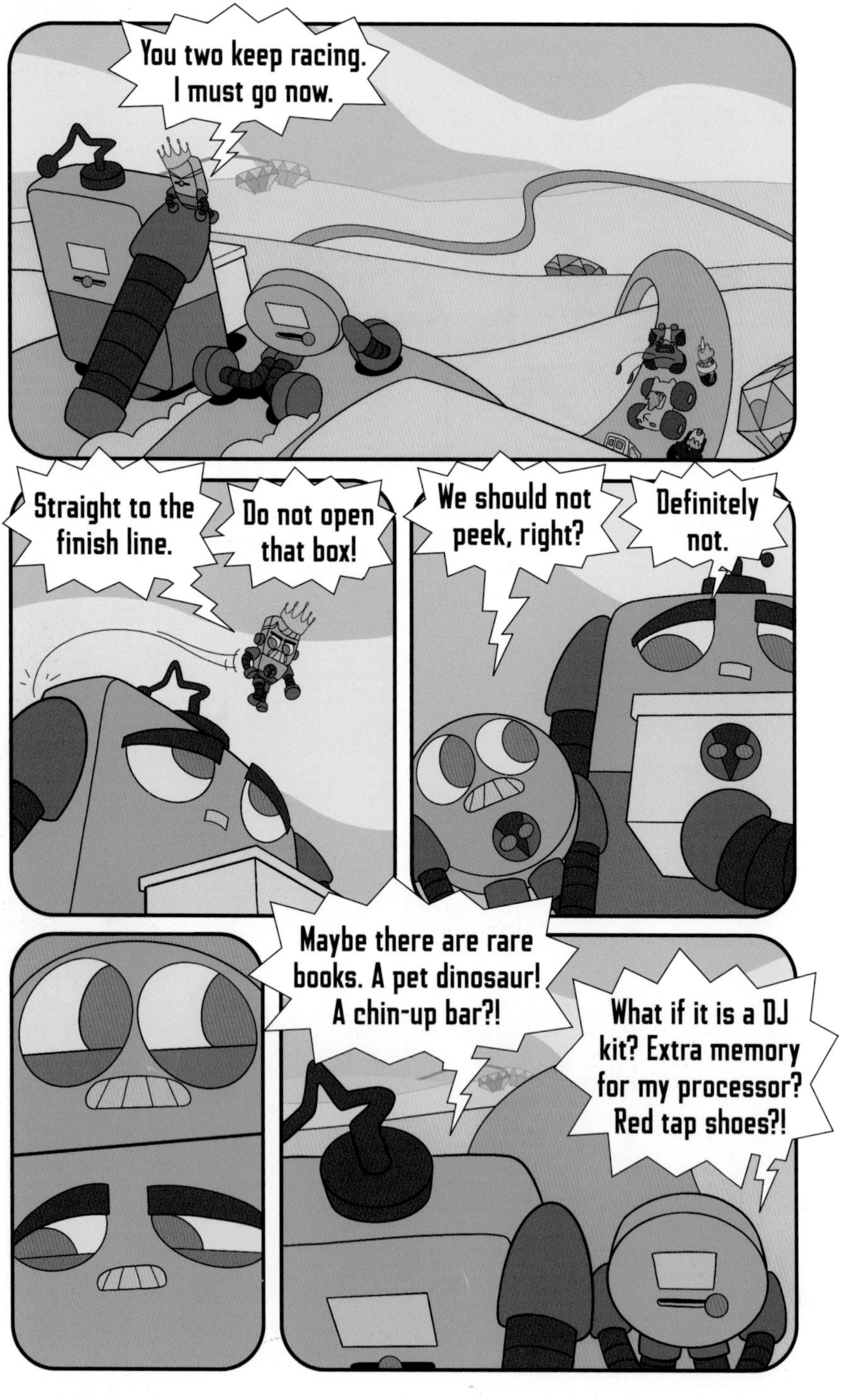
You two keep racing. I must go now.
Straight to the finish line.
Do not open that box!
We should not peek, right?
Definitely not.
Maybe there are rare books. A pet dinosaur! A chin-up bar?!
What if it is a DJ kit? Extra memory for my processor? Red tap shoes?!

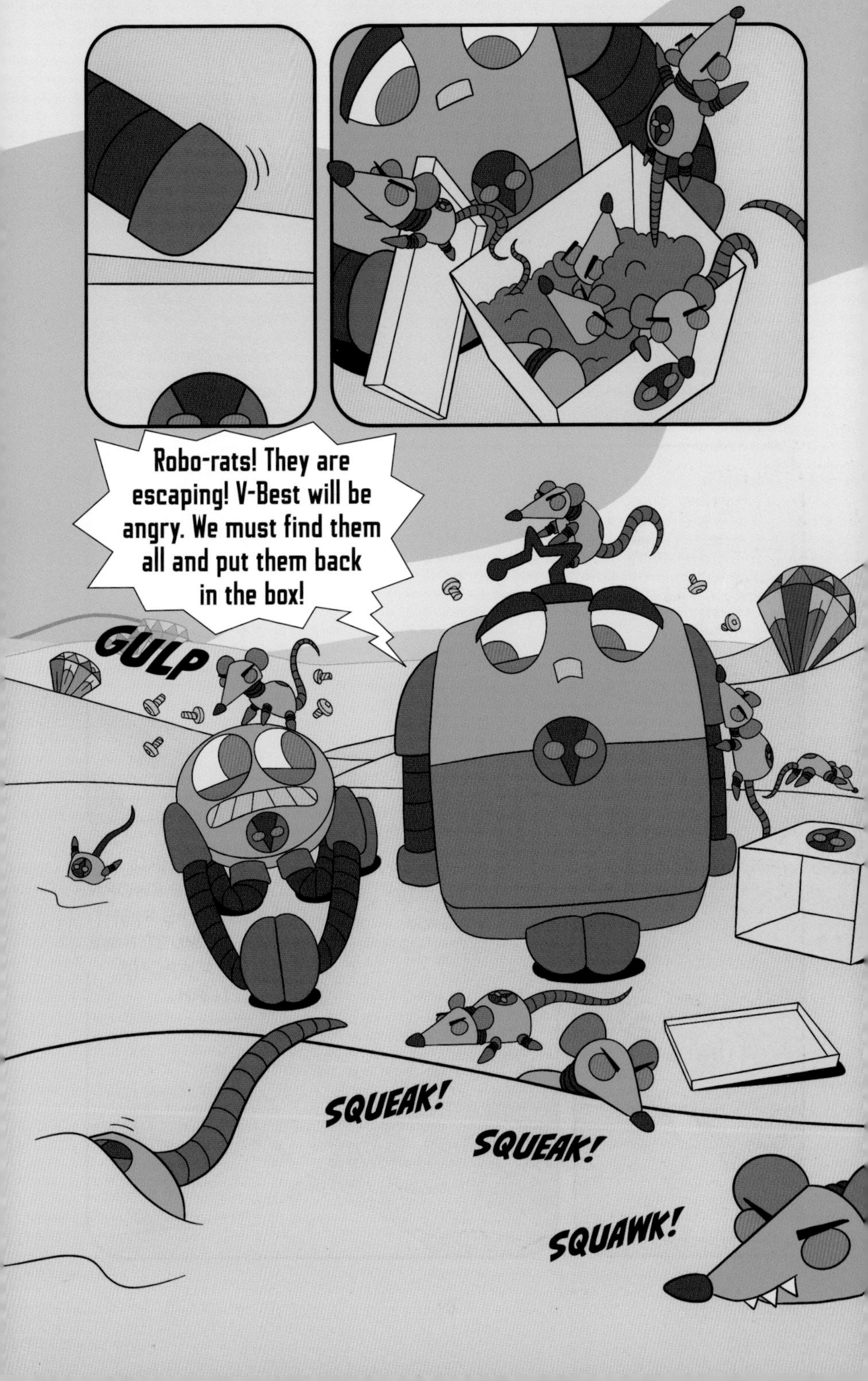
Robo-rats! They are escaping! V-Best will be angry. We must find them all and put them back in the box!
GULP
SQUEAK!
SQUEAK!
SQUAWK!

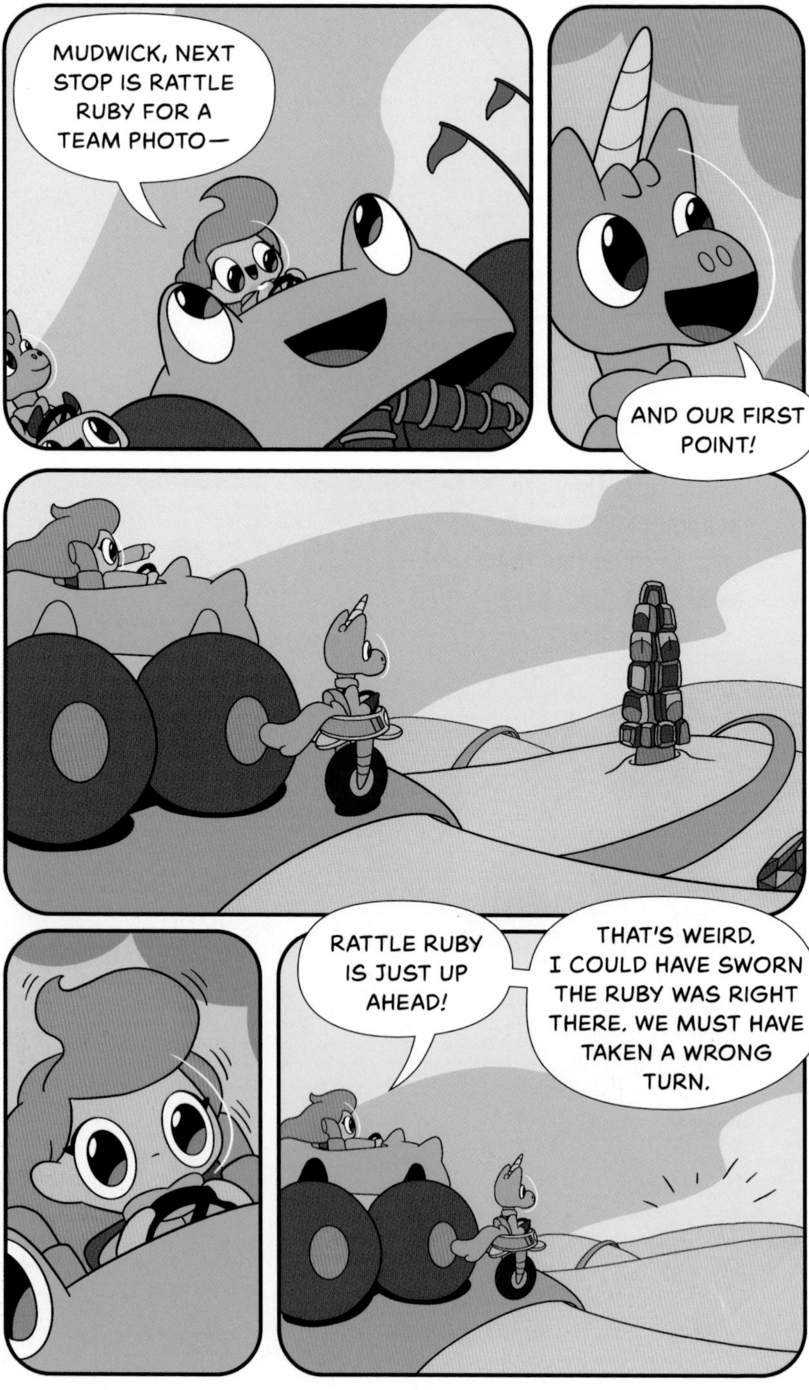
MUDWICK, NEXT STOP IS RATTLE RUBY FOR A TEAM PHOTO—
AND OUR FIRST POINT!
RATTLE RUBY IS JUST UP AHEAD!
THAT'S WEIRD. I COULD HAVE SWORN THE RUBY WAS RIGHT THERE. WE MUST HAVE TAKEN A WRONG TURN.

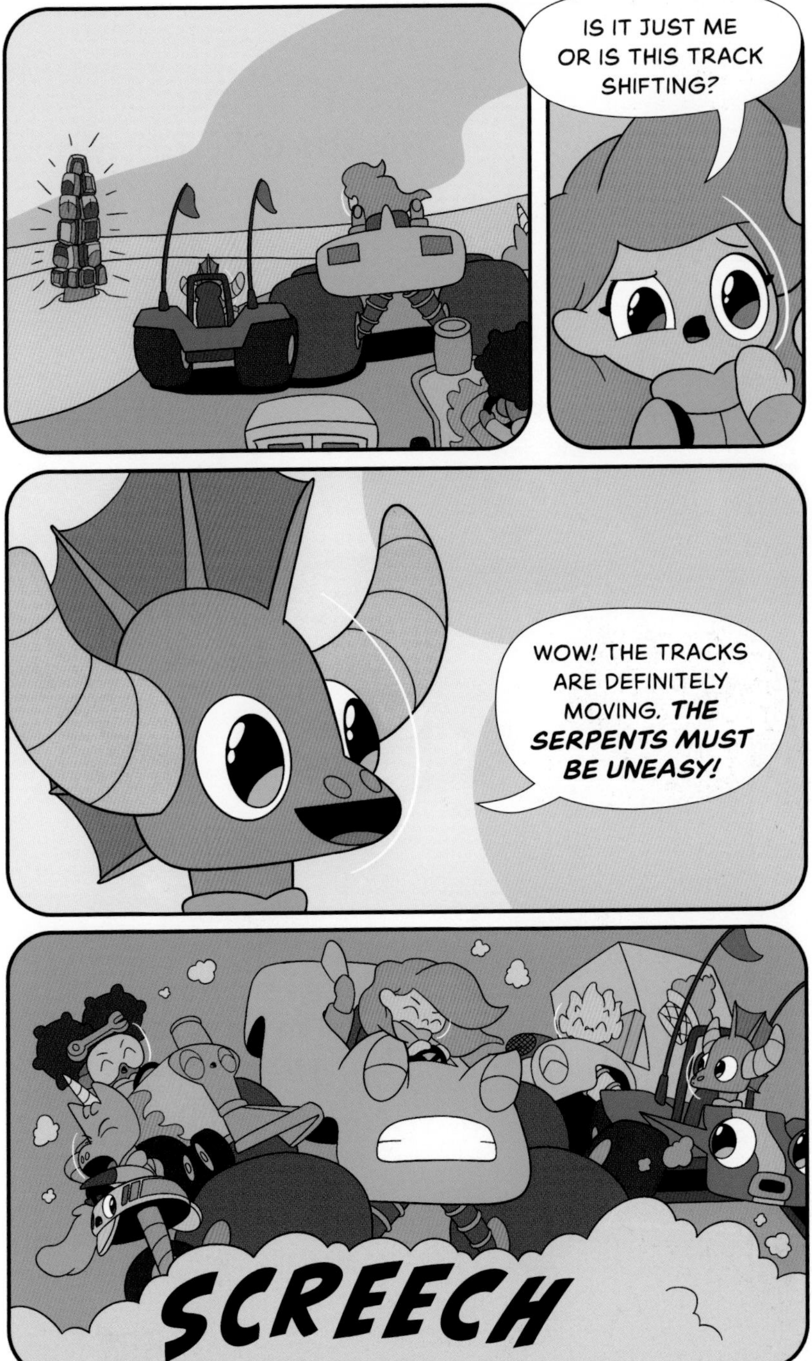
IS IT JUST ME OR IS THIS TRACK SHIFTING?
WOW! THE TRACKS ARE DEFINITELY MOVING. THE SERPENTS MUST BE UNEASY!
SCREECH

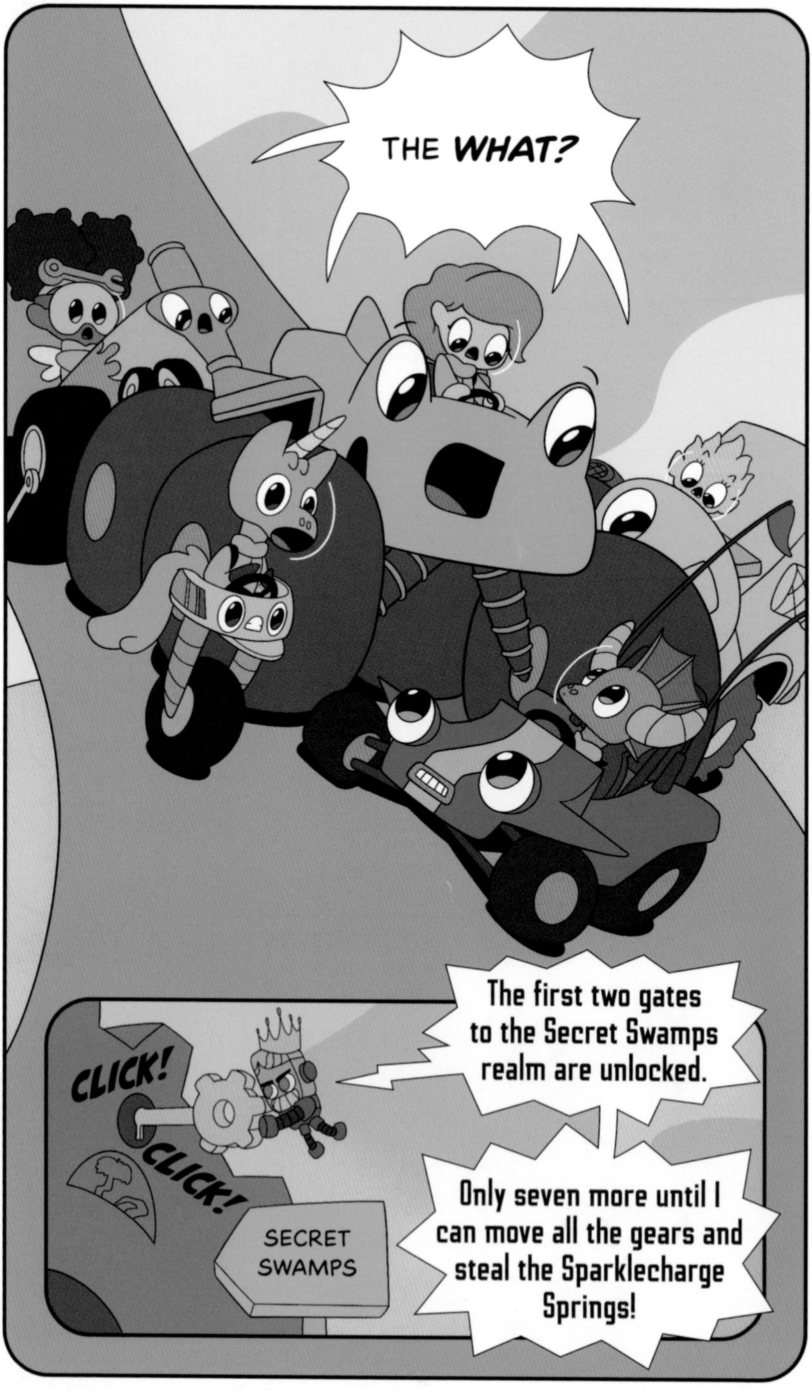
THE WHAT?
The first two gates to the Secret Swamps realm are unlocked.
CLICK!
CLICK!
SECRET SWAMPS
Only seven more until I can move all the gears and steal the Sparklecharge Springs!

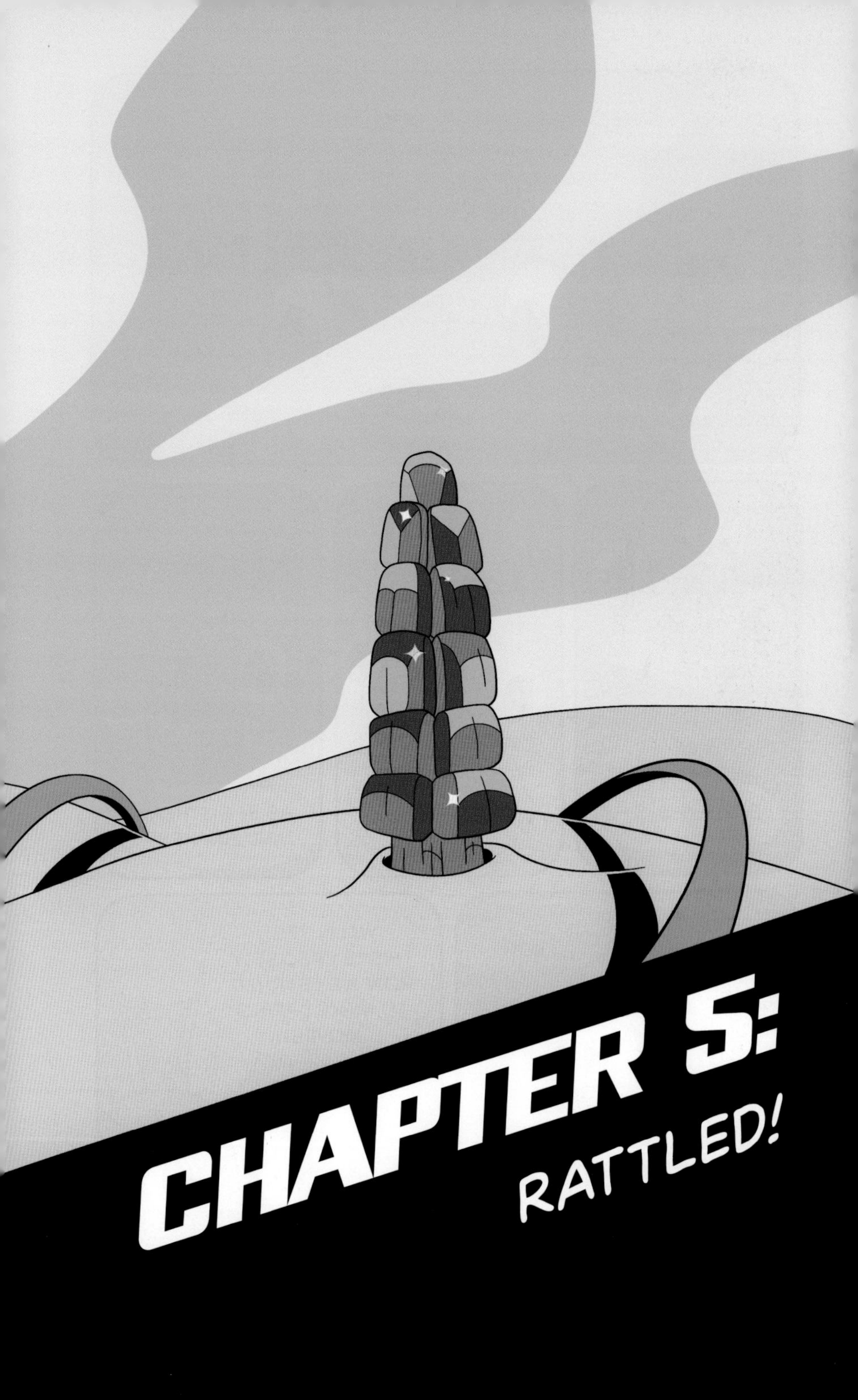
CHAPTER 5:
RATTLED!

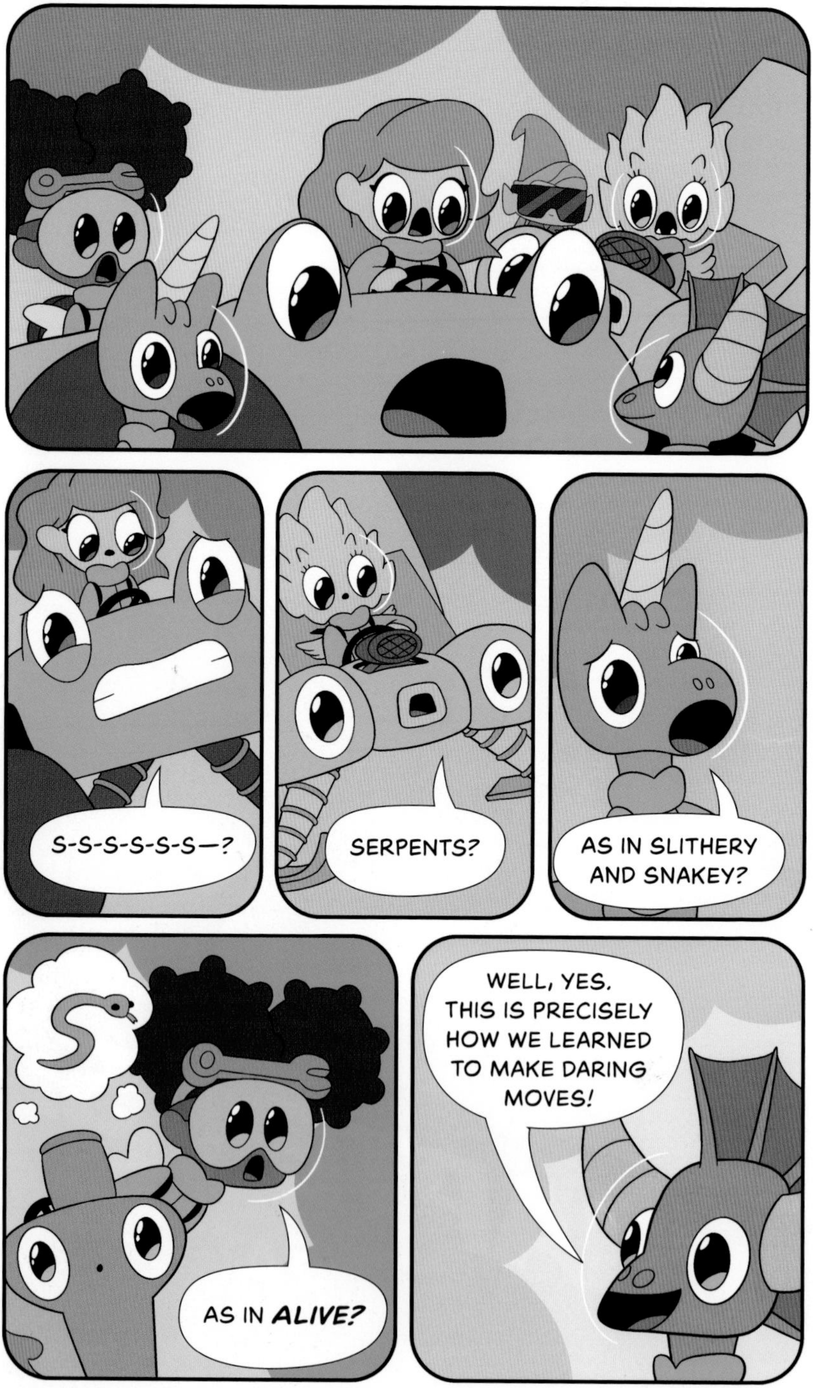
S-S-S-S-S-S—?
SERPENTS?
AS IN SLITHERY AND SNAKEY?
AS IN ALIVE?
WELL, YES. THIS IS PRECISELY HOW WE LEARNED TO MAKE DARING MOVES!

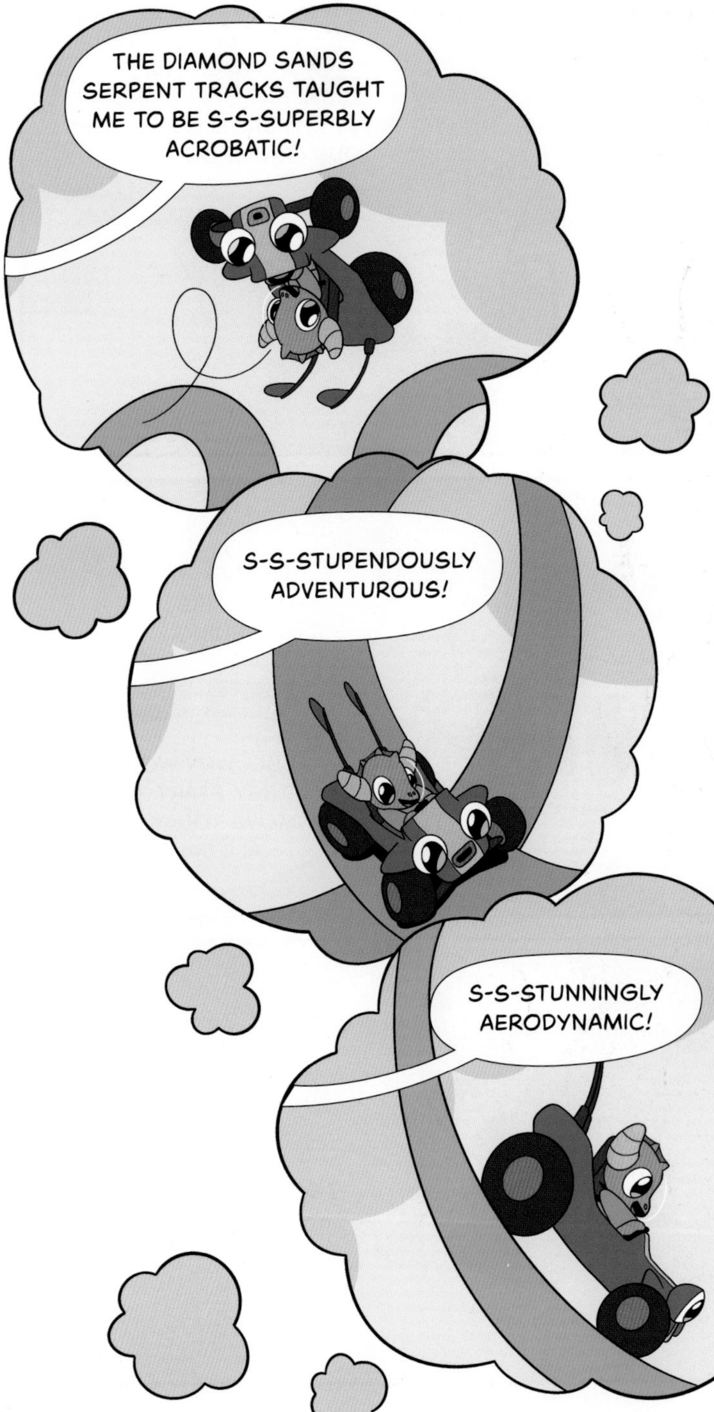
THE DIAMOND SANDS SERPENT TRACKS TAUGHT ME TO BE S-S-SUPERBLY ACROBATIC!
S-S-STUPENDOUSLY ADVENTUROUS!
S-S-STUNNINGLY AERODYNAMIC!

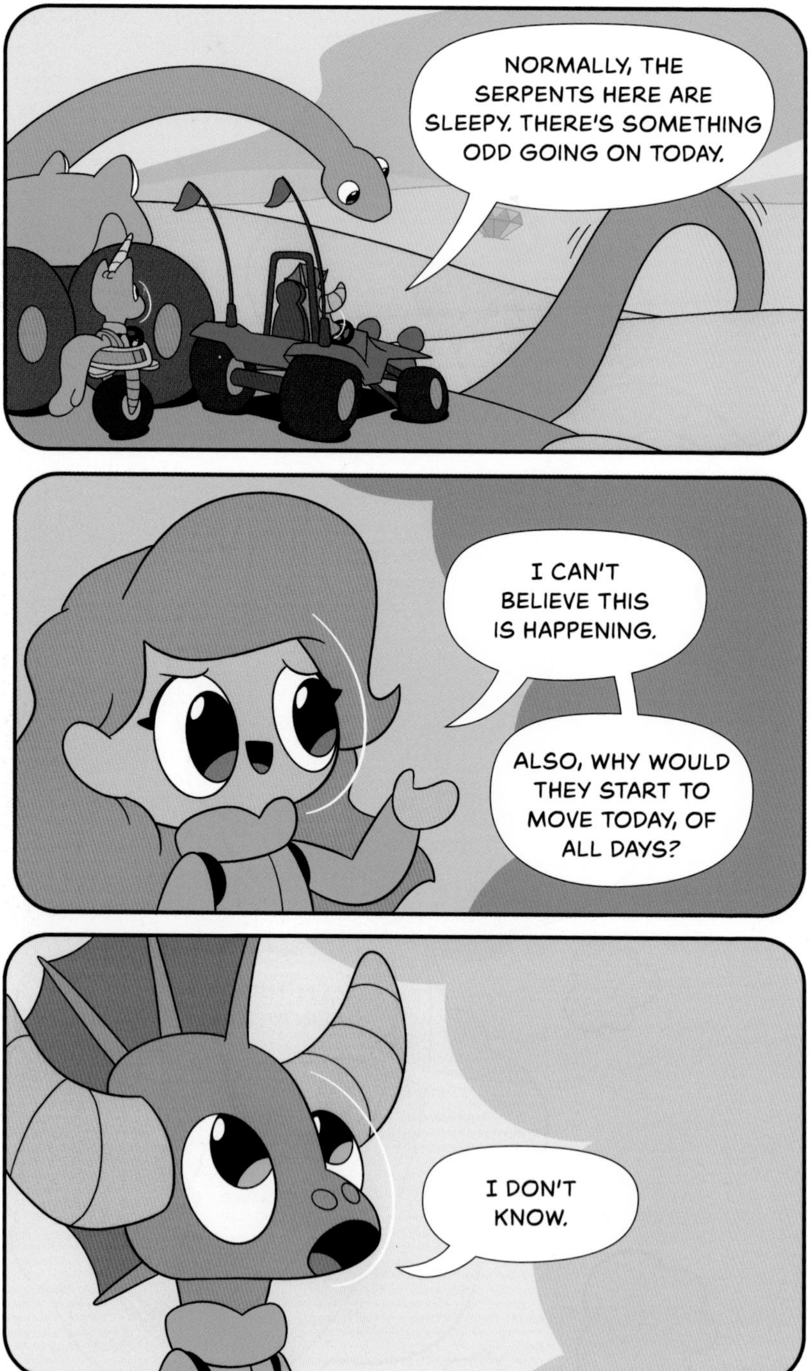
NORMALLY, THE SERPENTS HERE ARE SLEEPY. THERE'S SOMETHING ODD GOING ON TODAY.
I CAN'T BELIEVE THIS IS HAPPENING.
ALSO, WHY WOULD THEY START TO MOVE TODAY, OF ALL DAYS?
I DON'T KNOW.

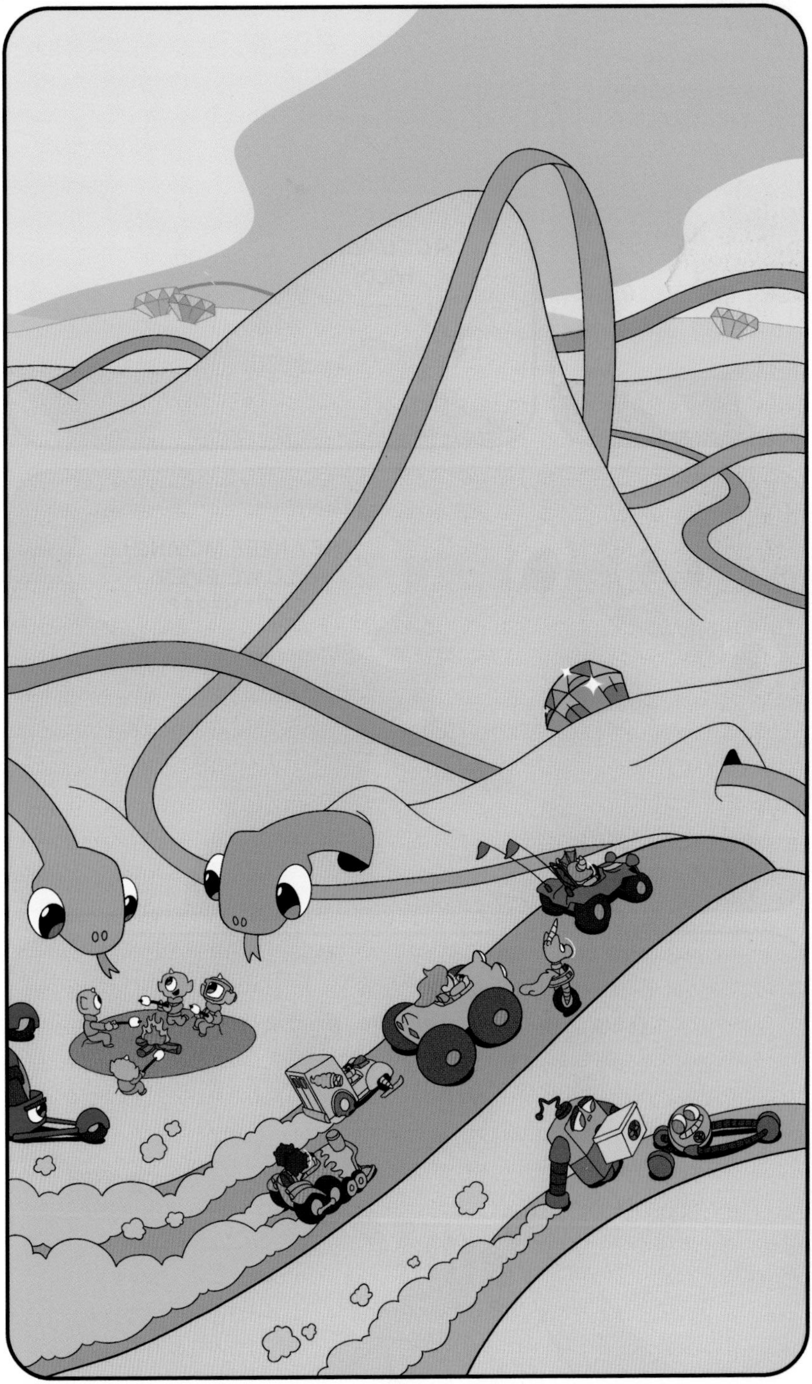

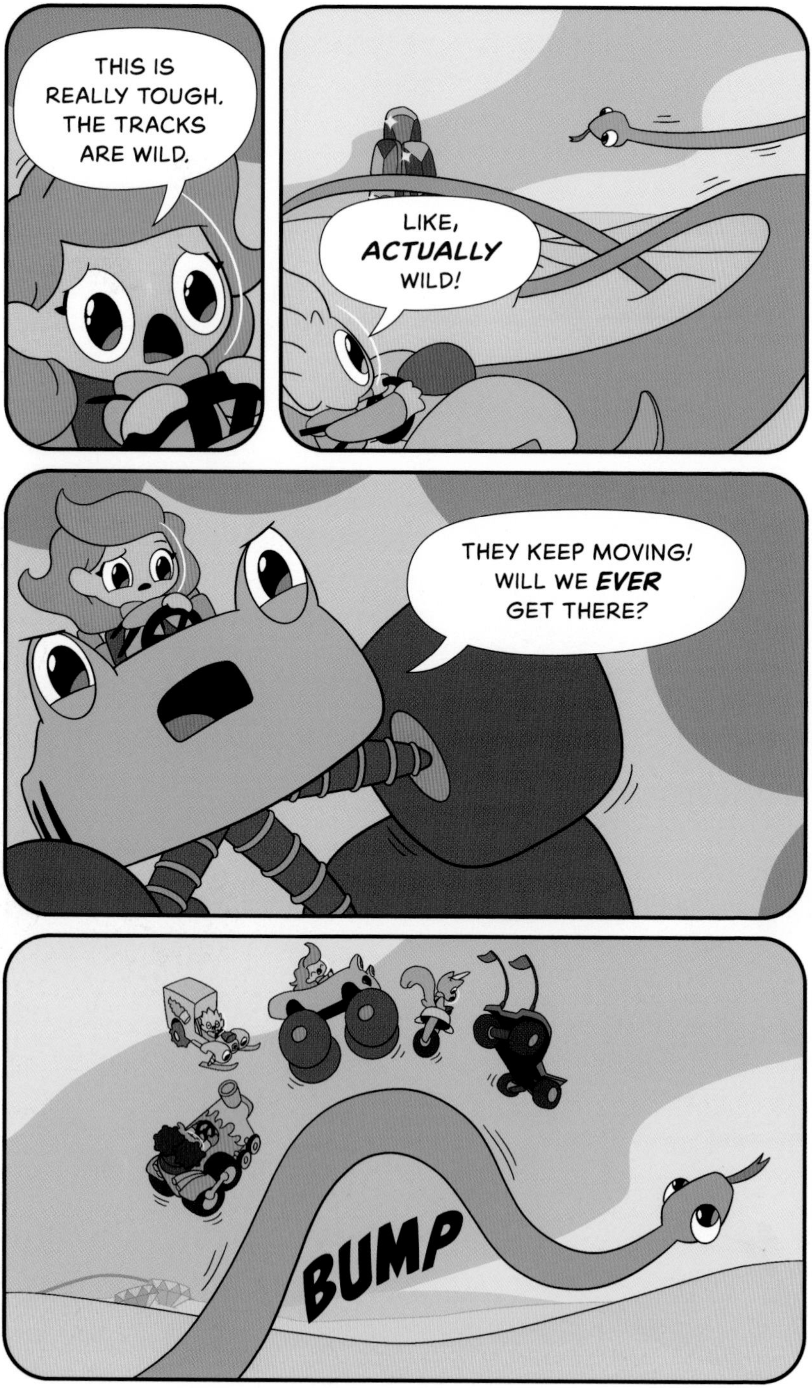
THIS IS REALLY TOUGH. THE TRACKS ARE WILD.
LIKE, ACTUALLY WILD!
THEY KEEP MOVING! WILL WE EVER GET THERE?
BUMP

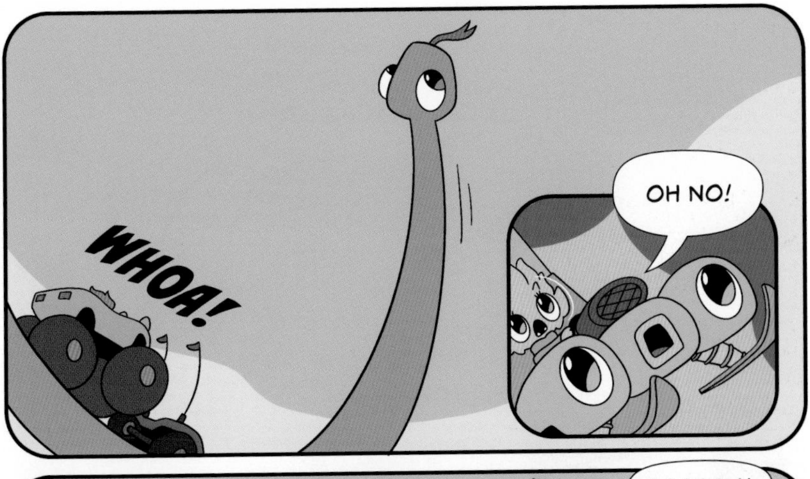
WHOA!
OH NO!

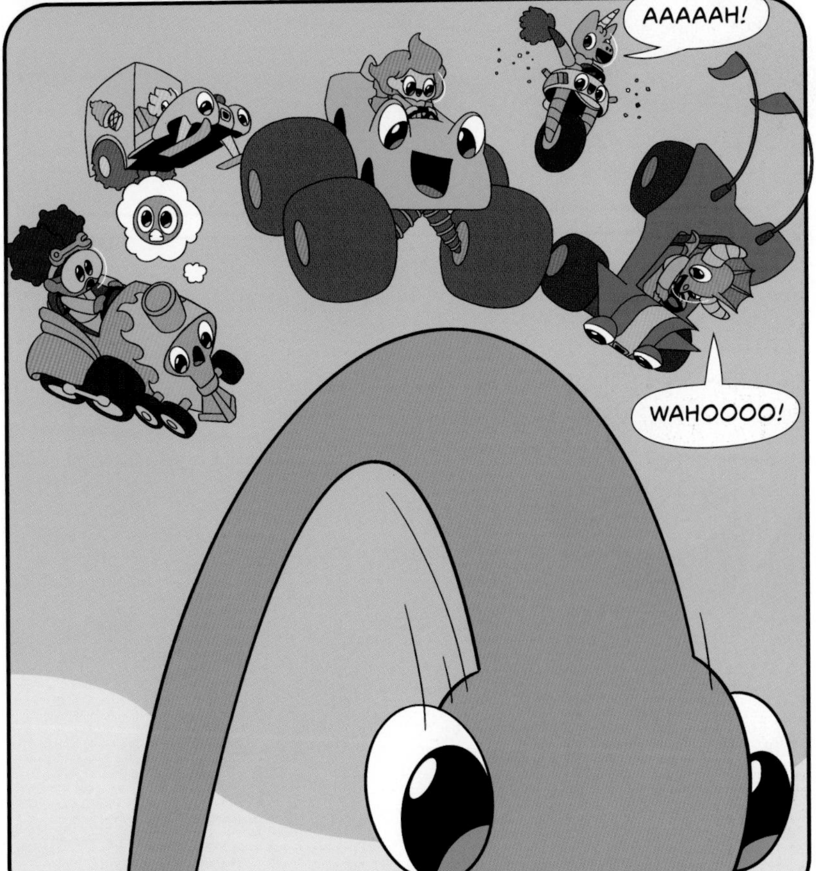
AAAAAH!
WAHOOOO!

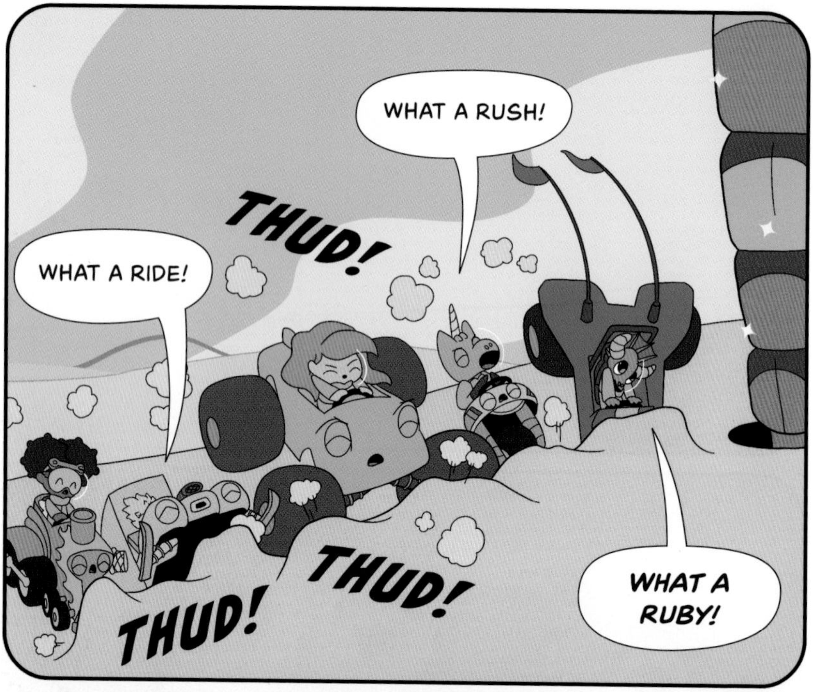
WHAT A RIDE!
WHAT A RUSH!
WHAT A RUBY!
THUD!
THUD!
THUD!

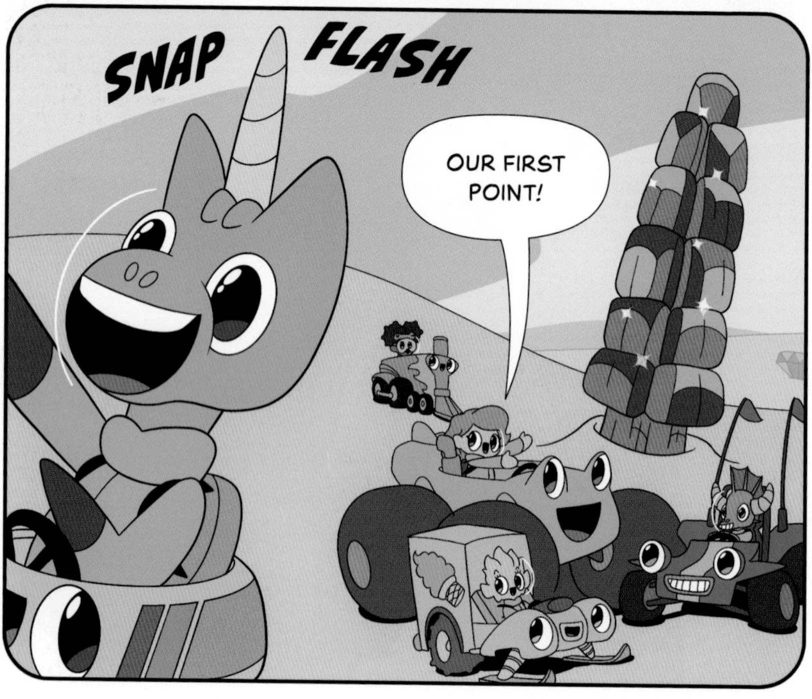
SNAP
FLASH
OUR FIRST POINT!

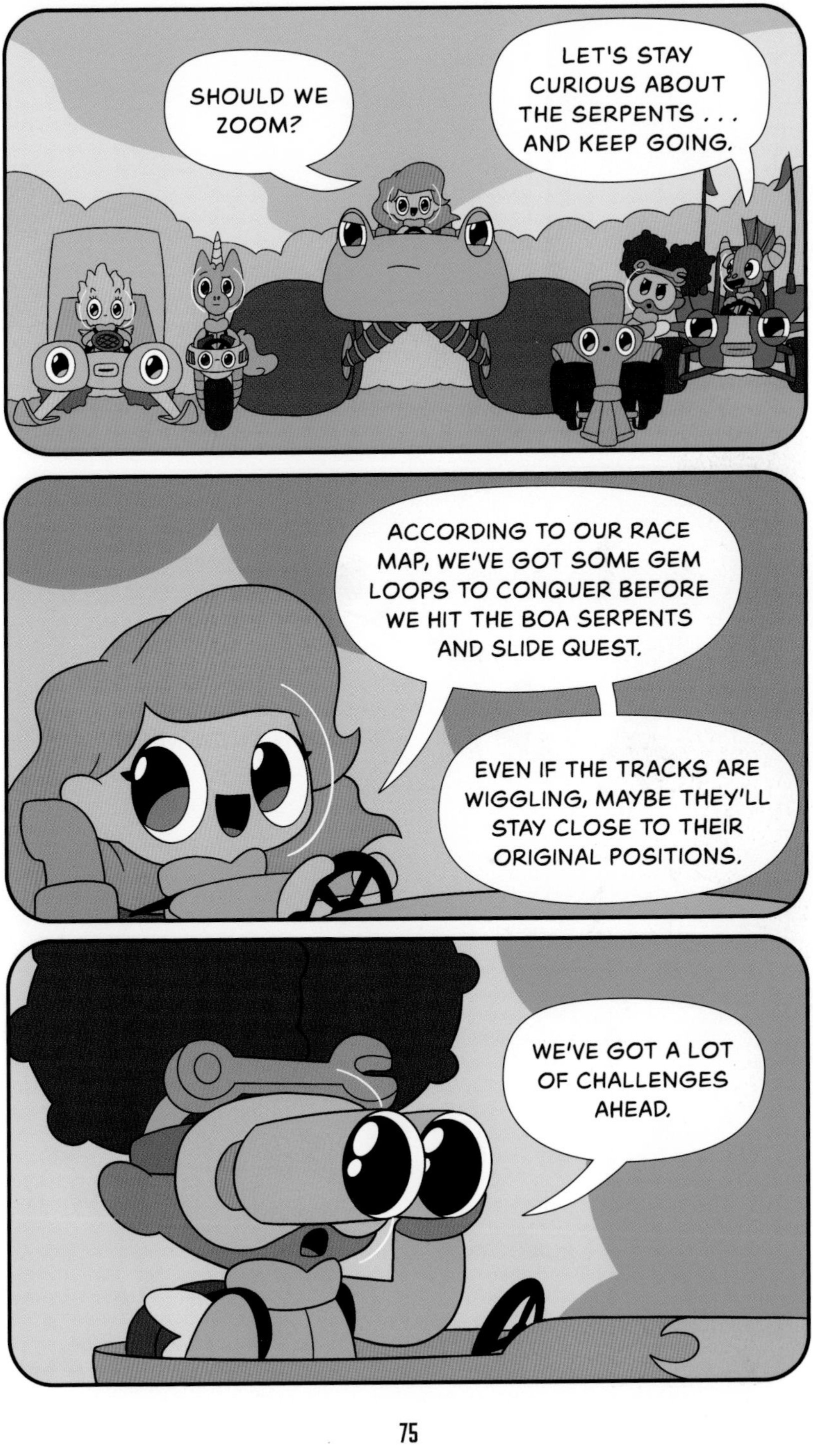
SHOULD WE ZOOM?
LET'S STAY CURIOUS ABOUT THE SERPENTS . . . AND KEEP GOING.
ACCORDING TO OUR RACE MAP, WE'VE GOT SOME GEM LOOPS TO CONQUER BEFORE WE HIT THE BOA SERPENTS AND SLIDE QUEST.
EVEN IF THE TRACKS ARE WIGGLING, MAYBE THEY'LL STAY CLOSE TO THEIR ORIGINAL POSITIONS.
WE'VE GOT A LOT OF CHALLENGES AHEAD.

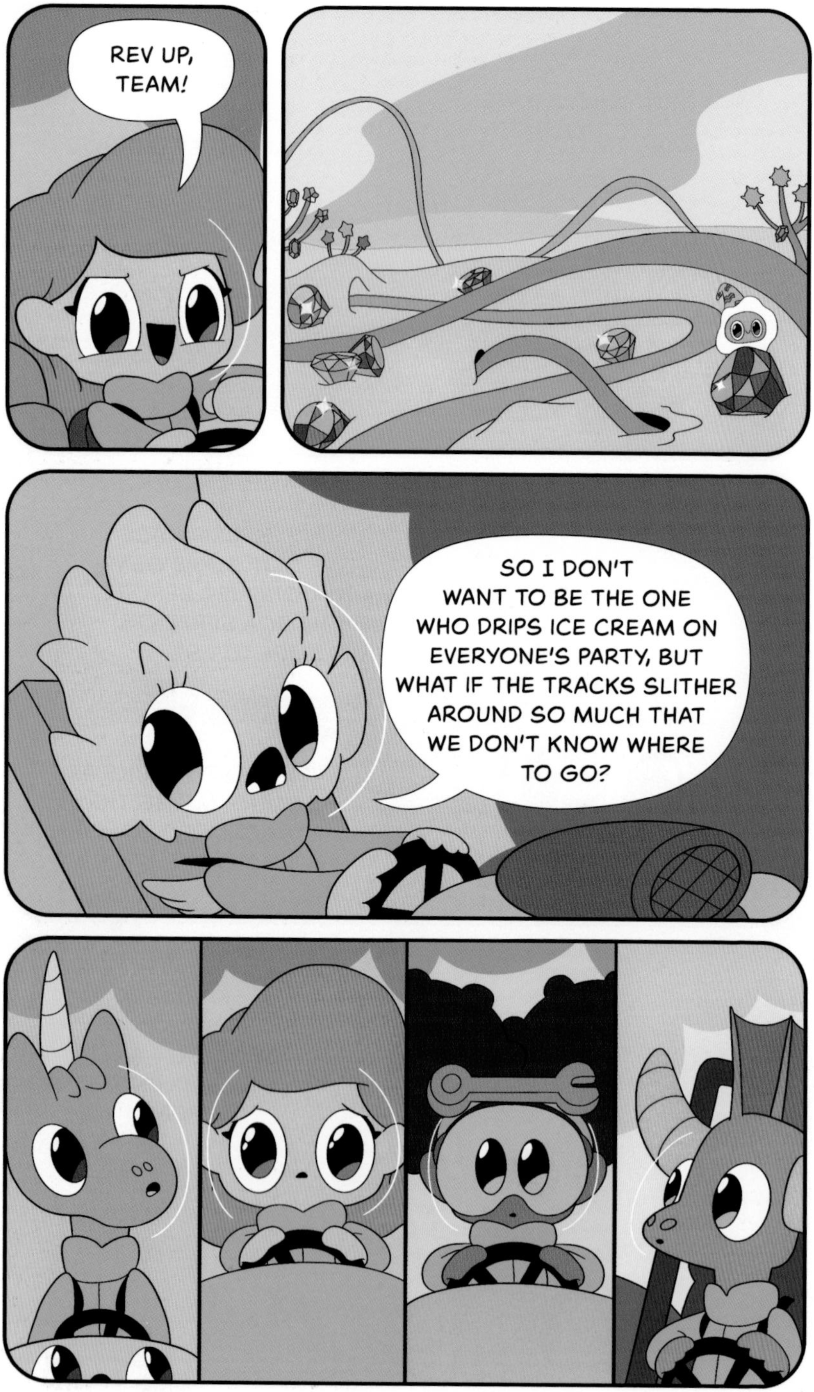
REV UP, TEAM!
SO I DON'T WANT TO BE THE ONE WHO DRIPS ICE CREAM ON EVERYONE'S PARTY, BUT WHAT IF THE TRACKS SLITHER AROUND SO MUCH THAT WE DON'T KNOW WHERE TO GO?

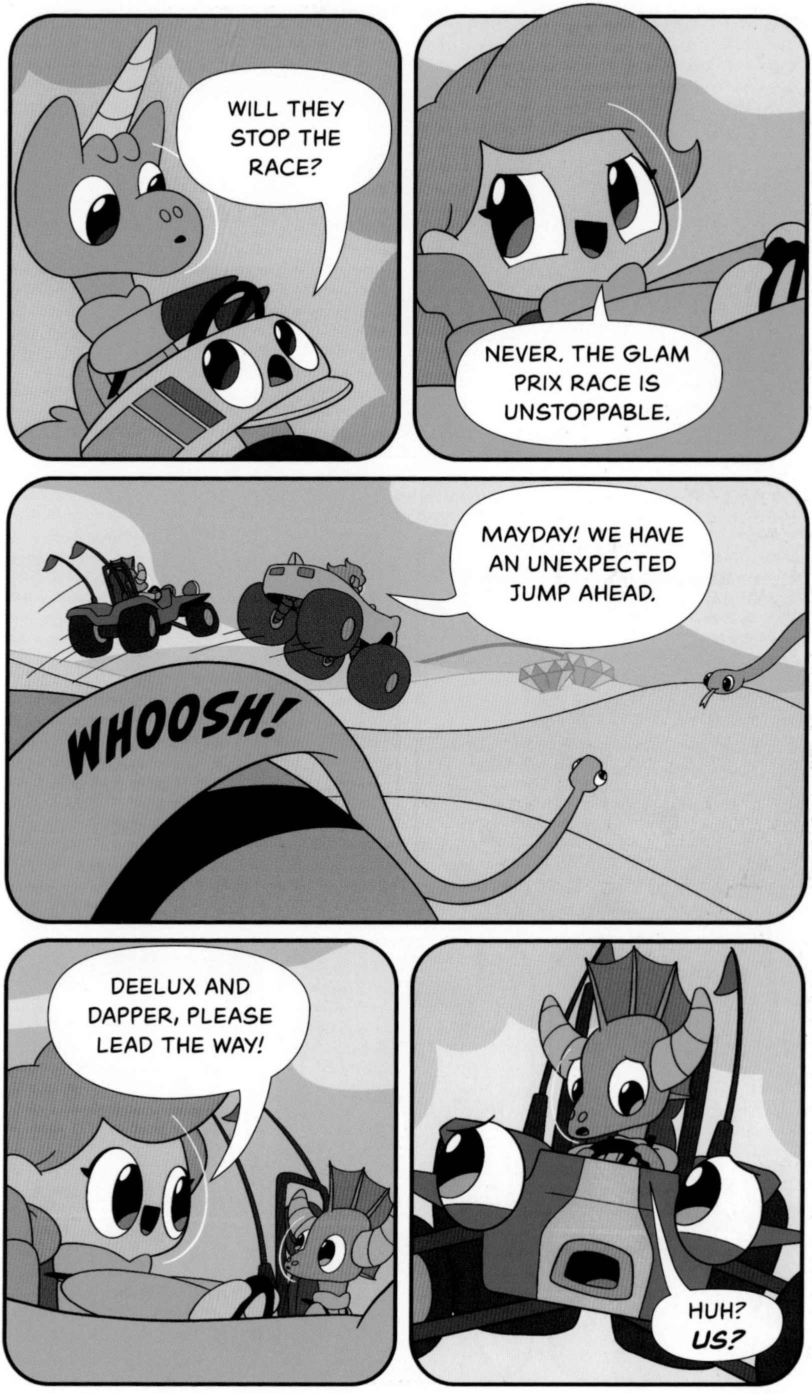
WILL THEY STOP THE RACE?
NEVER. THE GLAM PRIX RACE IS UNSTOPPABLE.
MAYDAY! WE HAVE AN UNEXPECTED JUMP AHEAD.
WHOOSH!
DEELUX AND DAPPER, PLEASE LEAD THE WAY!
HUH? *US?*

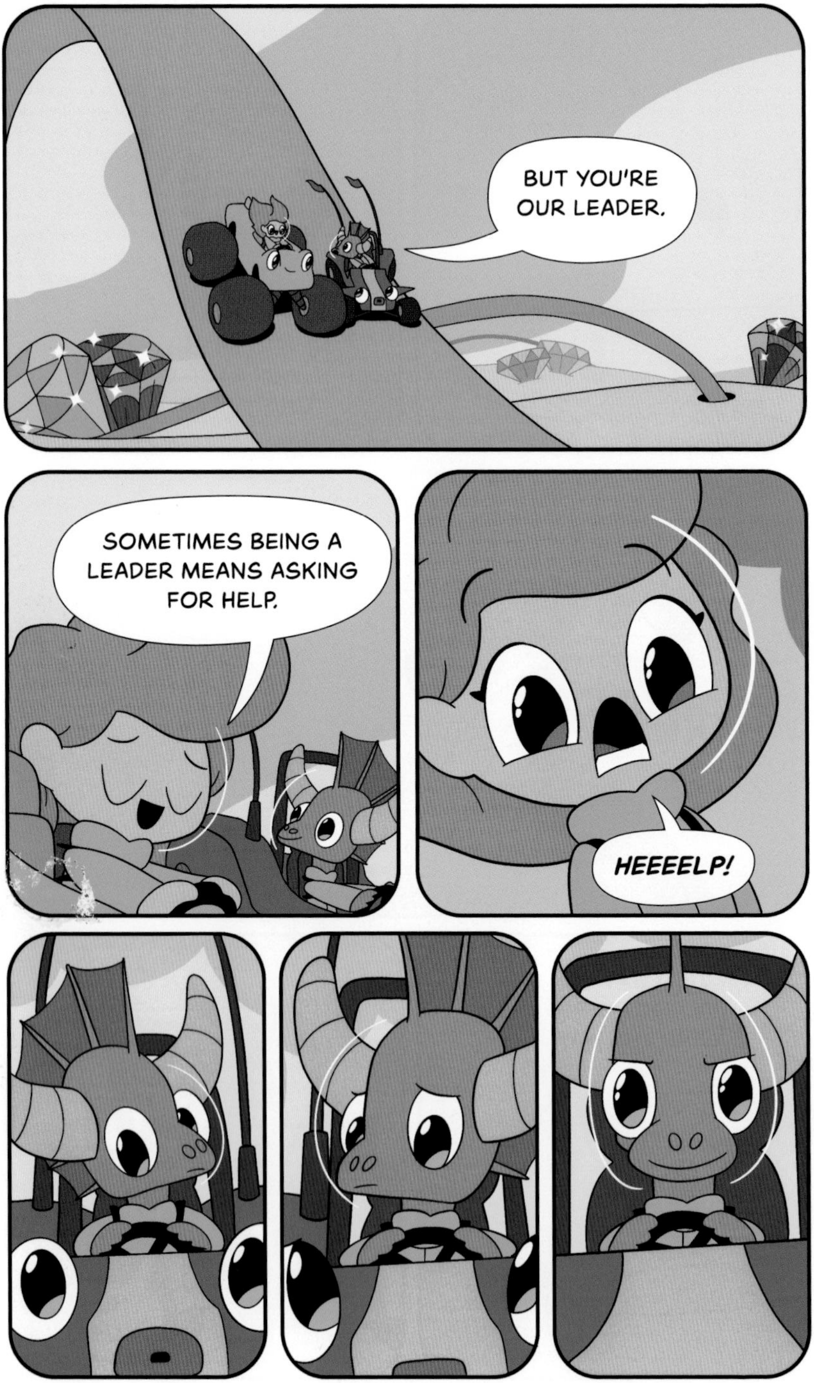
BUT YOU'RE OUR LEADER.
SOMETIMES BEING A LEADER MEANS ASKING FOR HELP.
HEEEELP!

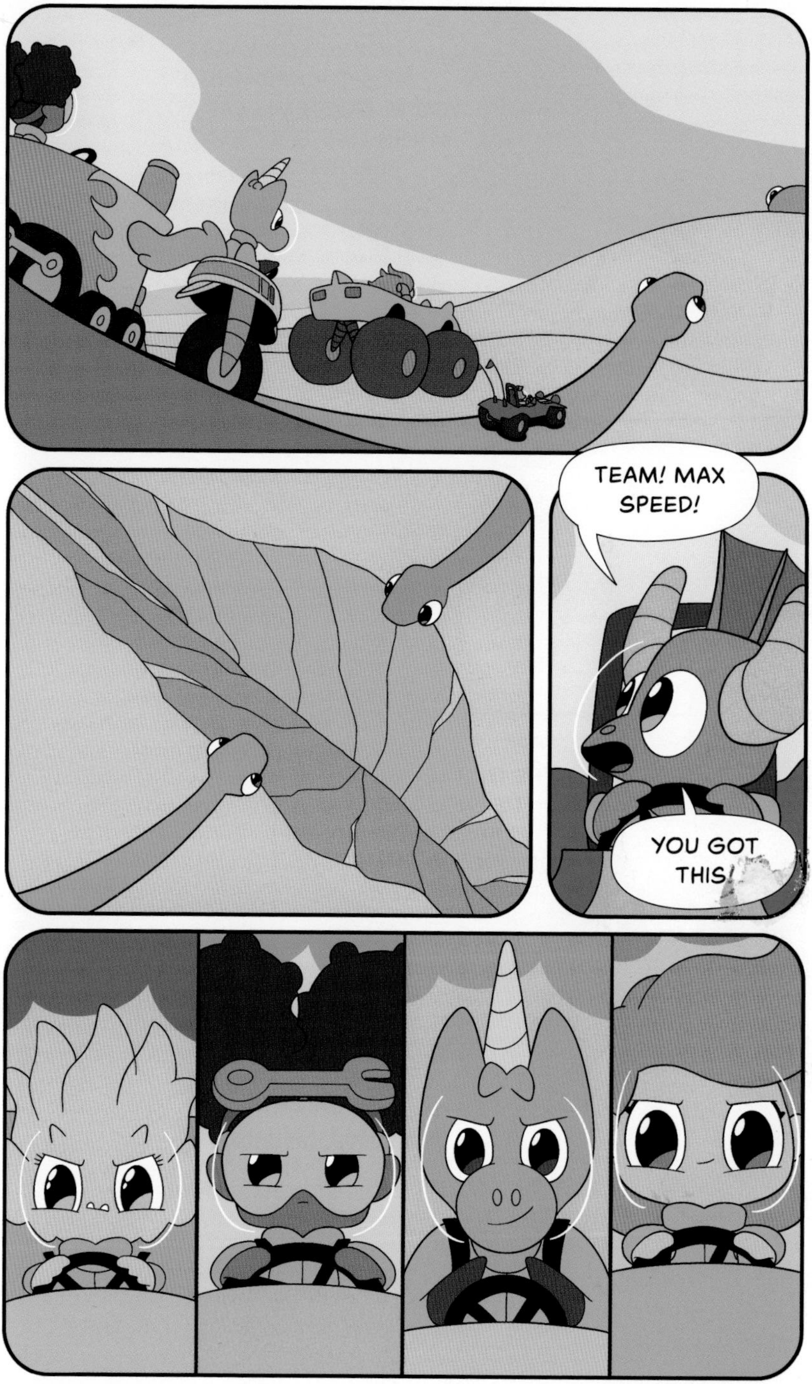
TEAM! MAX SPEED!
YOU GOT THIS!

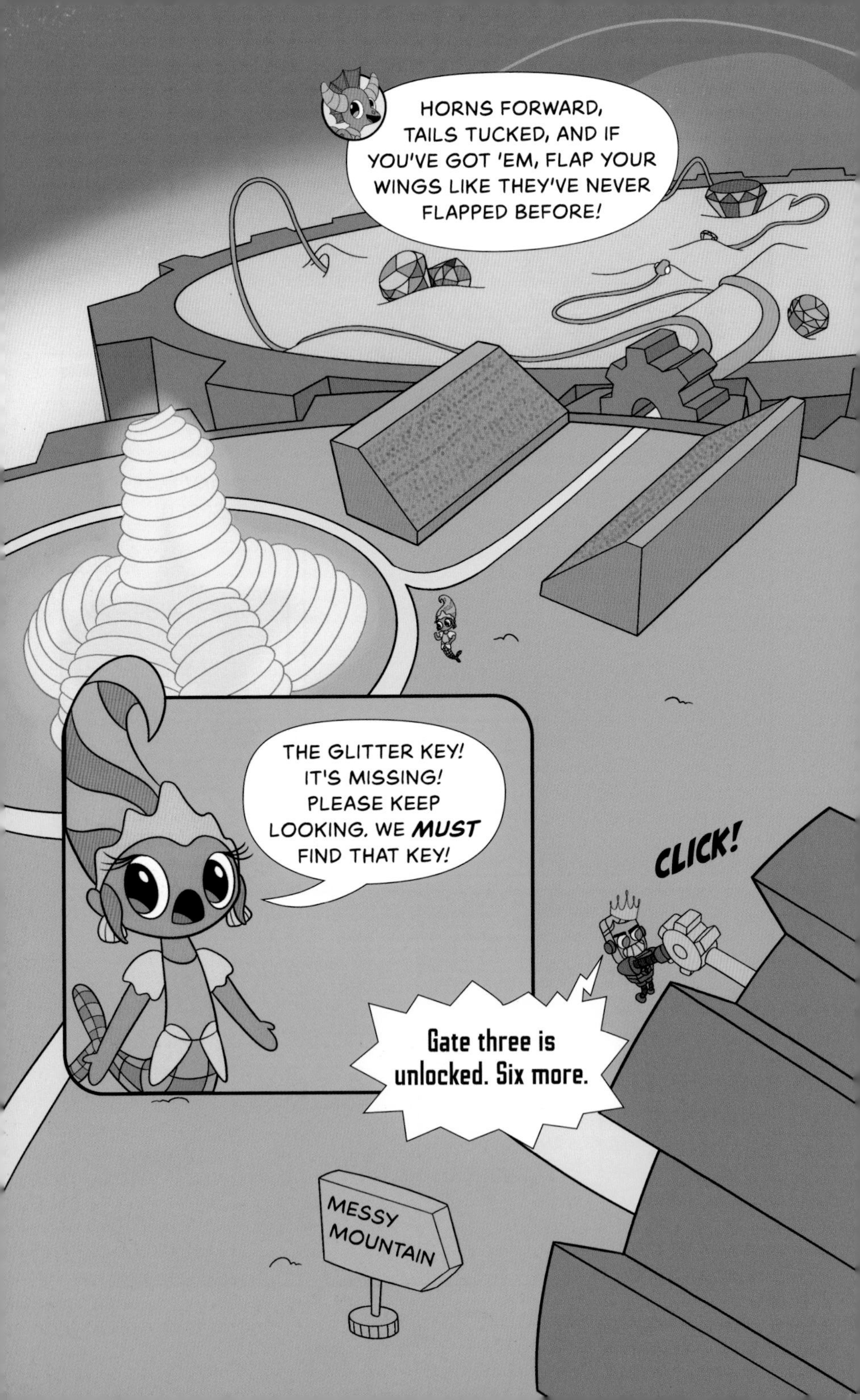
HORNS FORWARD, TAILS TUCKED, AND IF YOU'VE GOT 'EM, FLAP YOUR WINGS LIKE THEY'VE NEVER FLAPPED BEFORE!
THE GLITTER KEY! IT'S MISSING! PLEASE KEEP LOOKING. WE ***MUST*** FIND THAT KEY!
CLICK!
Gate three is unlocked. Six more.
MESSY MOUNTAIN

CHAPTER 6:
S-S-SLIDE QUEST!

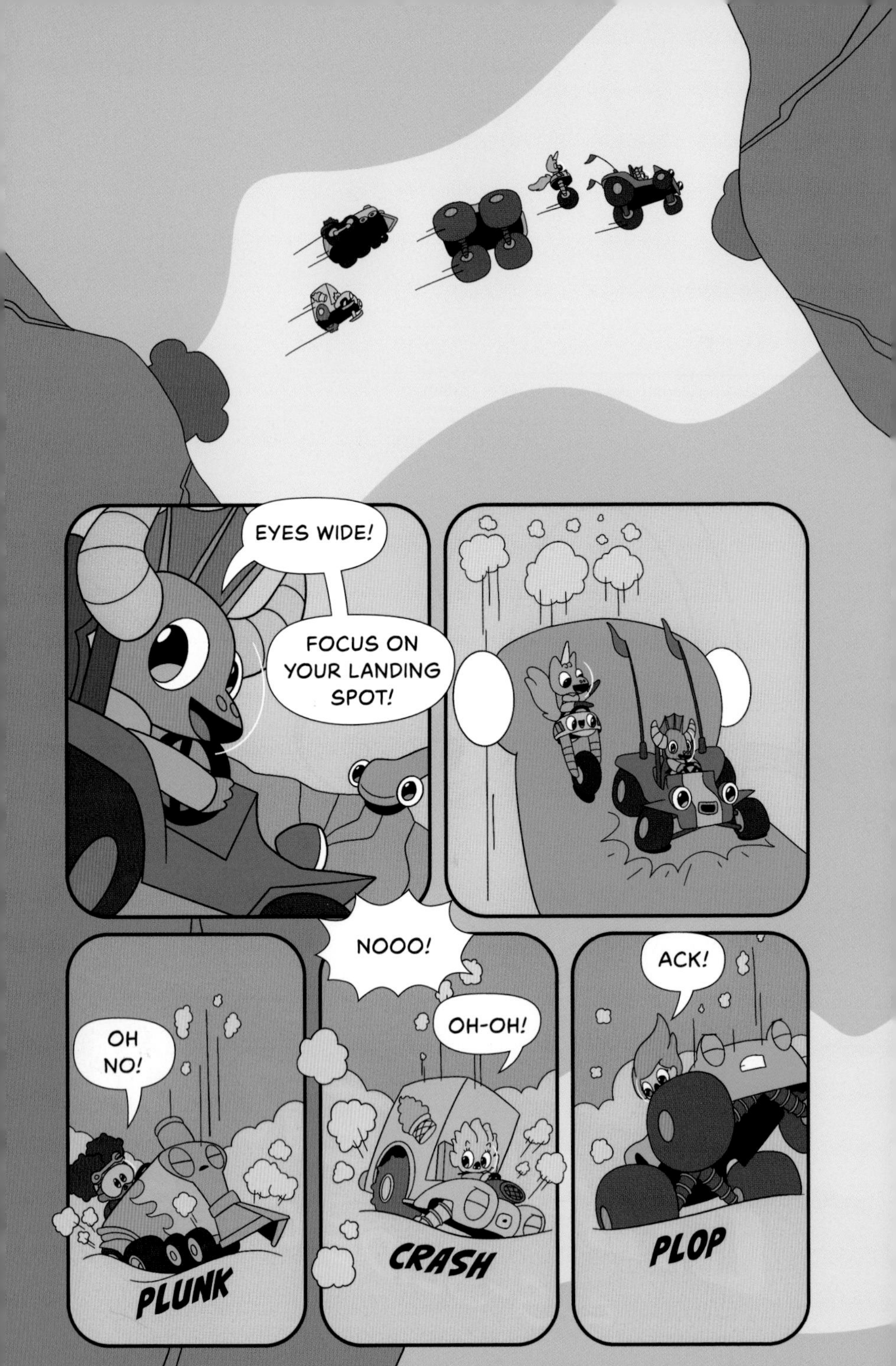
EYES WIDE!
FOCUS ON YOUR LANDING SPOT!
NOOO!
OH NO!
PLUNK
OH-OH!
CRASH
ACK!
PLOP

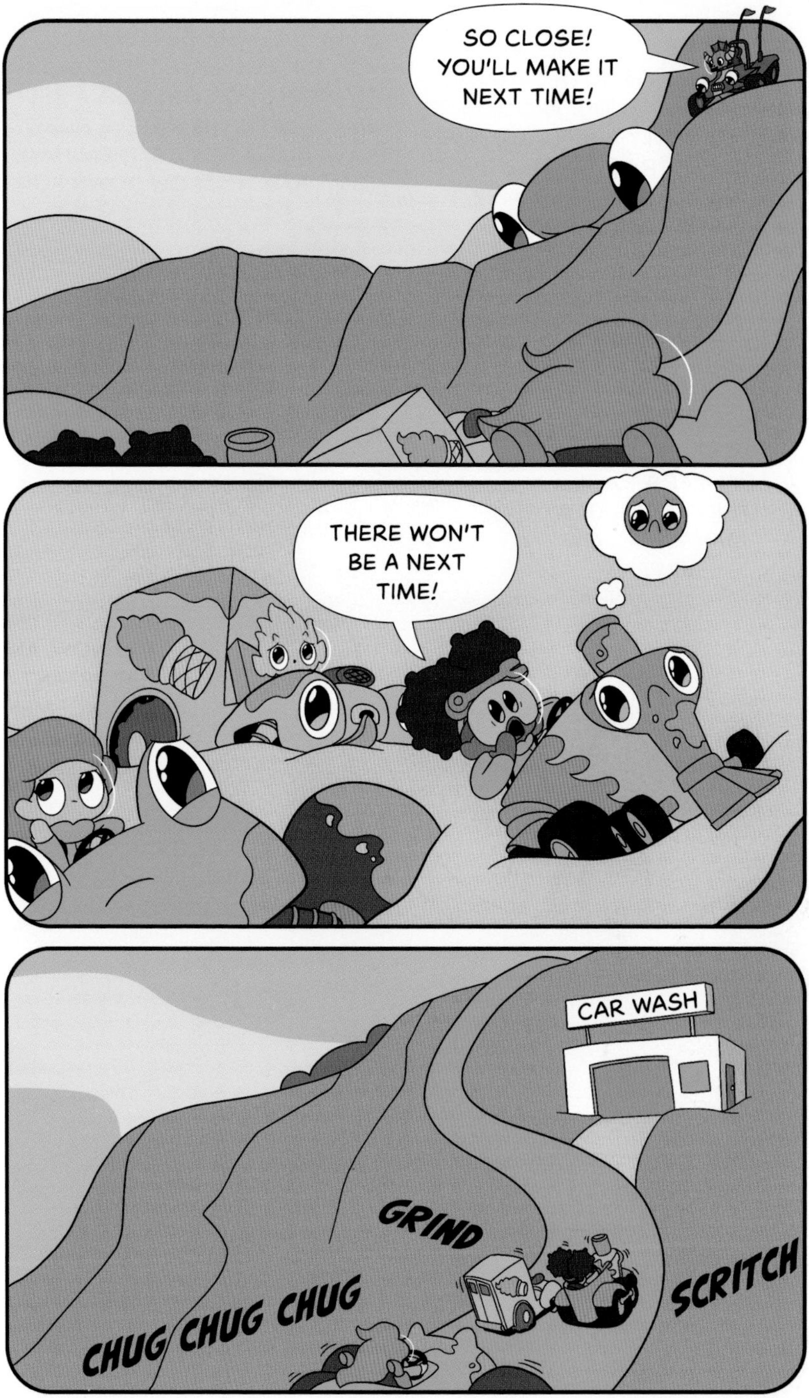
SO CLOSE! YOU'LL MAKE IT NEXT TIME!
THERE WON'T BE A NEXT TIME!
CAR WASH
GRIND
CHUG CHUG CHUG
SCRITCH

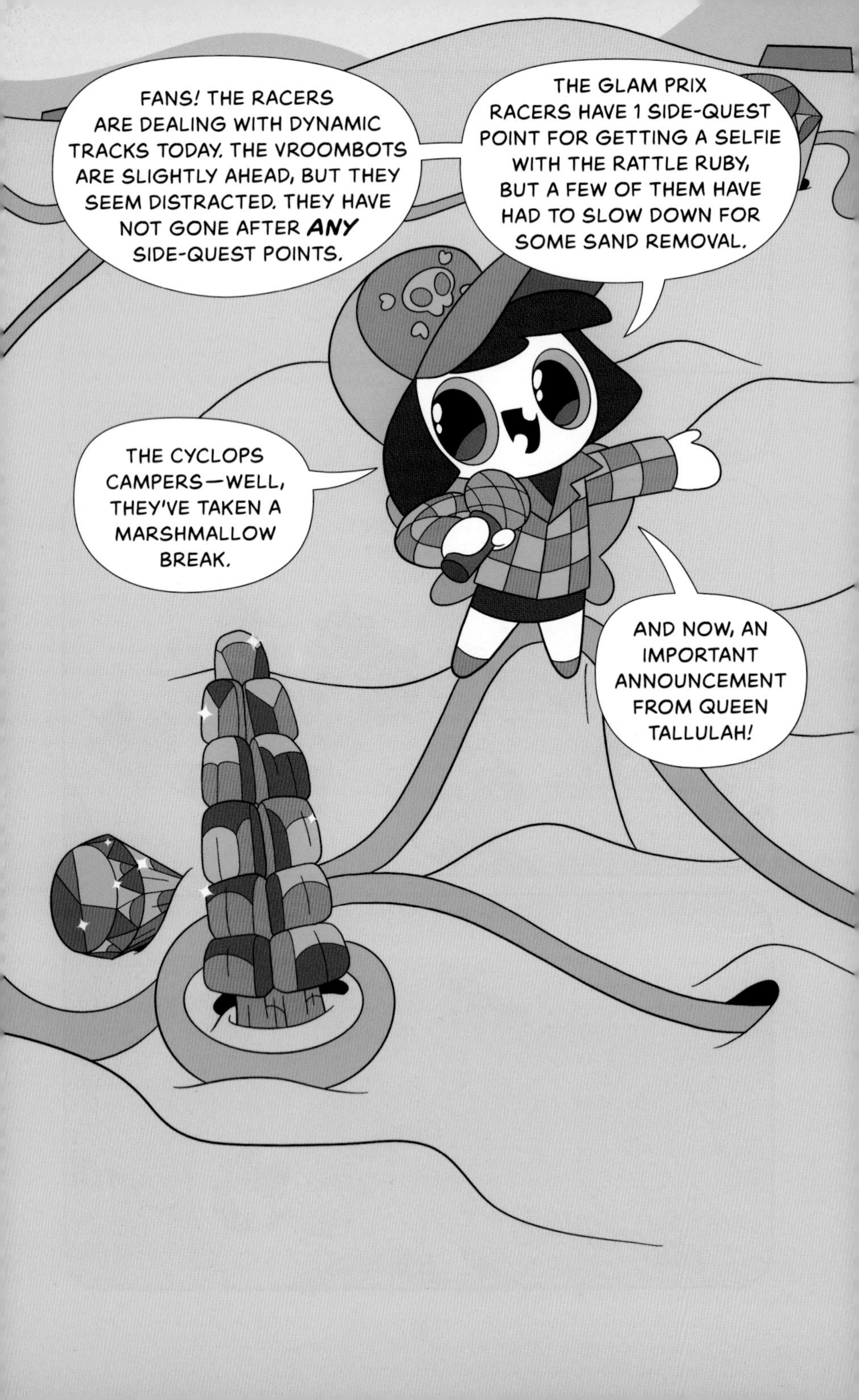
FANS! THE RACERS ARE DEALING WITH DYNAMIC TRACKS TODAY. THE VROOMBOTS ARE SLIGHTLY AHEAD, BUT THEY SEEM DISTRACTED. THEY HAVE NOT GONE AFTER ***ANY*** SIDE-QUEST POINTS.
THE GLAM PRIX RACERS HAVE 1 SIDE-QUEST POINT FOR GETTING A SELFIE WITH THE RATTLE RUBY, BUT A FEW OF THEM HAVE HAD TO SLOW DOWN FOR SOME SAND REMOVAL.
THE CYCLOPS CAMPERS—WELL, THEY'VE TAKEN A MARSHMALLOW BREAK.
AND NOW, AN IMPORTANT ANNOUNCEMENT FROM QUEEN TALLULAH!

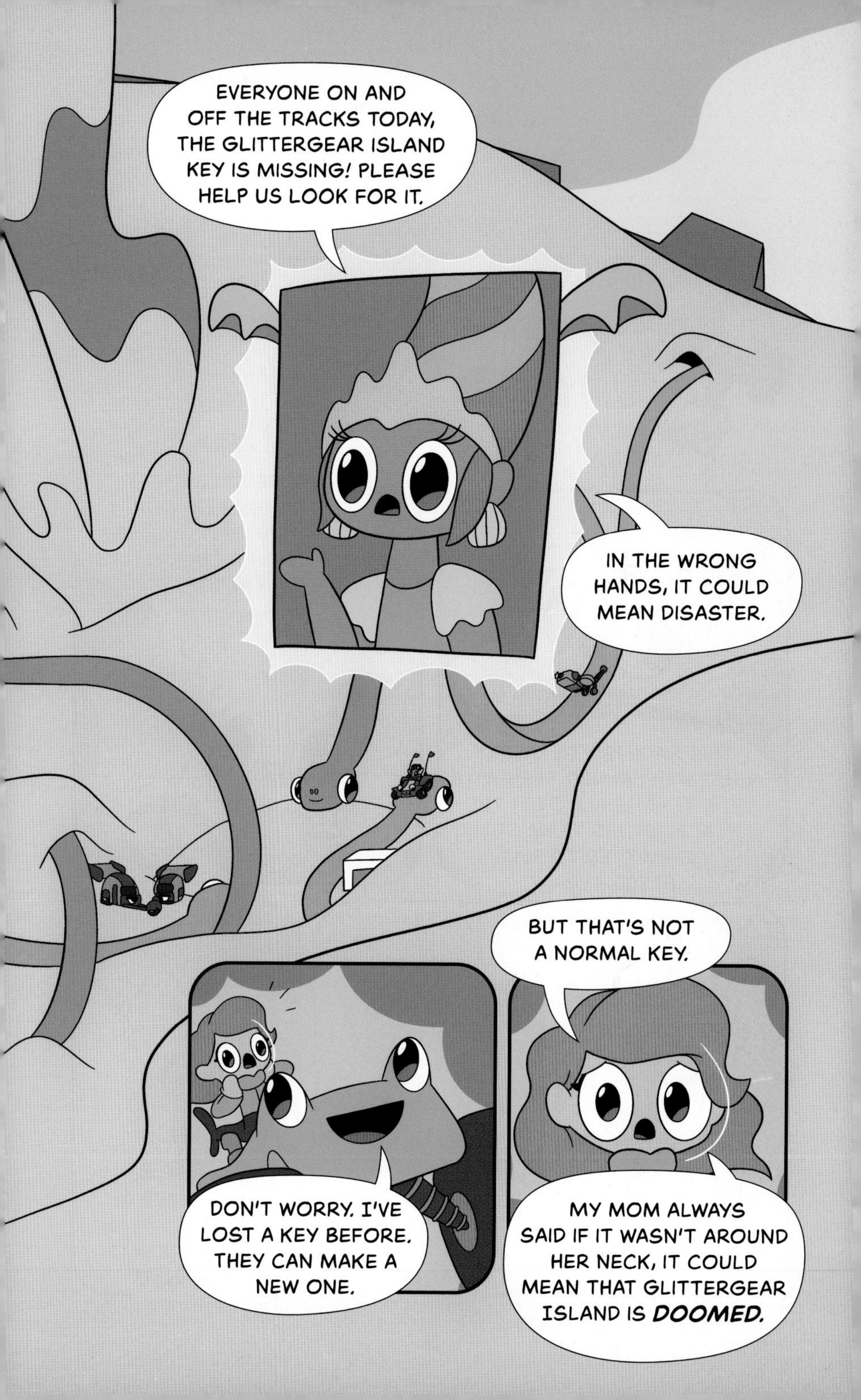
EVERYONE ON AND OFF THE TRACKS TODAY, THE GLITTERGEAR ISLAND KEY IS MISSING! PLEASE HELP US LOOK FOR IT.
IN THE WRONG HANDS, IT COULD MEAN DISASTER.
DON'T WORRY. I'VE LOST A KEY BEFORE. THEY CAN MAKE A NEW ONE.
BUT THAT'S NOT A NORMAL KEY.
MY MOM ALWAYS SAID IF IT WASN'T AROUND HER NECK, IT COULD MEAN THAT GLITTERGEAR ISLAND IS ***DOOMED.***

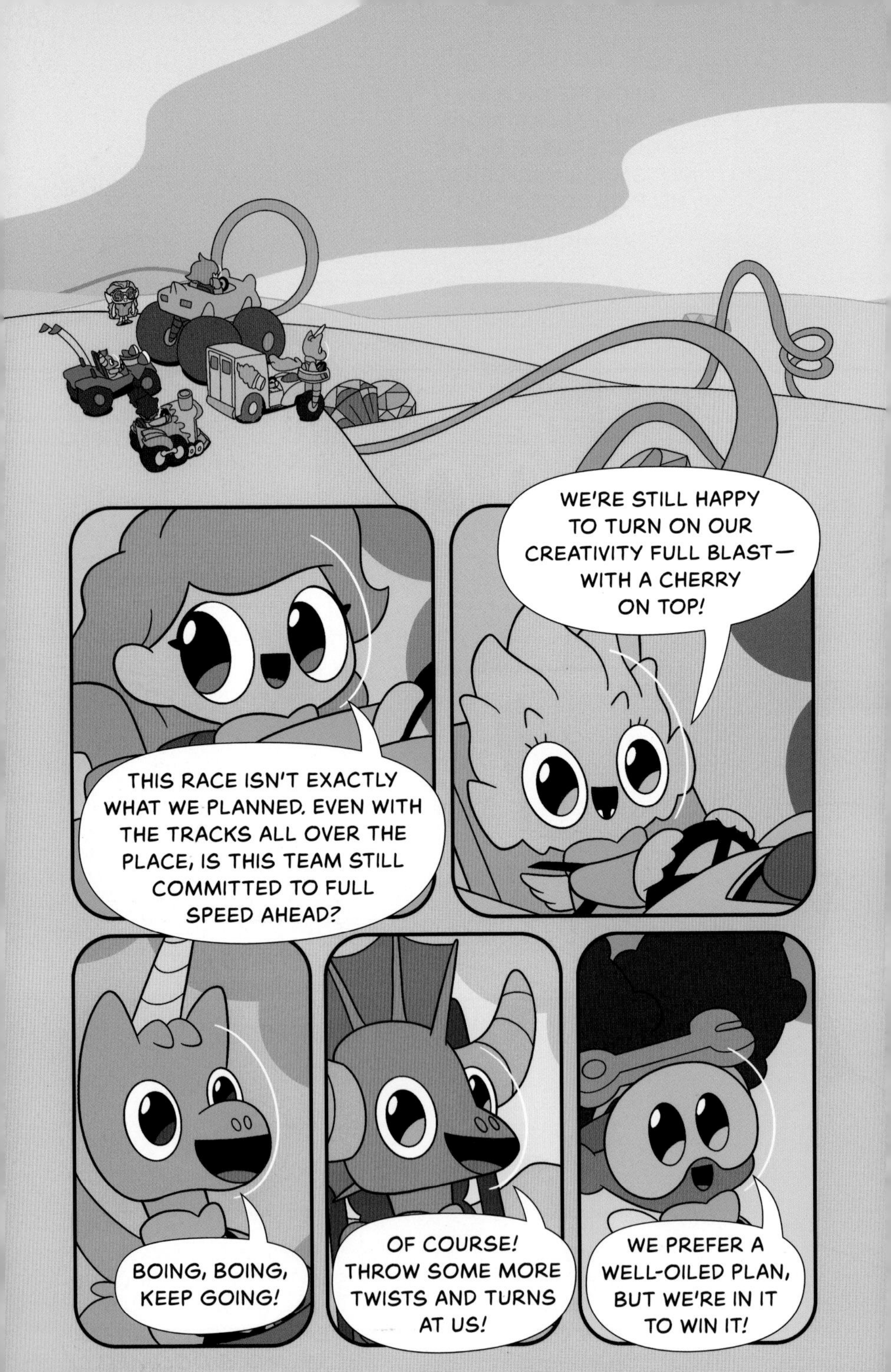
THIS RACE ISN'T EXACTLY WHAT WE PLANNED. EVEN WITH THE TRACKS ALL OVER THE PLACE, IS THIS TEAM STILL COMMITTED TO FULL SPEED AHEAD?
WE'RE STILL HAPPY TO TURN ON OUR CREATIVITY FULL BLAST—WITH A CHERRY ON TOP!
BOING, BOING, KEEP GOING!
OF COURSE! THROW SOME MORE TWISTS AND TURNS AT US!
WE PREFER A WELL-OILED PLAN, BUT WE'RE IN IT TO WIN IT!

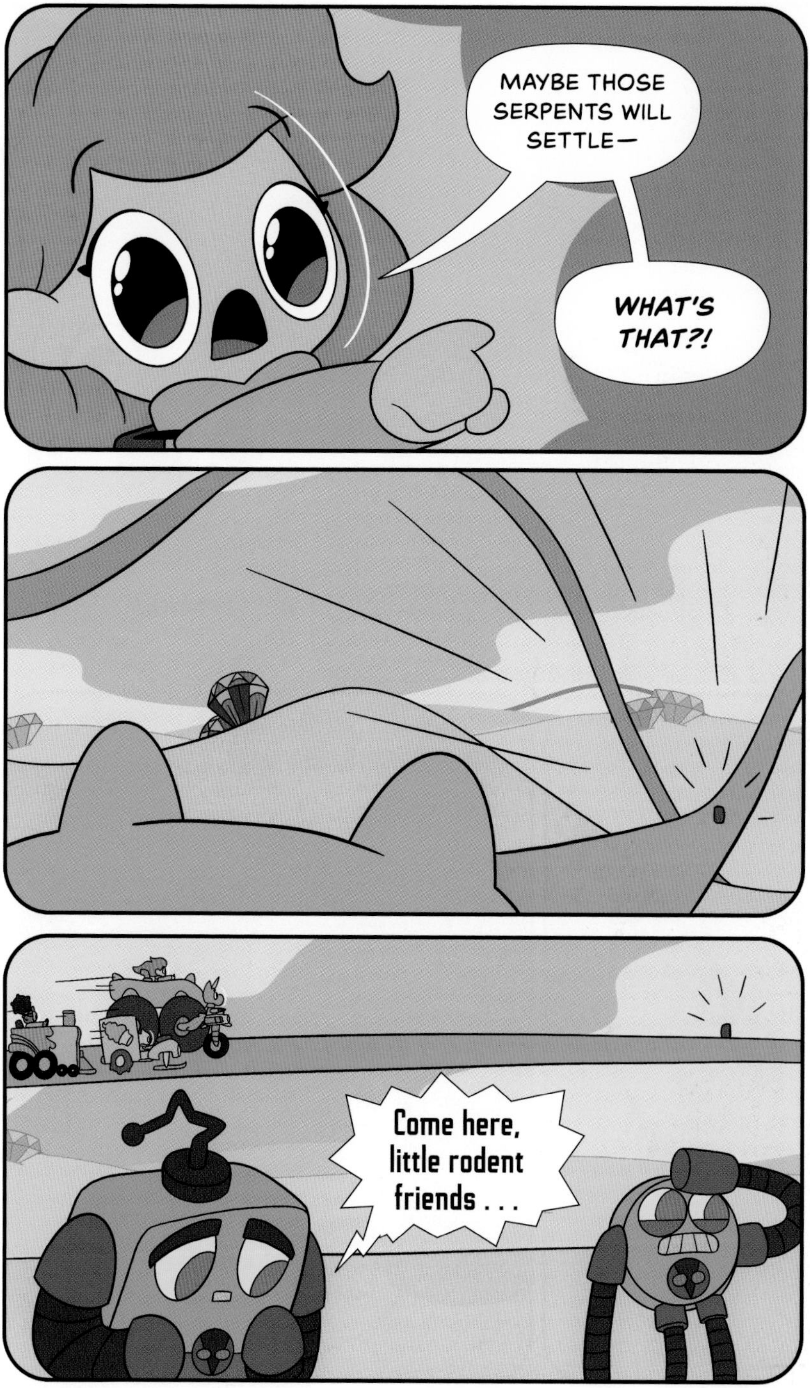
MAYBE THOSE SERPENTS WILL SETTLE—
WHAT'S THAT?!
Come here, little rodent friends . . .

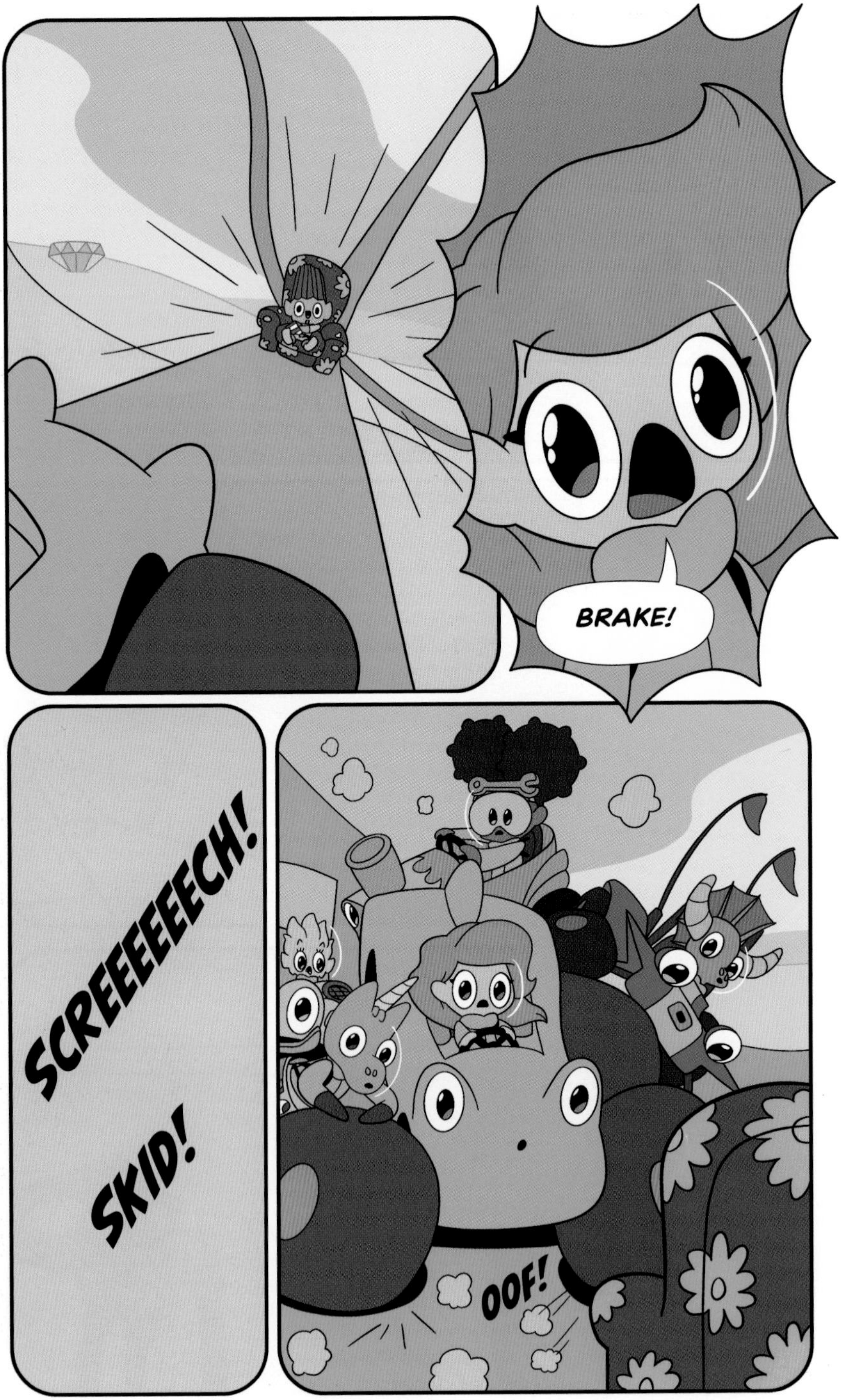
BRAKE!
SCREEEEEEECH!
SKID!
OOF!

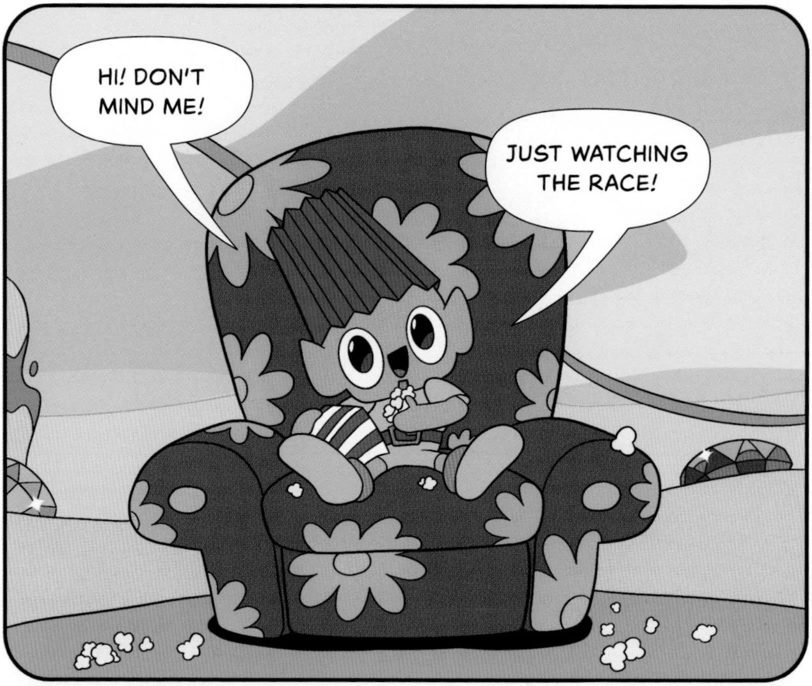
HI! DON'T
MIND ME!
JUST WATCHING
THE RACE!

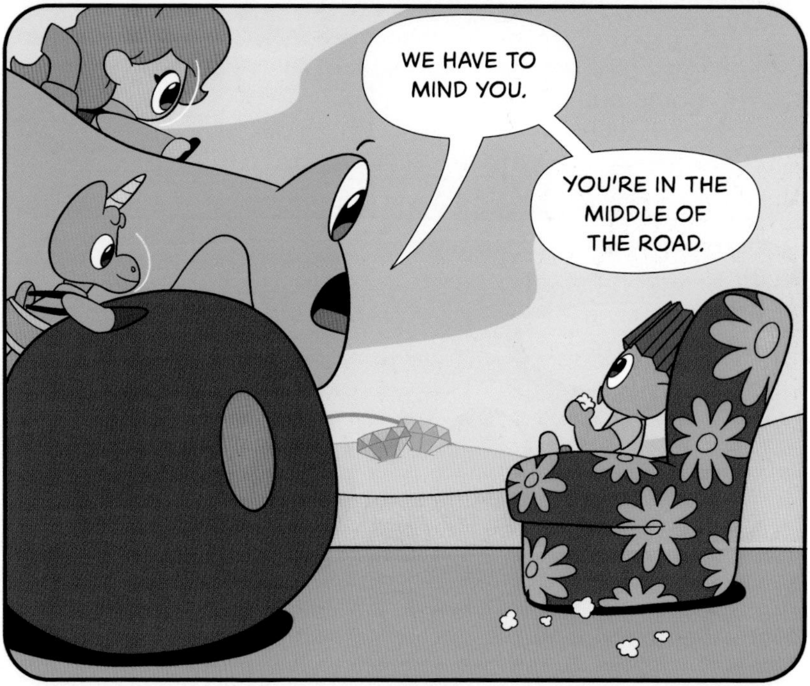
WE HAVE TO
MIND YOU.
YOU'RE IN THE
MIDDLE OF
THE ROAD.

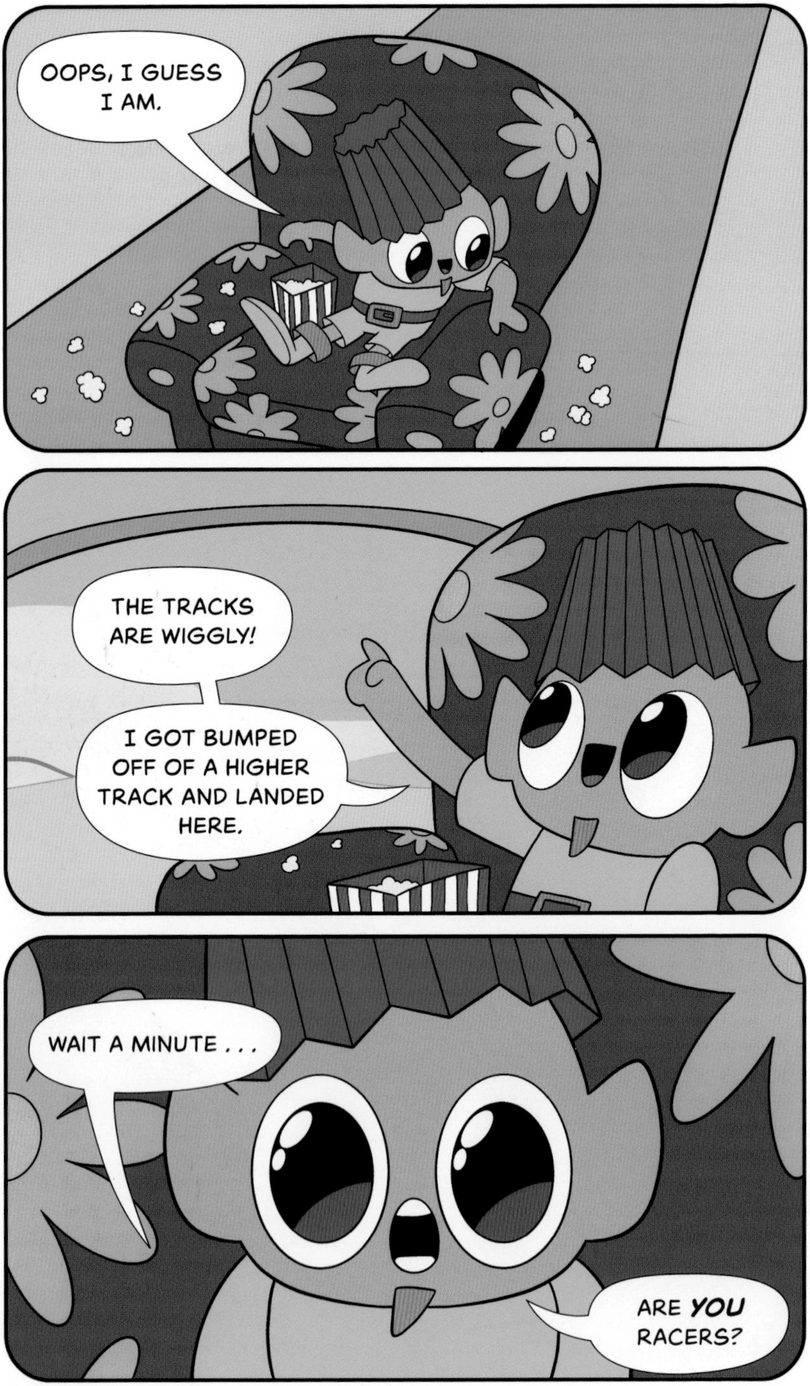
OOPS, I GUESS I AM.
THE TRACKS ARE WIGGLY!
I GOT BUMPED OFF OF A HIGHER TRACK AND LANDED HERE.
WAIT A MINUTE . . .
ARE *YOU* RACERS?

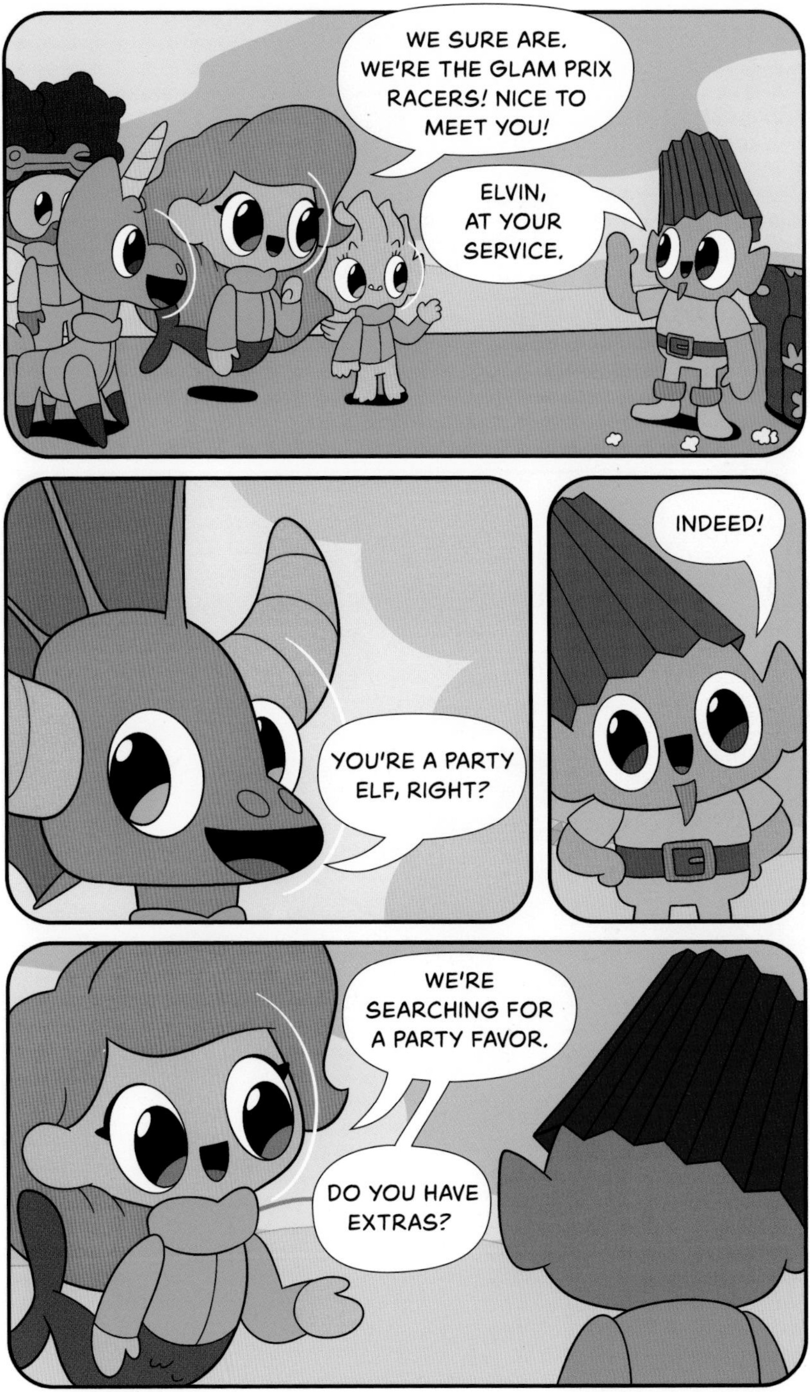
WE SURE ARE. WE'RE THE GLAM PRIX RACERS! NICE TO MEET YOU!
ELVIN, AT YOUR SERVICE.
YOU'RE A PARTY ELF, RIGHT?
INDEED!
WE'RE SEARCHING FOR A PARTY FAVOR.
DO YOU HAVE EXTRAS?

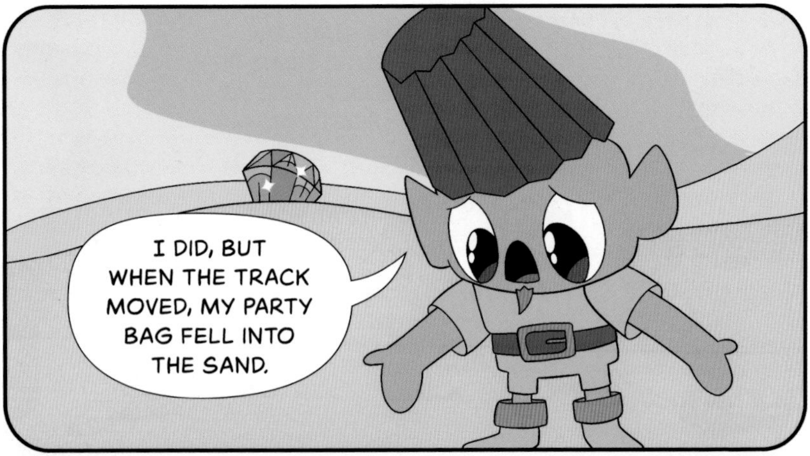
I DID, BUT WHEN THE TRACK MOVED, MY PARTY BAG FELL INTO THE SAND.

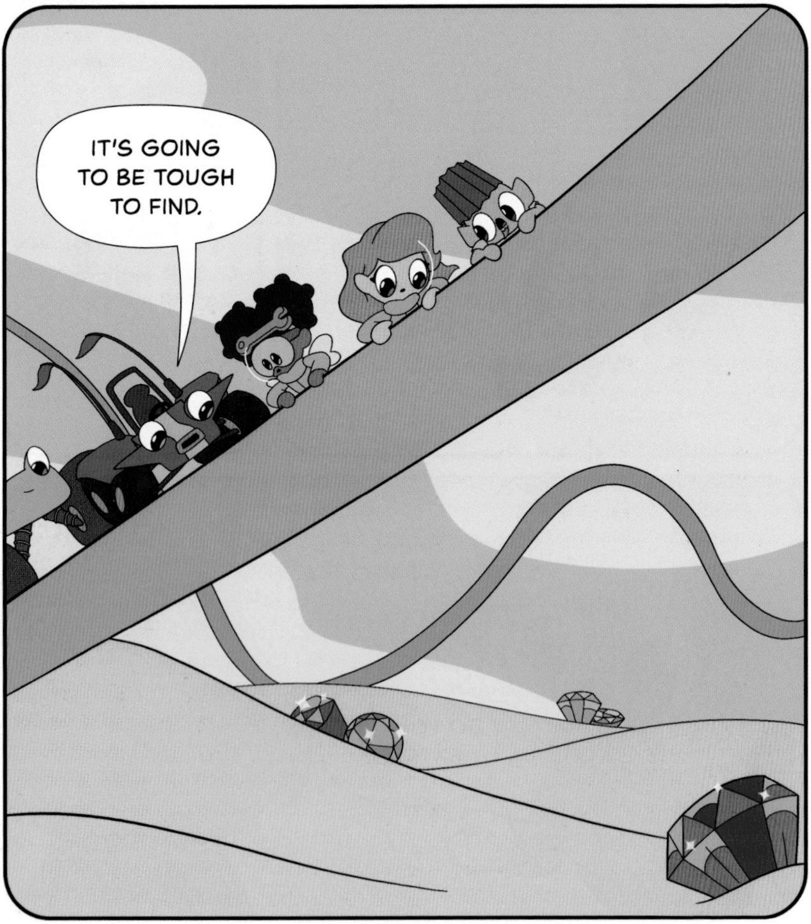
IT'S GOING TO BE TOUGH TO FIND.

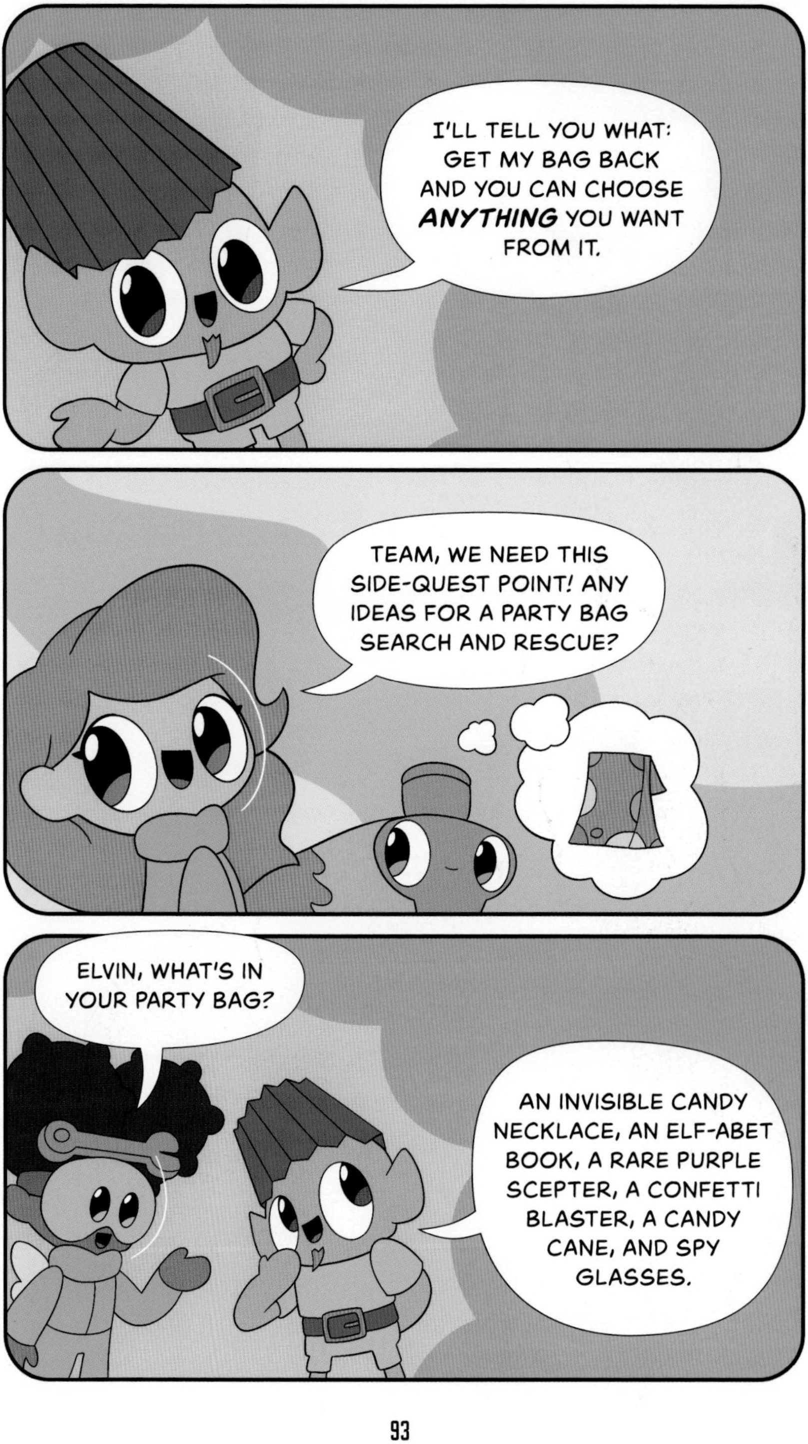
I'LL TELL YOU WHAT: GET MY BAG BACK AND YOU CAN CHOOSE **ANYTHING** YOU WANT FROM IT.
TEAM, WE NEED THIS SIDE-QUEST POINT! ANY IDEAS FOR A PARTY BAG SEARCH AND RESCUE?
ELVIN, WHAT'S IN YOUR PARTY BAG?
AN INVISIBLE CANDY NECKLACE, AN ELF-ABET BOOK, A RARE PURPLE SCEPTER, A CONFETTI BLASTER, A CANDY CANE, AND SPY GLASSES.

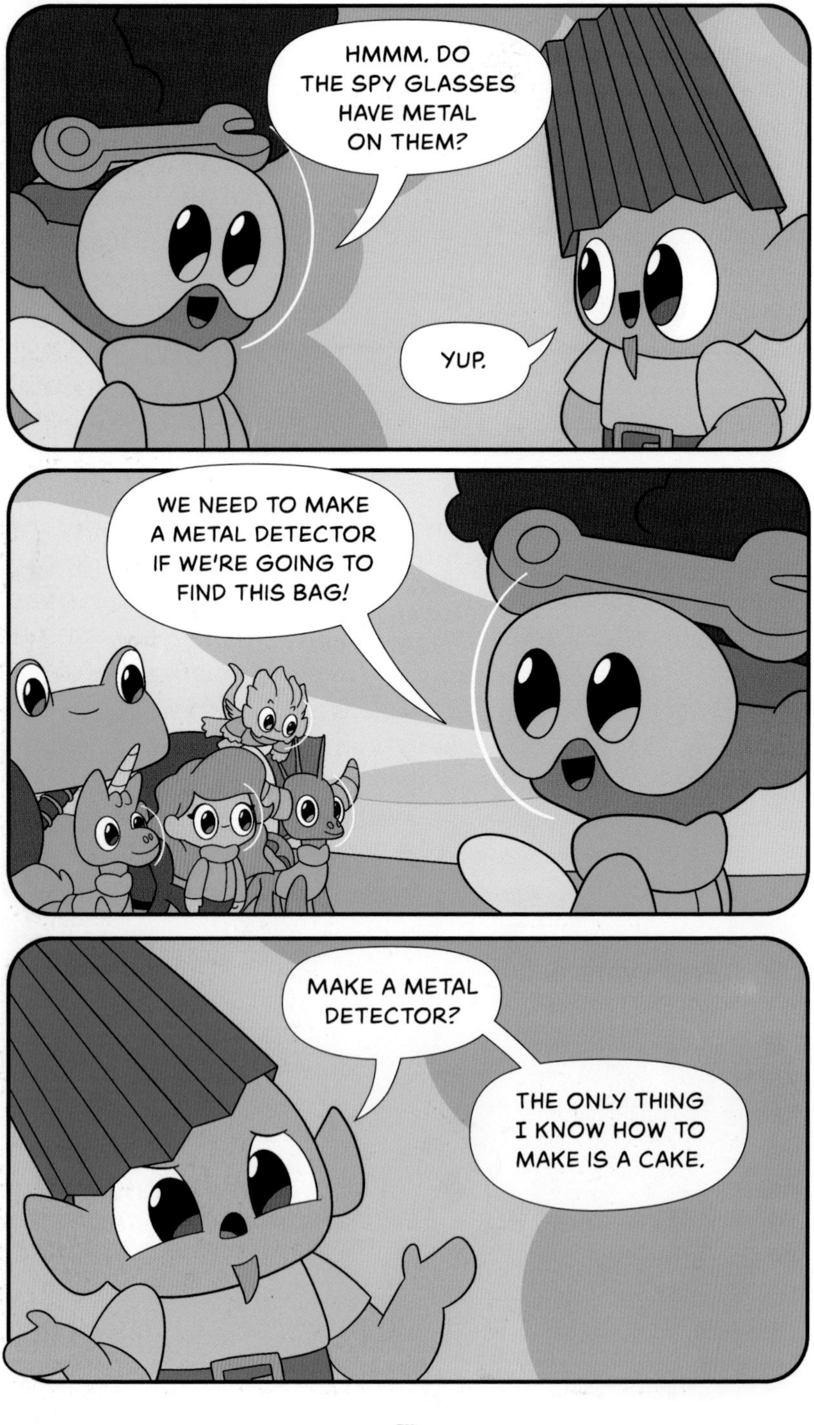
HMMM. DO THE SPY GLASSES HAVE METAL ON THEM?
YUP.
WE NEED TO MAKE A METAL DETECTOR IF WE'RE GOING TO FIND THIS BAG!
MAKE A METAL DETECTOR?
THE ONLY THING I KNOW HOW TO MAKE IS A CAKE.

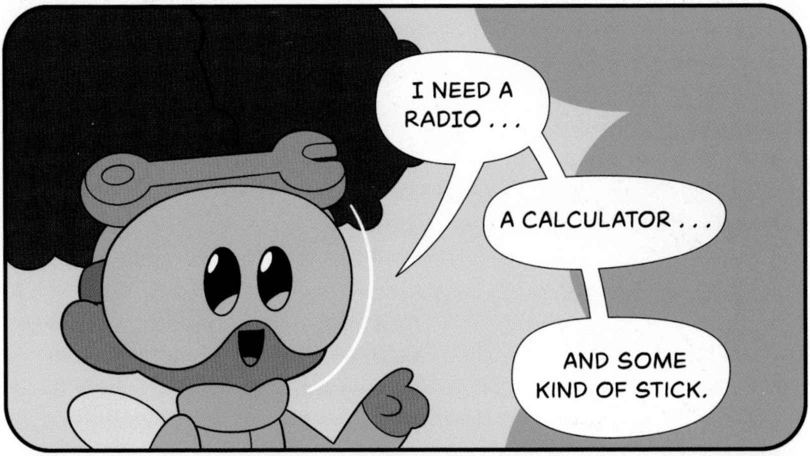
I NEED A RADIO . . .
A CALCULATOR . . .
AND SOME KIND OF STICK.

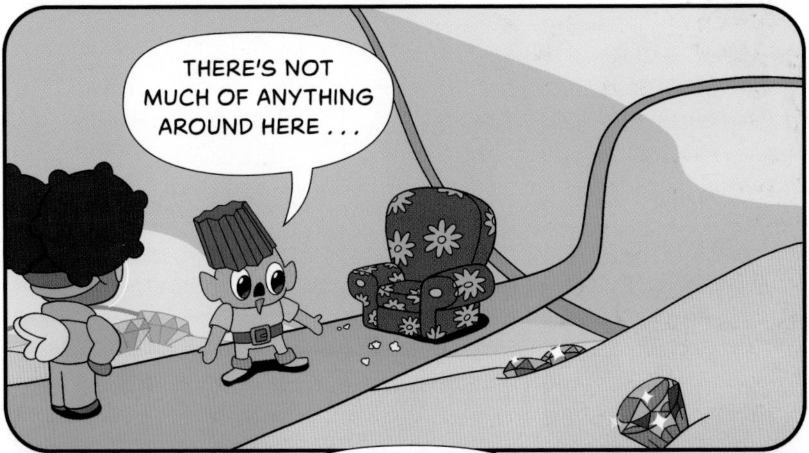
THERE'S NOT MUCH OF ANYTHING AROUND HERE . . .

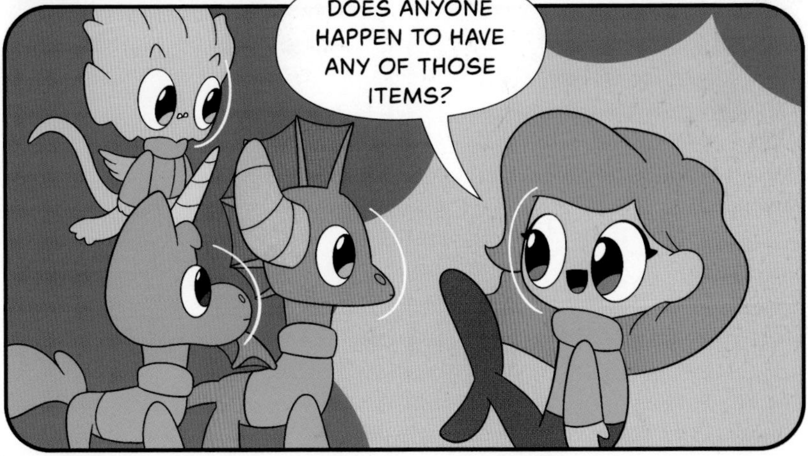
DOES ANYONE HAPPEN TO HAVE ANY OF THOSE ITEMS?

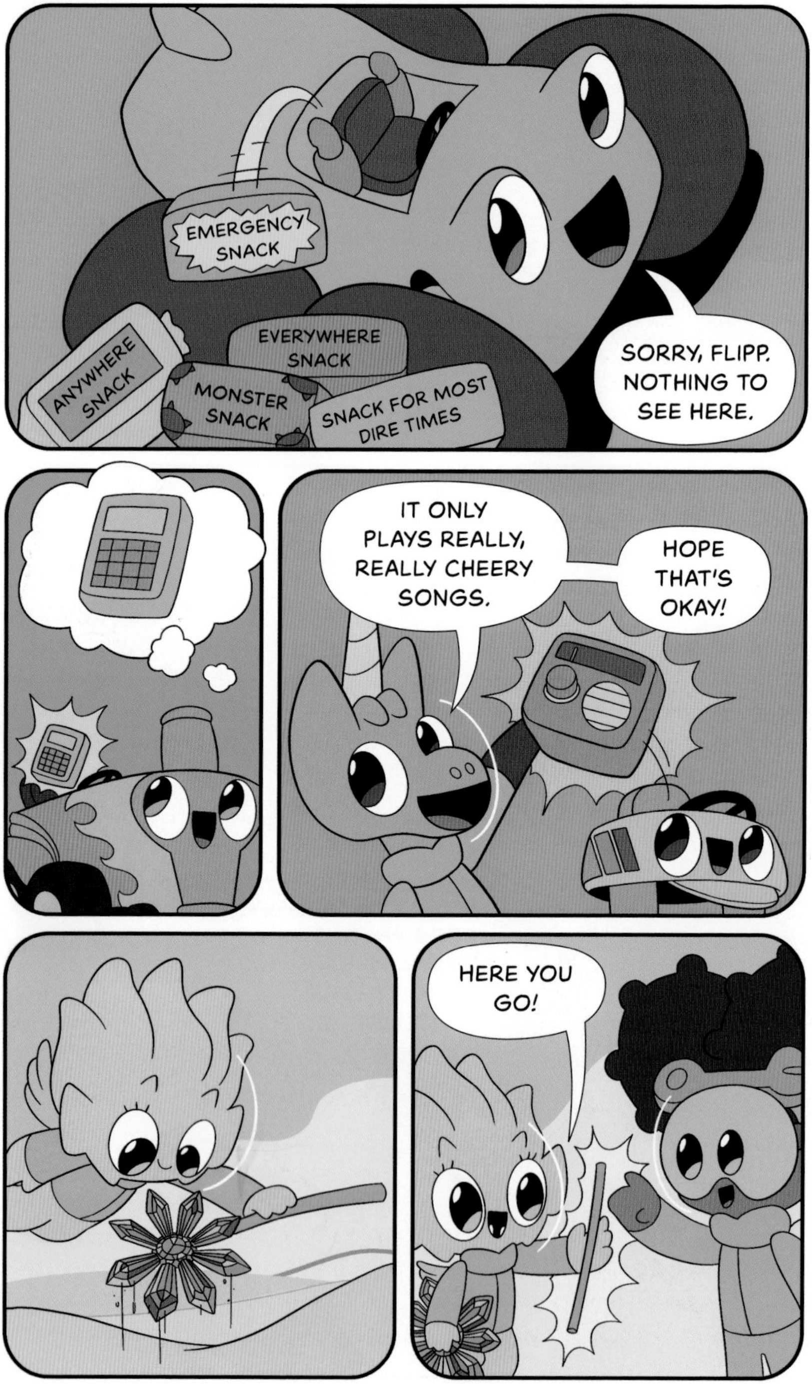
EMERGENCY SNACK
ANYWHERE SNACK
EVERYWHERE SNACK
MONSTER SNACK
SNACK FOR MOST DIRE TIMES
SORRY, FLIPP. NOTHING TO SEE HERE.
IT ONLY PLAYS REALLY, REALLY CHEERY SONGS.
HOPE THAT'S OKAY!
HERE YOU GO!

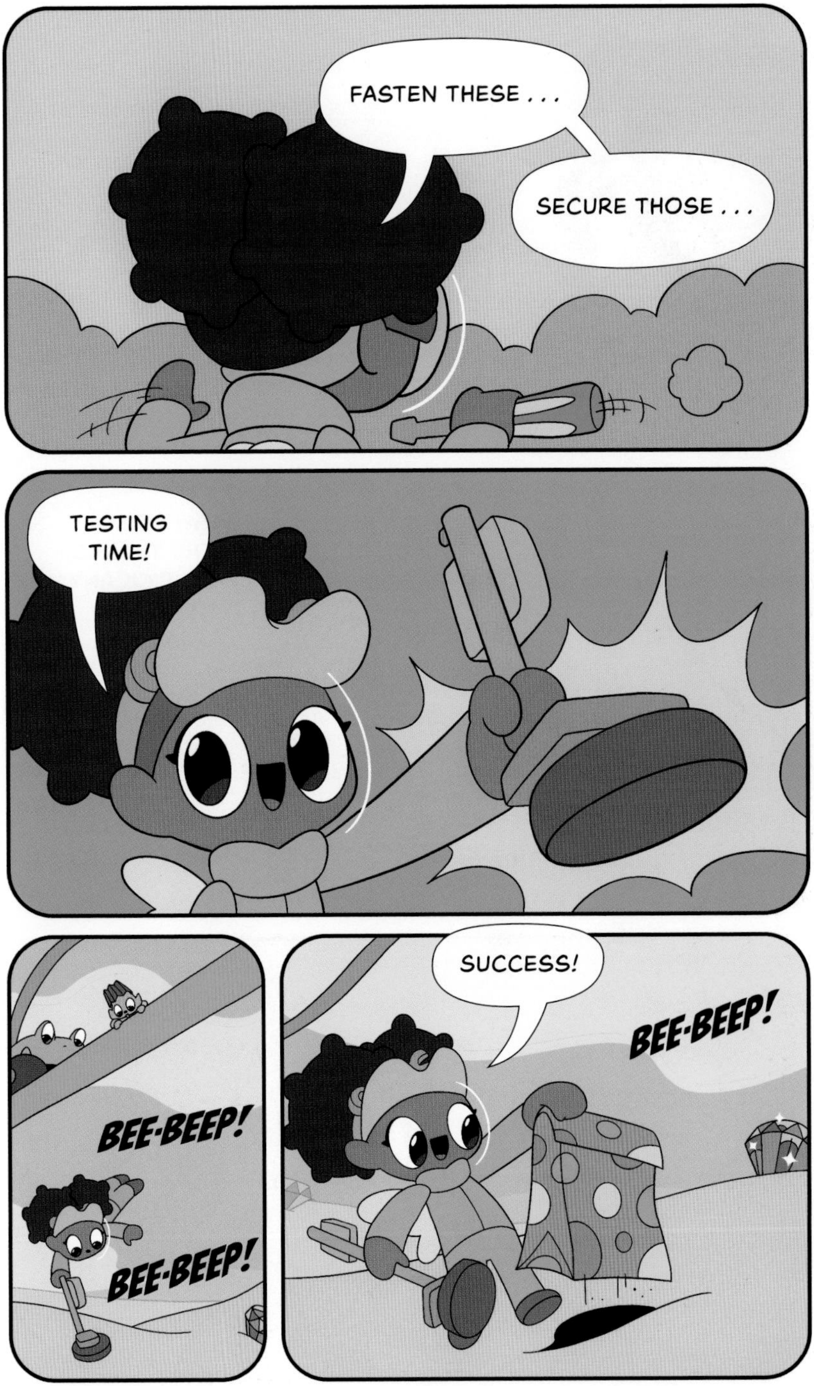
FASTEN THESE . . .
SECURE THOSE . . .
TESTING TIME!
BEE-BEEP!
BEE-BEEP!
SUCCESS!
BEE-BEEP!

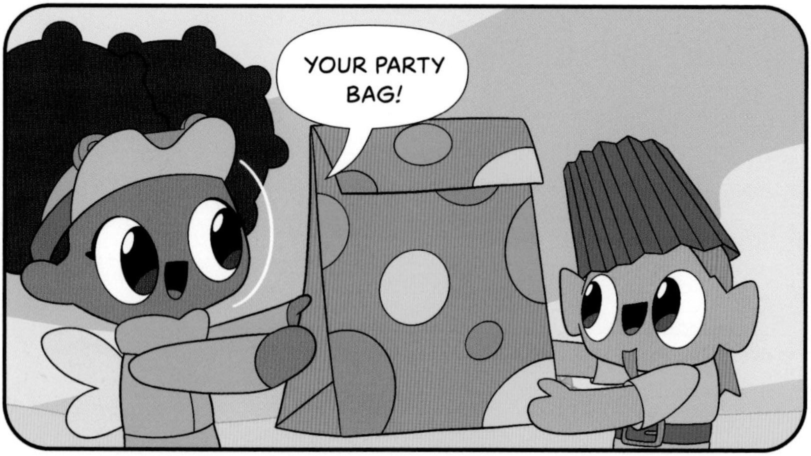
YOUR PARTY BAG!

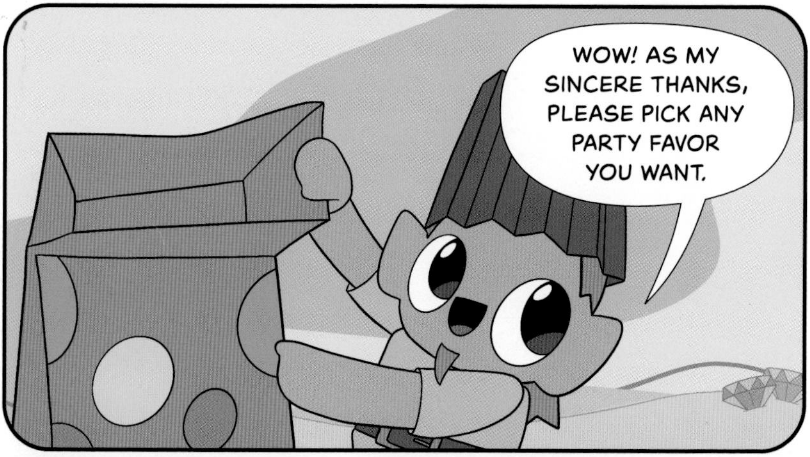
WOW! AS MY SINCERE THANKS, PLEASE PICK ANY PARTY FAVOR YOU WANT.

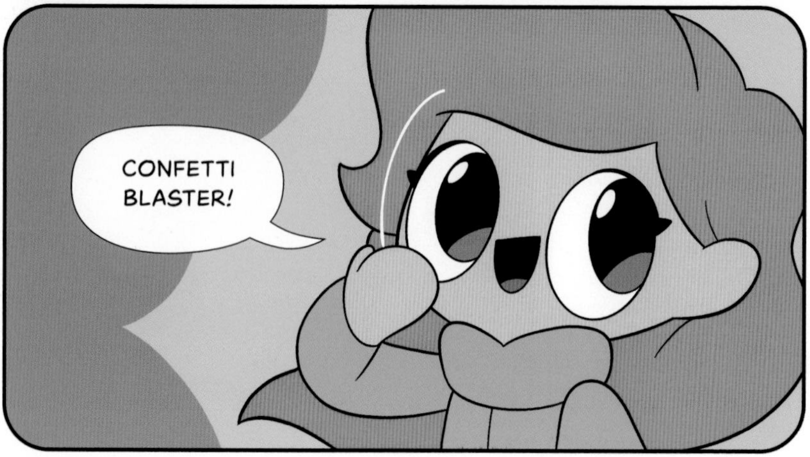
CONFETTI BLASTER!

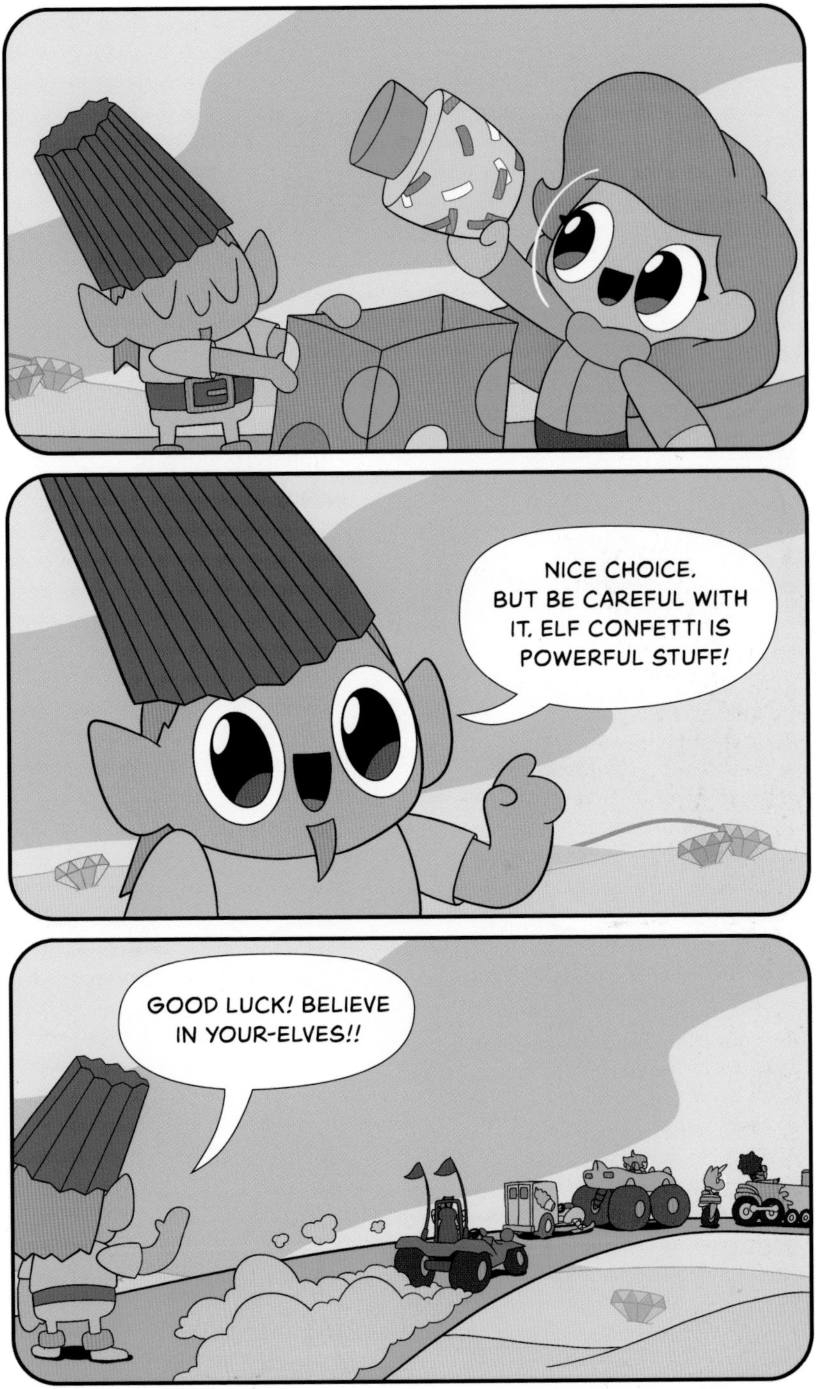
NICE CHOICE. BUT BE CAREFUL WITH IT. ELF CONFETTI IS POWERFUL STUFF!
GOOD LUCK! BELIEVE IN YOUR-ELVES!!

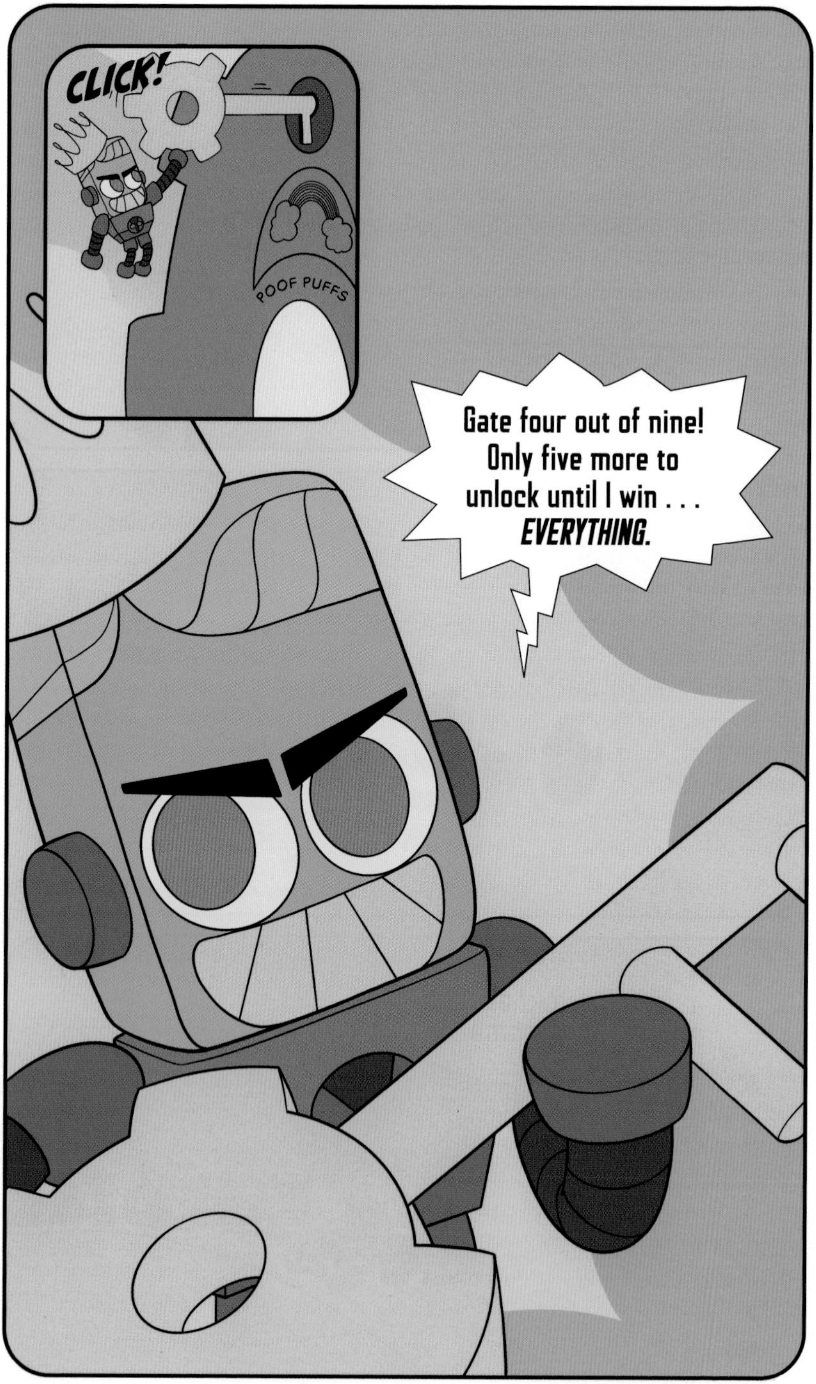
CLICK!
POOF PUFFS
Gate four out of nine! Only five more to unlock until I win . . . *EVERYTHING.*

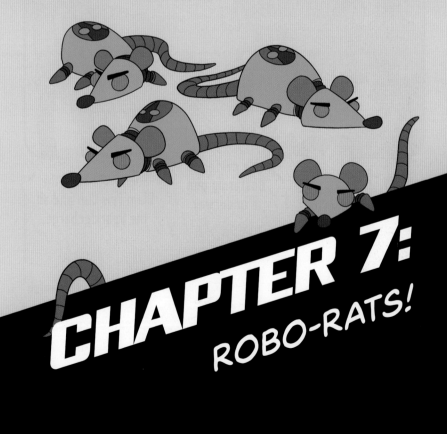

CHAPTER 7:
ROBO-RATS!

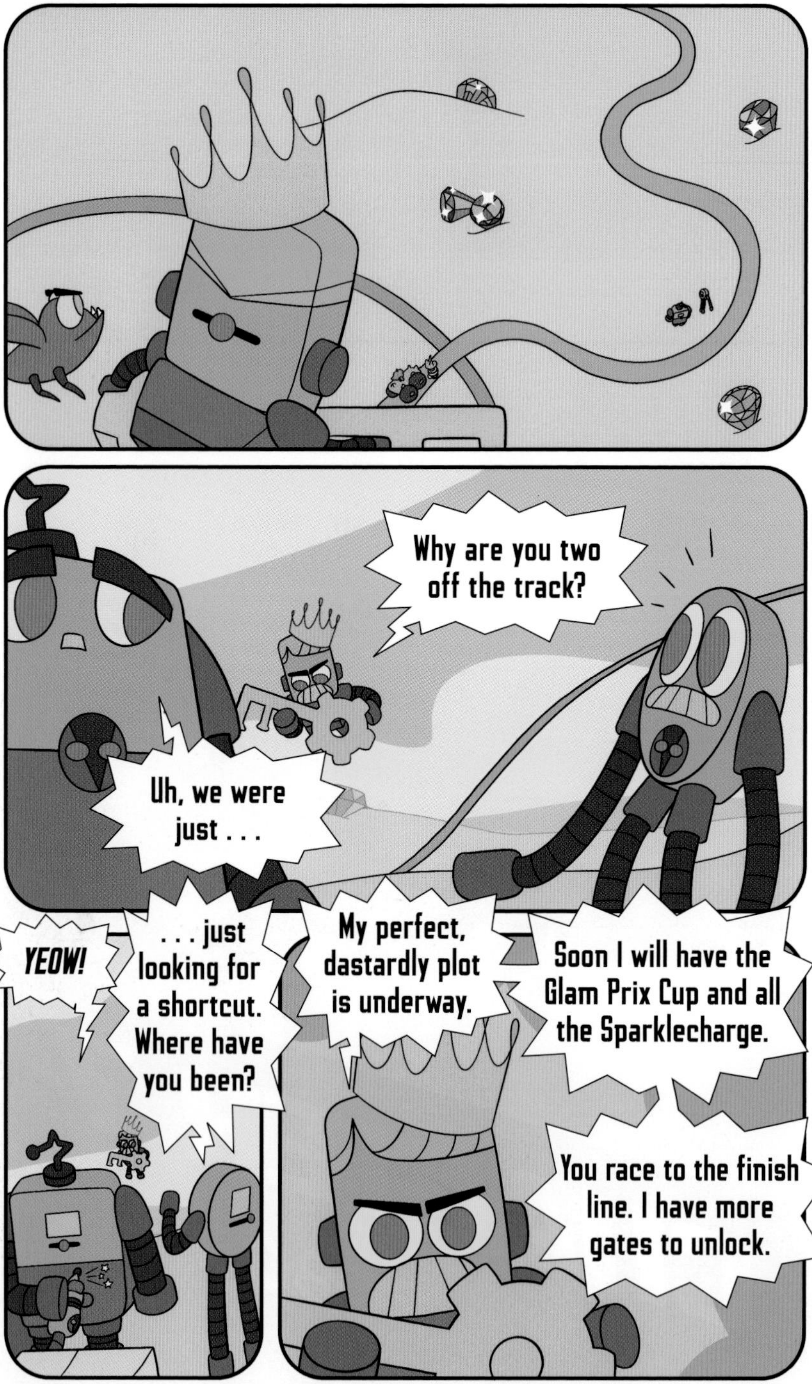
Why are you two off the track?
Uh, we were just . . .
YEOW!
. . . just looking for a shortcut. Where have you been?
My perfect, dastardly plot is underway.
Soon I will have the Glam Prix Cup and all the Sparklecharge.
You race to the finish line. I have more gates to unlock.

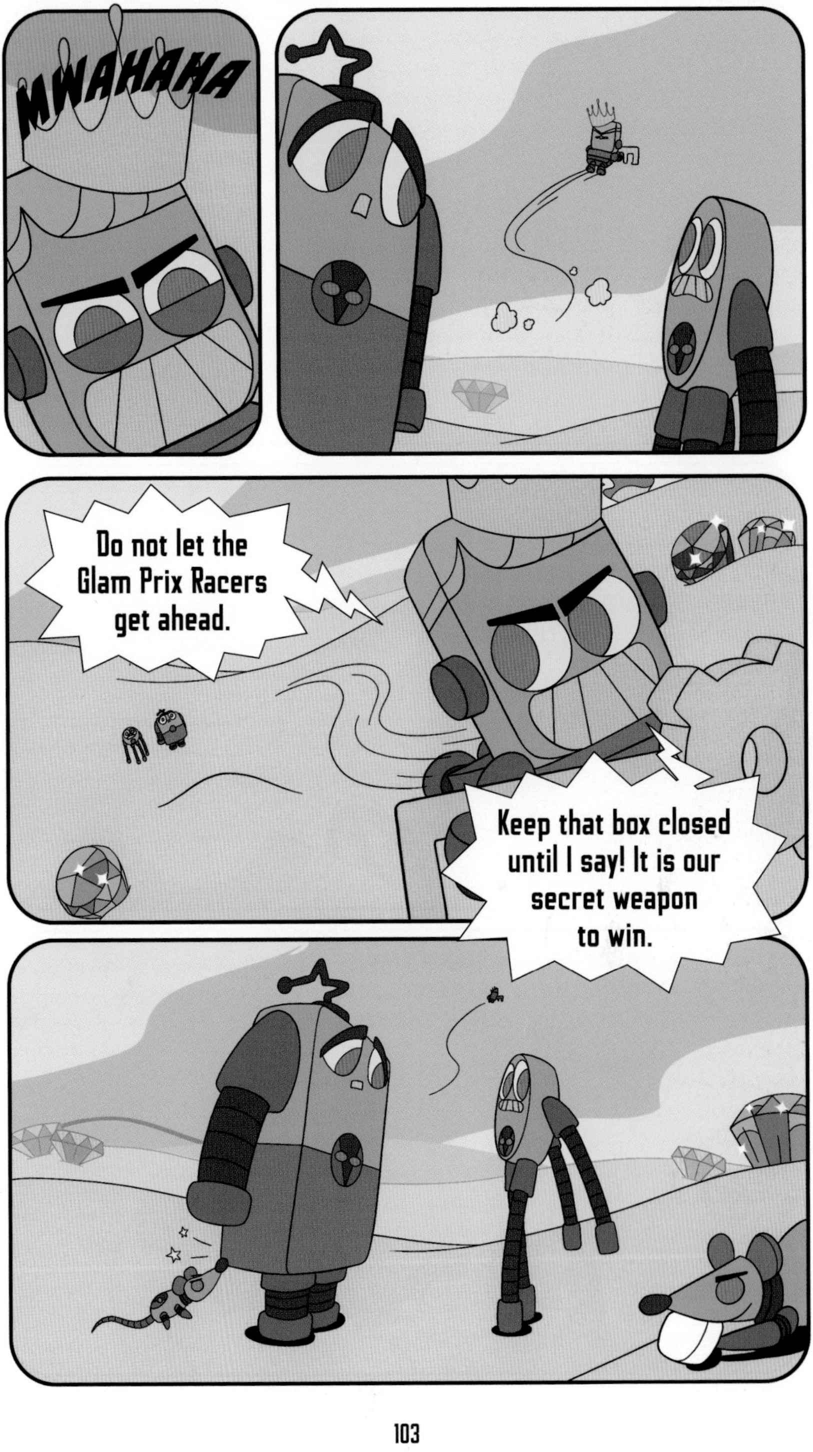
MWAHAHA
Do not let the Glam Prix Racers get ahead.
Keep that box closed until I say! It is our secret weapon to win.

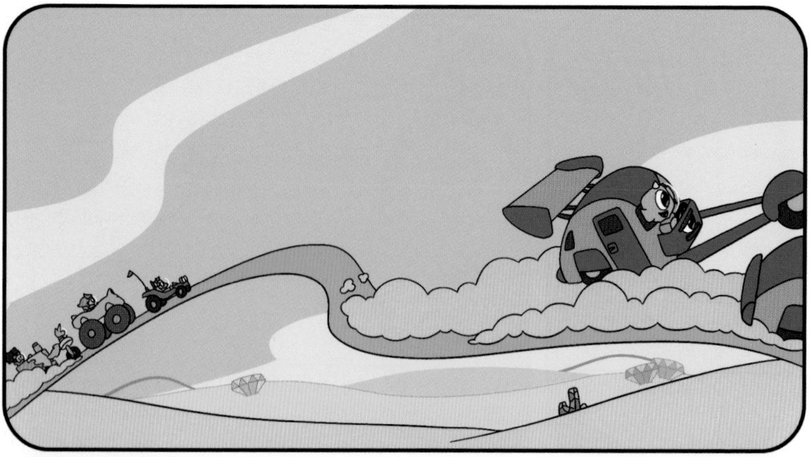

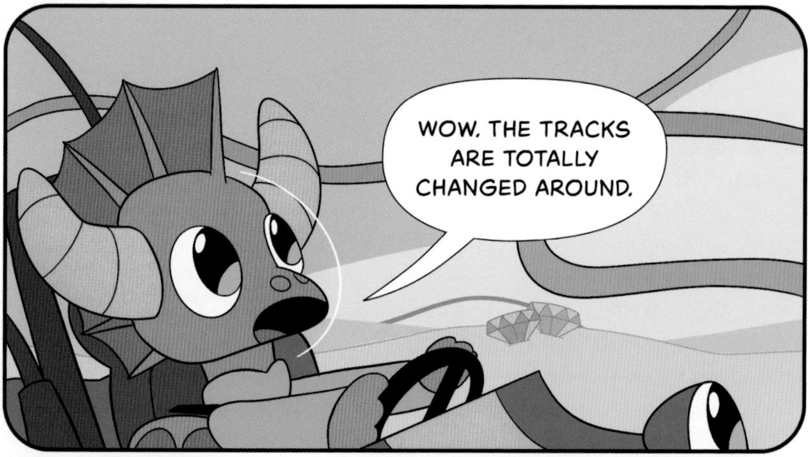
WOW. THE TRACKS ARE TOTALLY CHANGED AROUND.

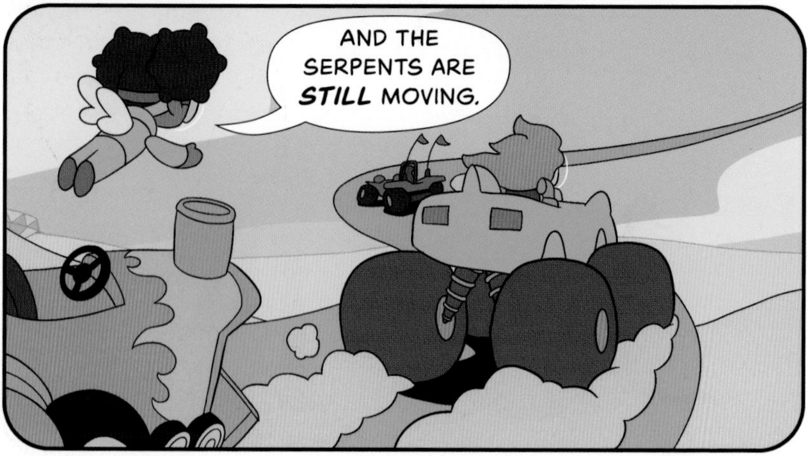
AND THE SERPENTS ARE *STILL* MOVING.

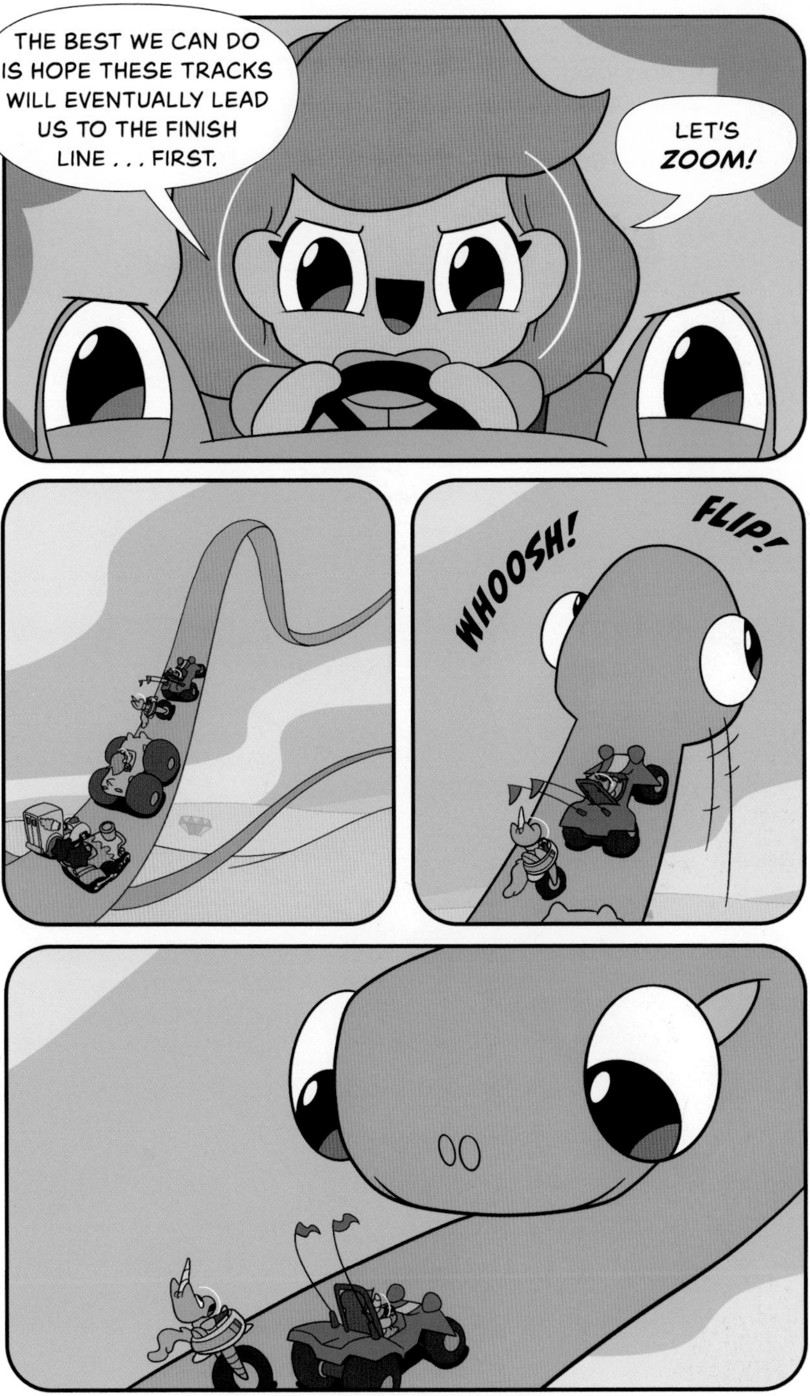
THE BEST WE CAN DO IS HOPE THESE TRACKS WILL EVENTUALLY LEAD US TO THE FINISH LINE . . . FIRST.
LET'S *ZOOM!*
WHOOSH!
FLIP!

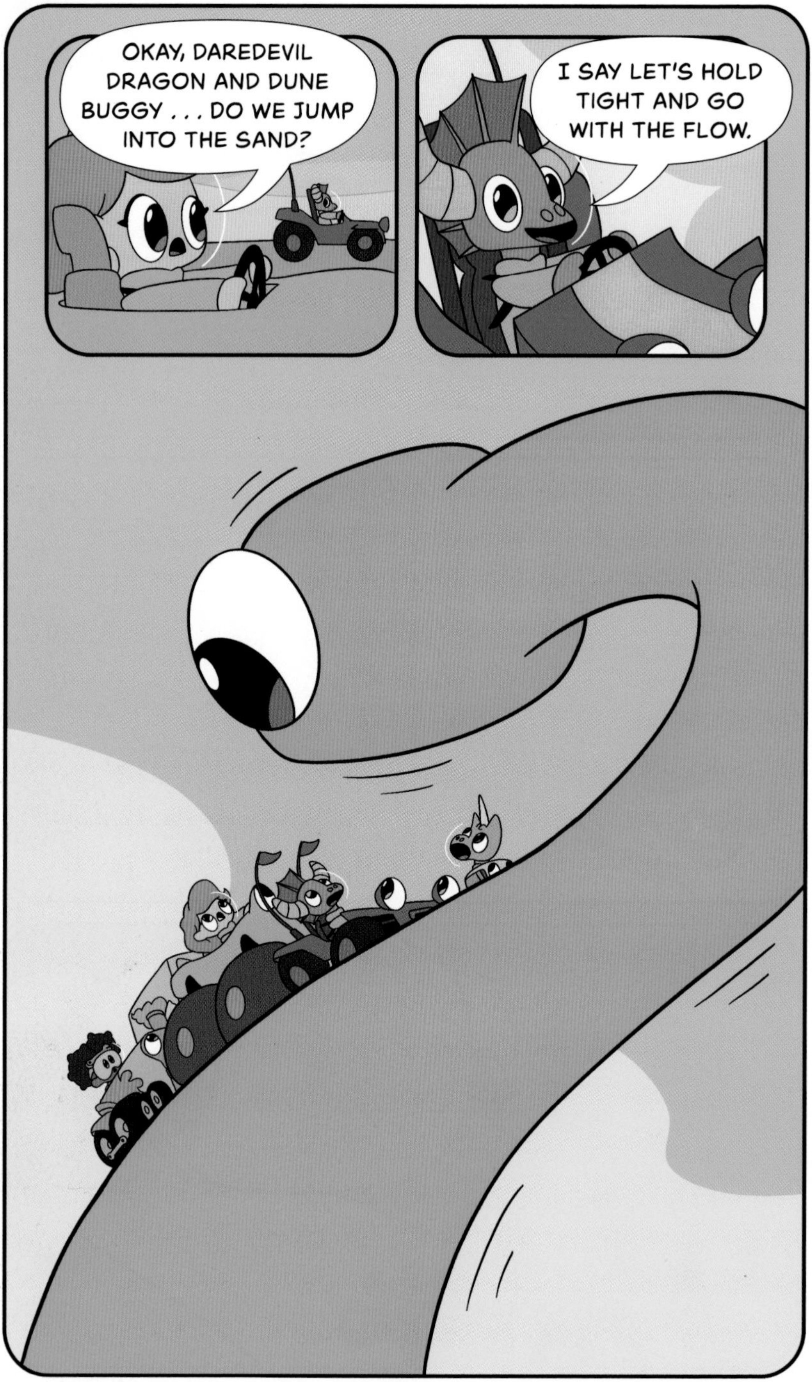
OKAY, DAREDEVIL DRAGON AND DUNE BUGGY . . . DO WE JUMP INTO THE SAND?
I SAY LET'S HOLD TIGHT AND GO WITH THE FLOW.

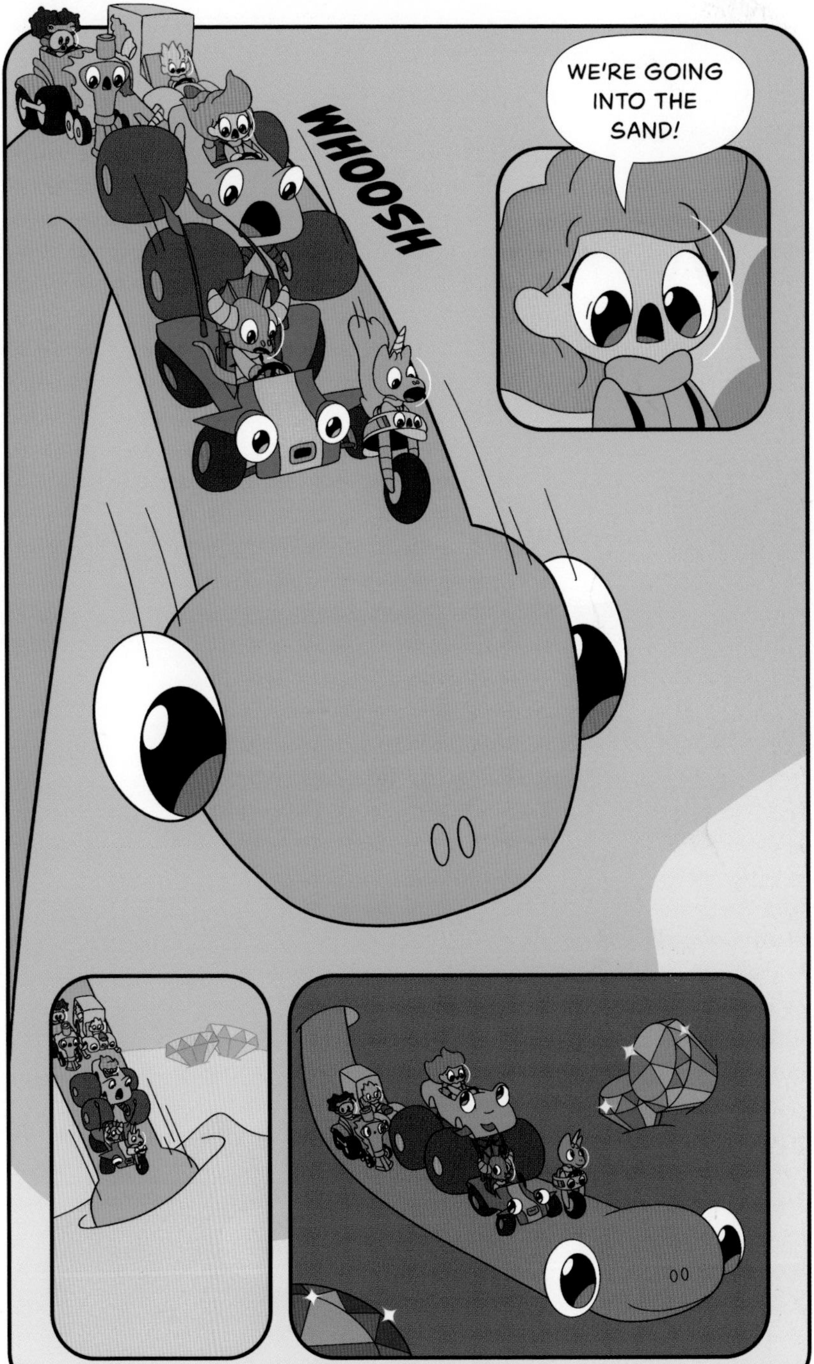
WHOOSH
WE'RE GOING INTO THE SAND!

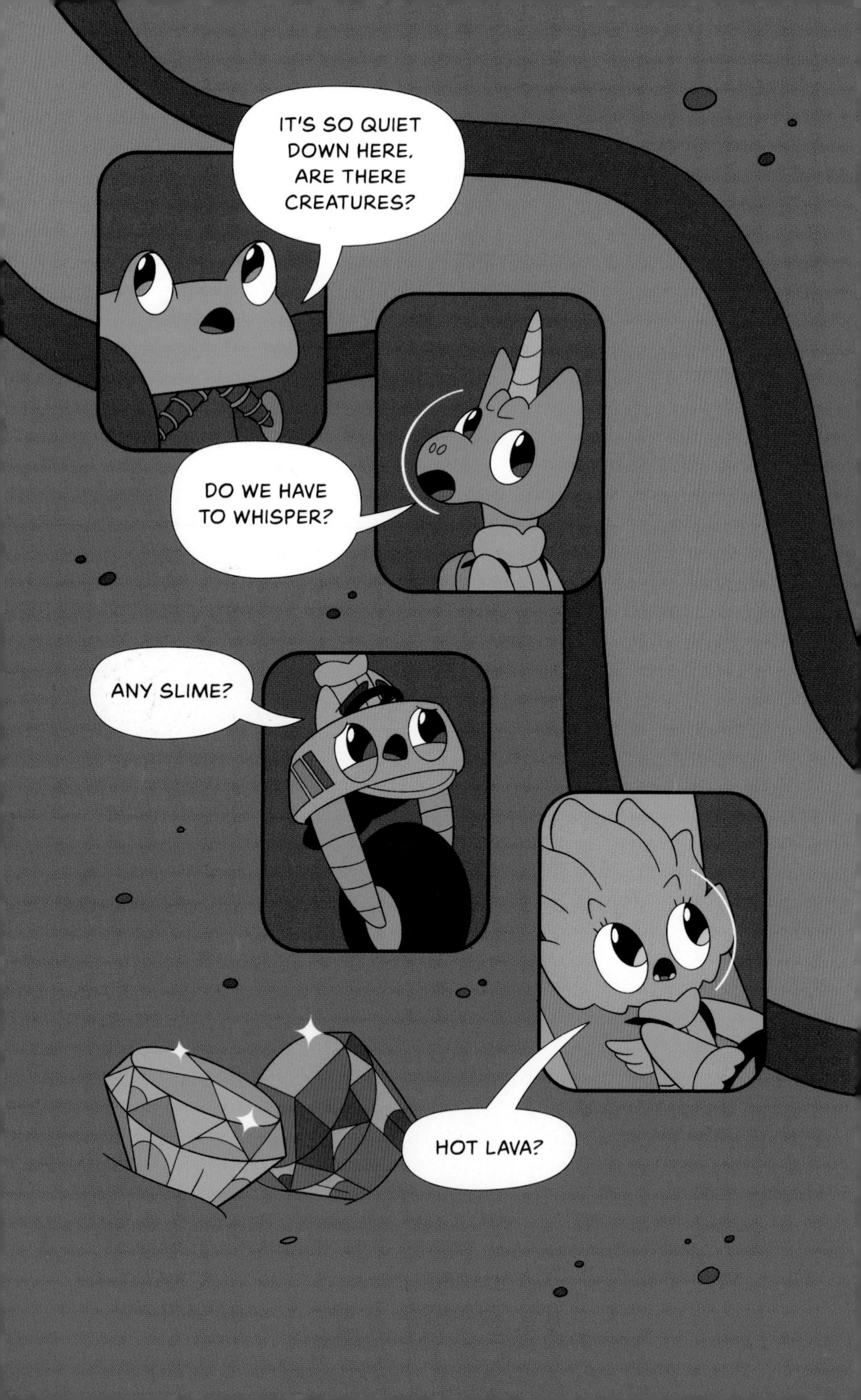
IT'S SO QUIET DOWN HERE. ARE THERE CREATURES?
DO WE HAVE TO WHISPER?
ANY SLIME?
HOT LAVA?

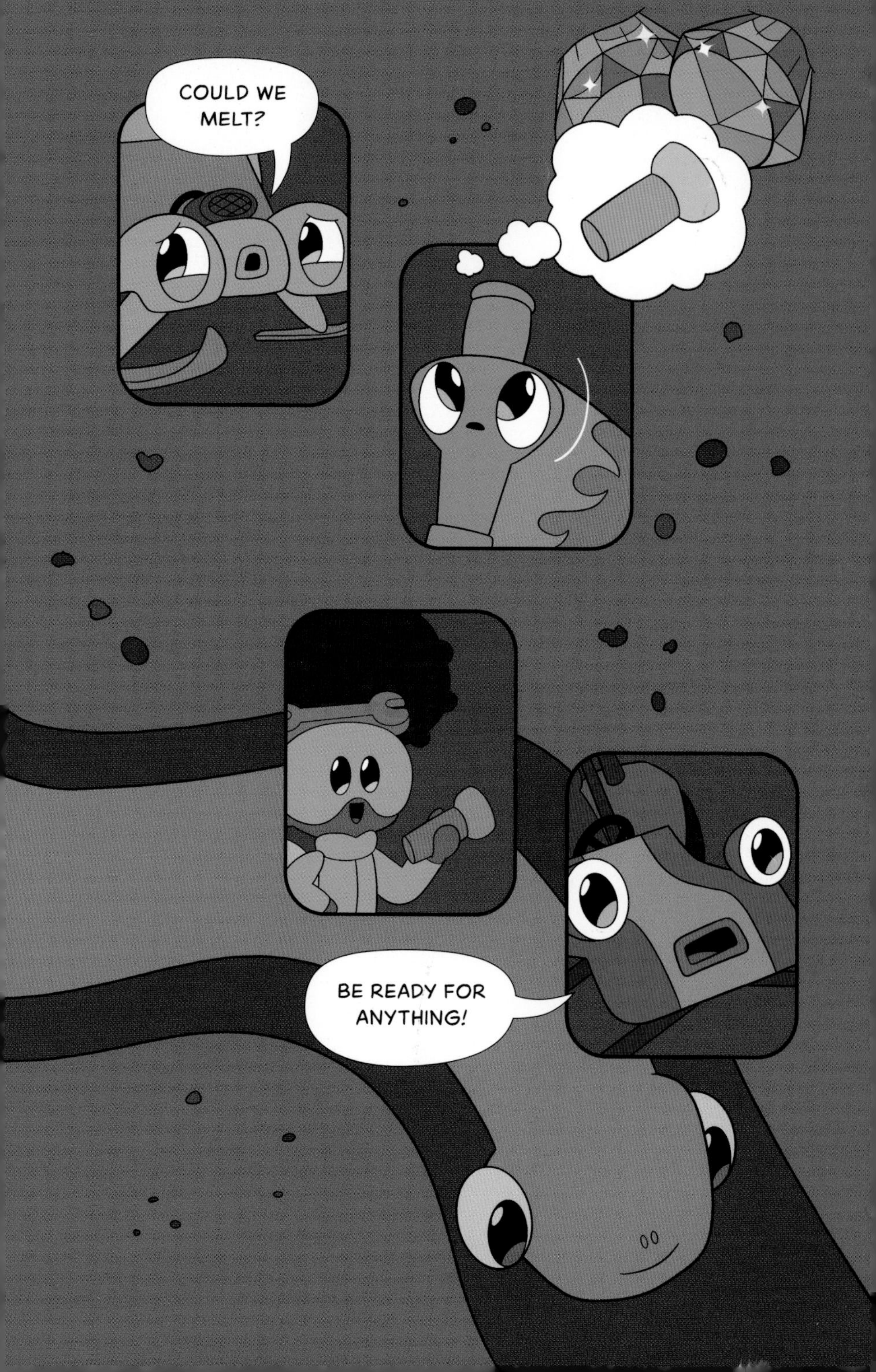
COULD WE
MELT?
BE READY FOR
ANYTHING!

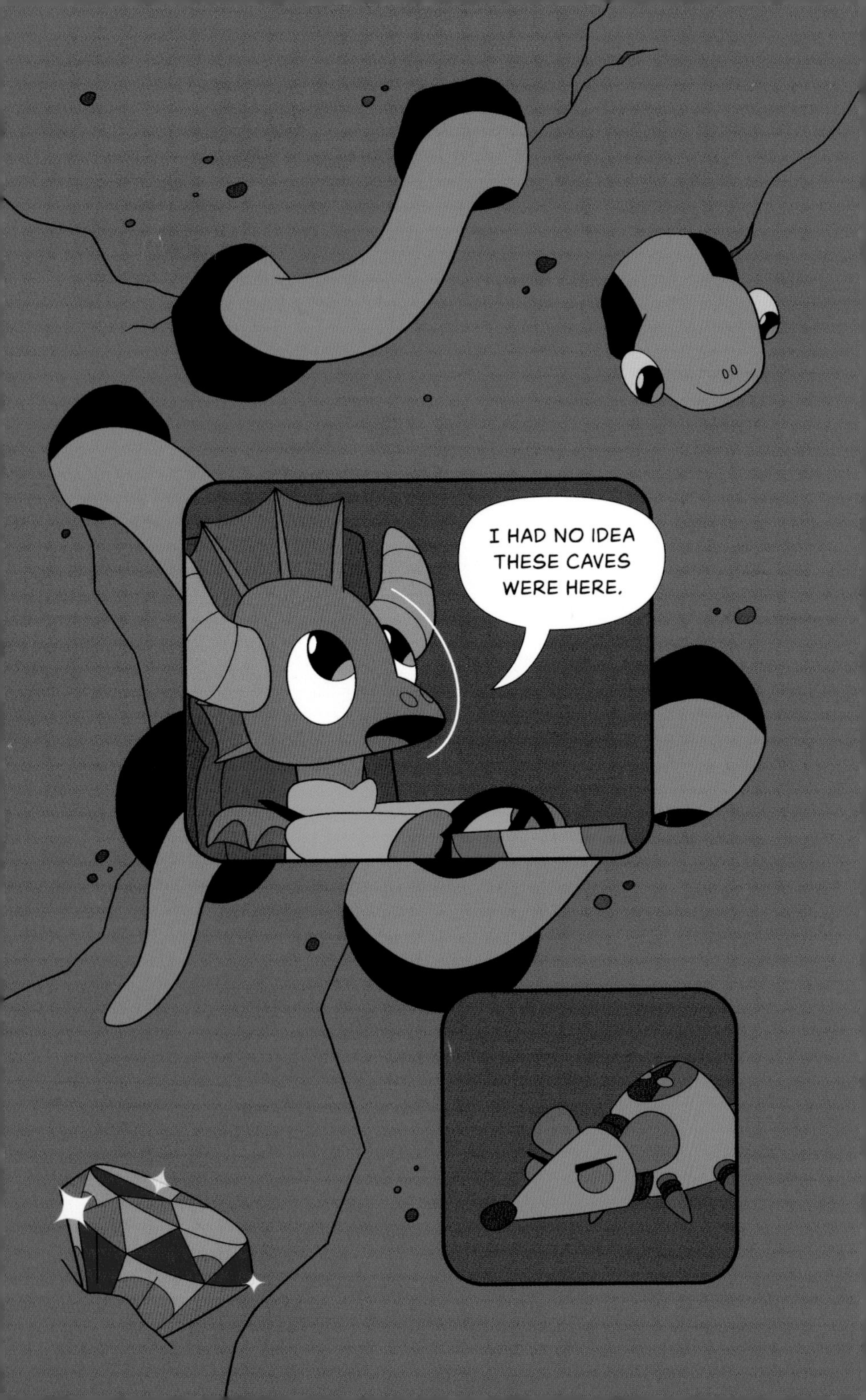
I HAD NO IDEA
THESE CAVES
WERE HERE.

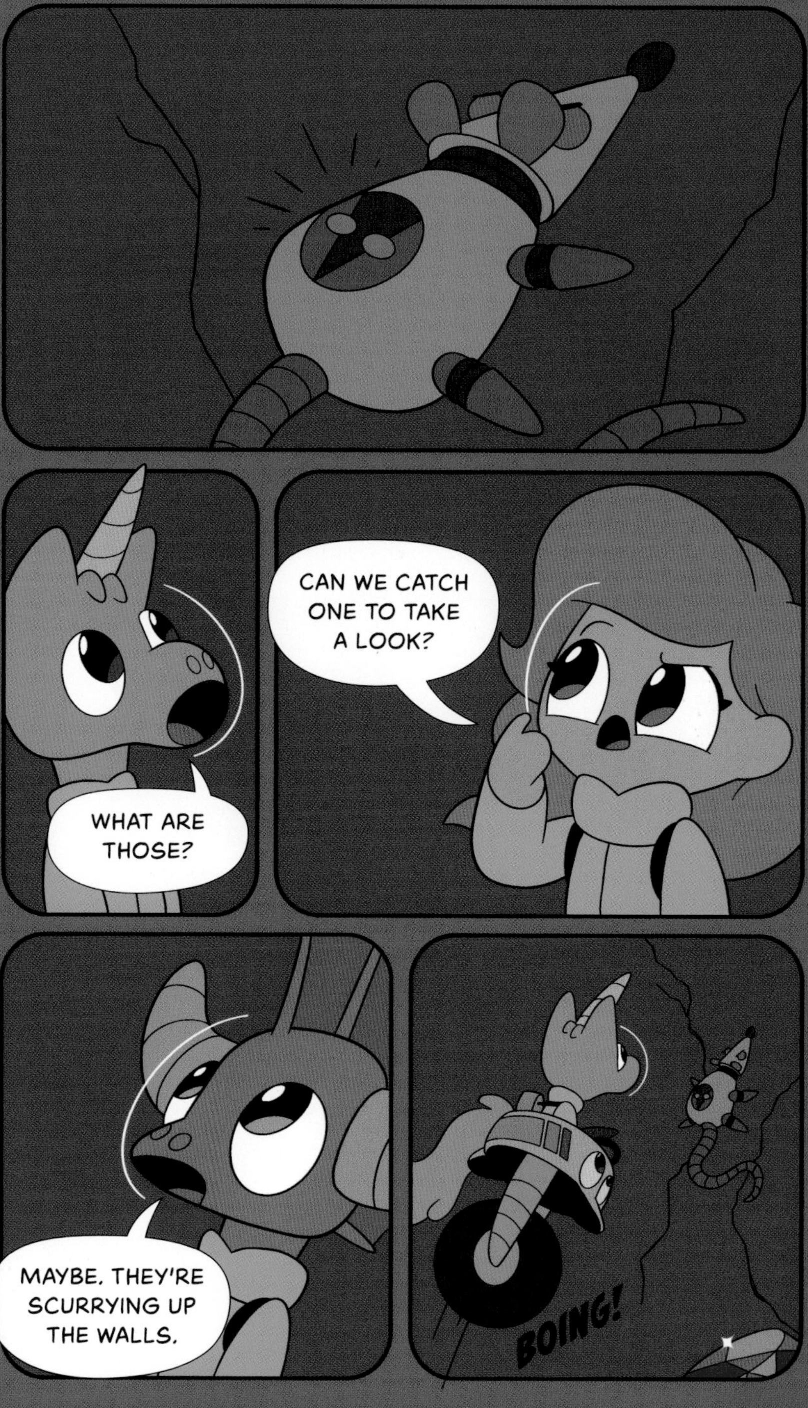
WHAT ARE THOSE?
CAN WE CATCH ONE TO TAKE A LOOK?
MAYBE. THEY'RE SCURRYING UP THE WALLS.
BOING!

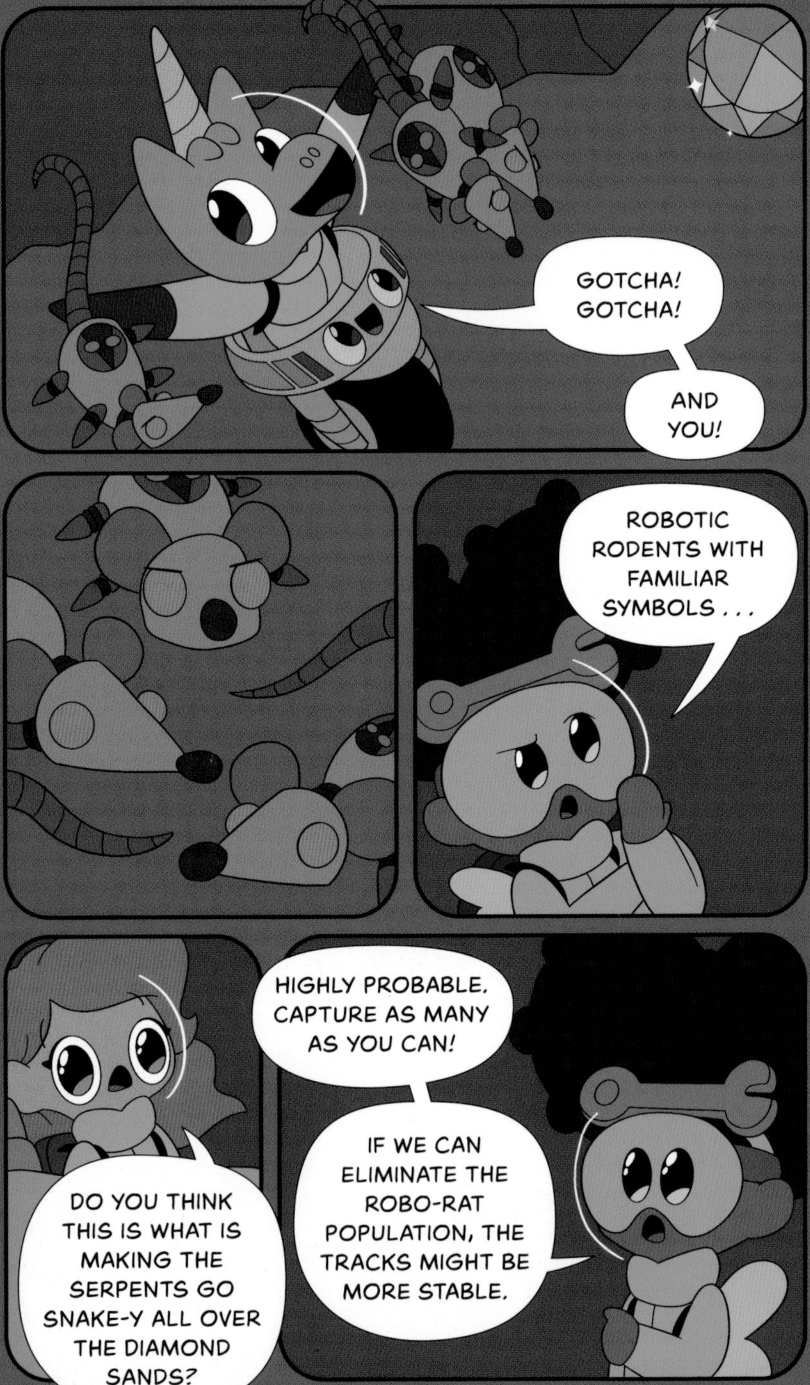
GOTCHA! GOTCHA!
AND YOU!
ROBOTIC RODENTS WITH FAMILIAR SYMBOLS . . .
DO YOU THINK THIS IS WHAT IS MAKING THE SERPENTS GO SNAKE-Y ALL OVER THE DIAMOND SANDS?
HIGHLY PROBABLE. CAPTURE AS MANY AS YOU CAN!
IF WE CAN ELIMINATE THE ROBO-RAT POPULATION, THE TRACKS MIGHT BE MORE STABLE.

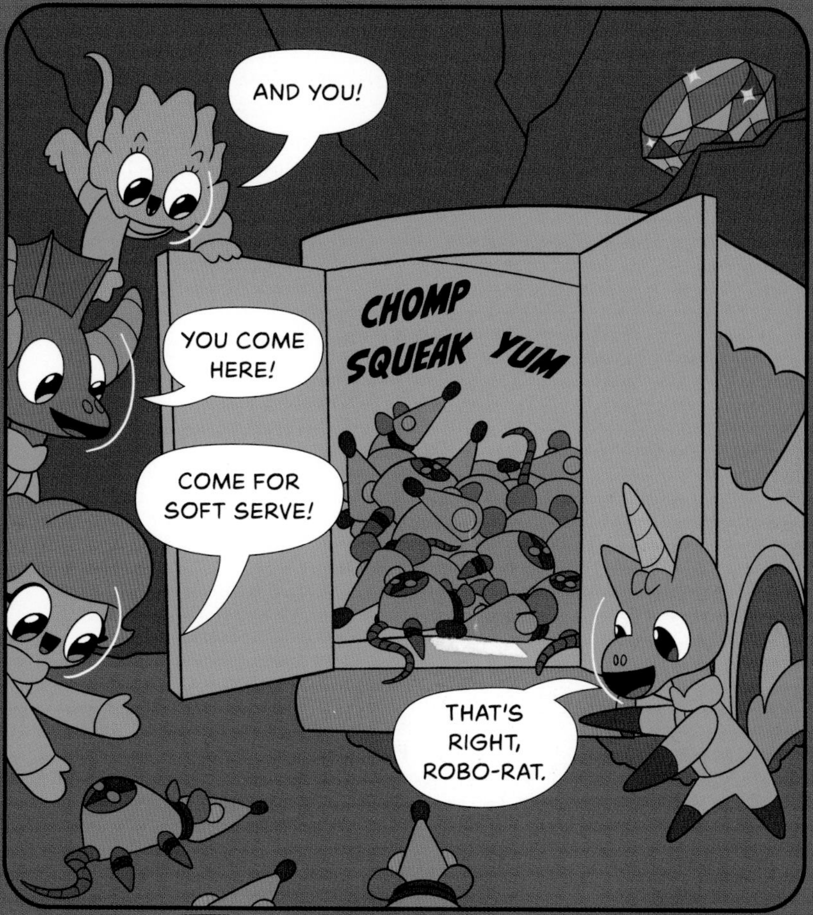
AND YOU!
YOU COME HERE!
COME FOR SOFT SERVE!
CHOMP
SQUEAK YUM
THAT'S RIGHT, ROBO-RAT.

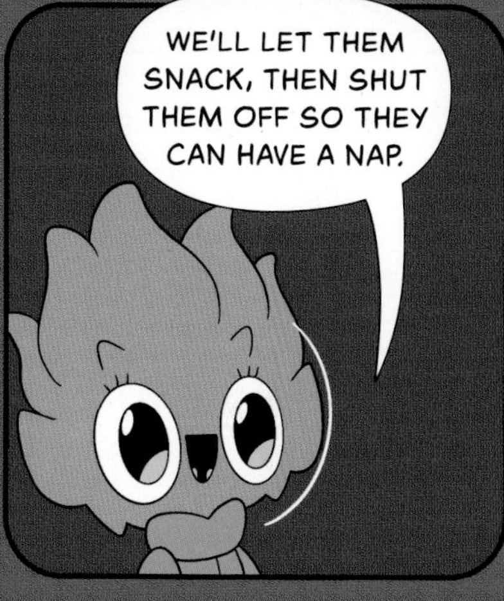
WE'LL LET THEM SNACK, THEN SHUT THEM OFF SO THEY CAN HAVE A NAP.

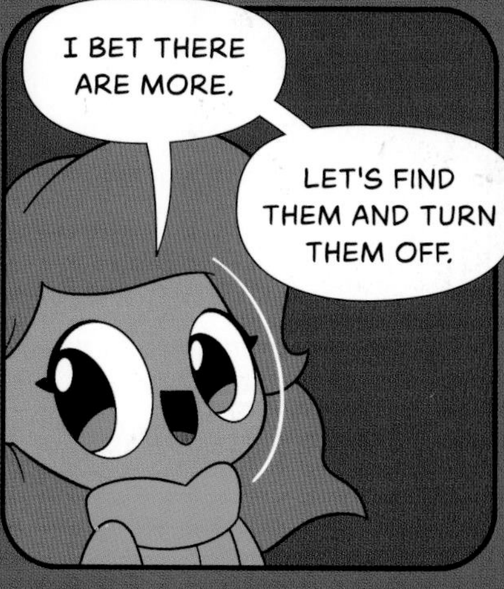
I BET THERE ARE MORE.
LET'S FIND THEM AND TURN THEM OFF.

IN THE HISTORY OF GLITTERGEAR ISLAND RACES, WE'VE NEVER SEEN THE KIND OF CHAOS THAT'S HAPPENING TODAY.

THE GLAM PRIX RACERS' WHEREABOUTS ARE UNKNOWN, BUT ONE OFFICIAL IS REPORTING THAT THEY WERE FORCED TO FOLLOW THE TRACK UNDERGROUND. WE'LL SEE WHERE THEY POP UP!

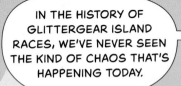

THE GLAM PRIX RACERS ALREADY EARNED 2 SIDE-QUEST POINTS AND THE CYCLOPS CAMPERS HAVE 1 SIDE-QUEST POINT. THE VROOMBOTS ARE STILL WELL AHEAD, BUT HAVE NO SIDE-QUEST POINTS. STAY TUNED!

Both Fancy Forest gates are unlocked.

Only three more to go until the Sparklecharge Springs are *MINE*.

CLICK!

CLICK!

FANCY FOREST

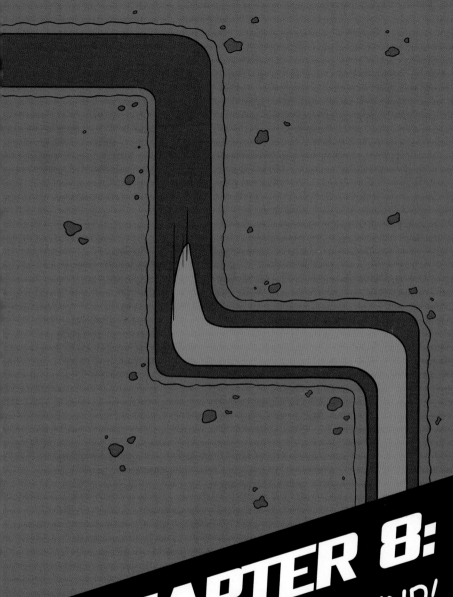

CHAPTER 8:
UNDERGROUND!

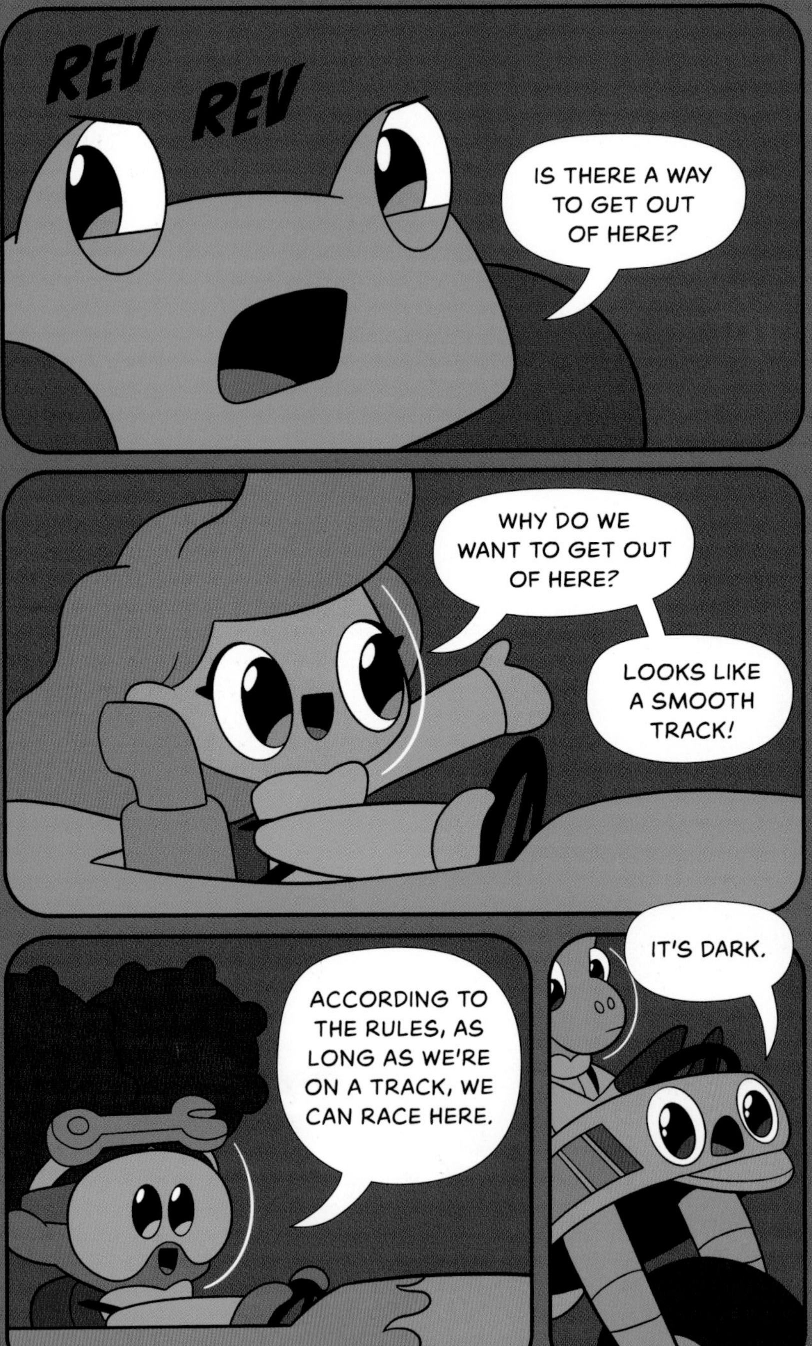
REV
REV
IS THERE A WAY TO GET OUT OF HERE?
WHY DO WE WANT TO GET OUT OF HERE?
LOOKS LIKE A SMOOTH TRACK!
ACCORDING TO THE RULES, AS LONG AS WE'RE ON A TRACK, WE CAN RACE HERE.
IT'S DARK.

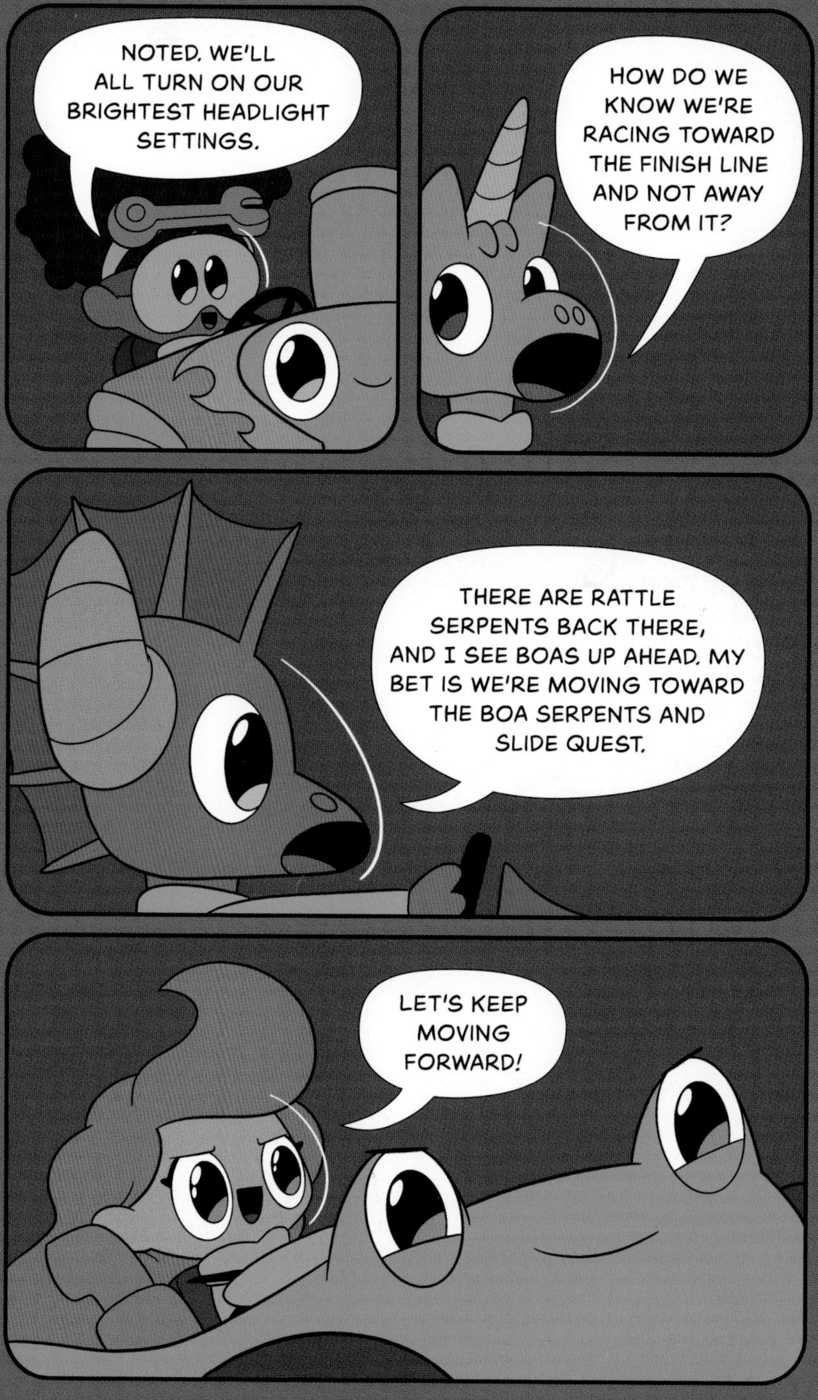
NOTED. WE'LL ALL TURN ON OUR BRIGHTEST HEADLIGHT SETTINGS.
HOW DO WE KNOW WE'RE RACING TOWARD THE FINISH LINE AND NOT AWAY FROM IT?
THERE ARE RATTLE SERPENTS BACK THERE, AND I SEE BOAS UP AHEAD. MY BET IS WE'RE MOVING TOWARD THE BOA SERPENTS AND SLIDE QUEST.
LET'S KEEP MOVING FORWARD!

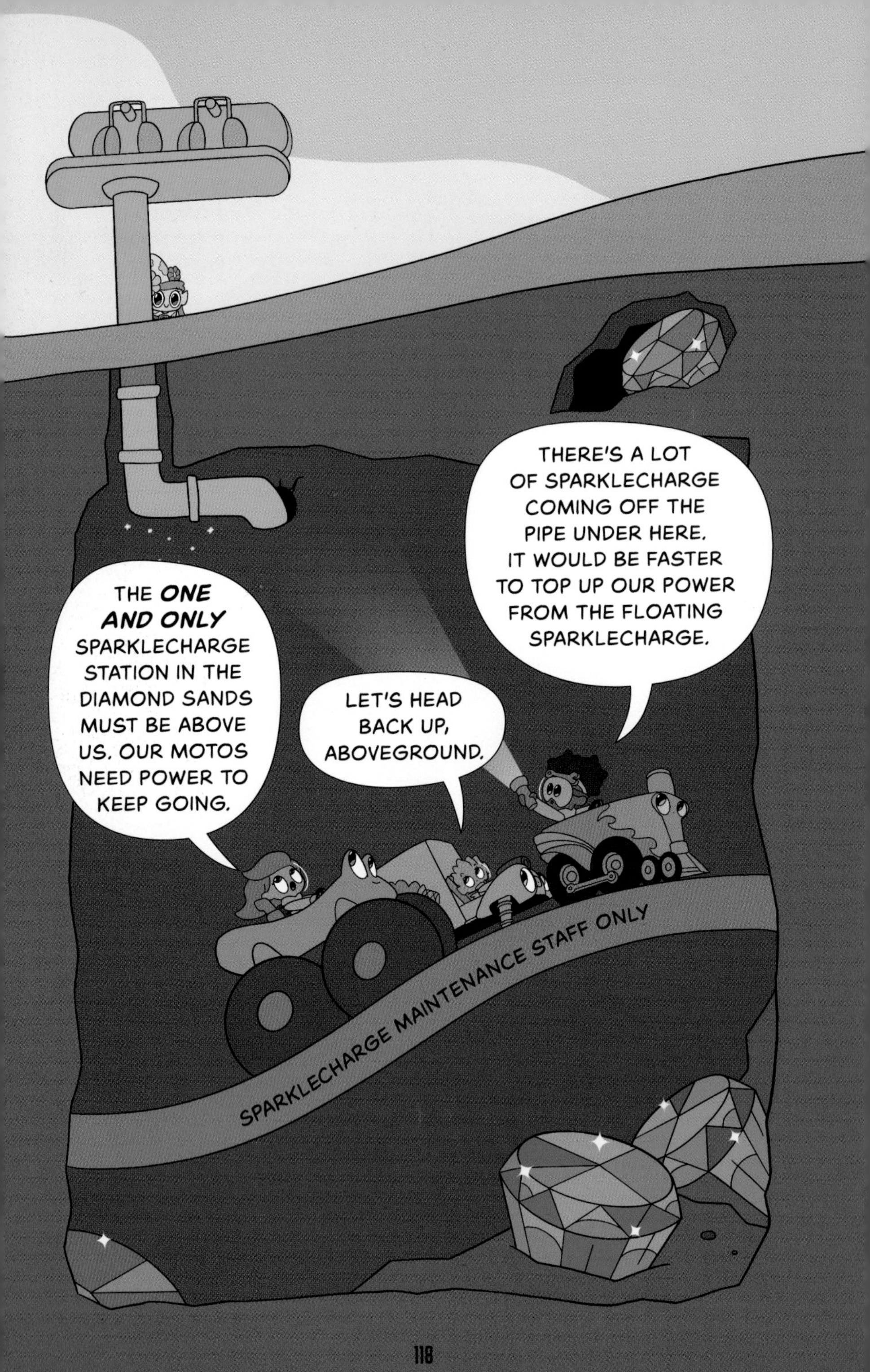
THE *ONE AND ONLY* SPARKLECHARGE STATION IN THE DIAMOND SANDS MUST BE ABOVE US. OUR MOTOS NEED POWER TO KEEP GOING.
LET'S HEAD BACK UP, ABOVEGROUND.
THERE'S A LOT OF SPARKLECHARGE COMING OFF THE PIPE UNDER HERE. IT WOULD BE FASTER TO TOP UP OUR POWER FROM THE FLOATING SPARKLECHARGE.
SPARKLECHARGE MAINTENANCE STAFF ONLY

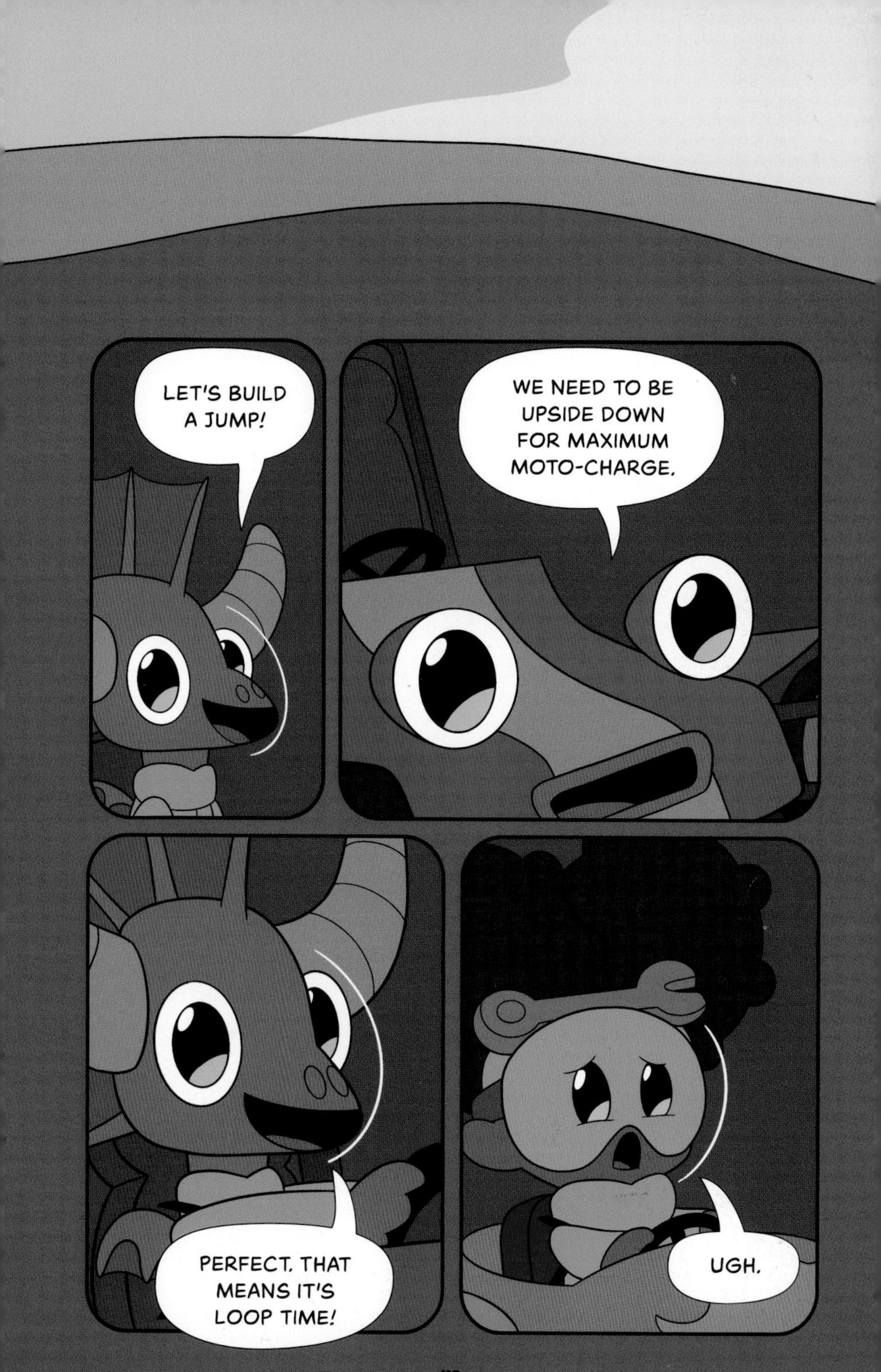
LET'S BUILD A JUMP!
WE NEED TO BE UPSIDE DOWN FOR MAXIMUM MOTO-CHARGE.
PERFECT. THAT MEANS IT'S LOOP TIME!
UGH.

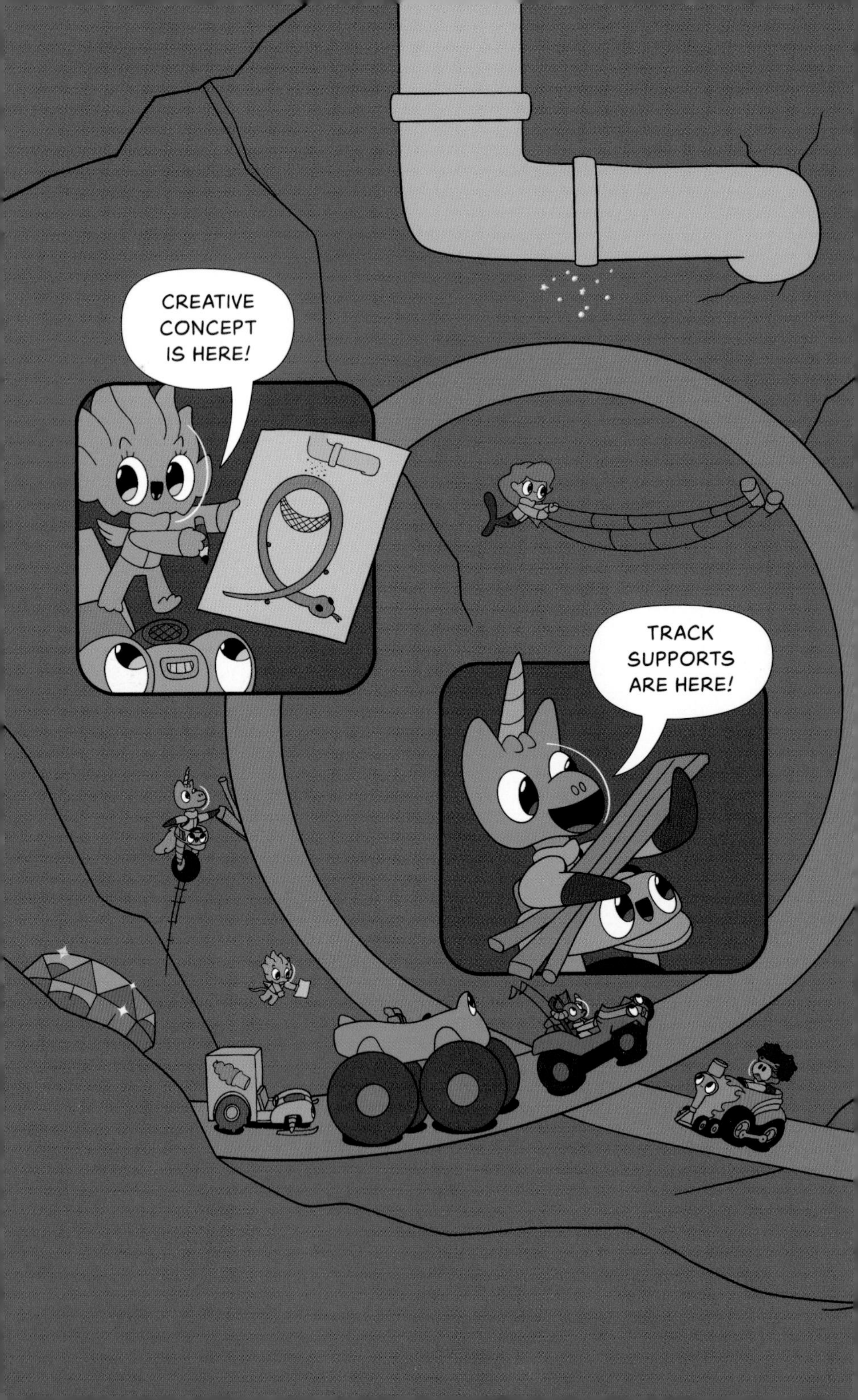

CREATIVE CONCEPT IS HERE!
TRACK SUPPORTS ARE HERE!

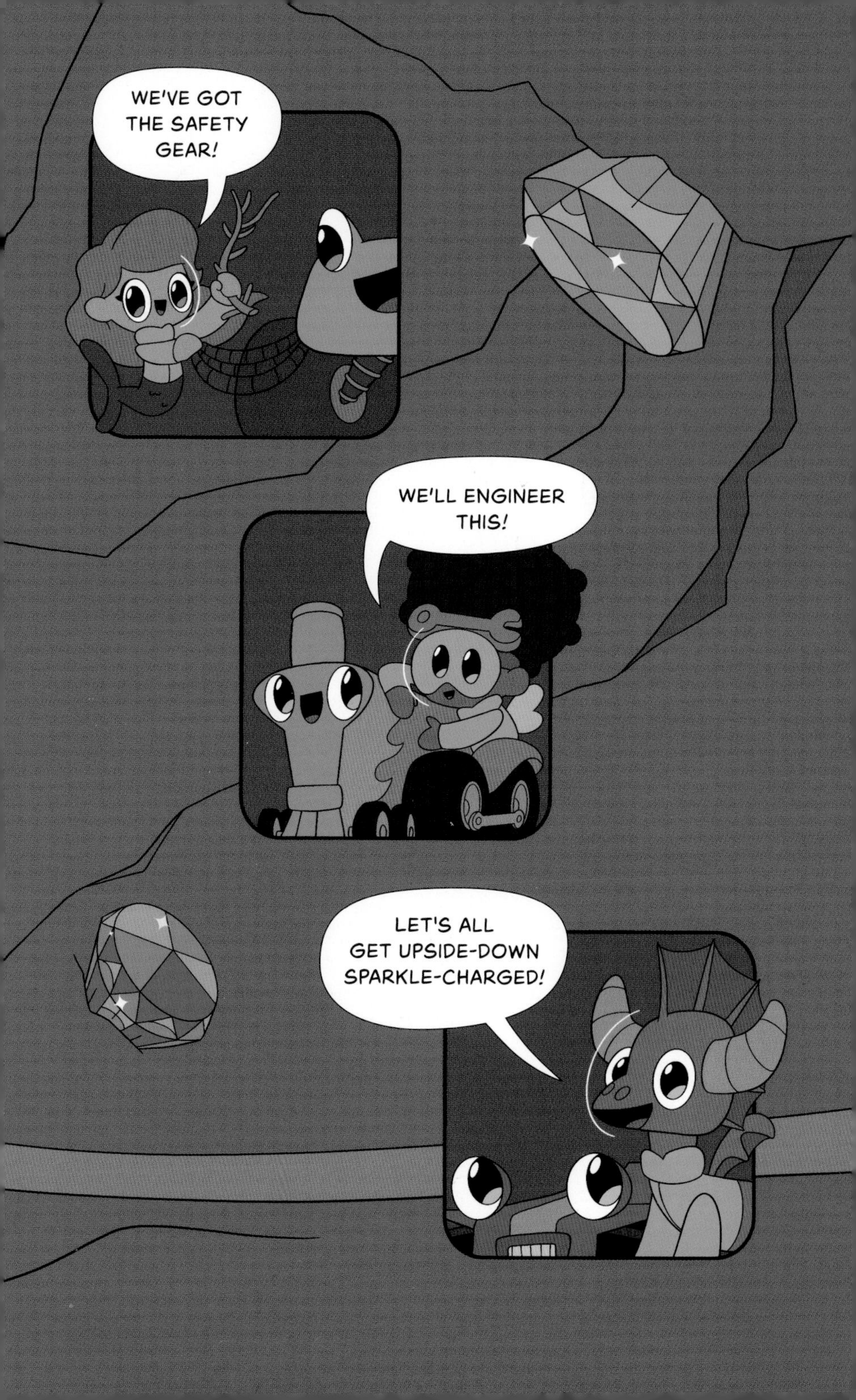
WE'VE GOT THE SAFETY GEAR!
WE'LL ENGINEER THIS!
LET'S ALL GET UPSIDE-DOWN SPARKLE-CHARGED!

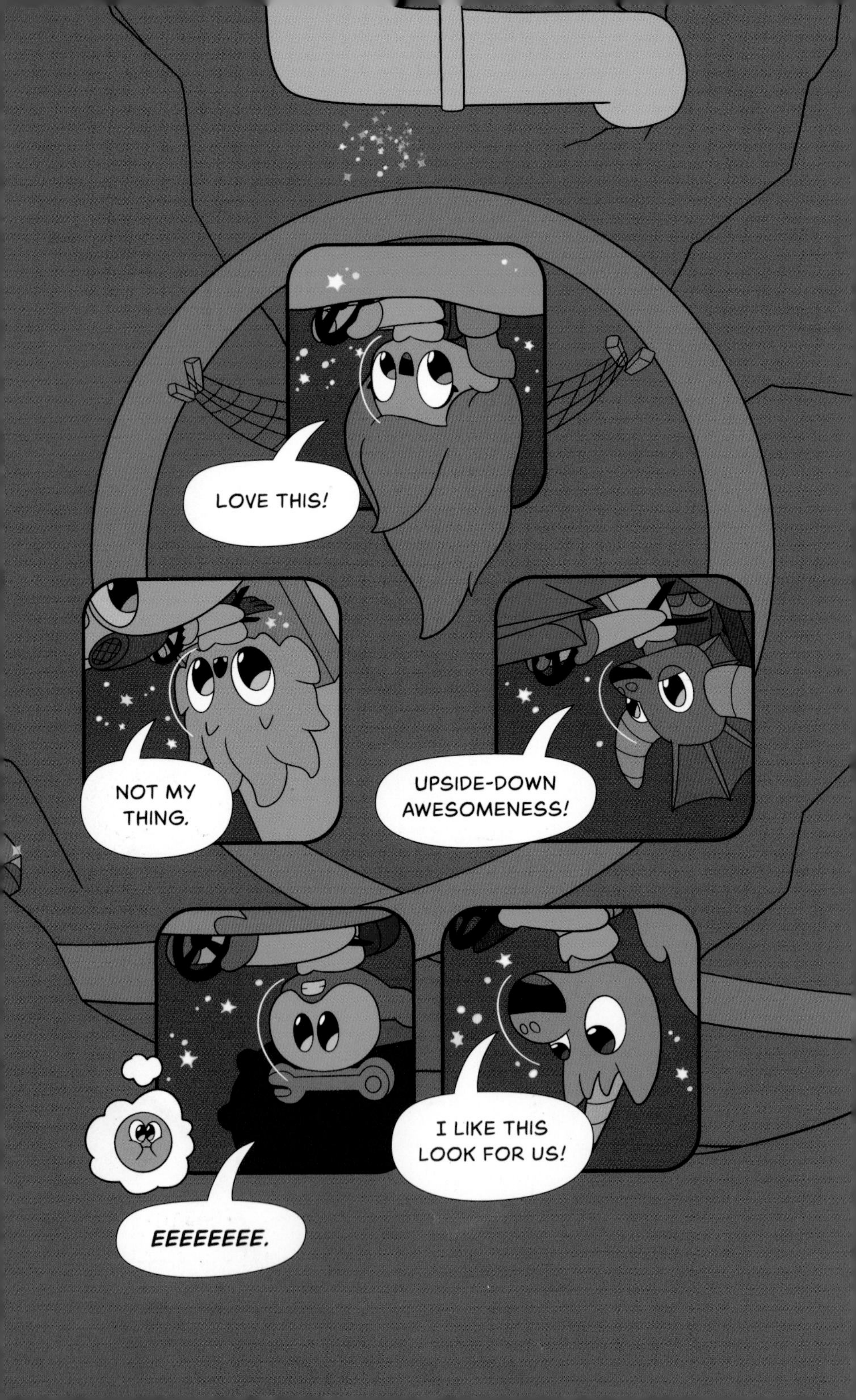
LOVE THIS!
NOT MY THING.
UPSIDE-DOWN AWESOMENESS!
EEEEEEEE.
I LIKE THIS LOOK FOR US!

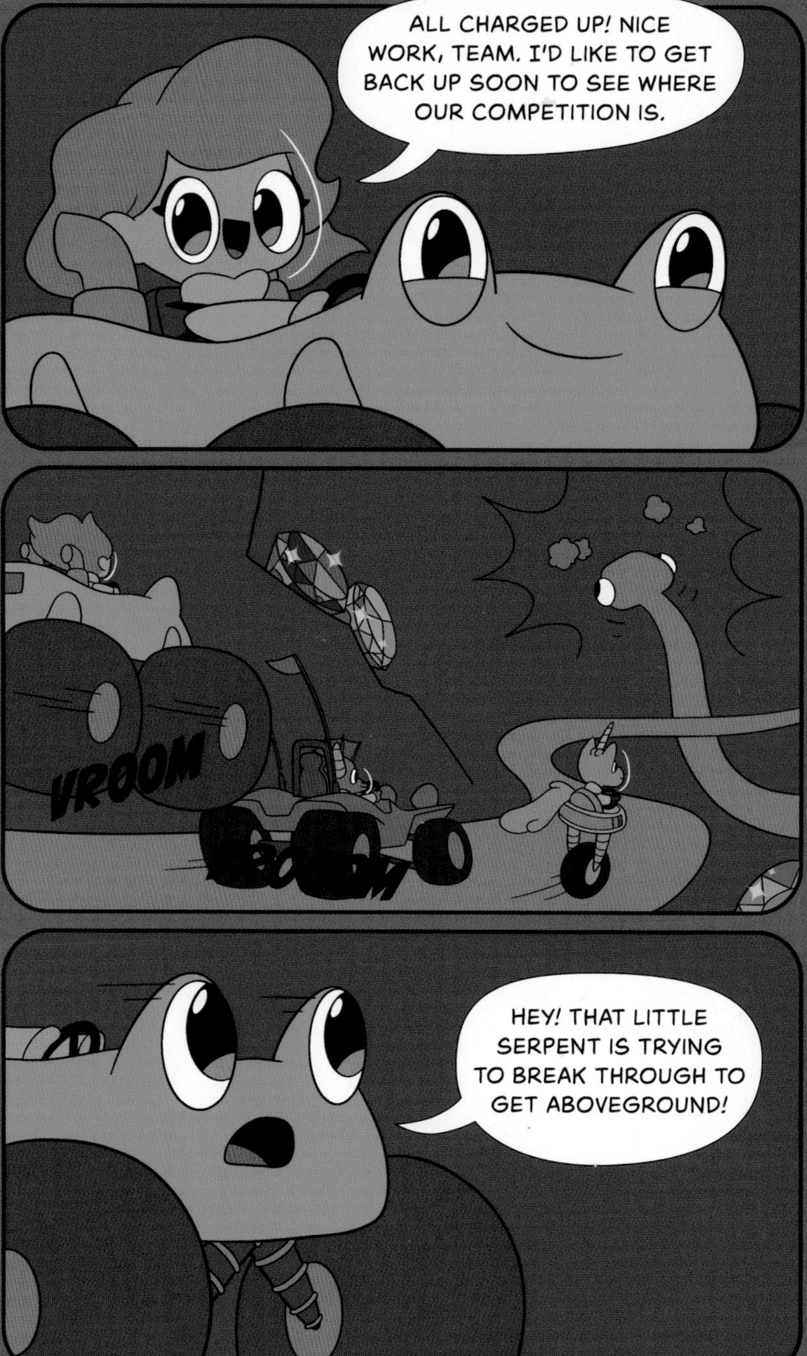
ALL CHARGED UP! NICE WORK, TEAM. I'D LIKE TO GET BACK UP SOON TO SEE WHERE OUR COMPETITION IS.
VROOM
HEY! THAT LITTLE SERPENT IS TRYING TO BREAK THROUGH TO GET ABOVEGROUND!

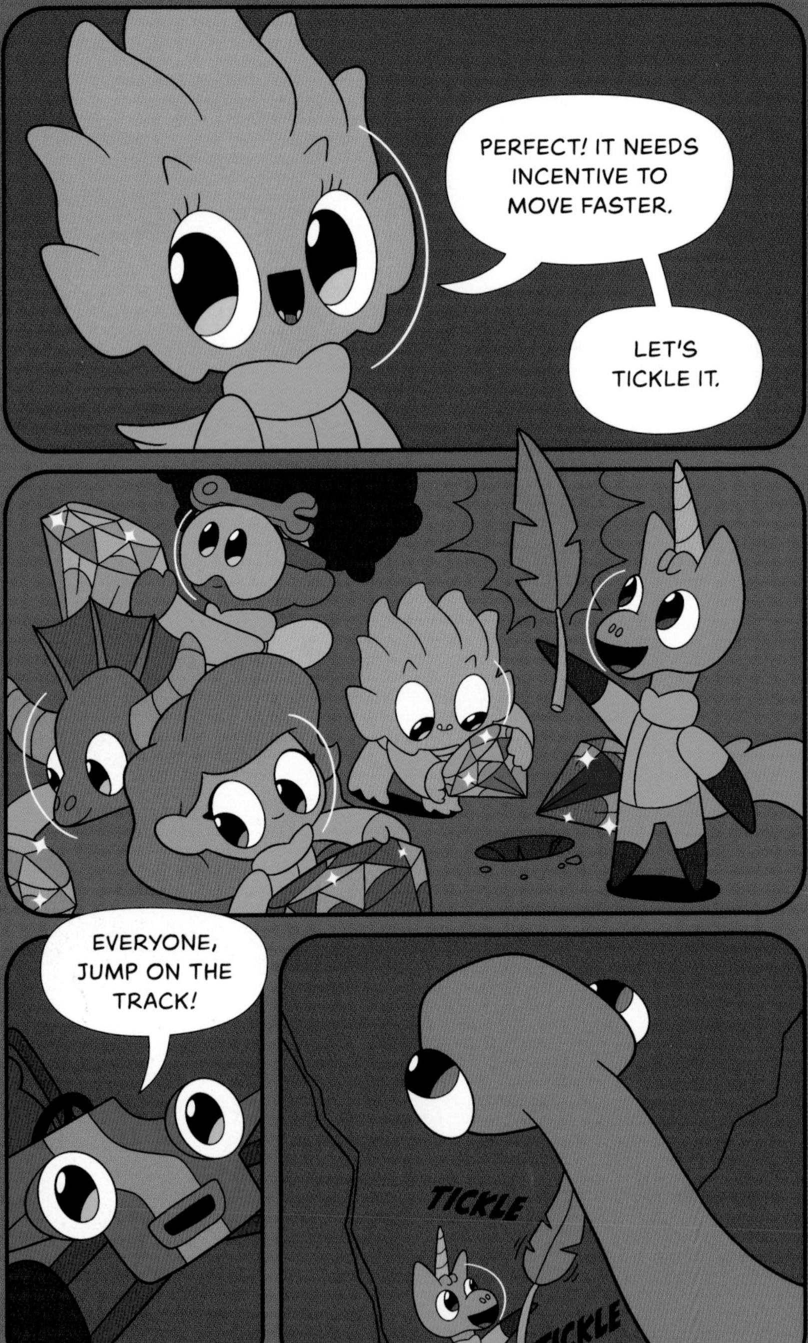
PERFECT! IT NEEDS INCENTIVE TO MOVE FASTER.
LET'S TICKLE IT.
EVERYONE, JUMP ON THE TRACK!
TICKLE
TICKLE

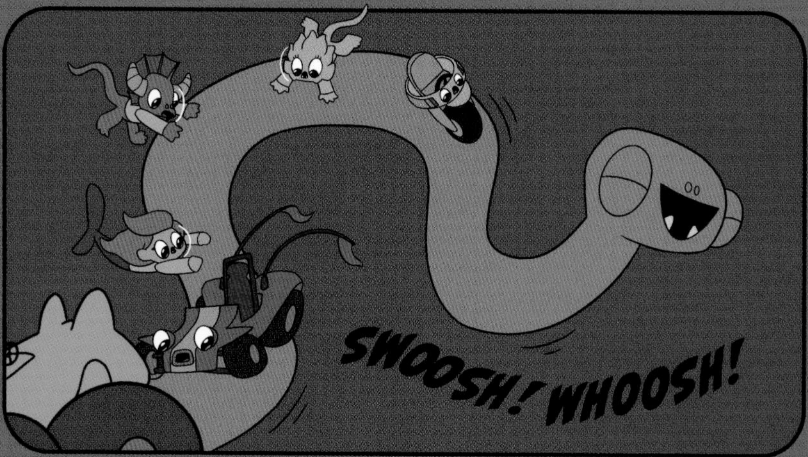
SWOOSH! WHOOSH!

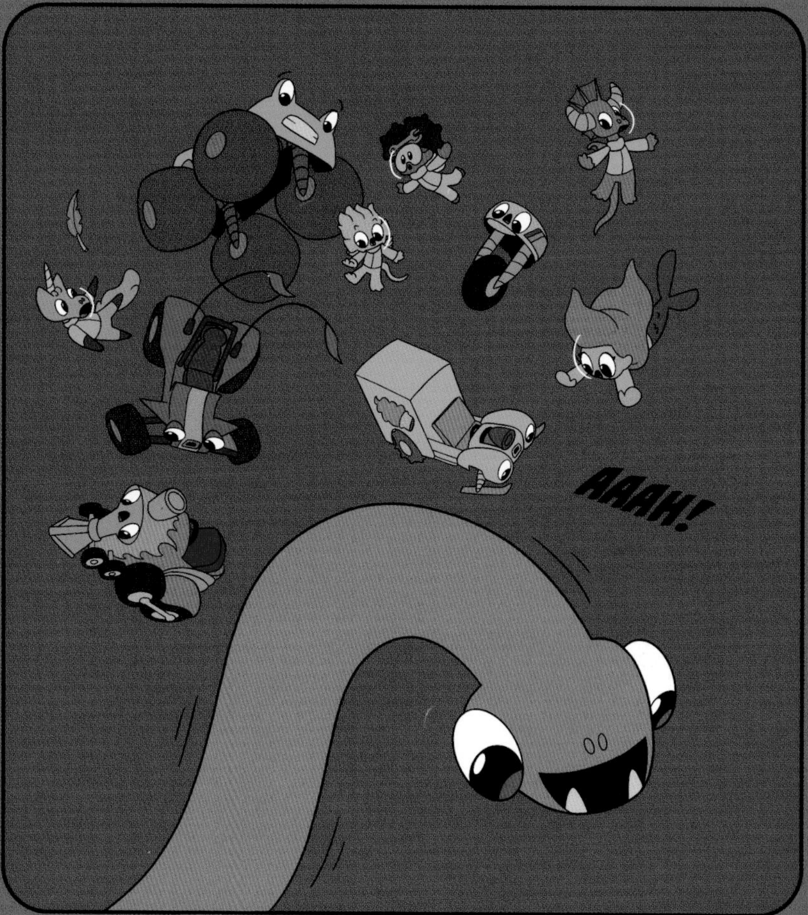
AAAH!

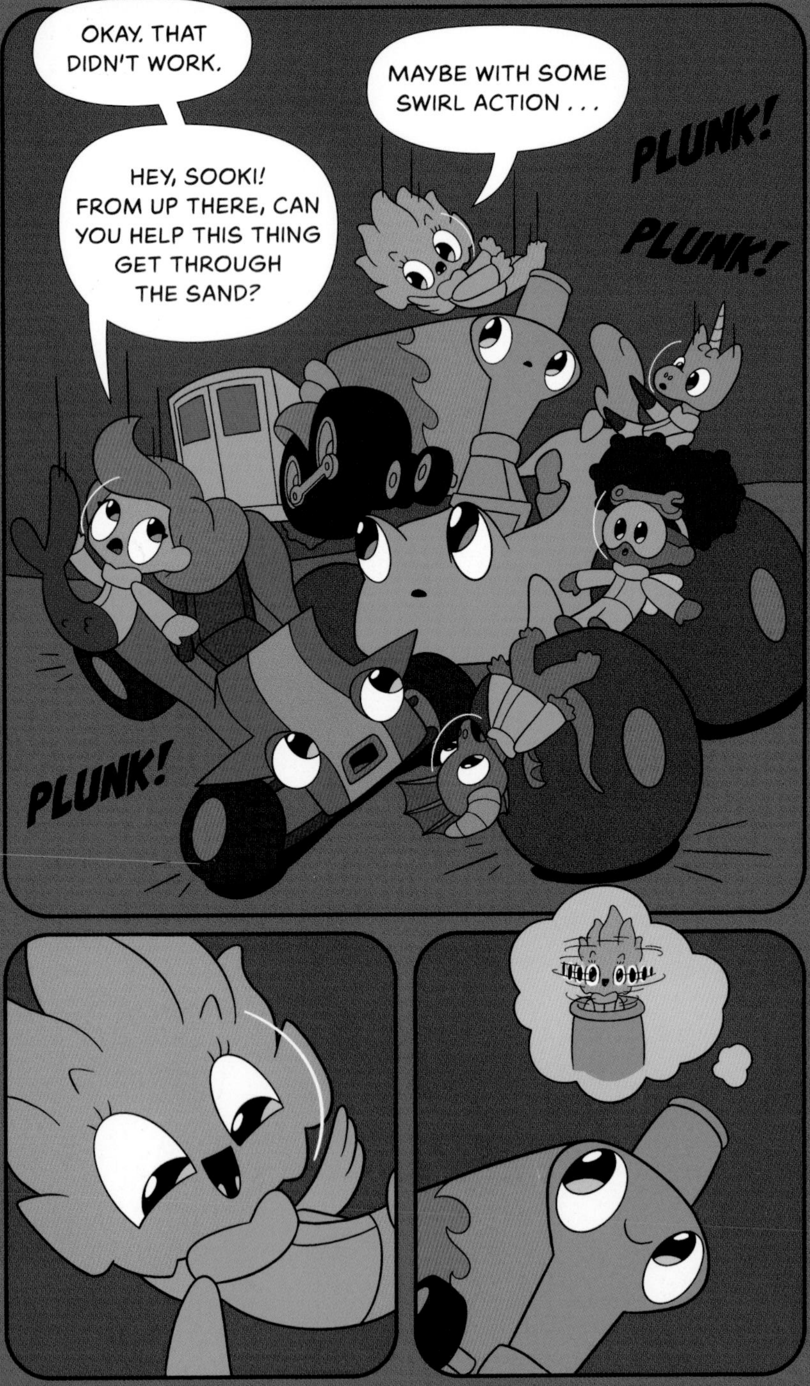
OKAY. THAT DIDN'T WORK.
HEY, SOOKI! FROM UP THERE, CAN YOU HELP THIS THING GET THROUGH THE SAND?
MAYBE WITH SOME SWIRL ACTION . . .
PLUNK!
PLUNK!
PLUNK!

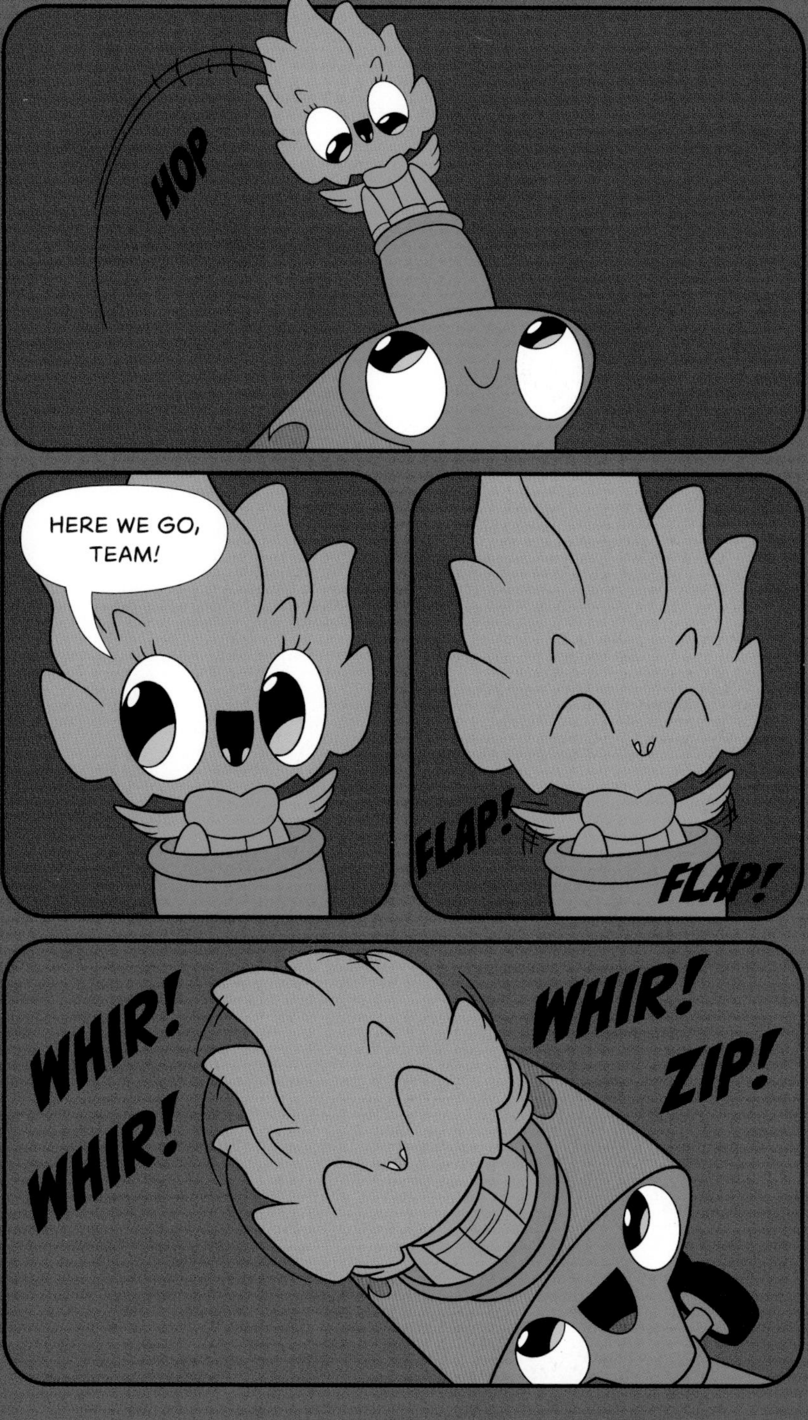
HOP
HERE WE GO, TEAM!
FLAP!
FLAP!
WHIR!
WHIR!
WHIR!
ZIP!

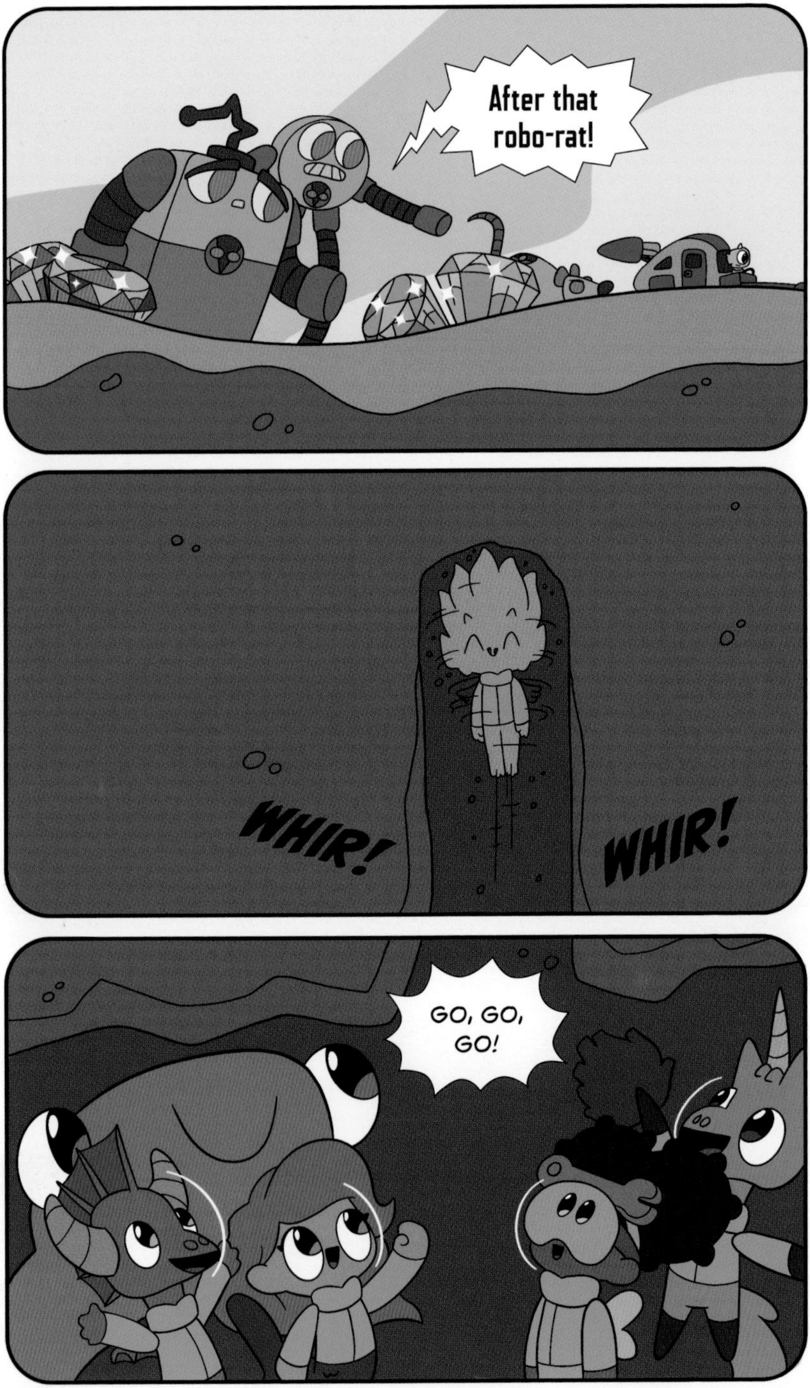
After that robo-rat!
WHIR!
WHIR!
GO, GO, GO!

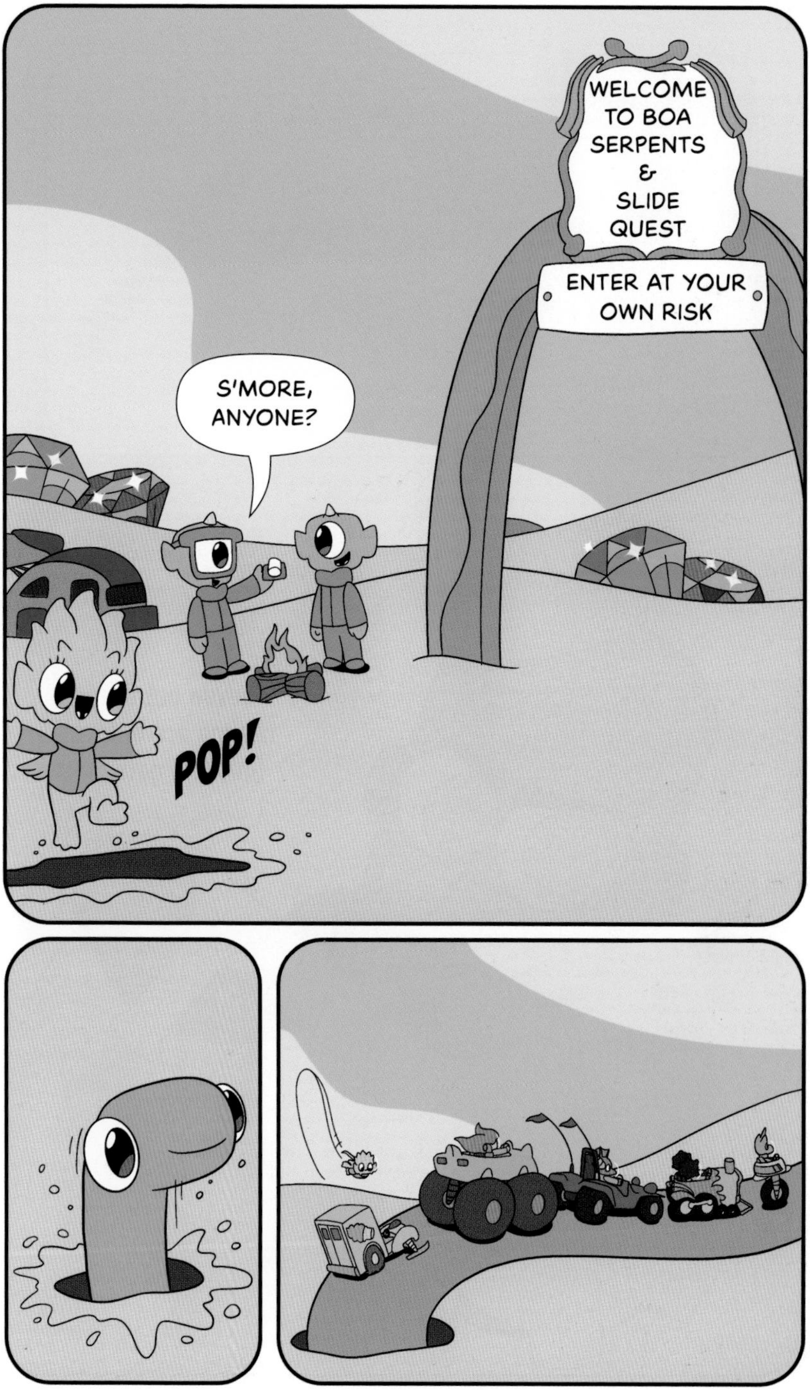
WELCOME TO BOA SERPENTS & SLIDE QUEST
ENTER AT YOUR OWN RISK
S'MORE, ANYONE?
POP!

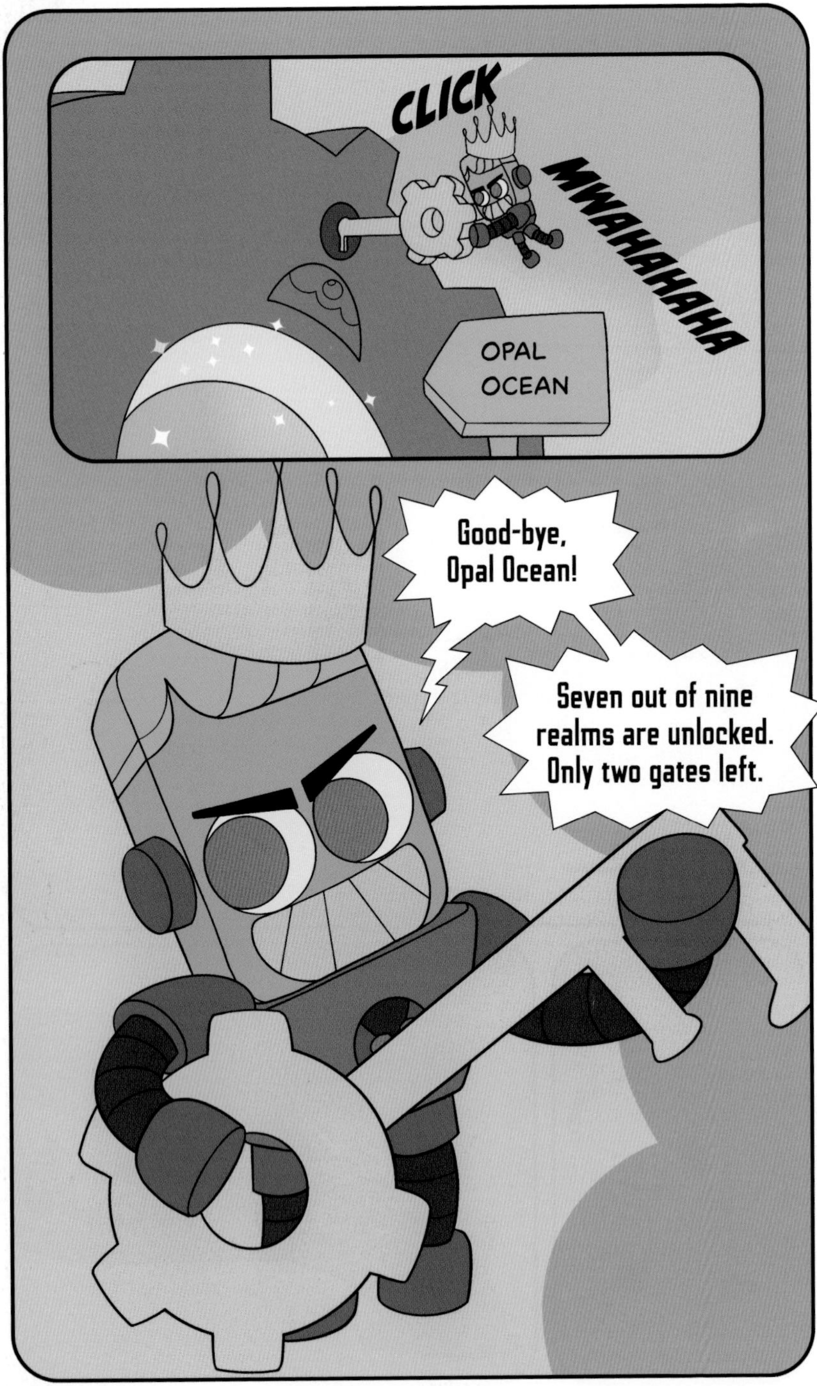
CLICK
MWAHAHAHA
OPAL OCEAN
Good-bye, Opal Ocean!
Seven out of nine realms are unlocked. Only two gates left.

CHAPTER 9:
BOA BOSS

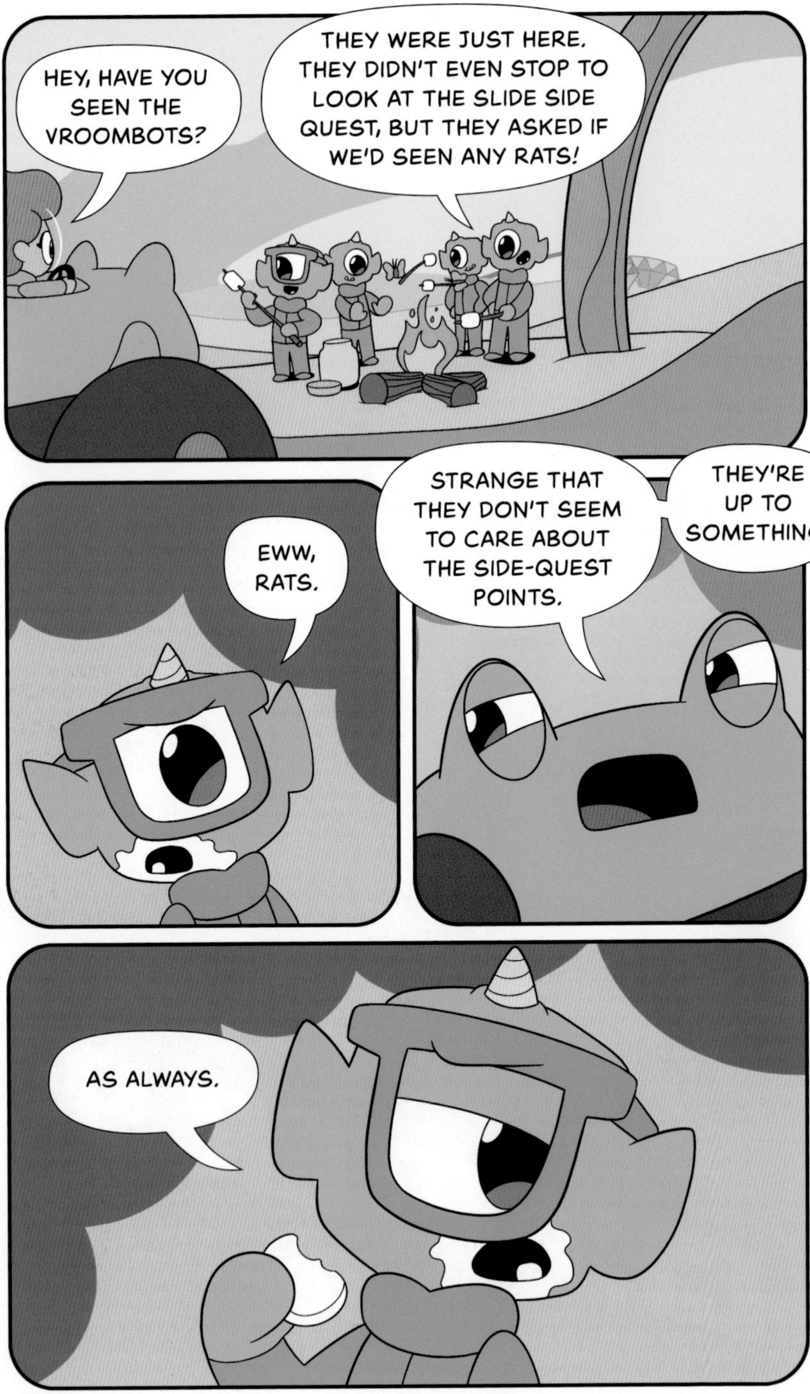
HEY, HAVE YOU SEEN THE VROOMBOTS?
THEY WERE JUST HERE. THEY DIDN'T EVEN STOP TO LOOK AT THE SLIDE SIDE QUEST, BUT THEY ASKED IF WE'D SEEN ANY RATS!
EWW, RATS.
STRANGE THAT THEY DON'T SEEM TO CARE ABOUT THE SIDE-QUEST POINTS.
THEY'RE UP TO SOMETHING.
AS ALWAYS.

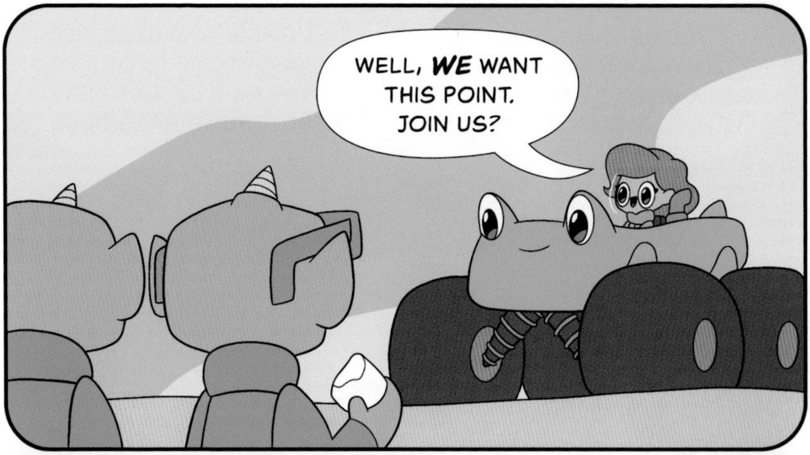
WELL, WE WANT THIS POINT. JOIN US?

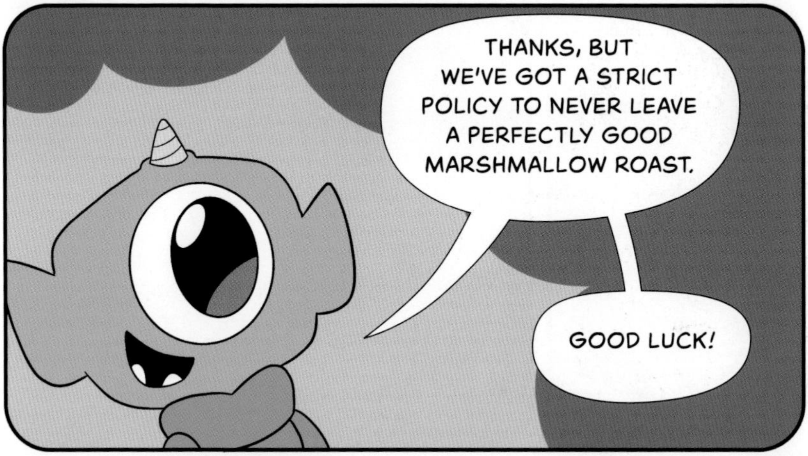
THANKS, BUT WE'VE GOT A STRICT POLICY TO NEVER LEAVE A PERFECTLY GOOD MARSHMALLOW ROAST.
GOOD LUCK!

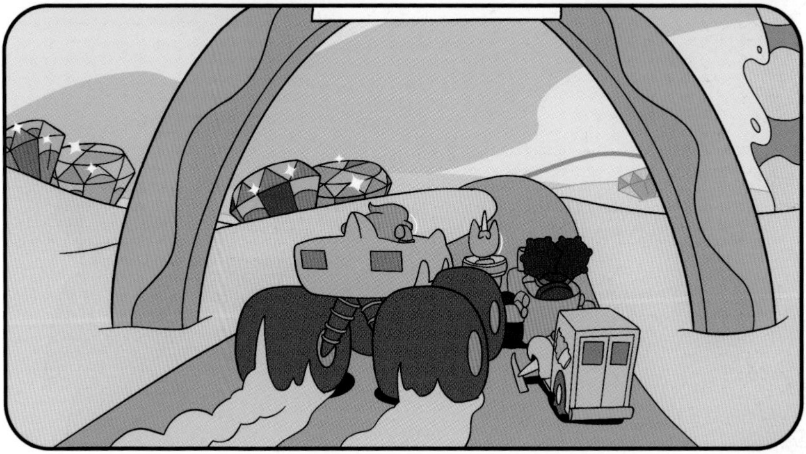

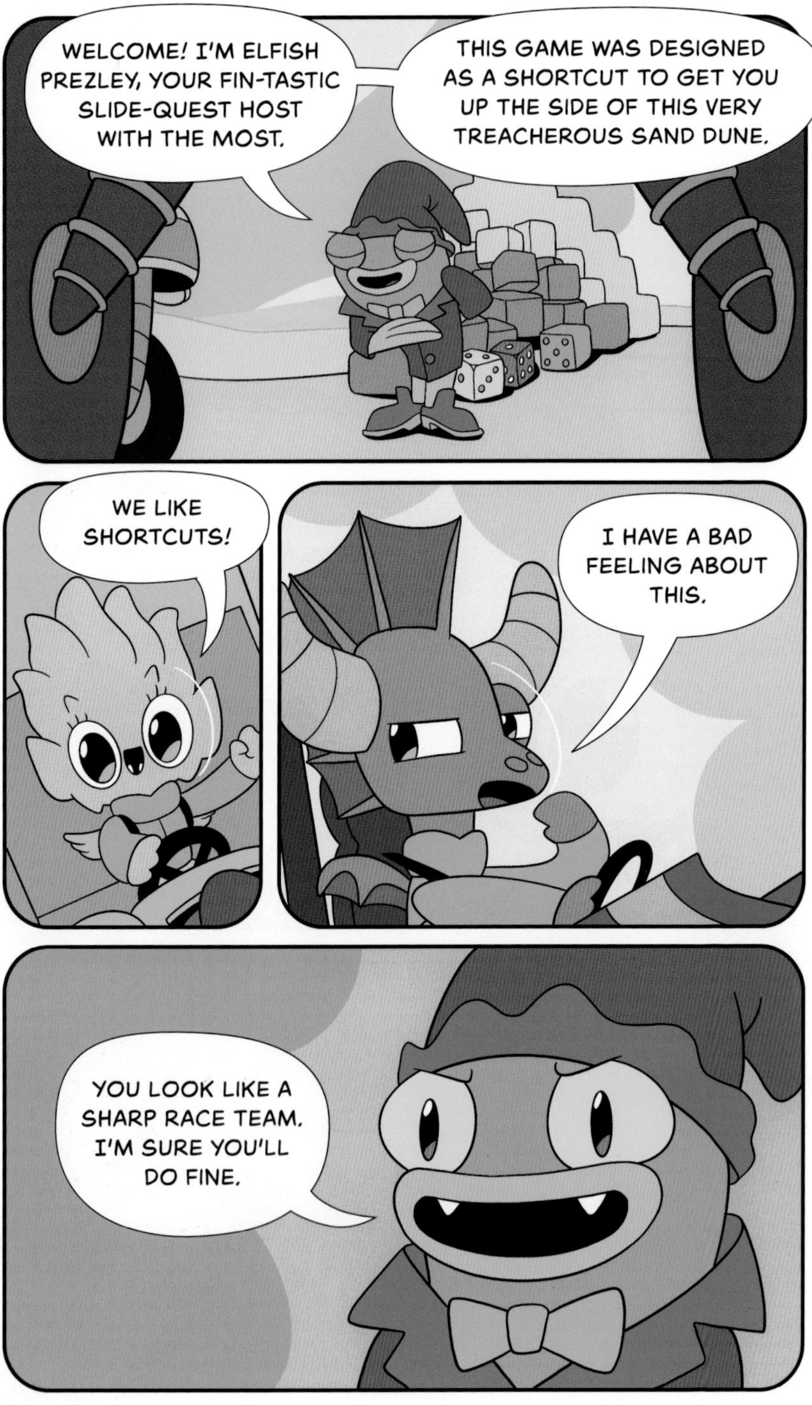
WELCOME! I'M ELFISH PREZLEY, YOUR FIN-TASTIC SLIDE-QUEST HOST WITH THE MOST.
THIS GAME WAS DESIGNED AS A SHORTCUT TO GET YOU UP THE SIDE OF THIS VERY TREACHEROUS SAND DUNE.
WE LIKE SHORTCUTS!
I HAVE A BAD FEELING ABOUT THIS.
YOU LOOK LIKE A SHARP RACE TEAM. I'M SURE YOU'LL DO FINE.

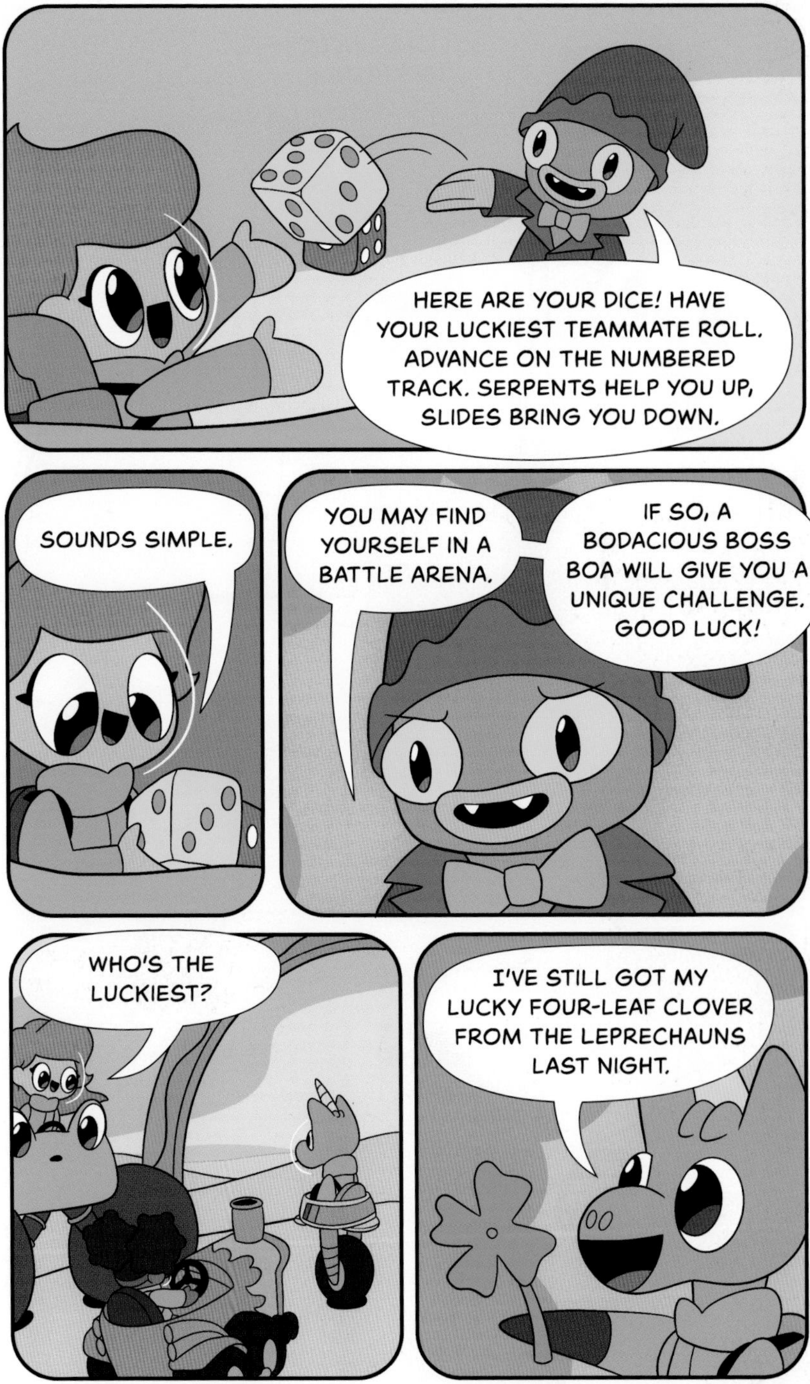
HERE ARE YOUR DICE! HAVE YOUR LUCKIEST TEAMMATE ROLL. ADVANCE ON THE NUMBERED TRACK. SERPENTS HELP YOU UP, SLIDES BRING YOU DOWN.
SOUNDS SIMPLE.
YOU MAY FIND YOURSELF IN A BATTLE ARENA.
IF SO, A BODACIOUS BOSS BOA WILL GIVE YOU A UNIQUE CHALLENGE. GOOD LUCK!
WHO'S THE LUCKIEST?
I'VE STILL GOT MY LUCKY FOUR-LEAF CLOVER FROM THE LEPRECHAUNS LAST NIGHT.

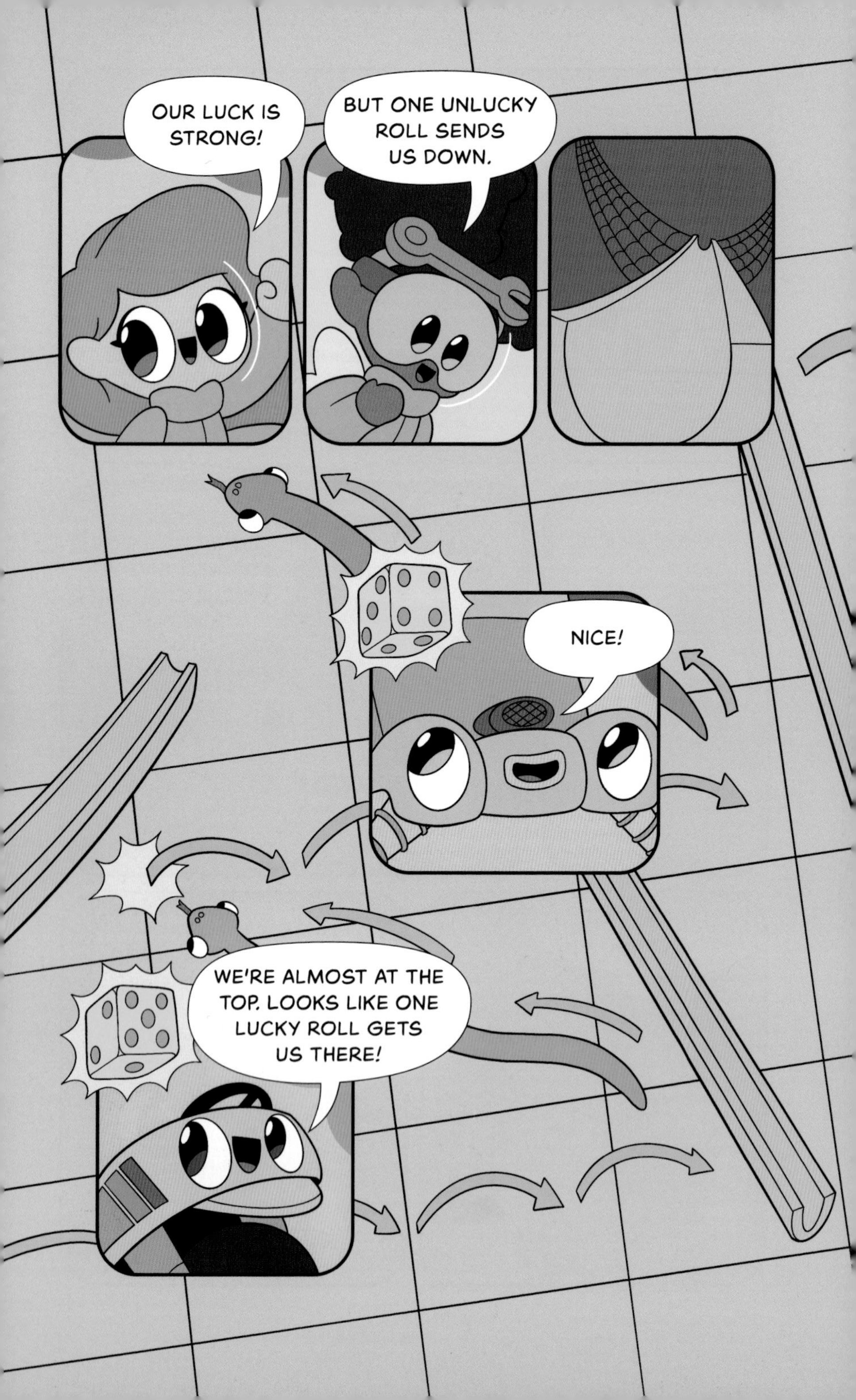
OUR LUCK IS STRONG!
BUT ONE UNLUCKY ROLL SENDS US DOWN.
NICE!
WE'RE ALMOST AT THE TOP. LOOKS LIKE ONE LUCKY ROLL GETS US THERE!

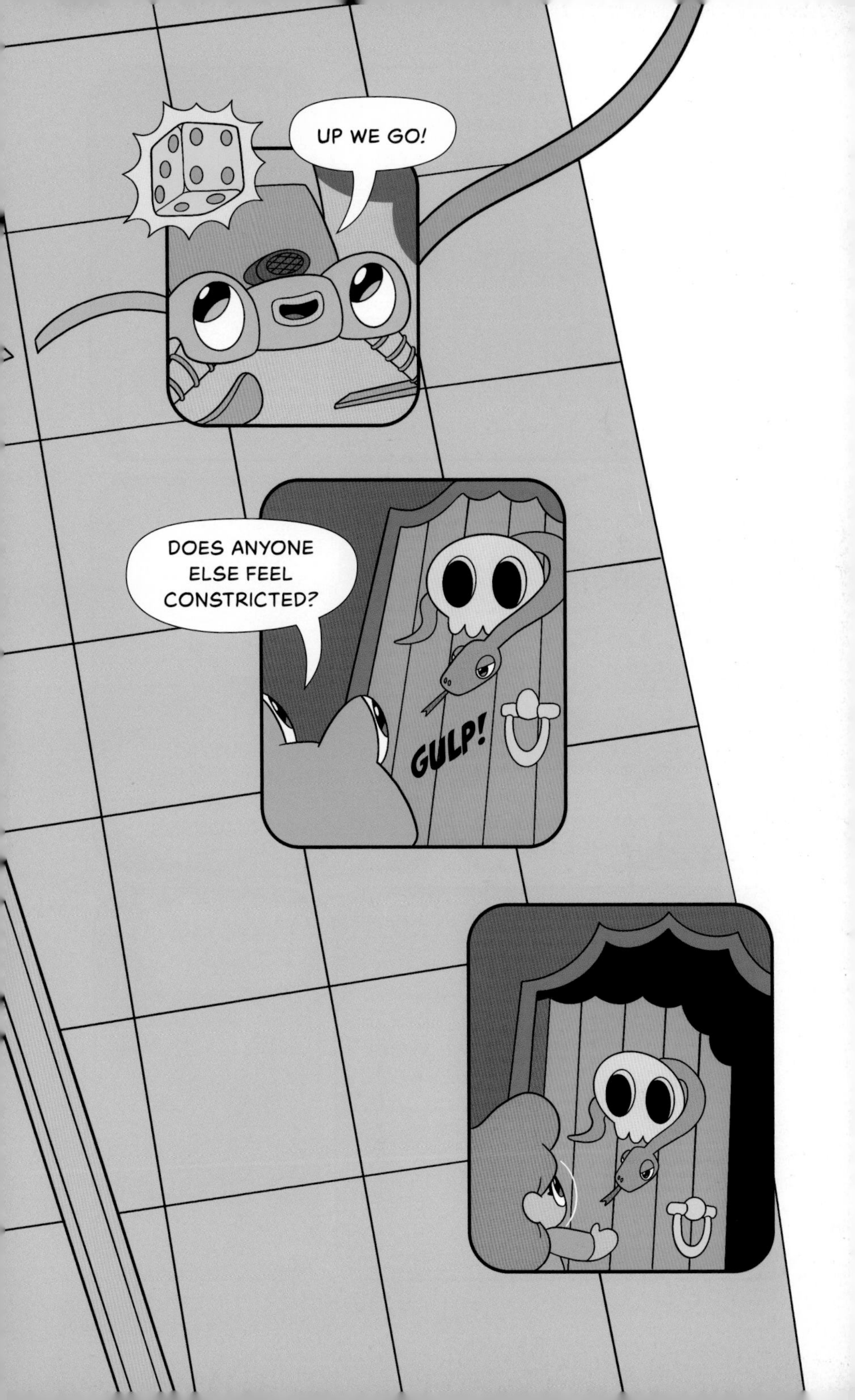
UP WE GO!
DOES ANYONE ELSE FEEL CONSTRICTED?
GULP!

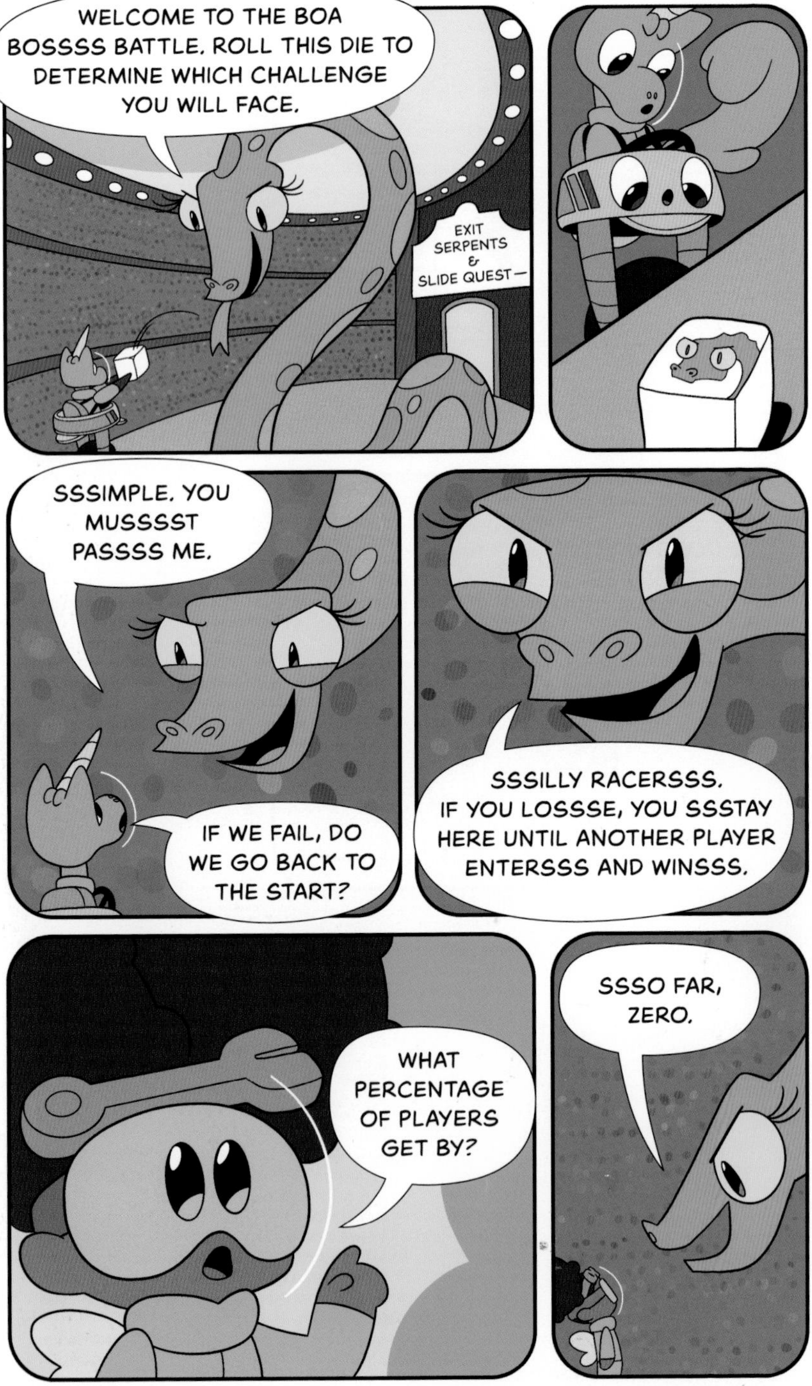
WELCOME TO THE BOA BOSSSS BATTLE. ROLL THIS DIE TO DETERMINE WHICH CHALLENGE YOU WILL FACE.
EXIT SERPENTS & SLIDE QUEST—
SSSIMPLE. YOU MUSSSST PASSSS ME.
IF WE FAIL, DO WE GO BACK TO THE START?
SSSILLY RACERSSS. IF YOU LOSSSE, YOU SSSTAY HERE UNTIL ANOTHER PLAYER ENTERSSS AND WINSSS.
WHAT PERCENTAGE OF PLAYERS GET BY?
SSSO FAR, ZERO.

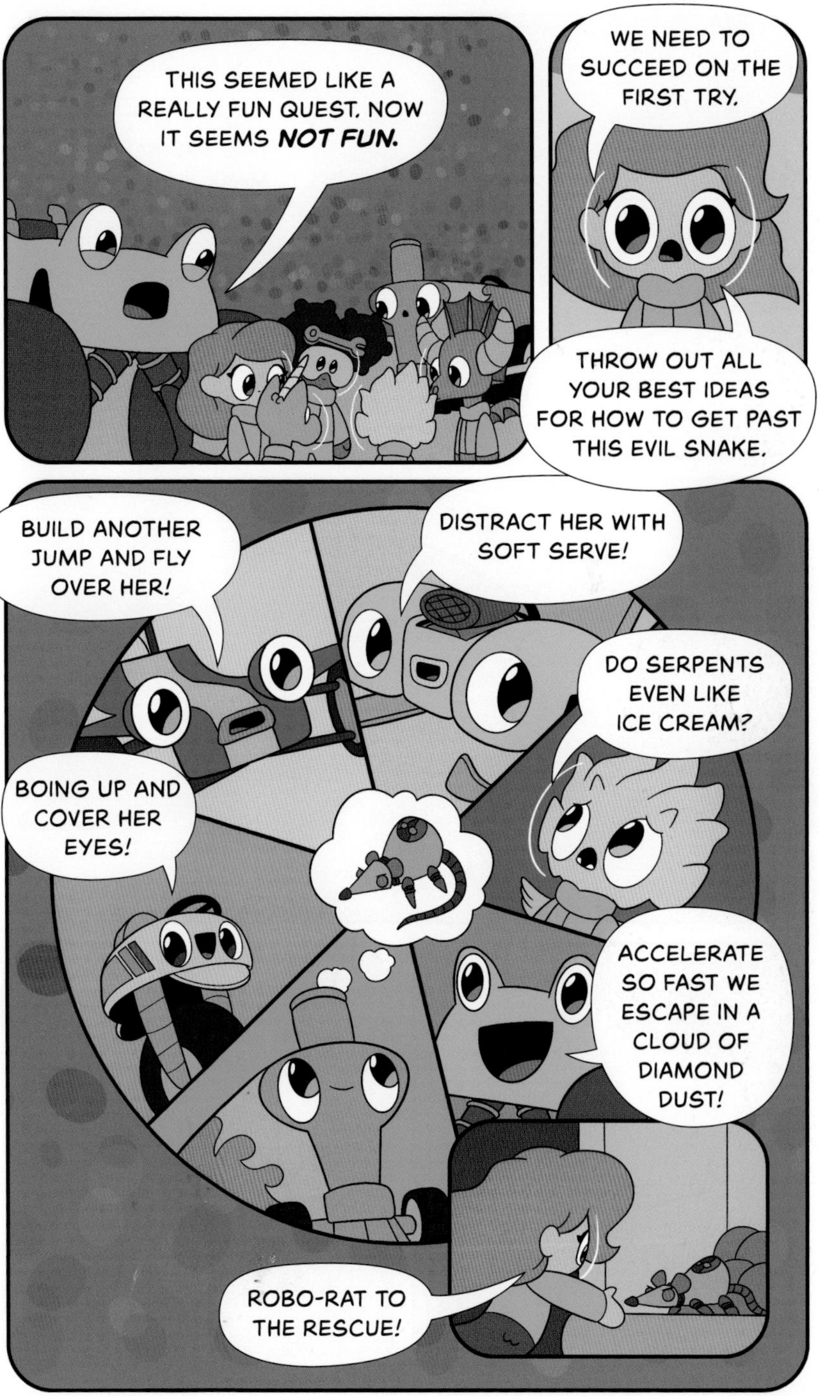
THIS SEEMED LIKE A REALLY FUN QUEST. NOW IT SEEMS **NOT FUN.**
WE NEED TO SUCCEED ON THE FIRST TRY.
THROW OUT ALL YOUR BEST IDEAS FOR HOW TO GET PAST THIS EVIL SNAKE.
BUILD ANOTHER JUMP AND FLY OVER HER!
DISTRACT HER WITH SOFT SERVE!
DO SERPENTS EVEN LIKE ICE CREAM?
BOING UP AND COVER HER EYES!
ACCELERATE SO FAST WE ESCAPE IN A CLOUD OF DIAMOND DUST!
ROBO-RAT TO THE RESCUE!

LET'S GET BY THIS BAD BOA AND MAKE HISSSTORY!

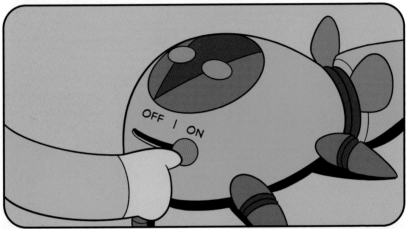

OFF | ON

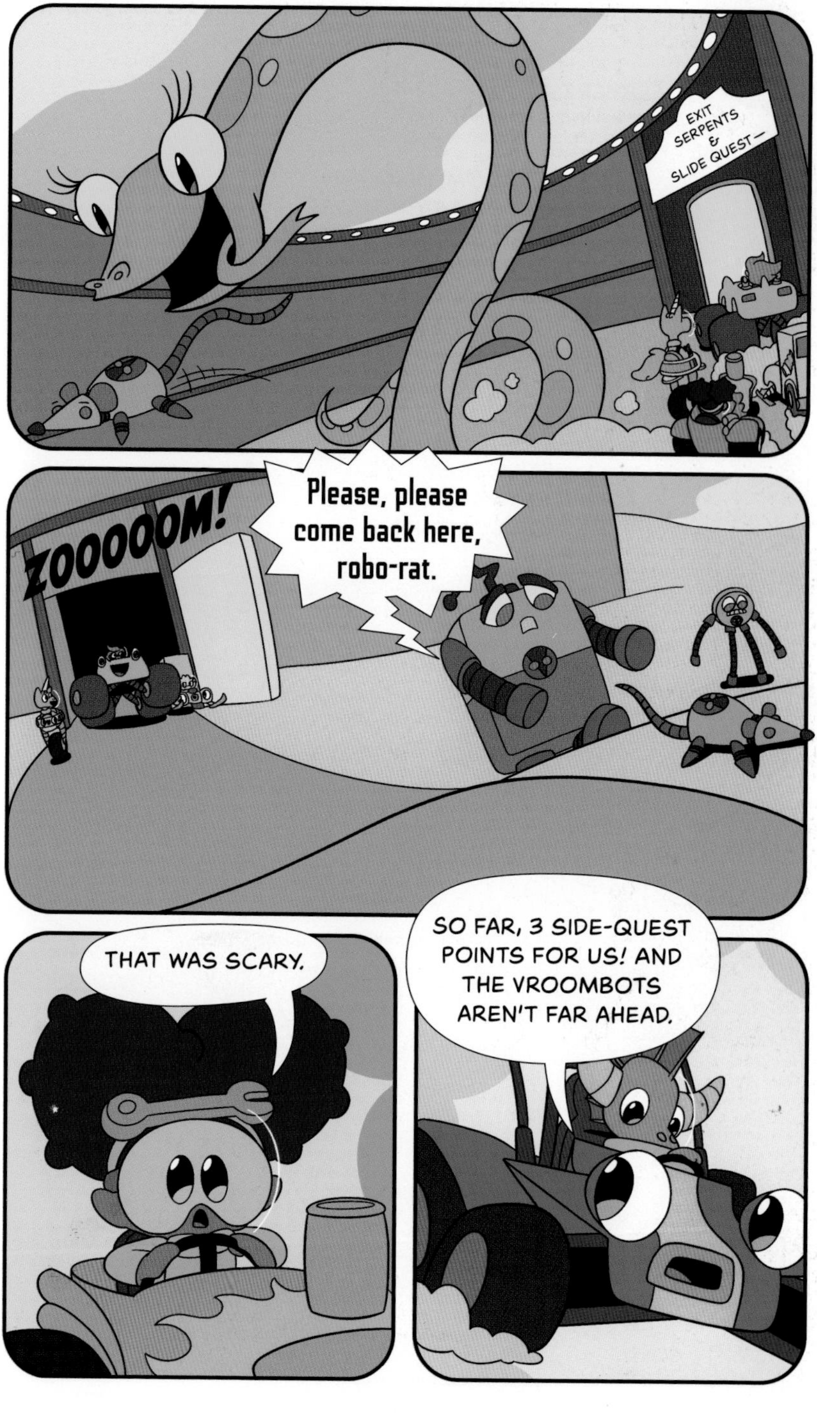
EXIT SERPENTS & SLIDE QUEST—
ZOOOOOM!
Please, please come back here, robo-rat.
THAT WAS SCARY.
SO FAR, 3 SIDE-QUEST POINTS FOR US! AND THE VROOMBOTS AREN'T FAR AHEAD.

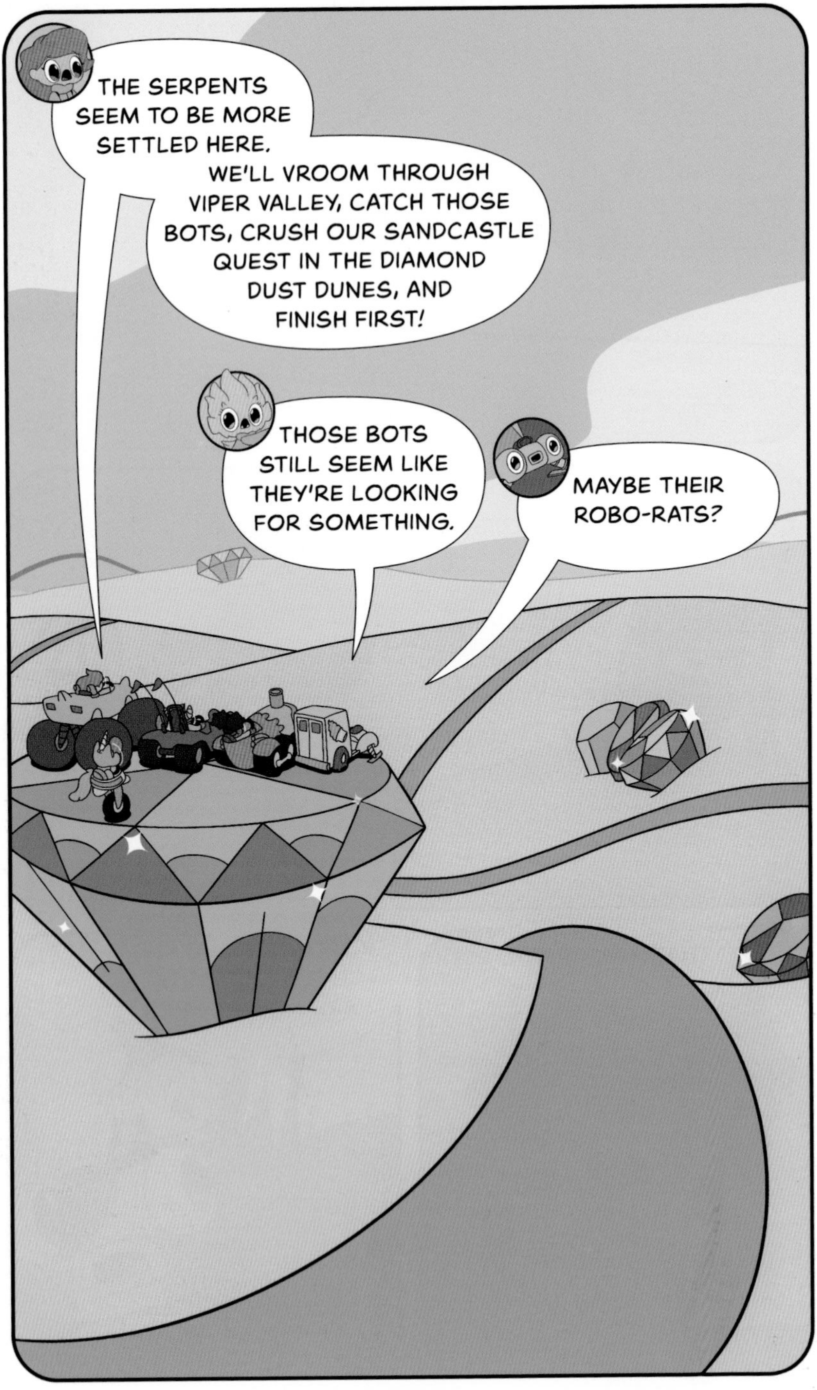
THE SERPENTS SEEM TO BE MORE SETTLED HERE.
WE'LL VROOM THROUGH VIPER VALLEY, CATCH THOSE BOTS, CRUSH OUR SANDCASTLE QUEST IN THE DIAMOND DUST DUNES, AND FINISH FIRST!
THOSE BOTS STILL SEEM LIKE THEY'RE LOOKING FOR SOMETHING.
MAYBE THEIR ROBO-RATS?

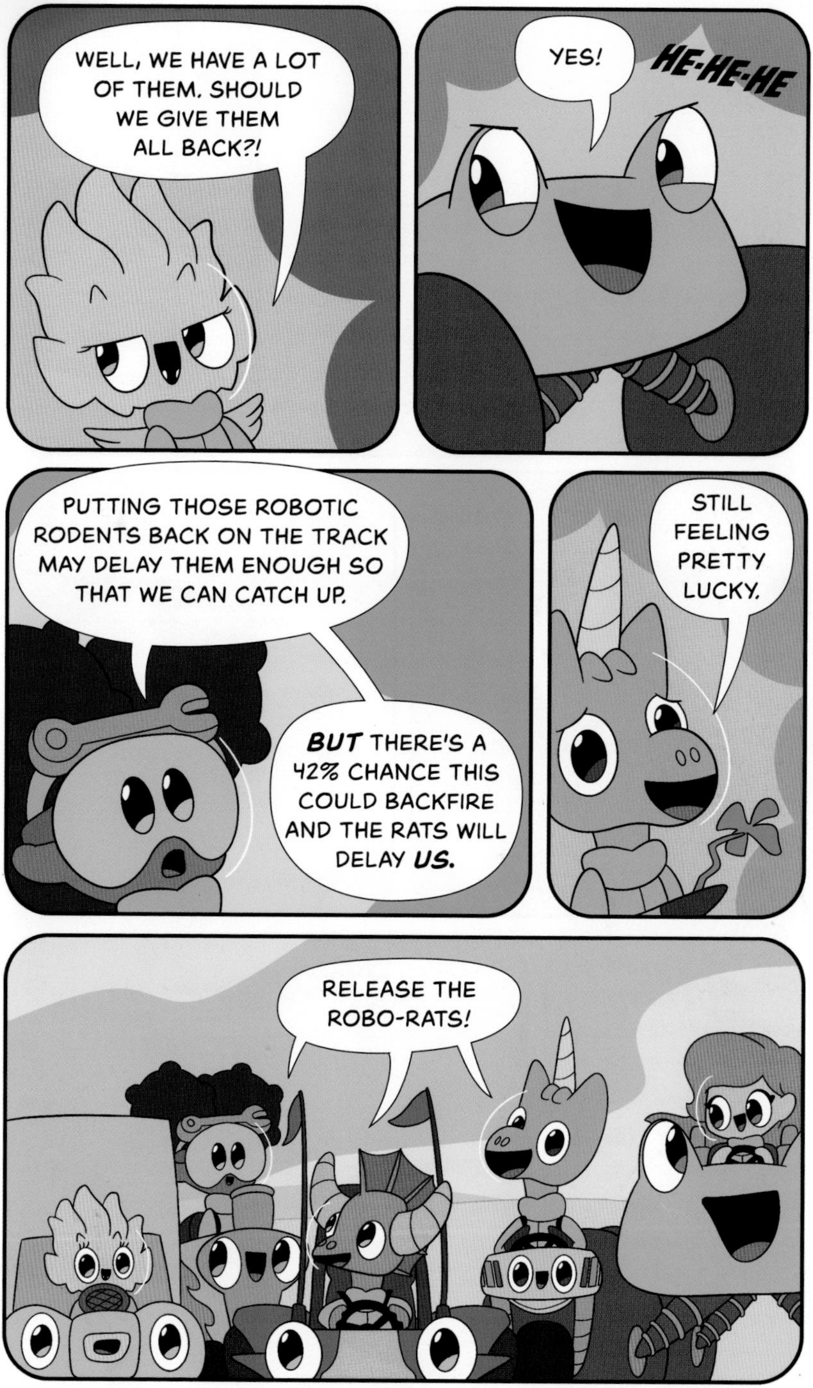
WELL, WE HAVE A LOT OF THEM. SHOULD WE GIVE THEM ALL BACK?!
YES!
HE-HE-HE
PUTTING THOSE ROBOTIC RODENTS BACK ON THE TRACK MAY DELAY THEM ENOUGH SO THAT WE CAN CATCH UP.
BUT THERE'S A 42% CHANCE THIS COULD BACKFIRE AND THE RATS WILL DELAY US.
STILL FEELING PRETTY LUCKY.
RELEASE THE ROBO-RATS!

LET THE RAT RACE BEGIN!

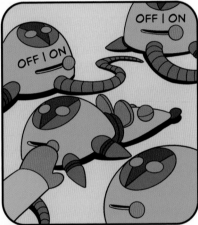

OFF | ON

OFF | ON

CLICK!

CLICK!

CLICK!

SQUEAK!
SQUAWK!

144

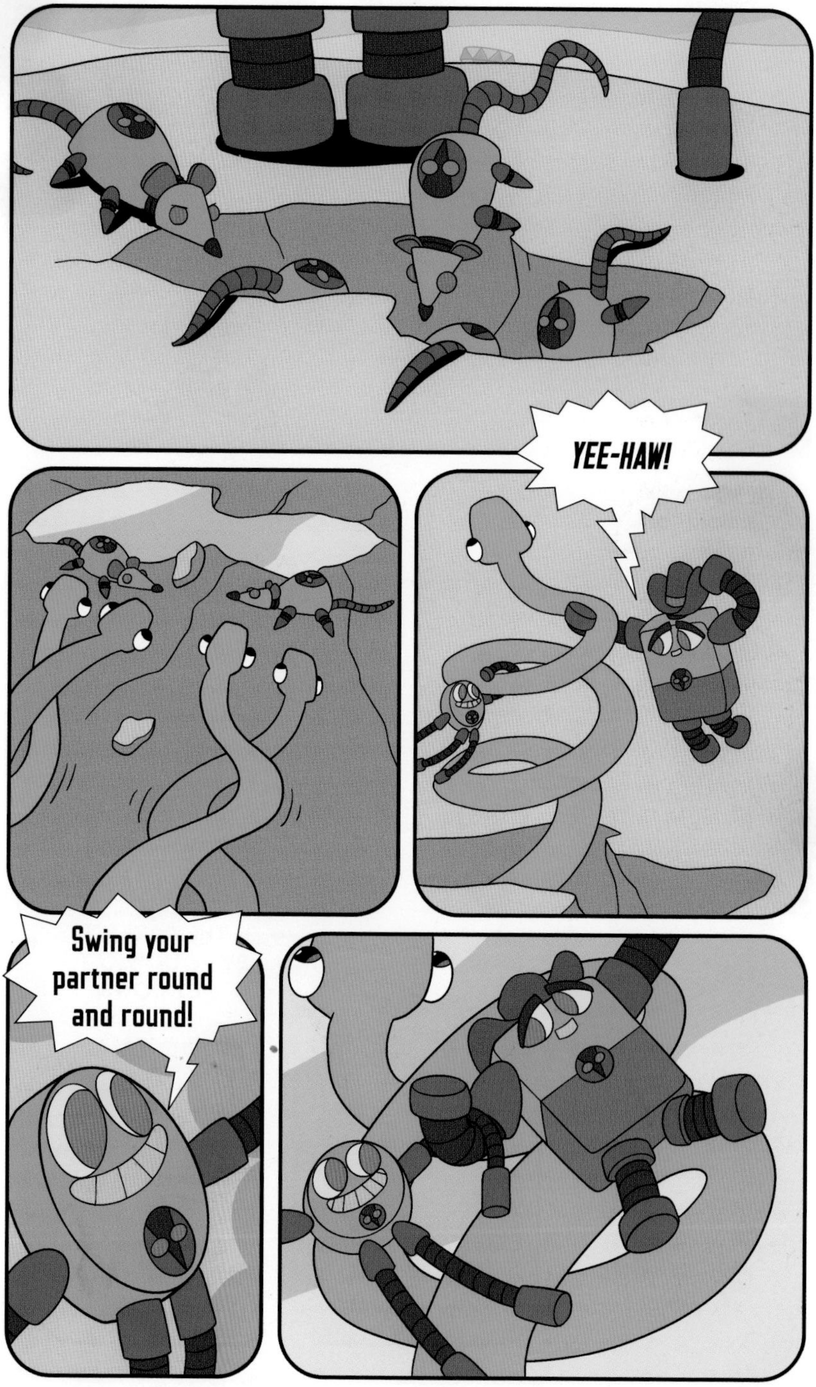
YEE-HAW!
Swing your partner round and round!

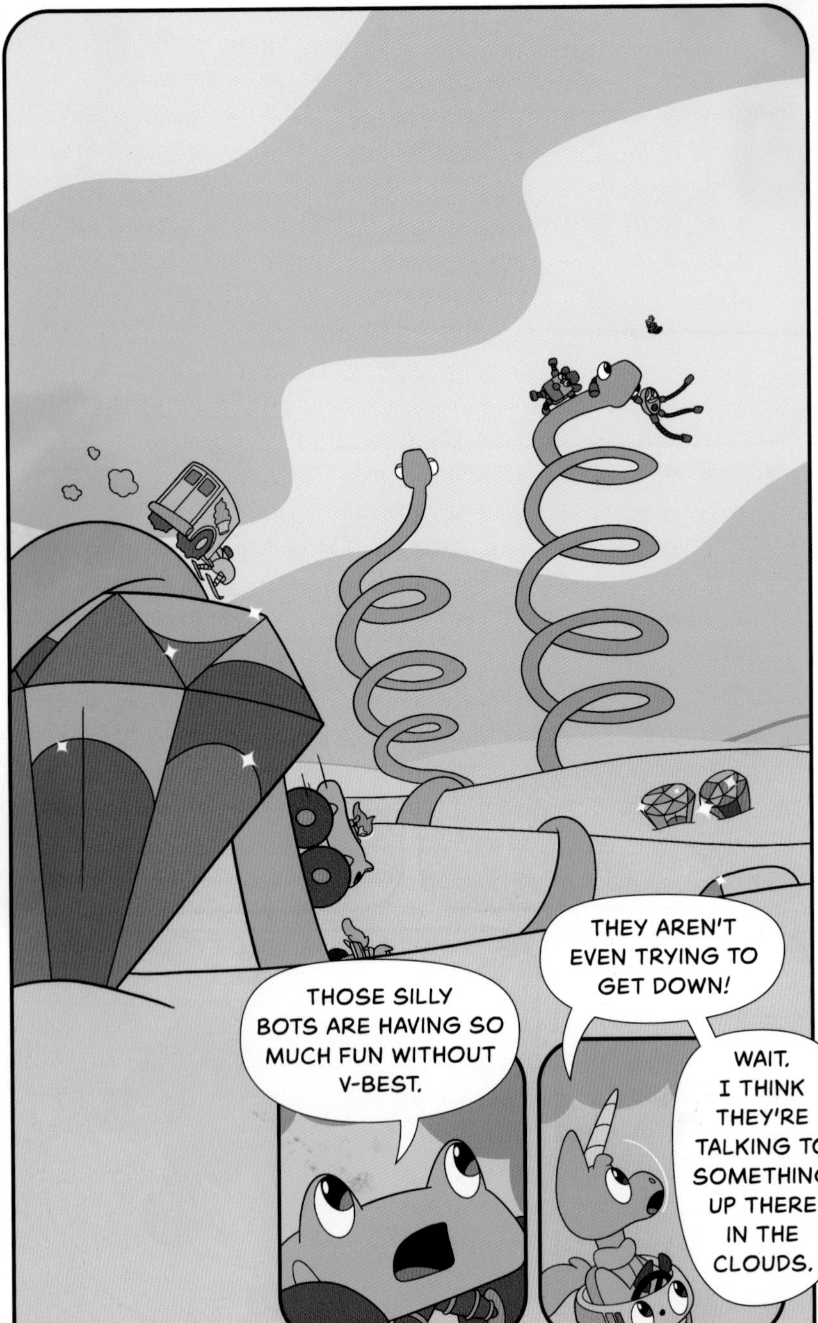
THOSE SILLY BOTS ARE HAVING SO MUCH FUN WITHOUT V-BEST.
THEY AREN'T EVEN TRYING TO GET DOWN!
WAIT. I THINK THEY'RE TALKING TO SOMETHING UP THERE IN THE CLOUDS.

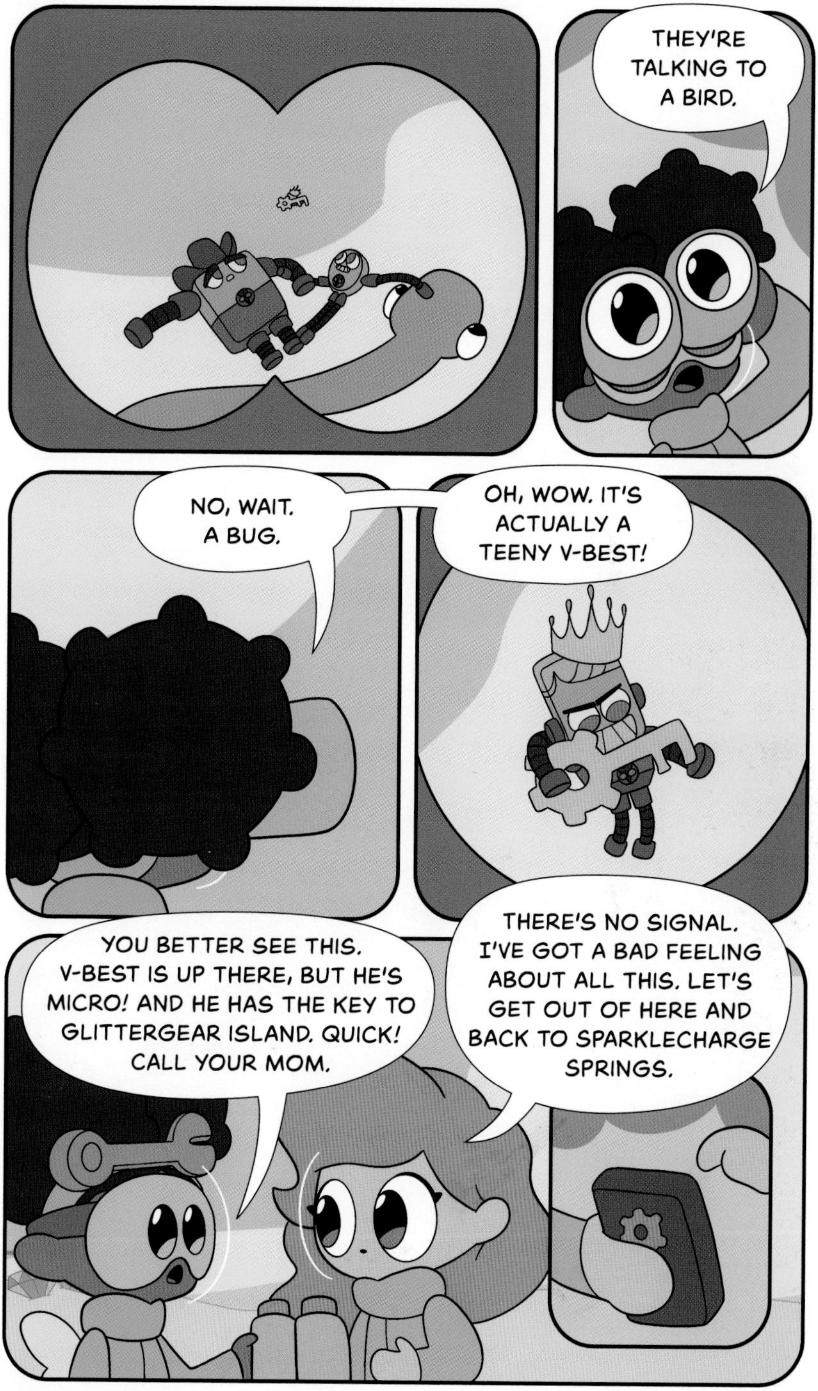
THEY'RE TALKING TO A BIRD.
NO, WAIT. A BUG.
OH, WOW. IT'S ACTUALLY A TEENY V-BEST!
YOU BETTER SEE THIS. V-BEST IS UP THERE, BUT HE'S MICRO! AND HE HAS THE KEY TO GLITTERGEAR ISLAND. QUICK! CALL YOUR MOM.
THERE'S NO SIGNAL. I'VE GOT A BAD FEELING ABOUT ALL THIS. LET'S GET OUT OF HERE AND BACK TO SPARKLECHARGE SPRINGS.

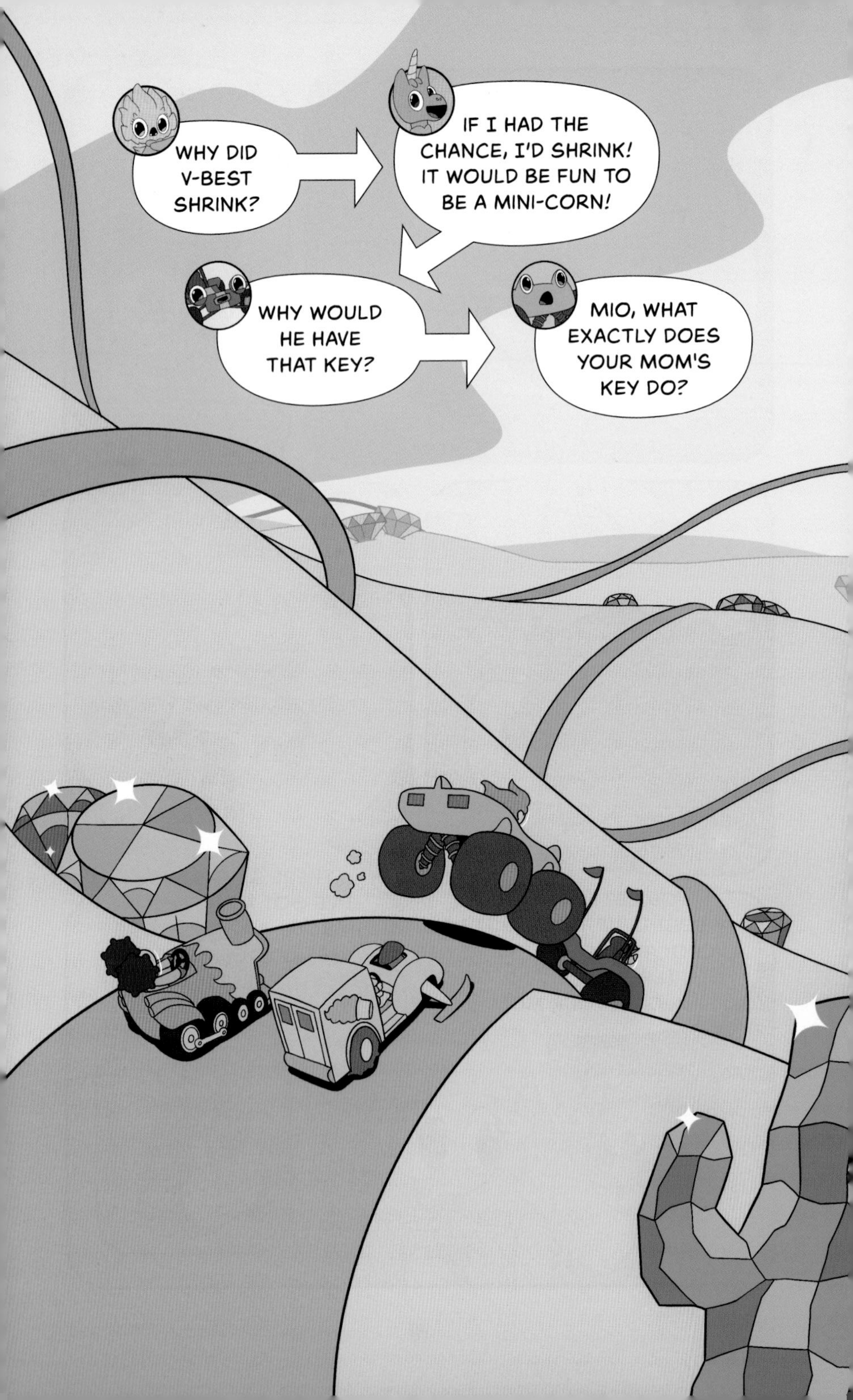
WHY DID V-BEST SHRINK?
IF I HAD THE CHANCE, I'D SHRINK! IT WOULD BE FUN TO BE A MINI-CORN!
WHY WOULD HE HAVE THAT KEY?
MIO, WHAT EXACTLY DOES YOUR MOM'S KEY DO?

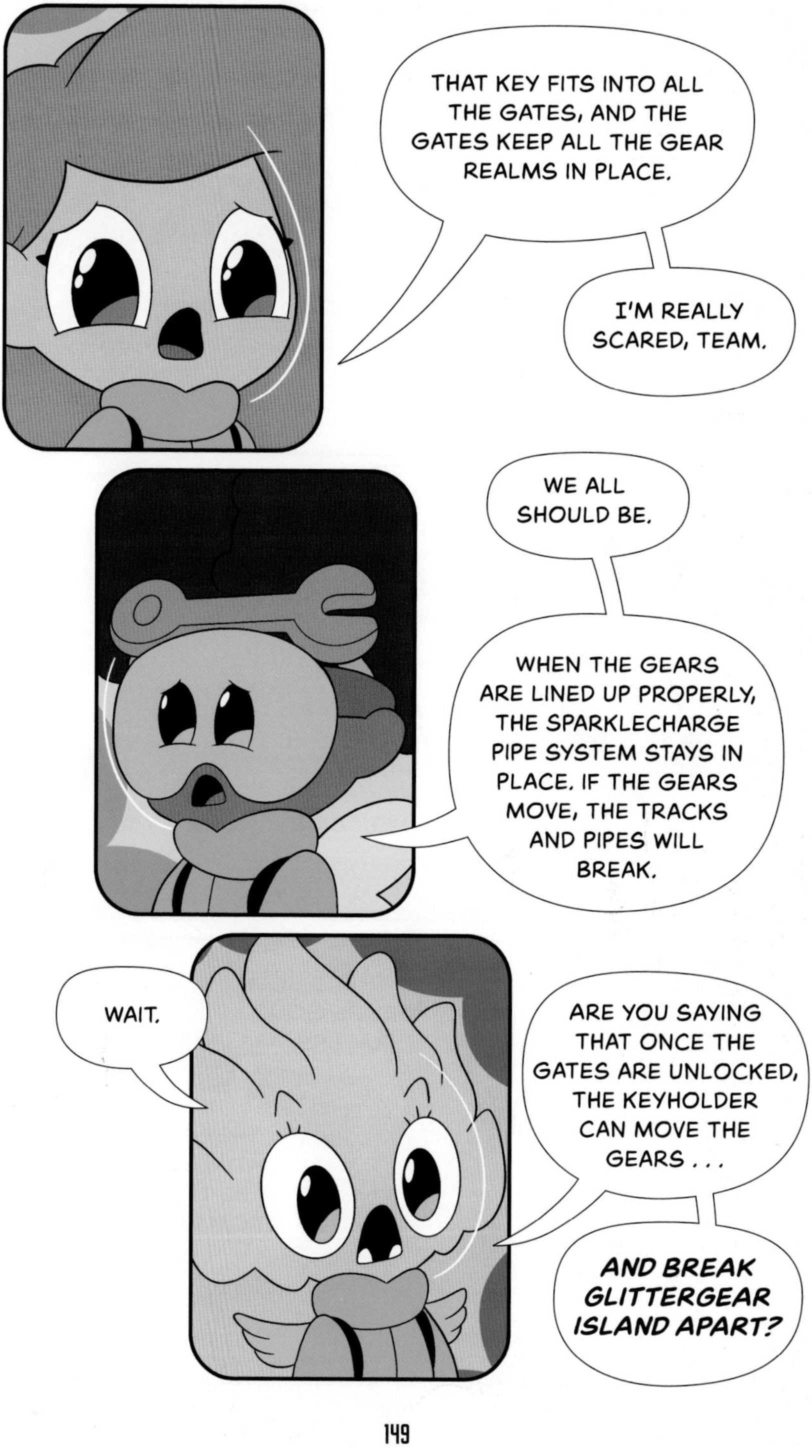
THAT KEY FITS INTO ALL THE GATES, AND THE GATES KEEP ALL THE GEAR REALMS IN PLACE.
I'M REALLY SCARED, TEAM.
WE ALL SHOULD BE.
WHEN THE GEARS ARE LINED UP PROPERLY, THE SPARKLECHARGE PIPE SYSTEM STAYS IN PLACE. IF THE GEARS MOVE, THE TRACKS AND PIPES WILL BREAK.
WAIT.
ARE YOU SAYING THAT ONCE THE GATES ARE UNLOCKED, THE KEYHOLDER CAN MOVE THE GEARS . . .
AND BREAK GLITTERGEAR ISLAND APART?

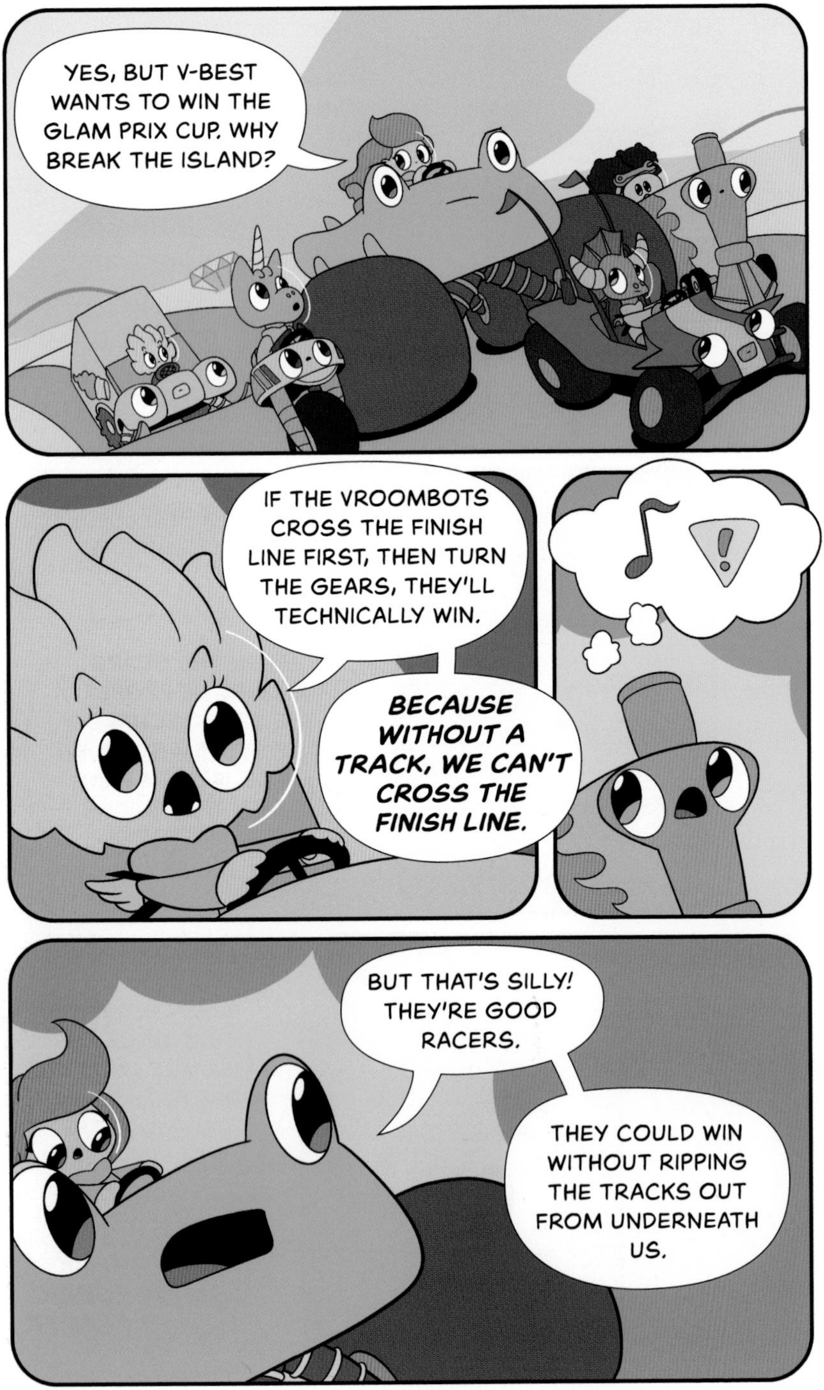
YES, BUT V-BEST WANTS TO WIN THE GLAM PRIX CUP. WHY BREAK THE ISLAND?
IF THE VROOMBOTS CROSS THE FINISH LINE FIRST, THEN TURN THE GEARS, THEY'LL TECHNICALLY WIN.
BECAUSE WITHOUT A TRACK, WE CAN'T CROSS THE FINISH LINE.
BUT THAT'S SILLY! THEY'RE GOOD RACERS.
THEY COULD WIN WITHOUT RIPPING THE TRACKS OUT FROM UNDERNEATH US.

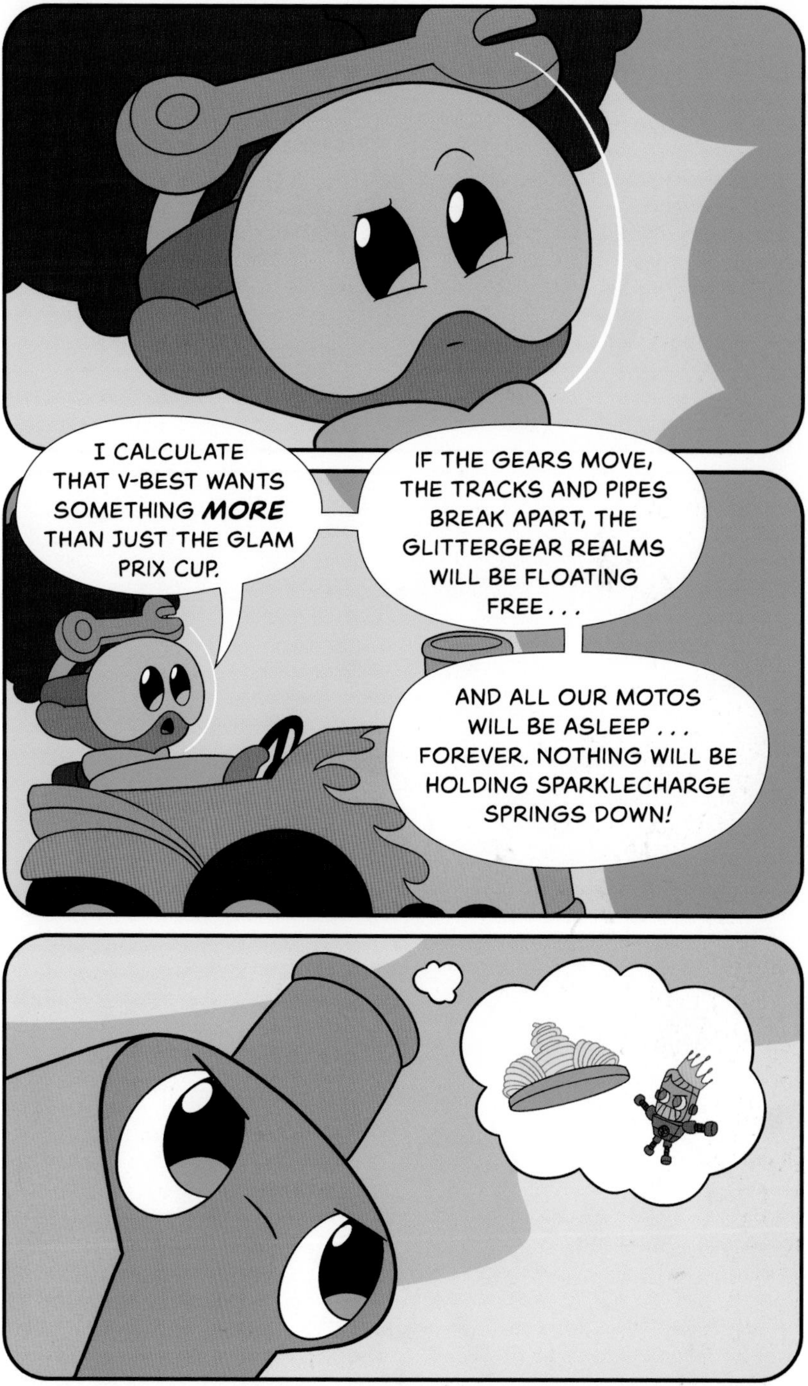
I CALCULATE THAT V-BEST WANTS SOMETHING *MORE* THAN JUST THE GLAM PRIX CUP.
IF THE GEARS MOVE, THE TRACKS AND PIPES BREAK APART, THE GLITTERGEAR REALMS WILL BE FLOATING FREE . . .
AND ALL OUR MOTOS WILL BE ASLEEP . . . FOREVER. NOTHING WILL BE HOLDING SPARKLECHARGE SPRINGS DOWN!

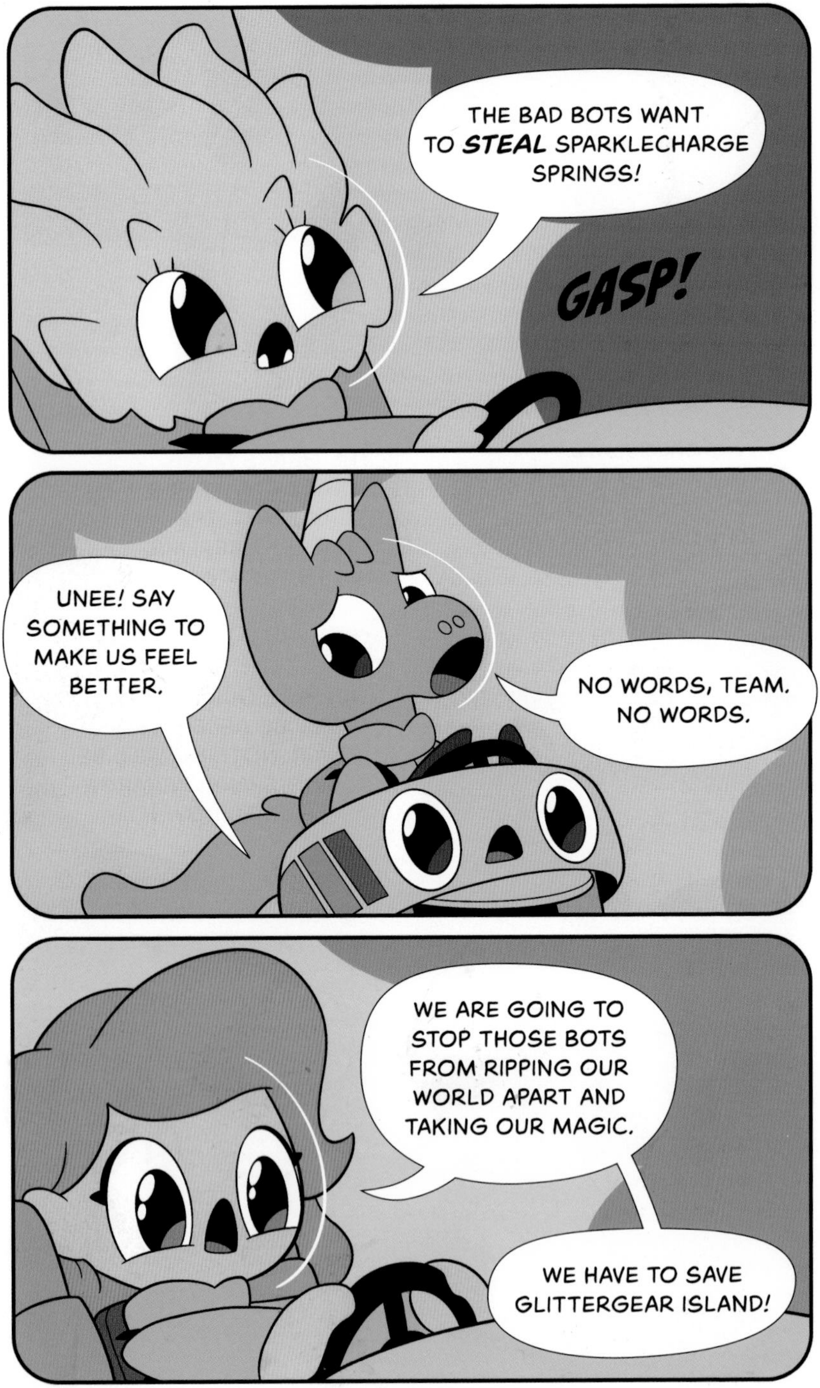
THE BAD BOTS WANT TO **STEAL** SPARKLECHARGE SPRINGS!
GASP!
UNEE! SAY SOMETHING TO MAKE US FEEL BETTER.
NO WORDS, TEAM. NO WORDS.
WE ARE GOING TO STOP THOSE BOTS FROM RIPPING OUR WORLD APART AND TAKING OUR MAGIC.
WE HAVE TO SAVE GLITTERGEAR ISLAND!

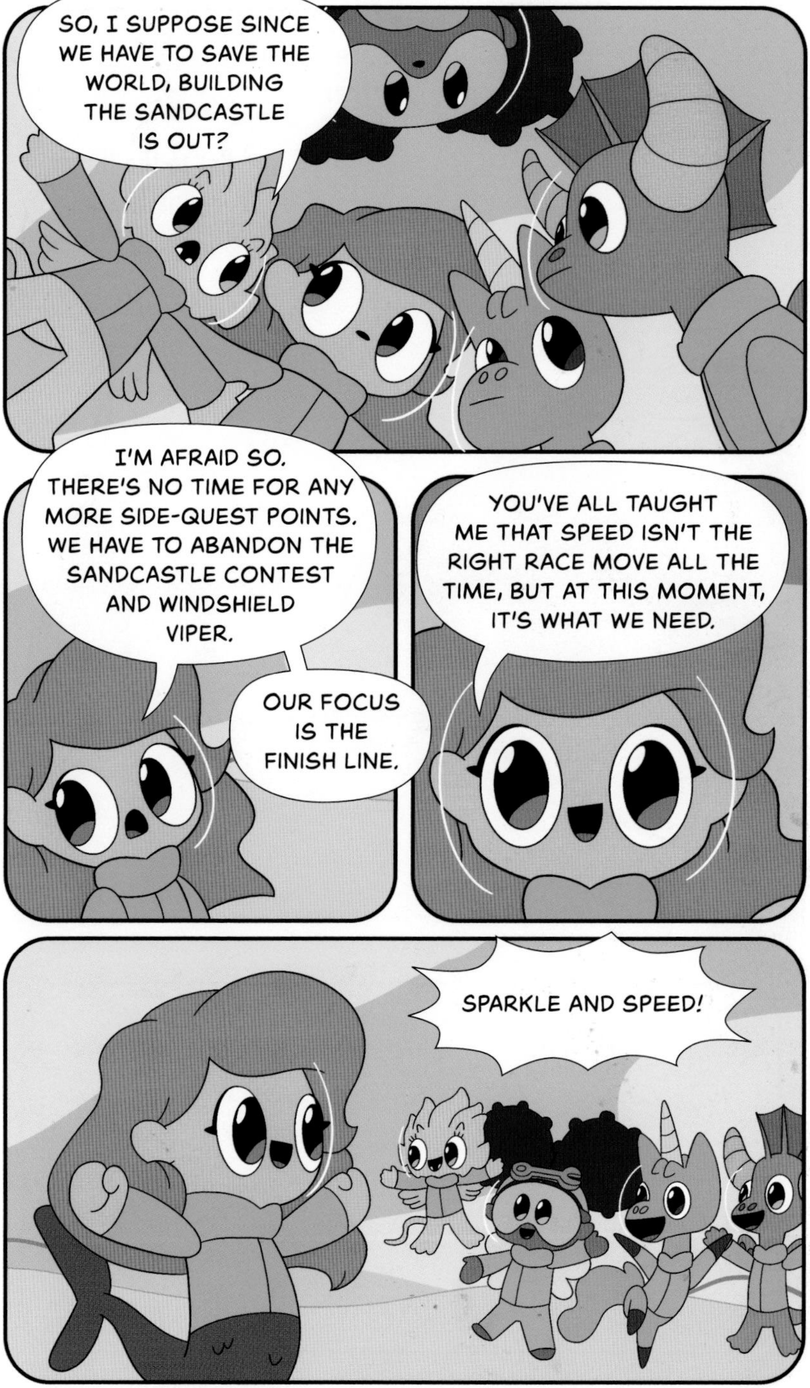
SO, I SUPPOSE SINCE WE HAVE TO SAVE THE WORLD, BUILDING THE SANDCASTLE IS OUT?
I'M AFRAID SO. THERE'S NO TIME FOR ANY MORE SIDE-QUEST POINTS. WE HAVE TO ABANDON THE SANDCASTLE CONTEST AND WINDSHIELD VIPER.
OUR FOCUS IS THE FINISH LINE.
YOU'VE ALL TAUGHT ME THAT SPEED ISN'T THE RIGHT RACE MOVE ALL THE TIME, BUT AT THIS MOMENT, IT'S WHAT WE NEED.
SPARKLE AND SPEED!

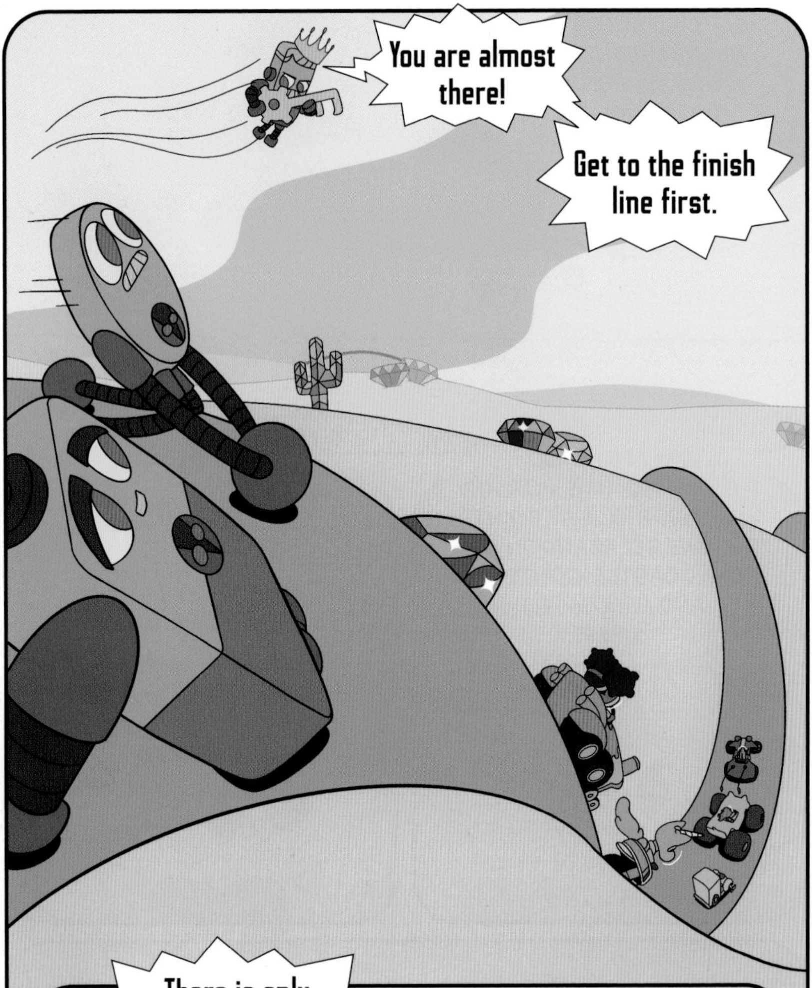
You are almost there!
Get to the finish line first.
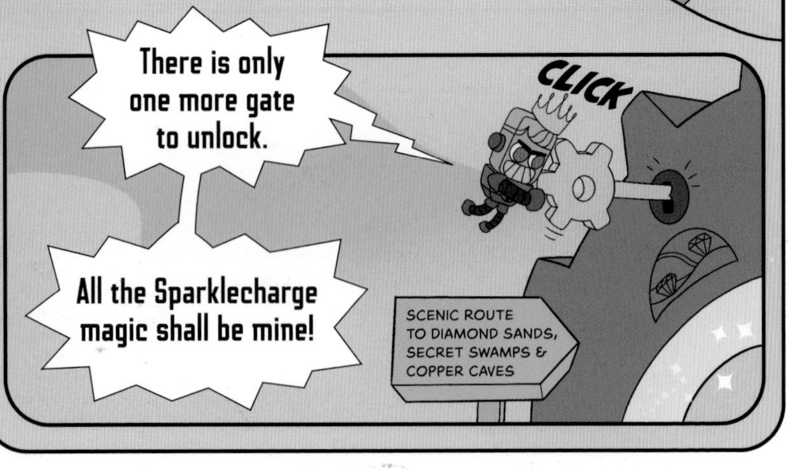
There is only one more gate to unlock.
All the Sparklecharge magic shall be mine!
CLICK
SCENIC ROUTE TO DIAMOND SANDS, SECRET SWAMPS & COPPER CAVES

CHAPTER 10:
DIAMOND DUST!

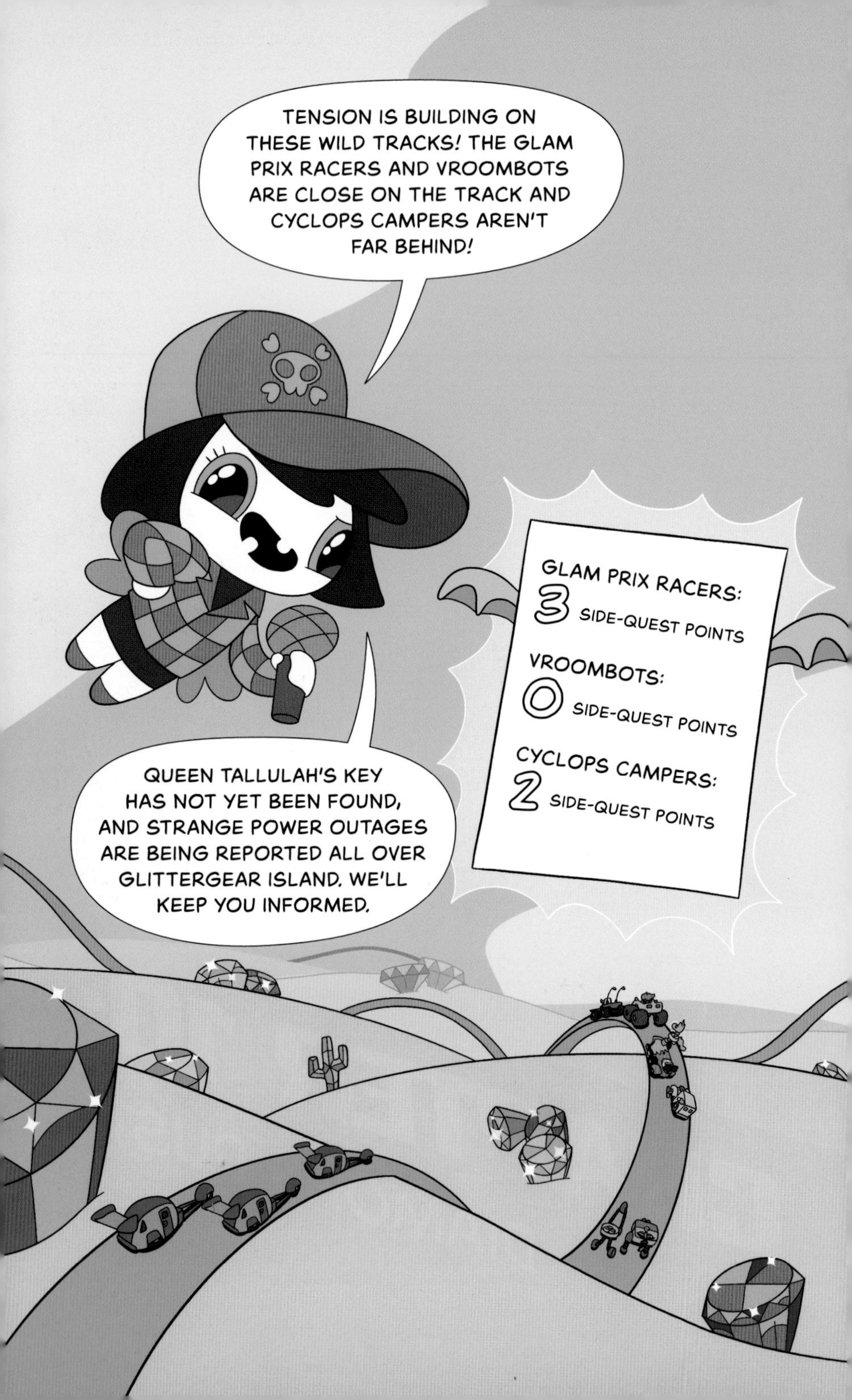
TENSION IS BUILDING ON THESE WILD TRACKS! THE GLAM PRIX RACERS AND VROOMBOTS ARE CLOSE ON THE TRACK AND CYCLOPS CAMPERS AREN'T FAR BEHIND!
GLAM PRIX RACERS: 3 SIDE-QUEST POINTS
VROOMBOTS: 0 SIDE-QUEST POINTS
CYCLOPS CAMPERS: 2 SIDE-QUEST POINTS
QUEEN TALLULAH'S KEY HAS NOT YET BEEN FOUND, AND STRANGE POWER OUTAGES ARE BEING REPORTED ALL OVER GLITTERGEAR ISLAND. WE'LL KEEP YOU INFORMED.

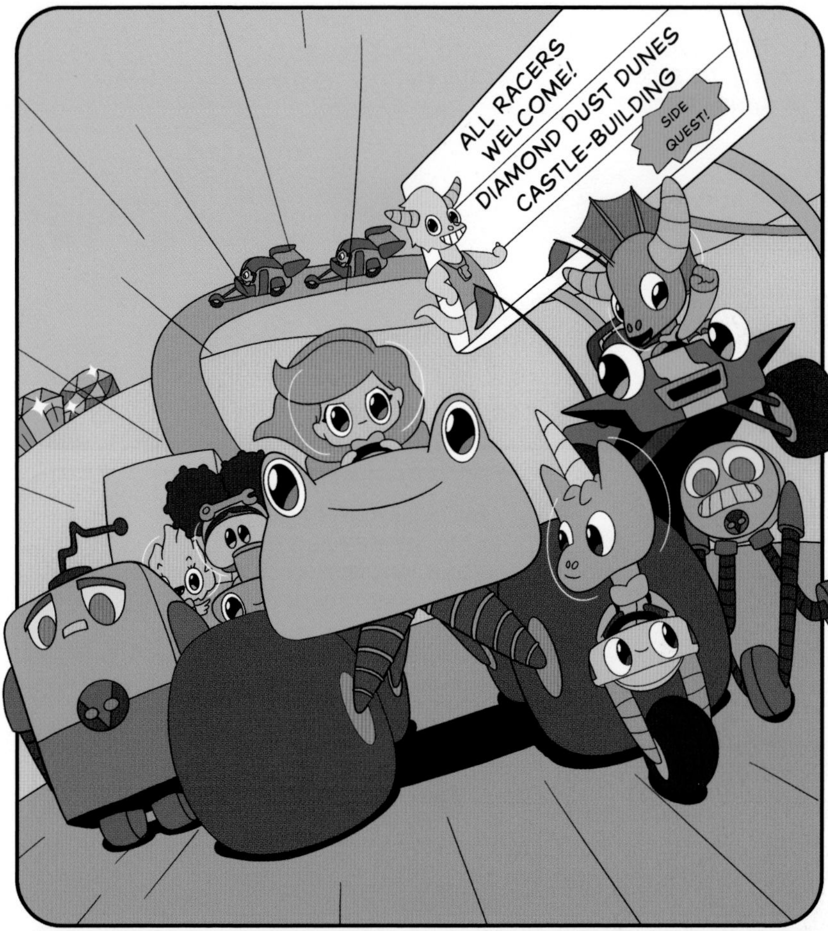
ALL RACERS WELCOME!
DIAMOND DUST DUNES CASTLE-BUILDING
SIDE QUEST!

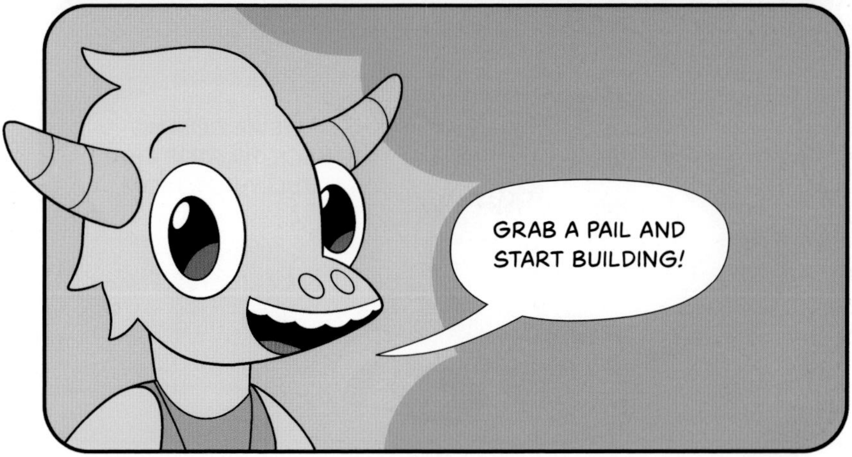
GRAB A PAIL AND START BUILDING!

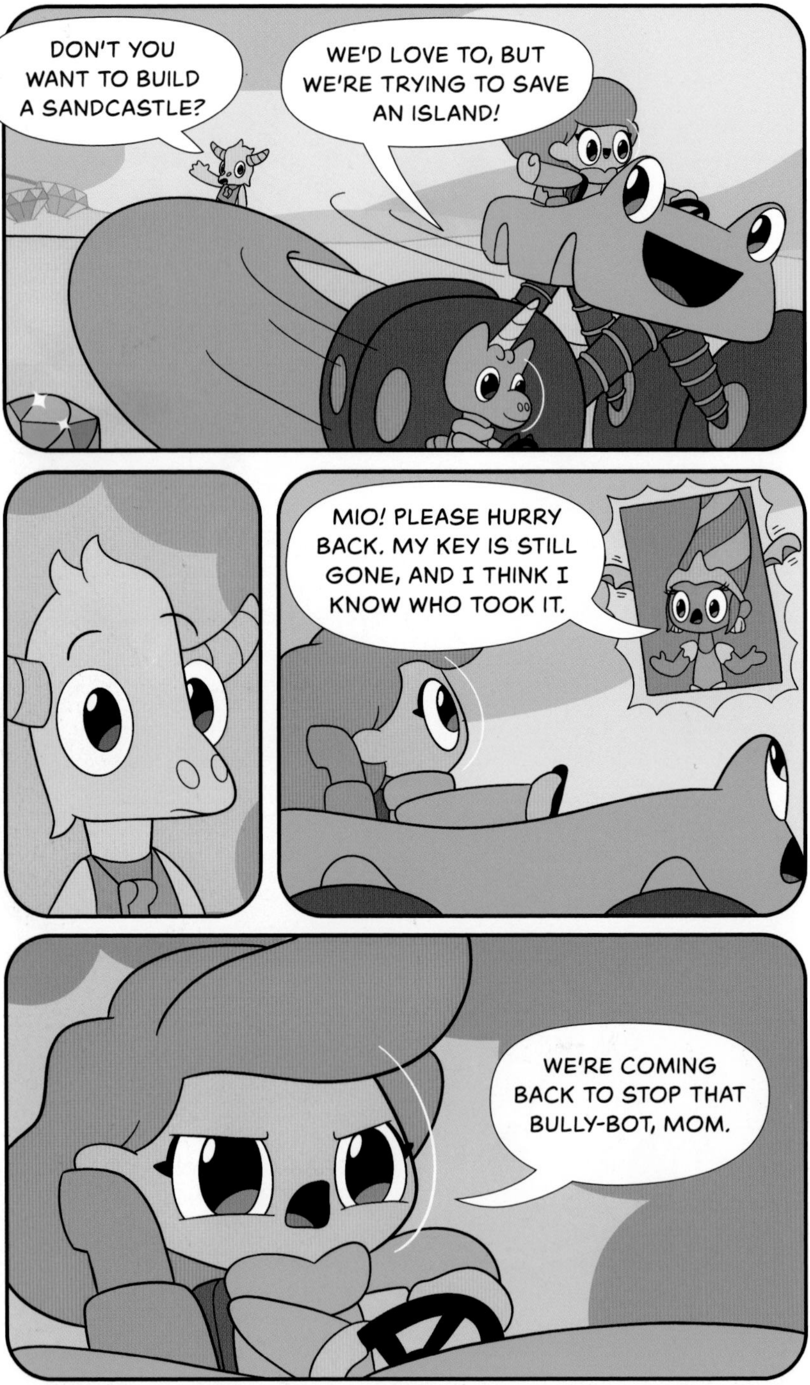
DON'T YOU WANT TO BUILD A SANDCASTLE?
WE'D LOVE TO, BUT WE'RE TRYING TO SAVE AN ISLAND!
MIO! PLEASE HURRY BACK. MY KEY IS STILL GONE, AND I THINK I KNOW WHO TOOK IT.
WE'RE COMING BACK TO STOP THAT BULLY-BOT, MOM.

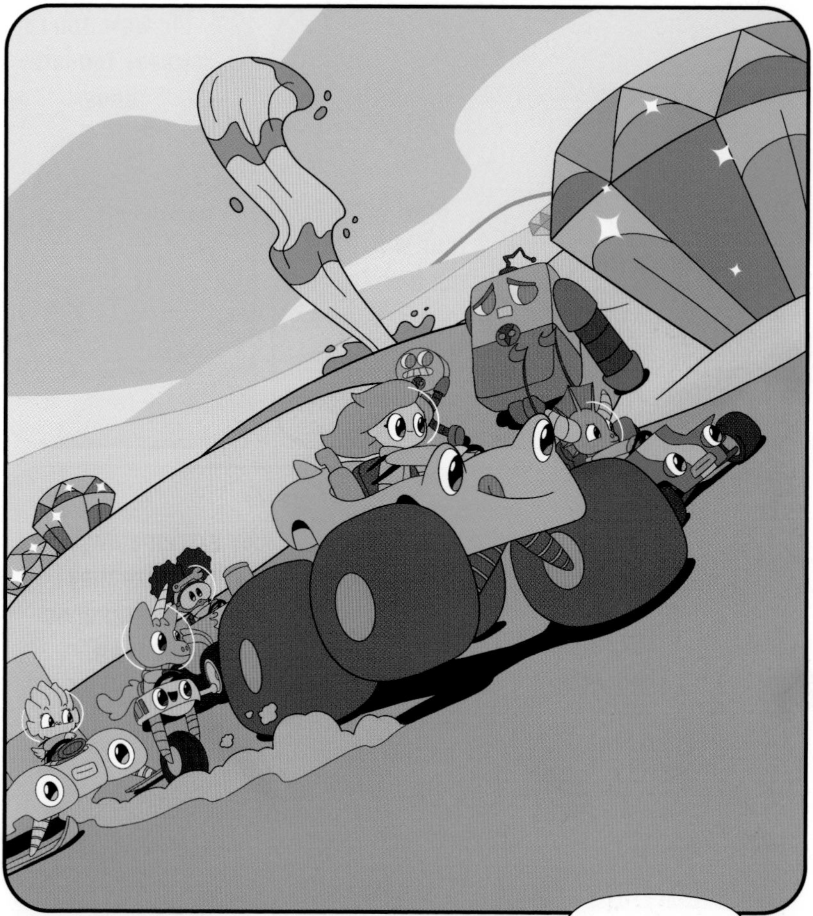

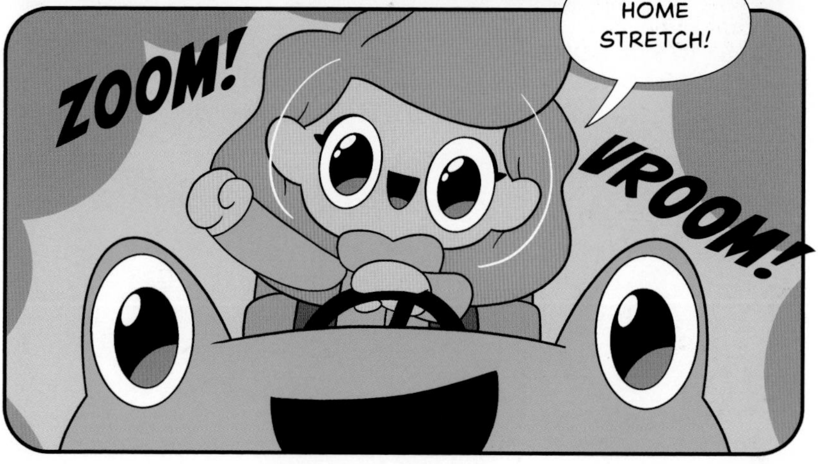
ZOOM!
HOME STRETCH!
VROOM!

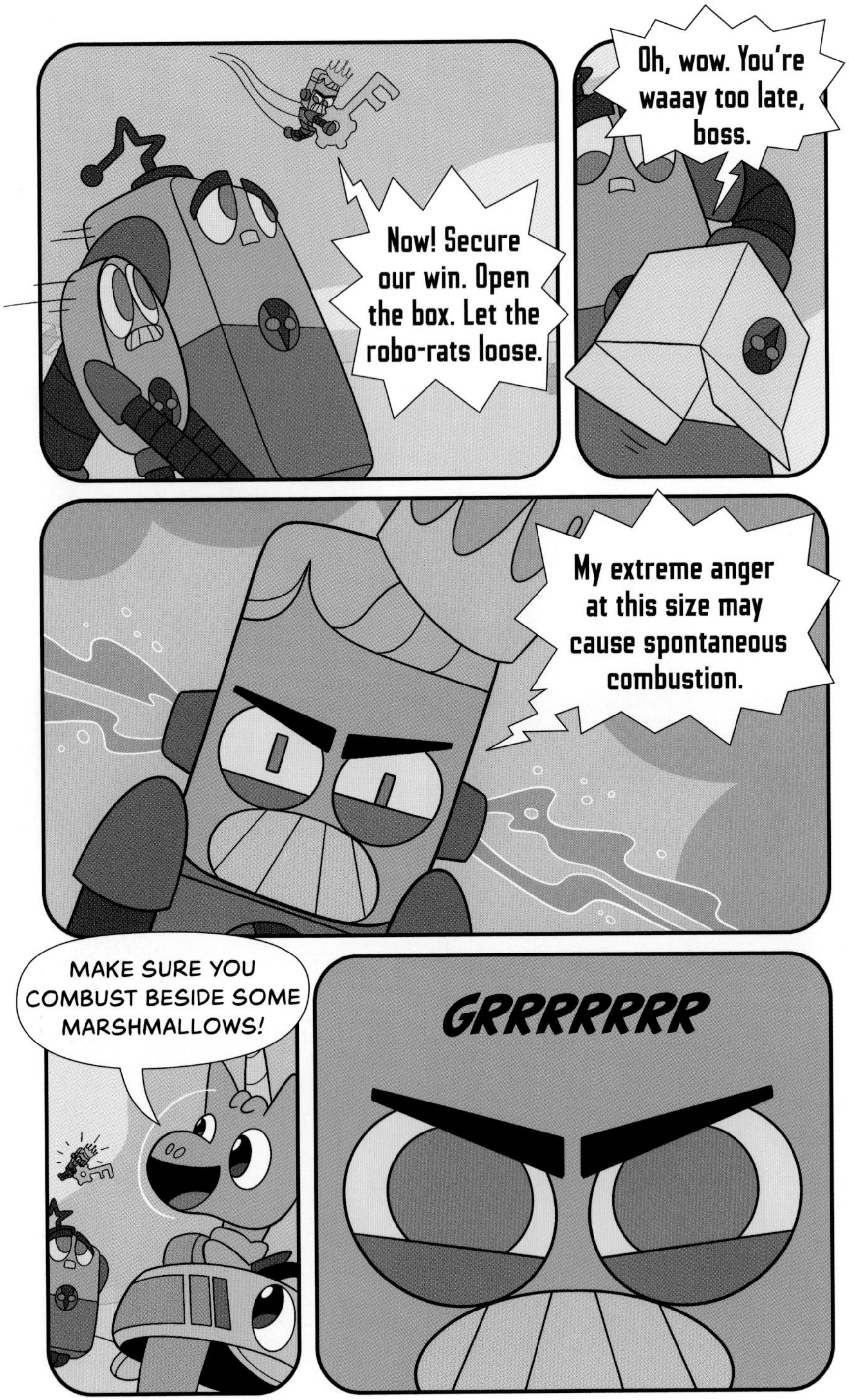
Now! Secure our win. Open the box. Let the robo-rats loose.
Oh, wow. You're waaay too late, boss.
My extreme anger at this size may cause spontaneous combustion.
MAKE SURE YOU COMBUST BESIDE SOME MARSHMALLOWS!
GRRRRRRR

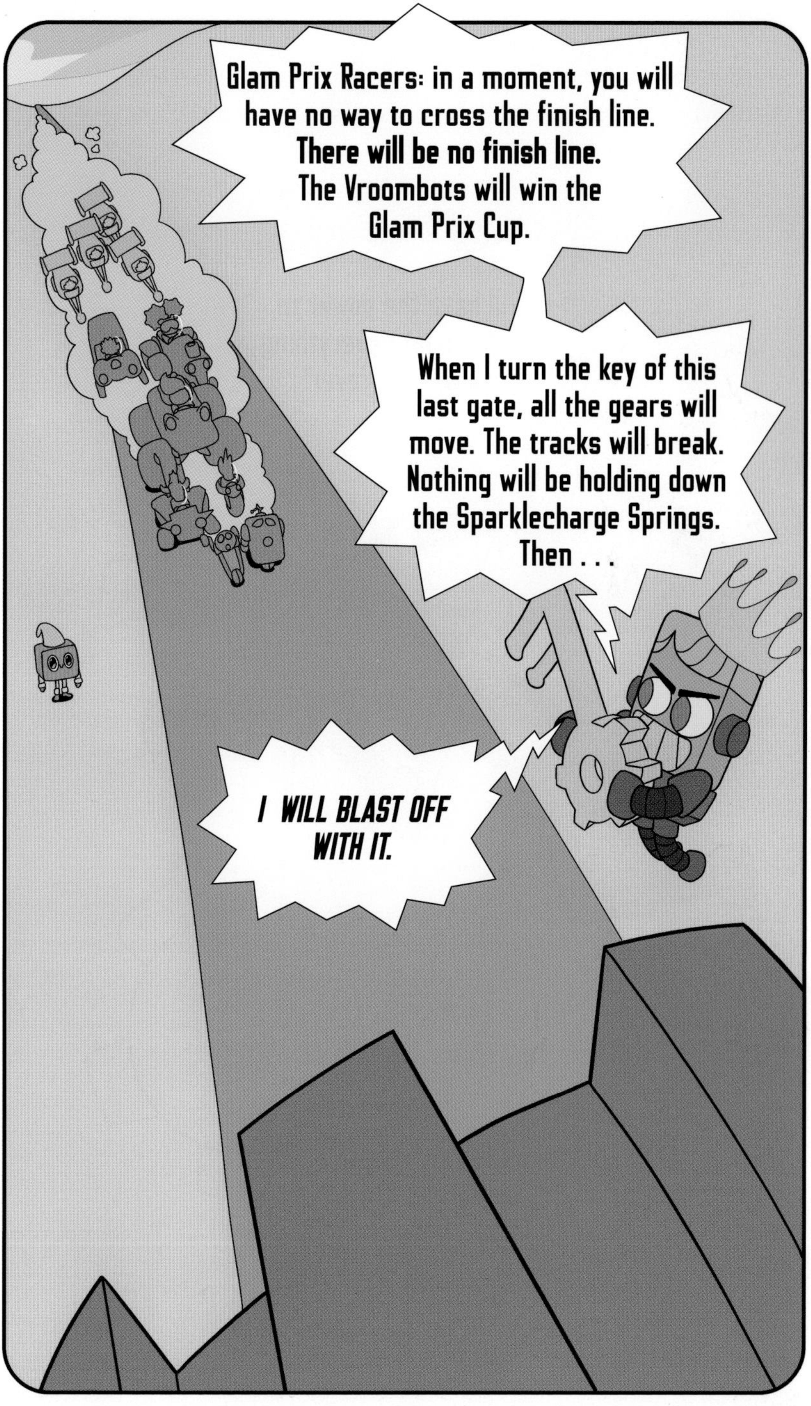
Glam Prix Racers: in a moment, you will have no way to cross the finish line. **There will be no finish line.** The Vroombots will win the Glam Prix Cup.
When I turn the key of this last gate, all the gears will move. The tracks will break. Nothing will be holding down the Sparklecharge Springs. Then . . .
I WILL BLAST OFF WITH IT.

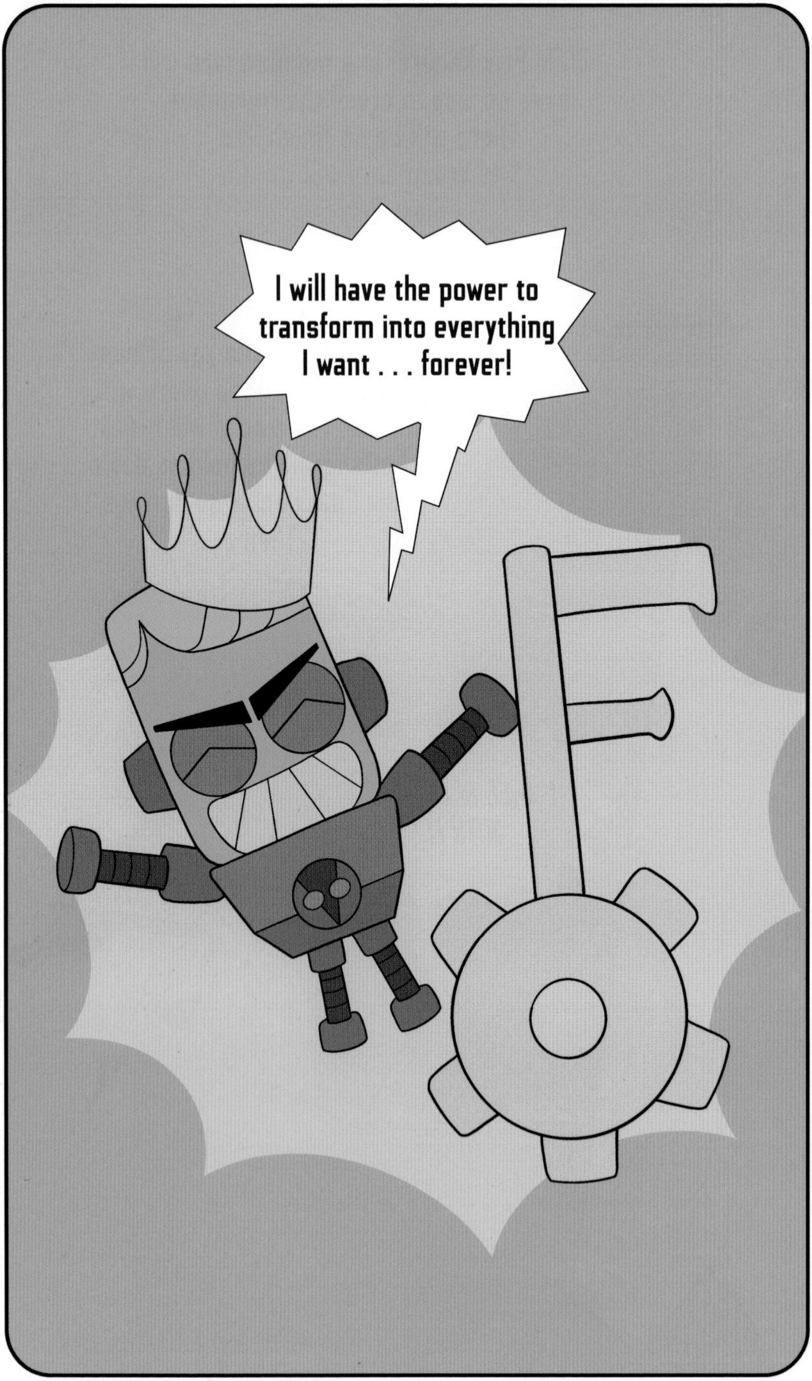
I will have the power to transform into everything I want . . . forever!

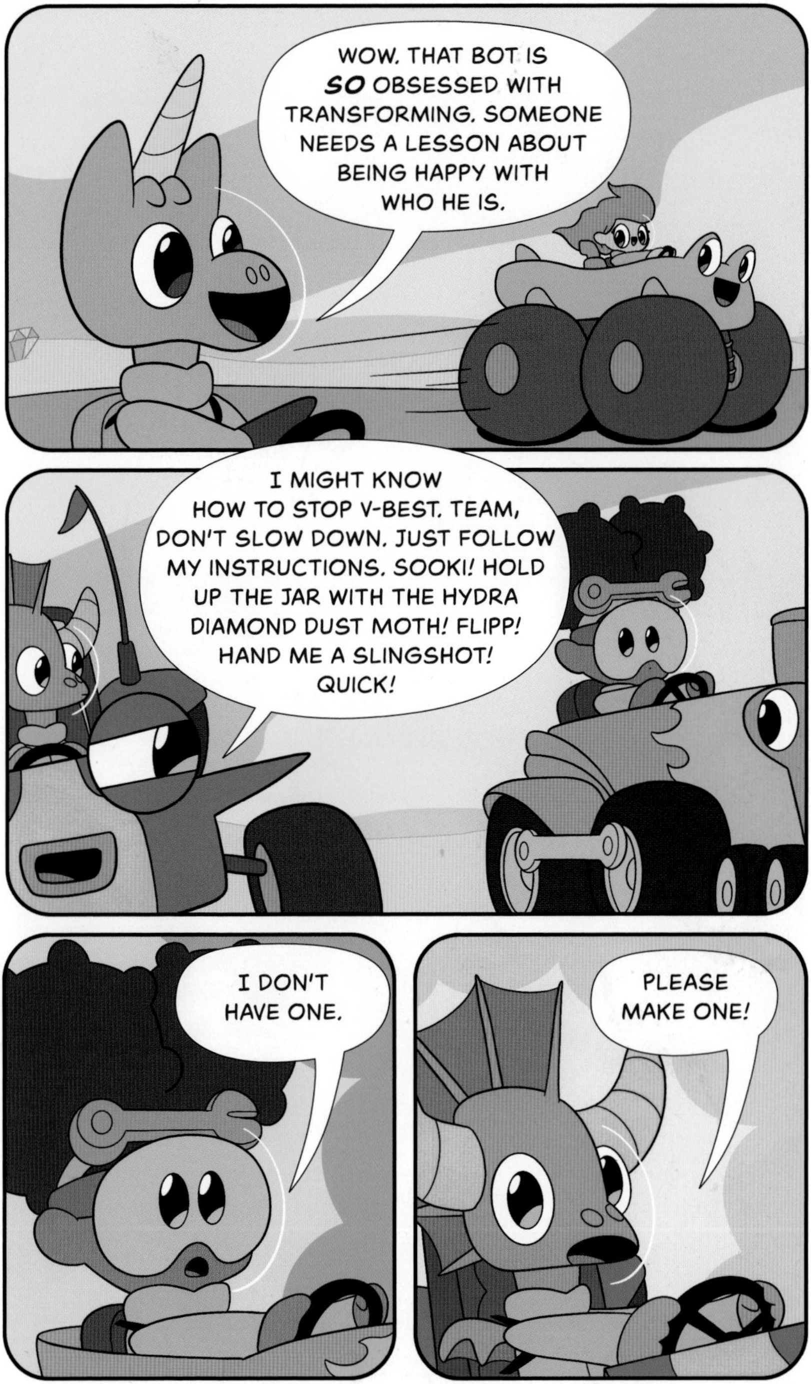
WOW, THAT BOT IS *SO* OBSESSED WITH TRANSFORMING. SOMEONE NEEDS A LESSON ABOUT BEING HAPPY WITH WHO HE IS.
I MIGHT KNOW HOW TO STOP V-BEST. TEAM, DON'T SLOW DOWN. JUST FOLLOW MY INSTRUCTIONS. SOOKI! HOLD UP THE JAR WITH THE HYDRA DIAMOND DUST MOTH! FLIPP! HAND ME A SLINGSHOT! QUICK!
I DON'T HAVE ONE.
PLEASE MAKE ONE!

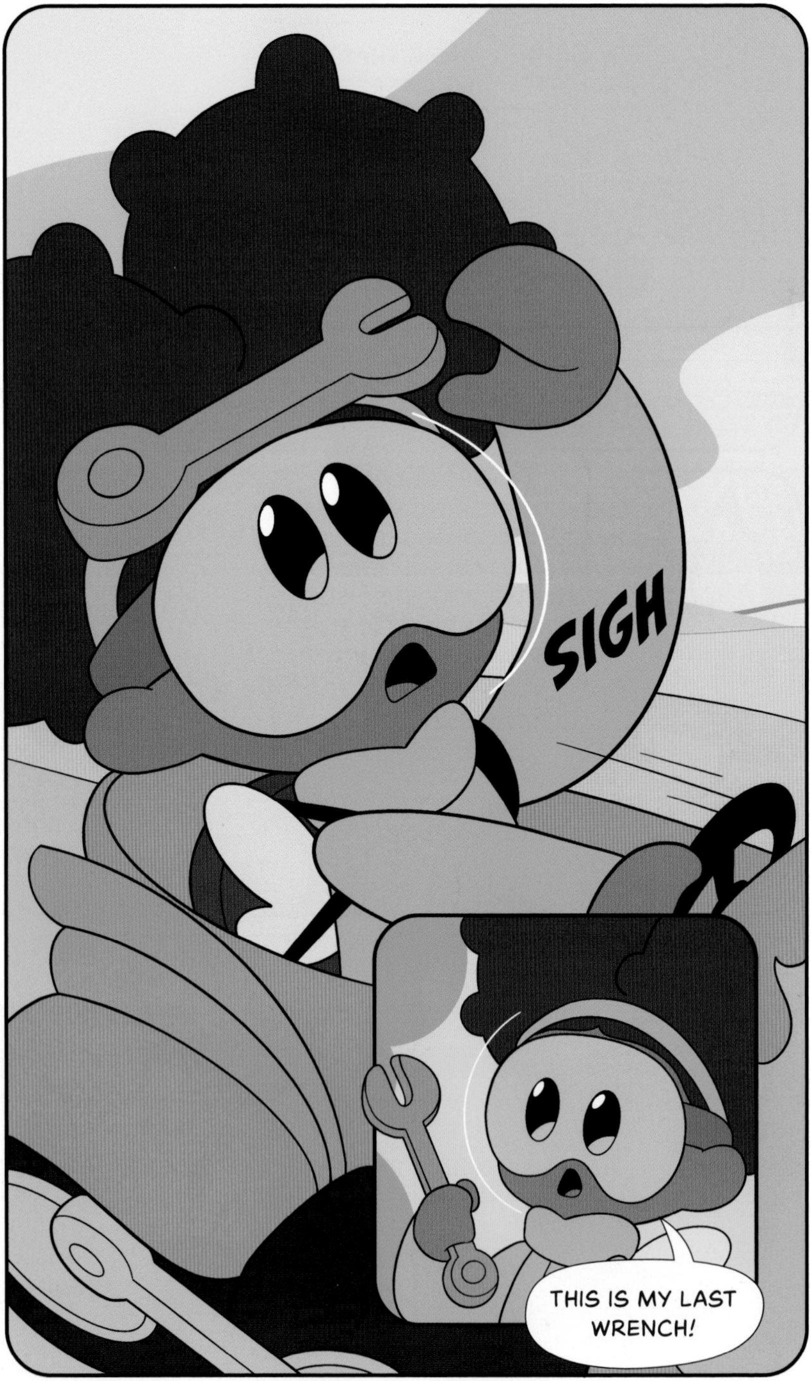
SIGH
THIS IS MY LAST WRENCH!

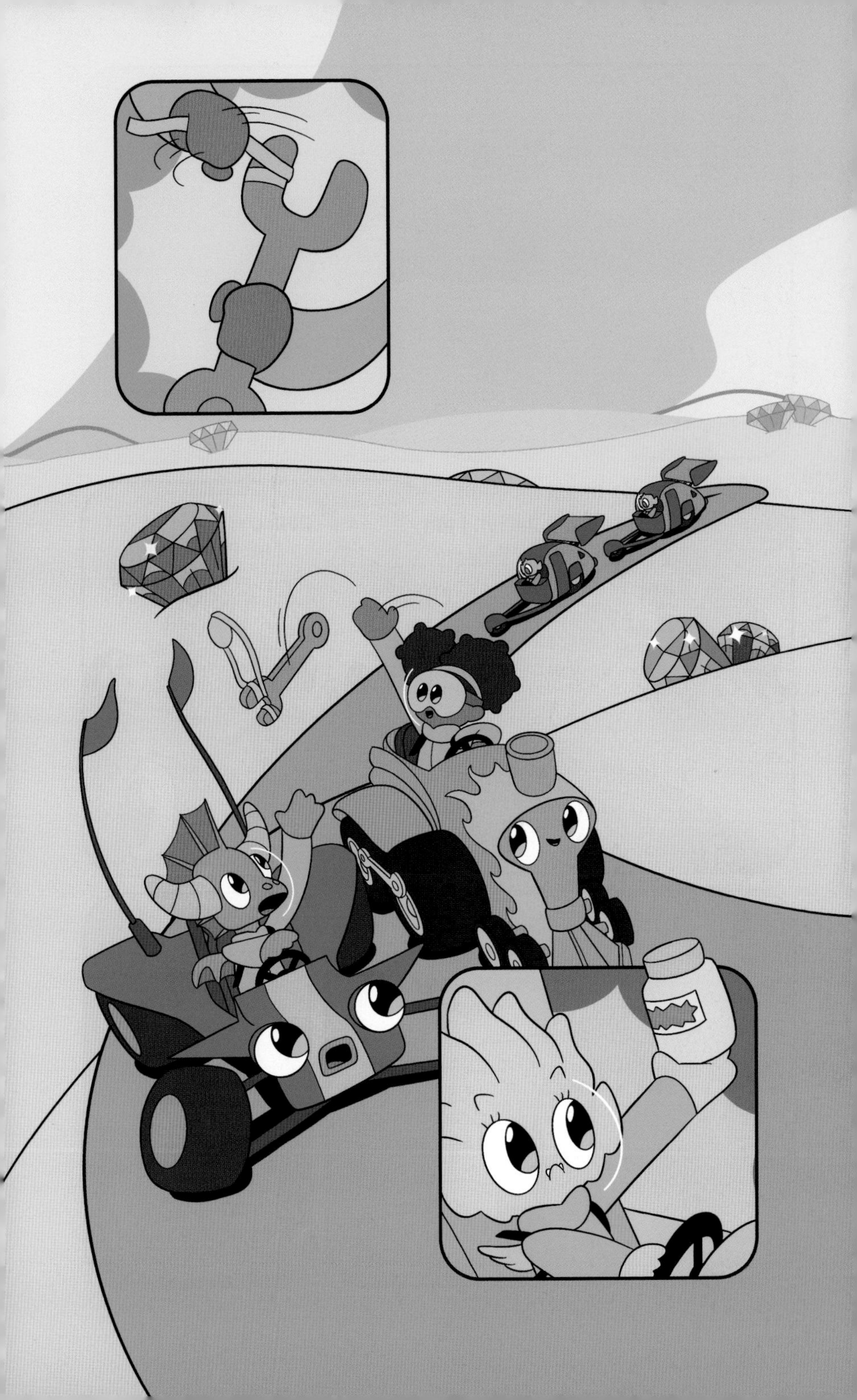

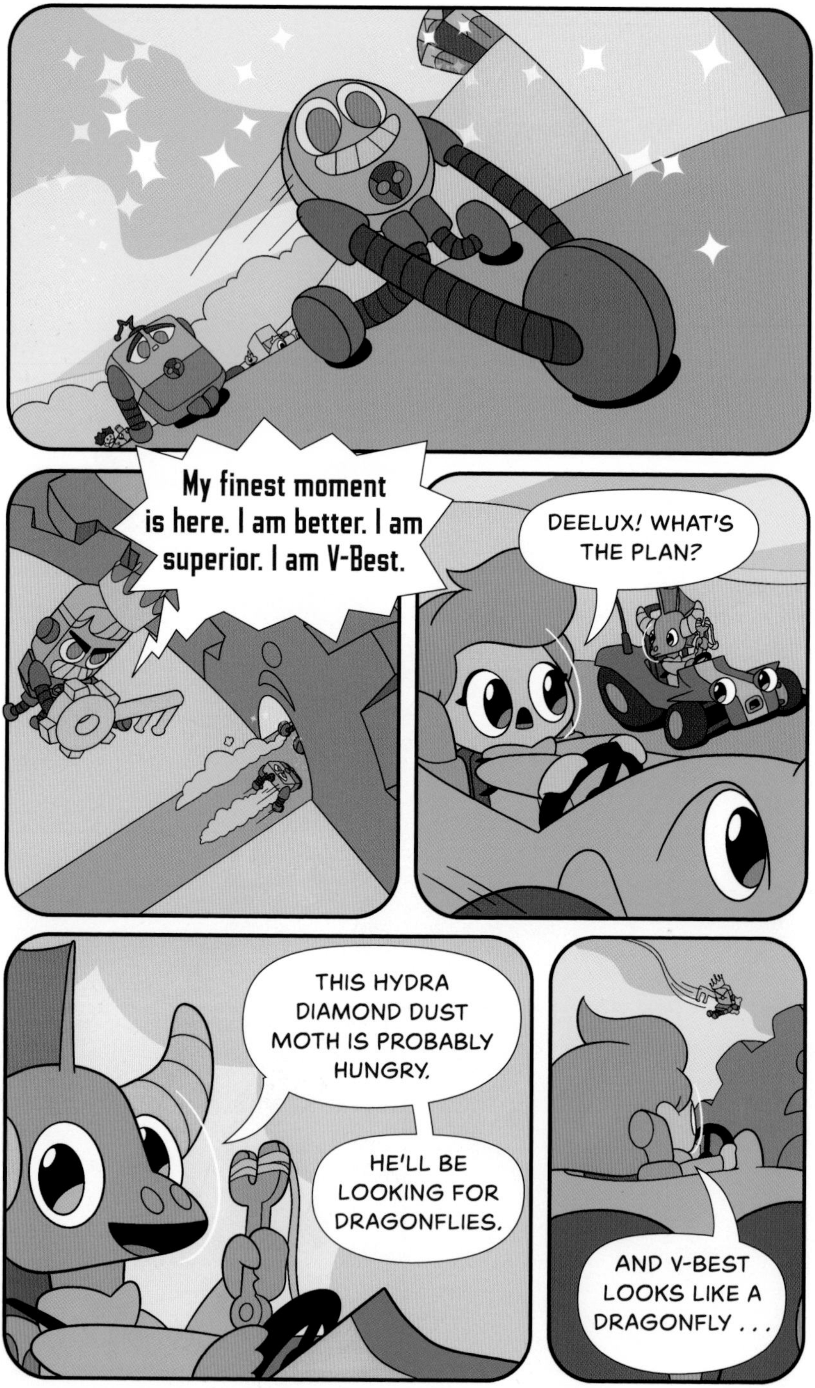
My finest moment is here. I am better. I am superior. I am V-Best.
DEELUX! WHAT'S THE PLAN?
THIS HYDRA DIAMOND DUST MOTH IS PROBABLY HUNGRY.
HE'LL BE LOOKING FOR DRAGONFLIES.
AND V-BEST LOOKS LIKE A DRAGONFLY . . .

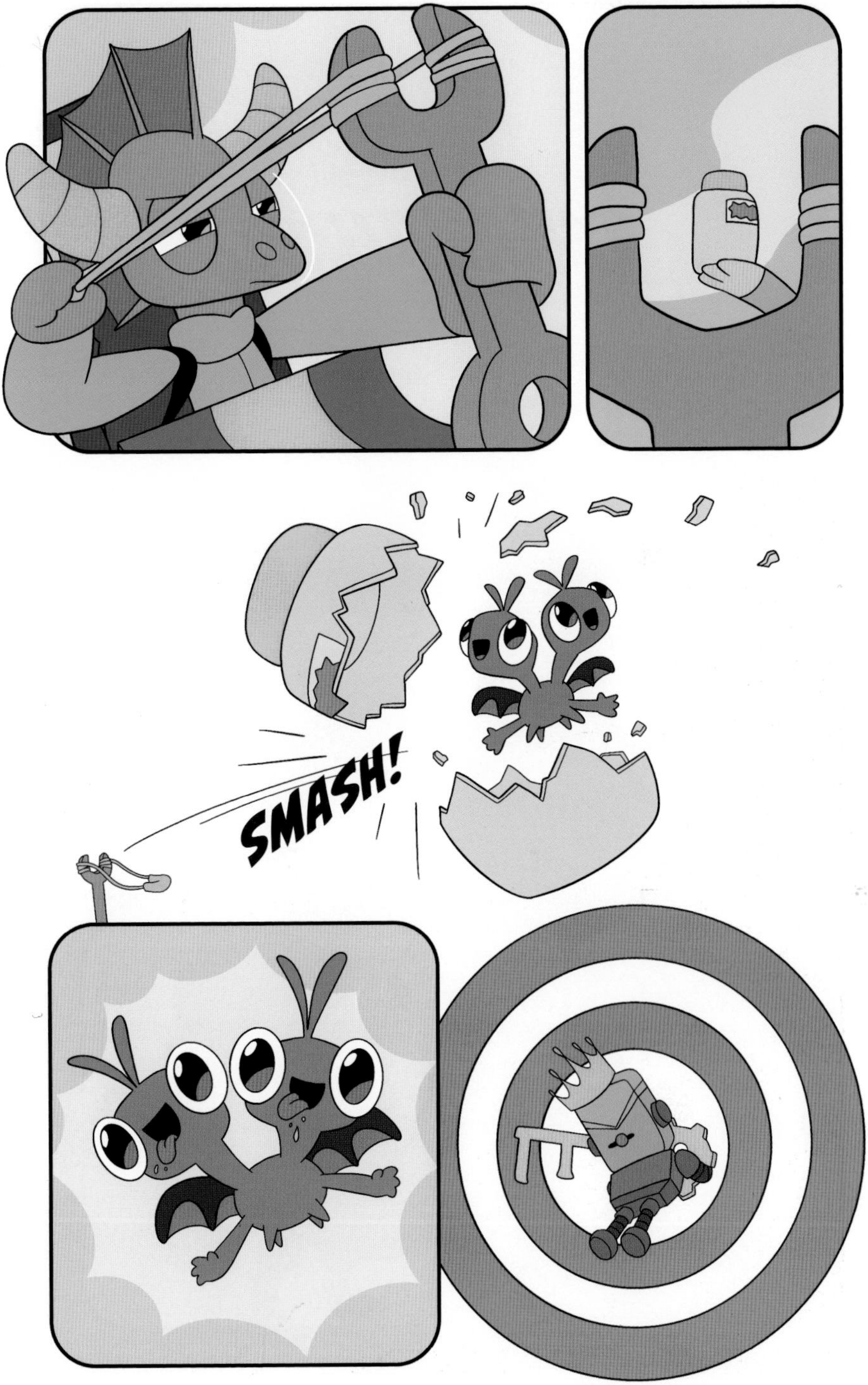
SMASH!

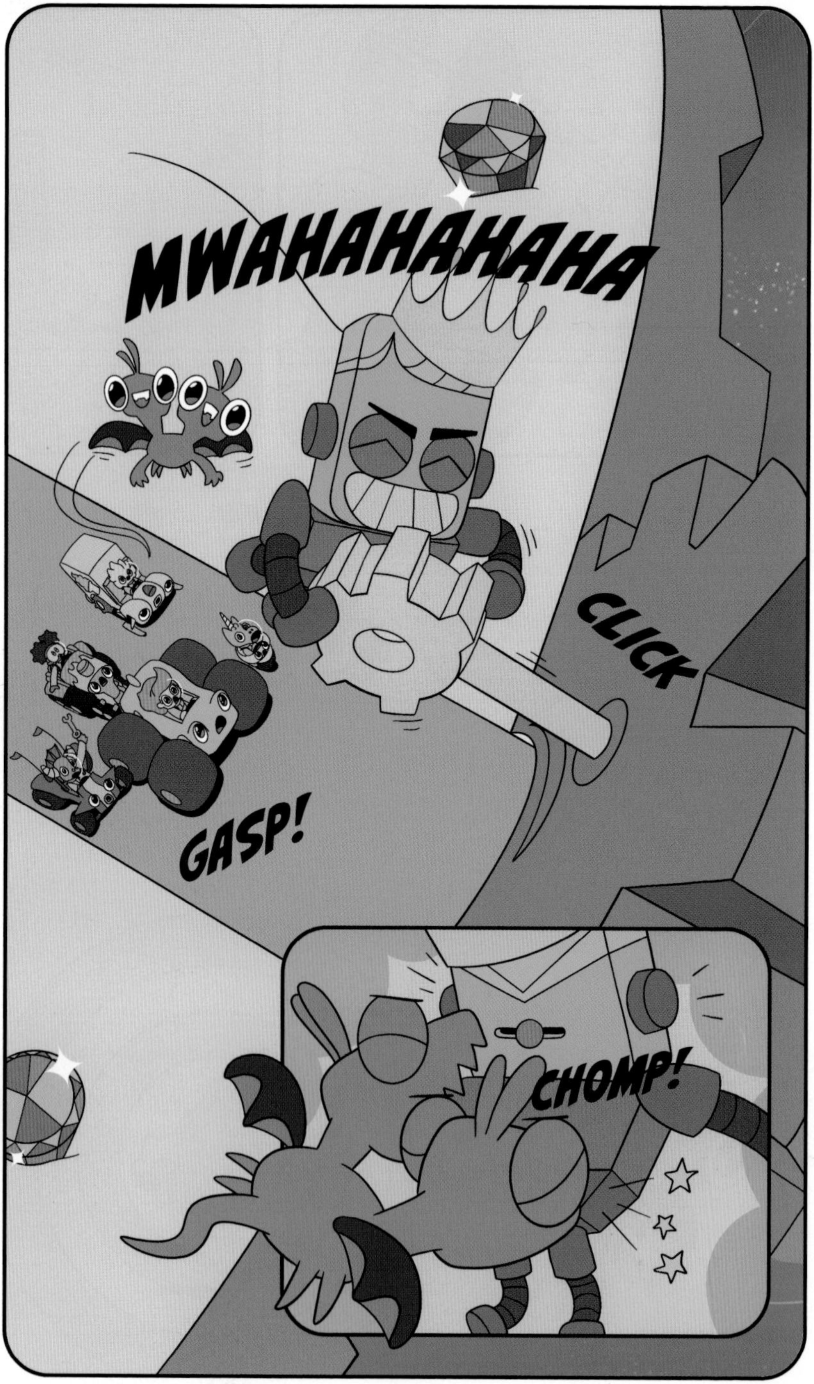
MWAHAHAHAHAHA
CLICK
GASP!
CHOMP!

CHAPTER 11:
DOOMED

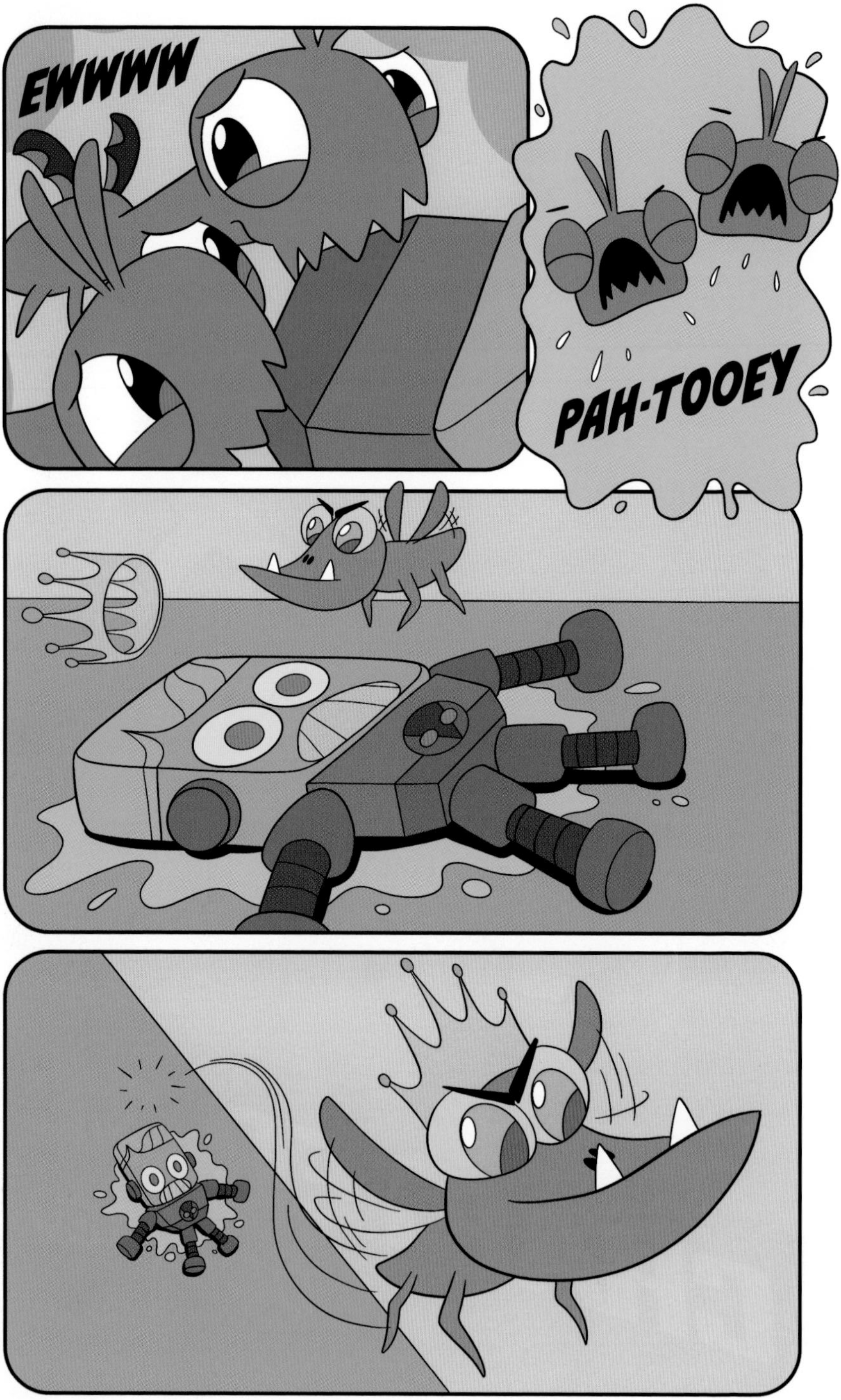
EWWWW
PAH-TOOEY

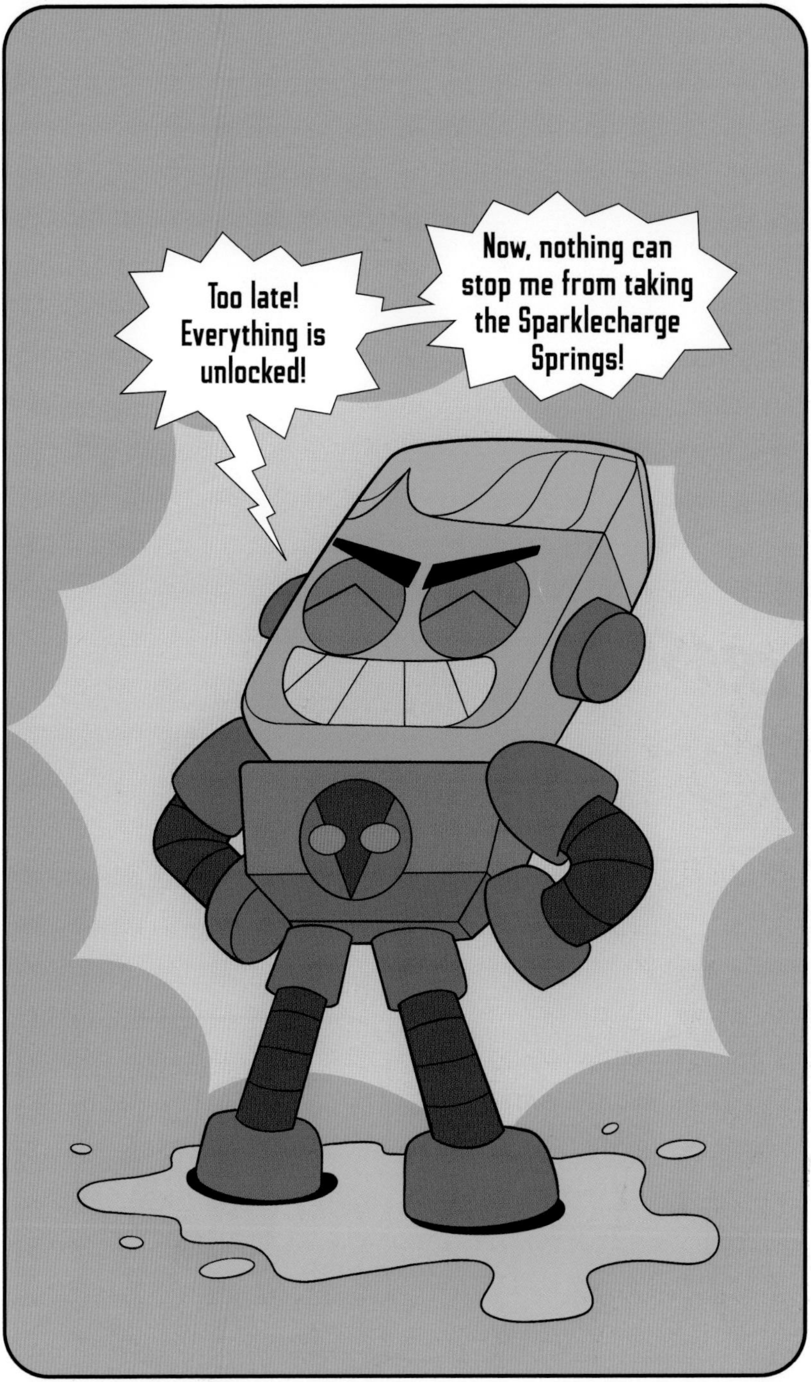
Too late! Everything is unlocked!
Now, nothing can stop me from taking the Sparklecharge Springs!

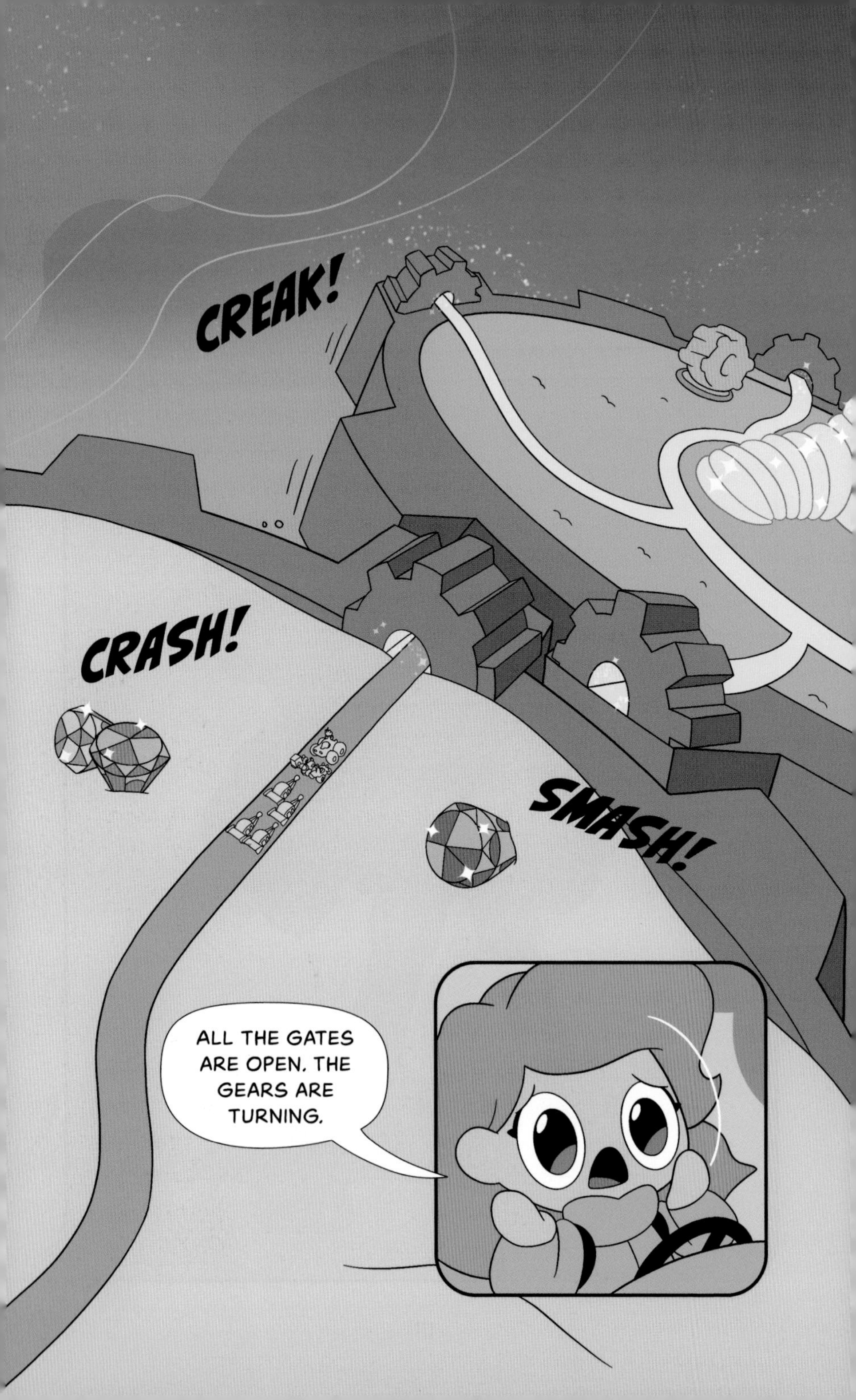
CREAK!
CRASH!
SMASH!
ALL THE GATES ARE OPEN. THE GEARS ARE TURNING.

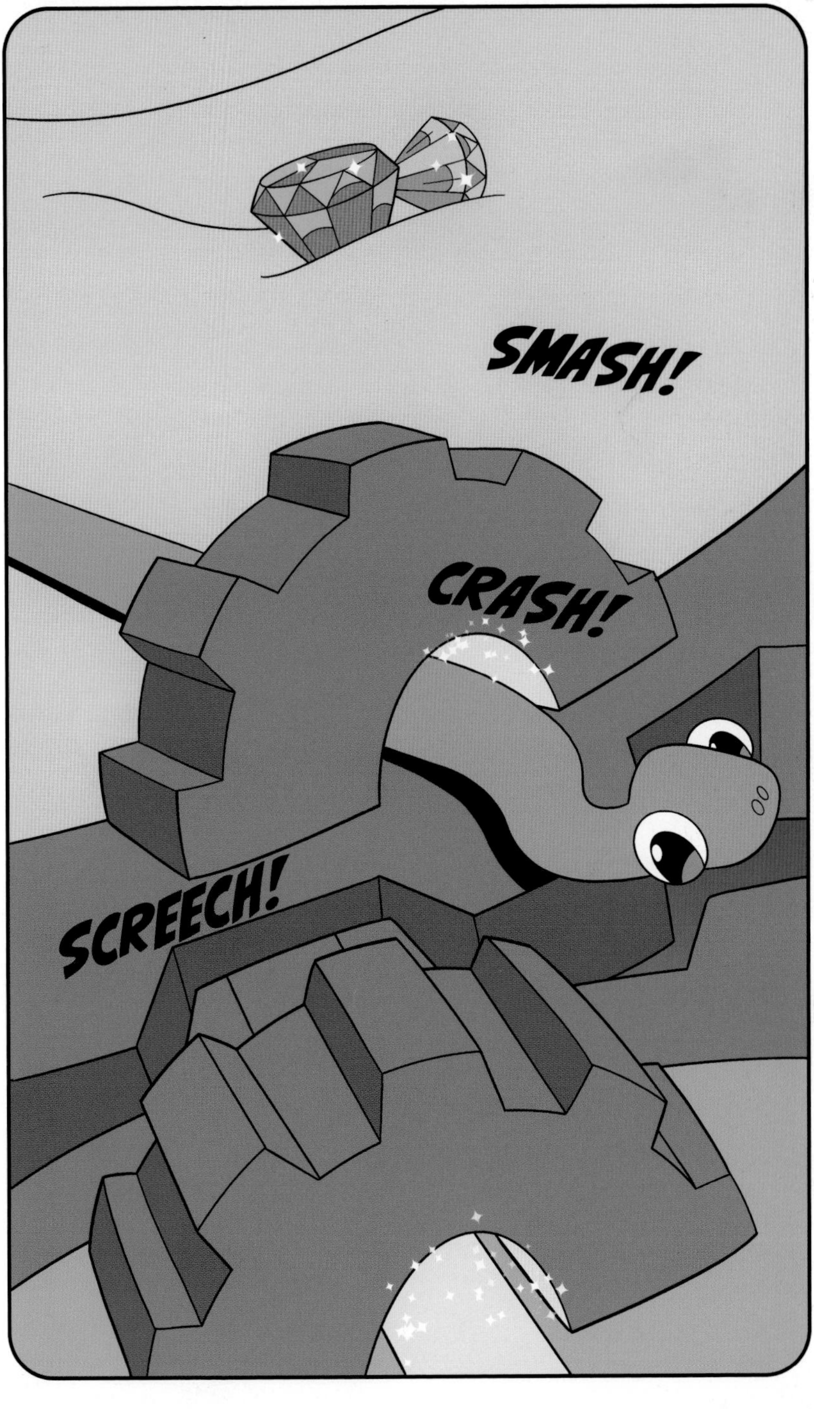
SMASH!
CRASH!
SCREECH!

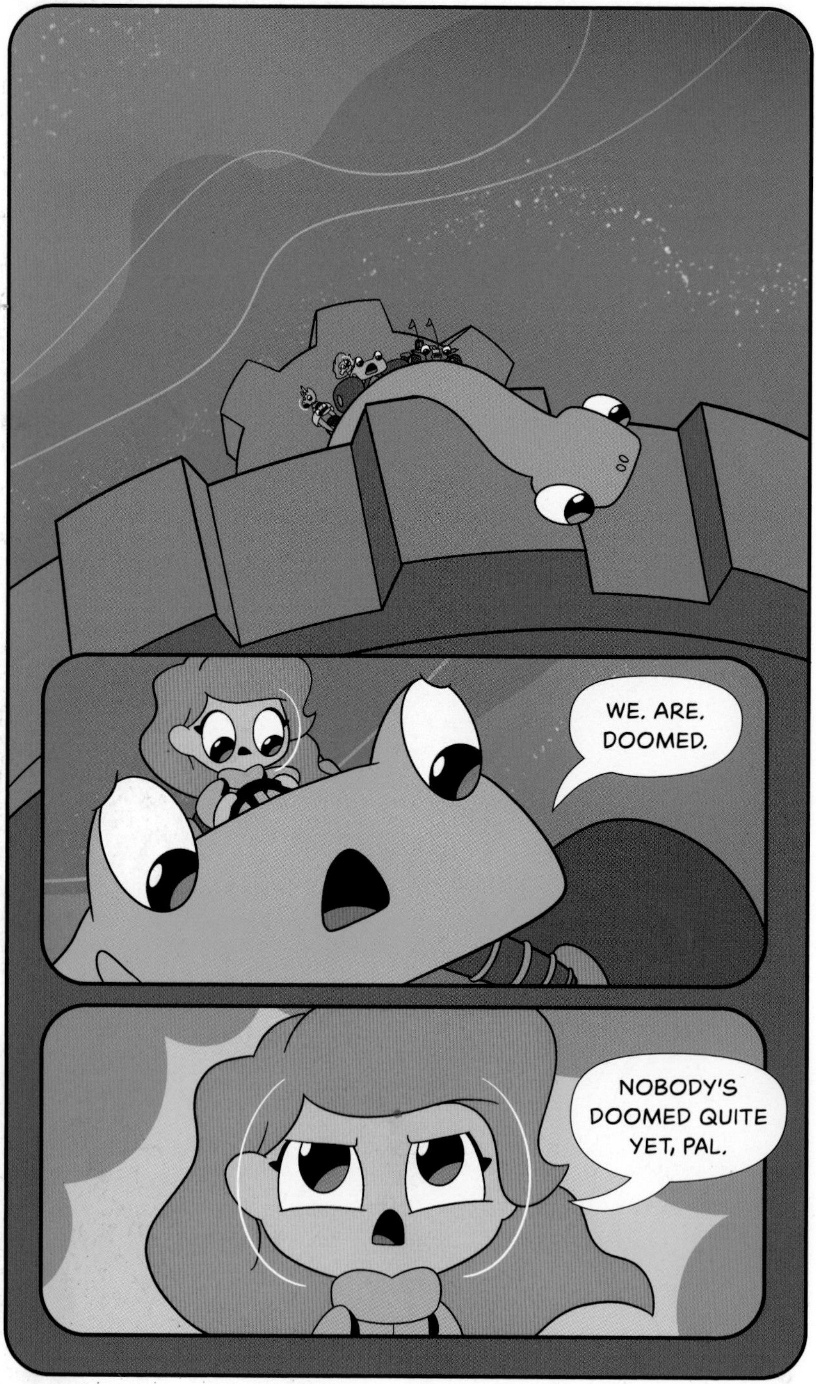
WE. ARE. DOOMED.
NOBODY'S DOOMED QUITE YET, PAL.

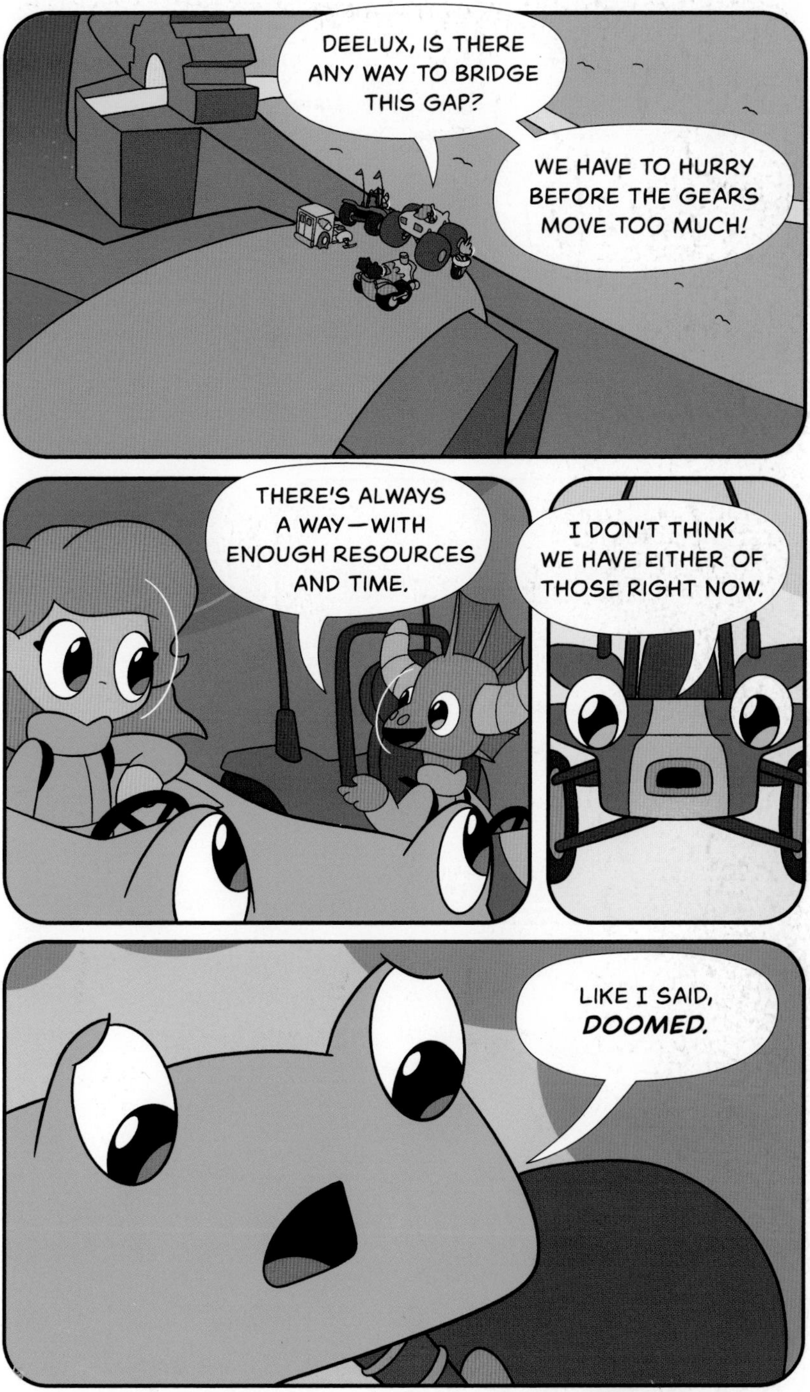
DEELUX, IS THERE ANY WAY TO BRIDGE THIS GAP?
WE HAVE TO HURRY BEFORE THE GEARS MOVE TOO MUCH!
THERE'S ALWAYS A WAY—WITH ENOUGH RESOURCES AND TIME.
I DON'T THINK WE HAVE EITHER OF THOSE RIGHT NOW.
LIKE I SAID, *DOOMED.*

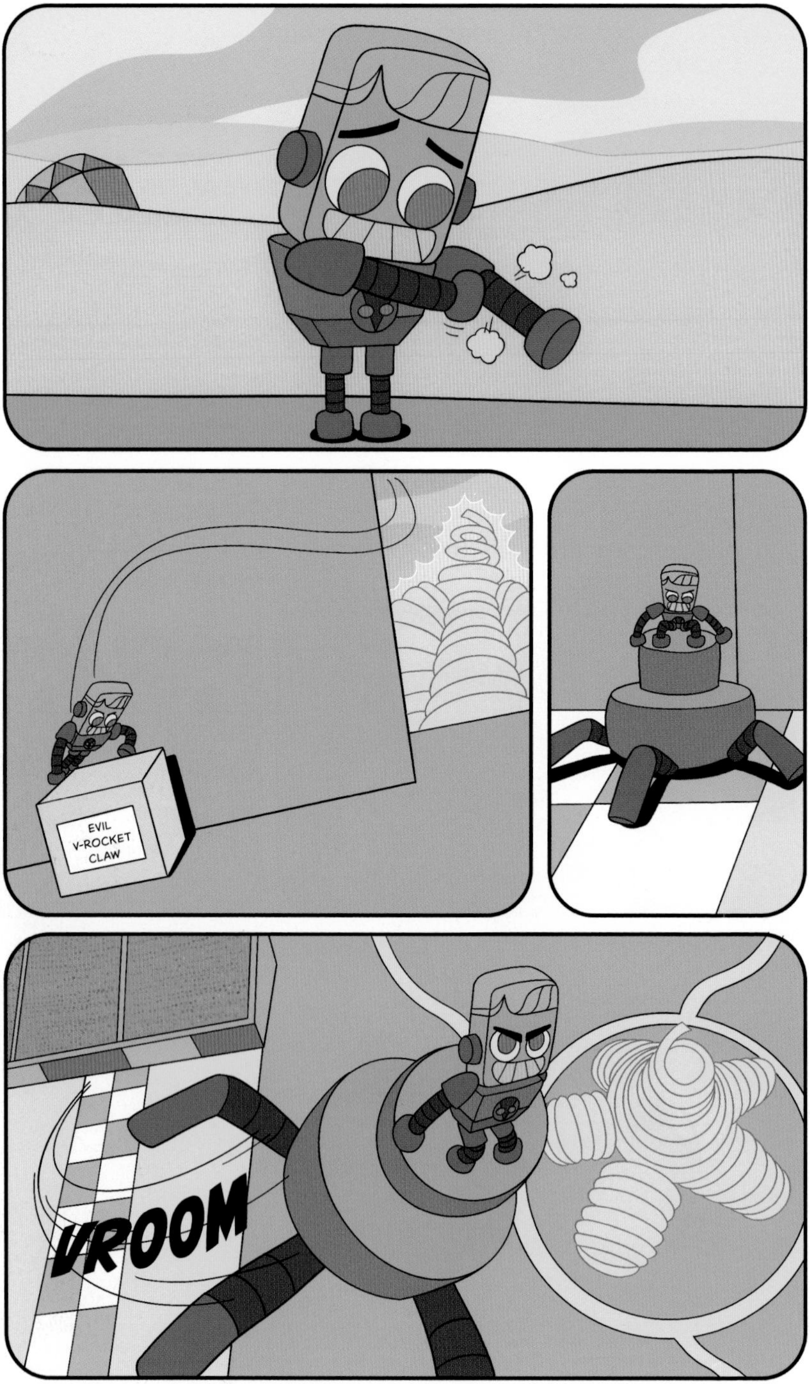
EVIL
V-ROCKET
CLAW
VROOM

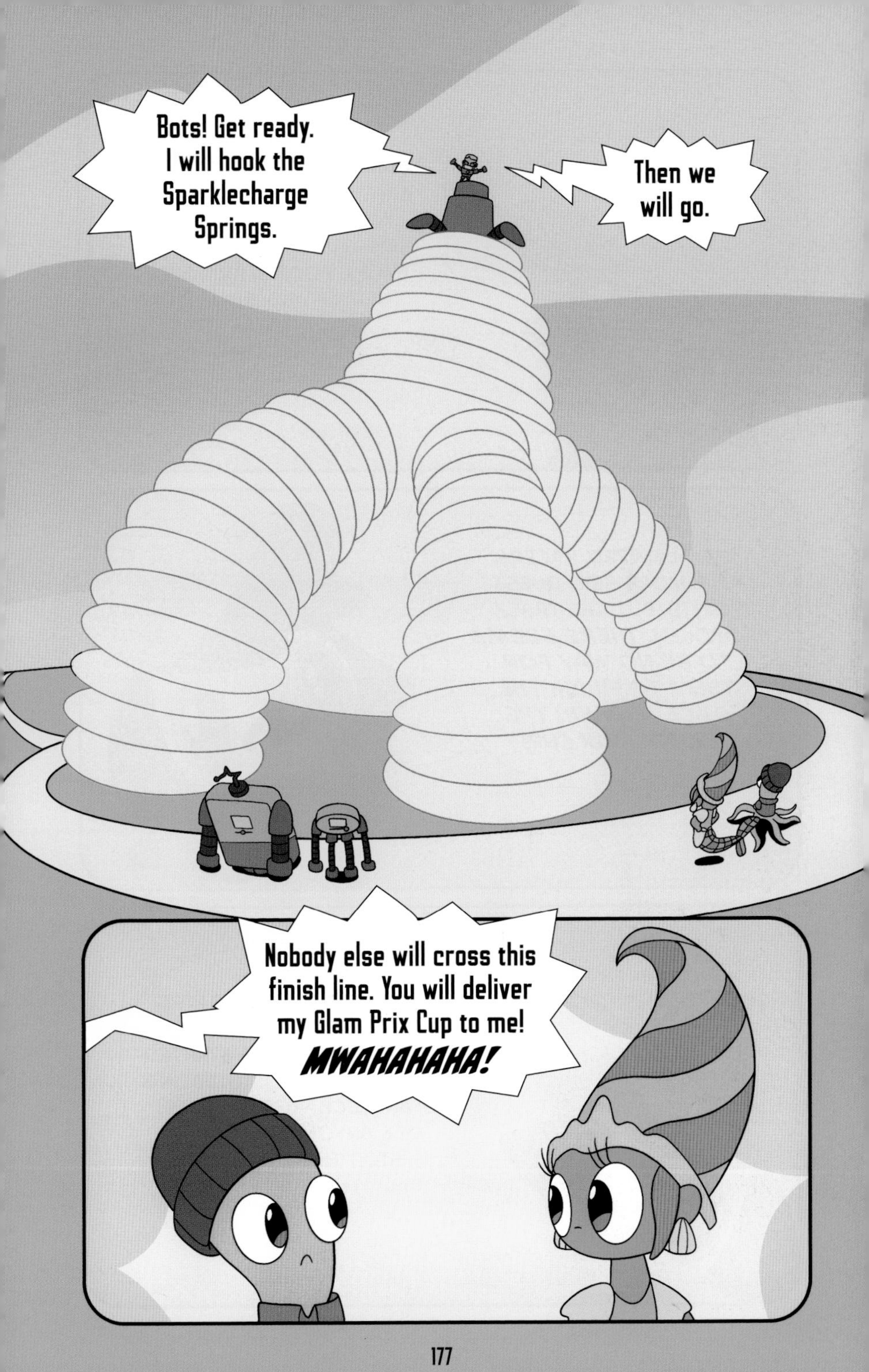
Bots! Get ready. I will hook the Sparklecharge Springs.
Then we will go.
Nobody else will cross this finish line. You will deliver my Glam Prix Cup to me! MWAHAHAHA!

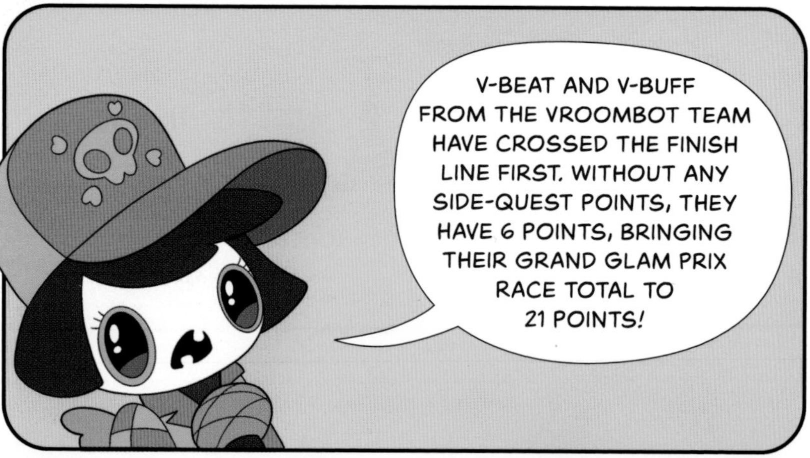
V-BEAT AND V-BUFF FROM THE VROOMBOT TEAM HAVE CROSSED THE FINISH LINE FIRST. WITHOUT ANY SIDE-QUEST POINTS, THEY HAVE 6 POINTS, BRINGING THEIR GRAND GLAM PRIX RACE TOTAL TO 21 POINTS!

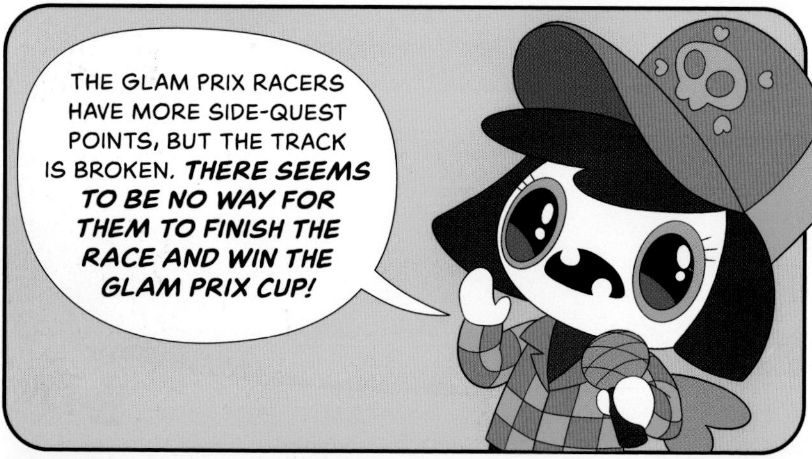
THE GLAM PRIX RACERS HAVE MORE SIDE-QUEST POINTS, BUT THE TRACK IS BROKEN. ***THERE SEEMS TO BE NO WAY FOR THEM TO FINISH THE RACE AND WIN THE GLAM PRIX CUP!***

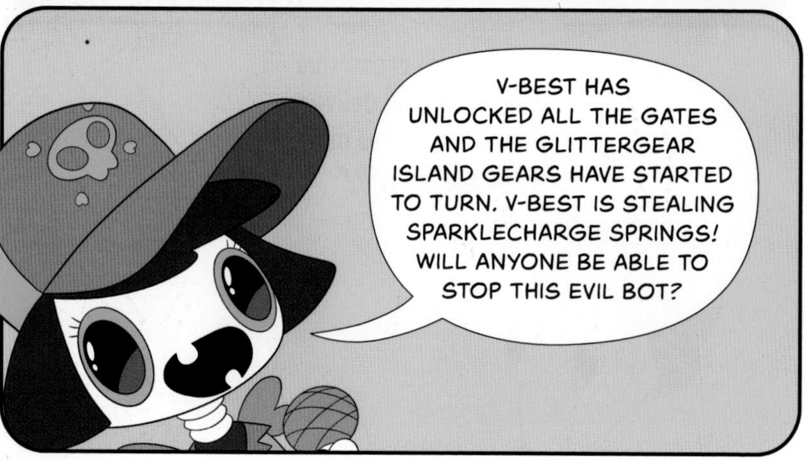
V-BEST HAS UNLOCKED ALL THE GATES AND THE GLITTERGEAR ISLAND GEARS HAVE STARTED TO TURN. V-BEST IS STEALING SPARKLECHARGE SPRINGS! WILL ANYONE BE ABLE TO STOP THIS EVIL BOT?

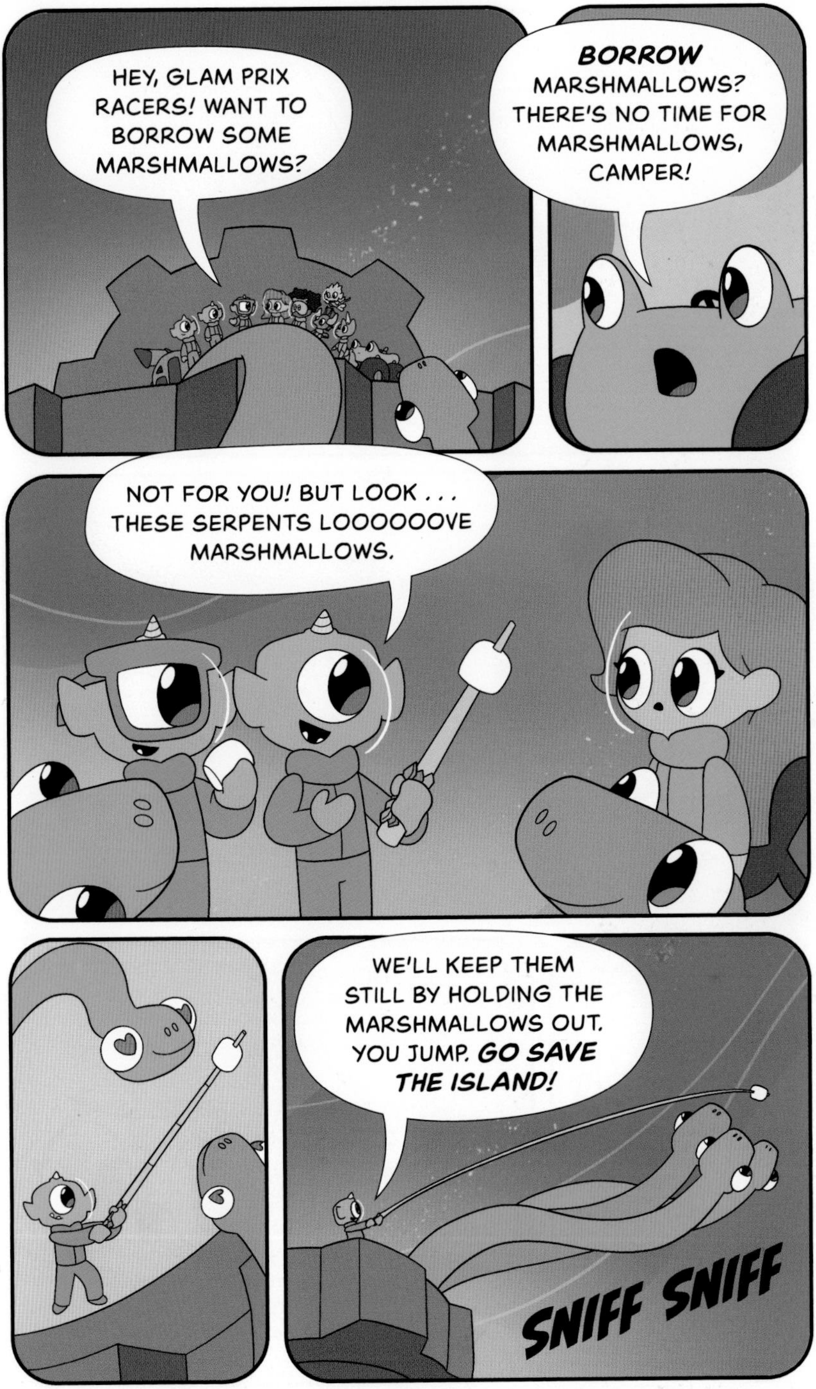
HEY, GLAM PRIX RACERS! WANT TO BORROW SOME MARSHMALLOWS?
BORROW MARSHMALLOWS? THERE'S NO TIME FOR MARSHMALLOWS, CAMPER!
NOT FOR YOU! BUT LOOK . . . THESE SERPENTS LOOOOOOVE MARSHMALLOWS.
WE'LL KEEP THEM STILL BY HOLDING THE MARSHMALLOWS OUT. YOU JUMP. *GO SAVE THE ISLAND!*
SNIFF SNIFF

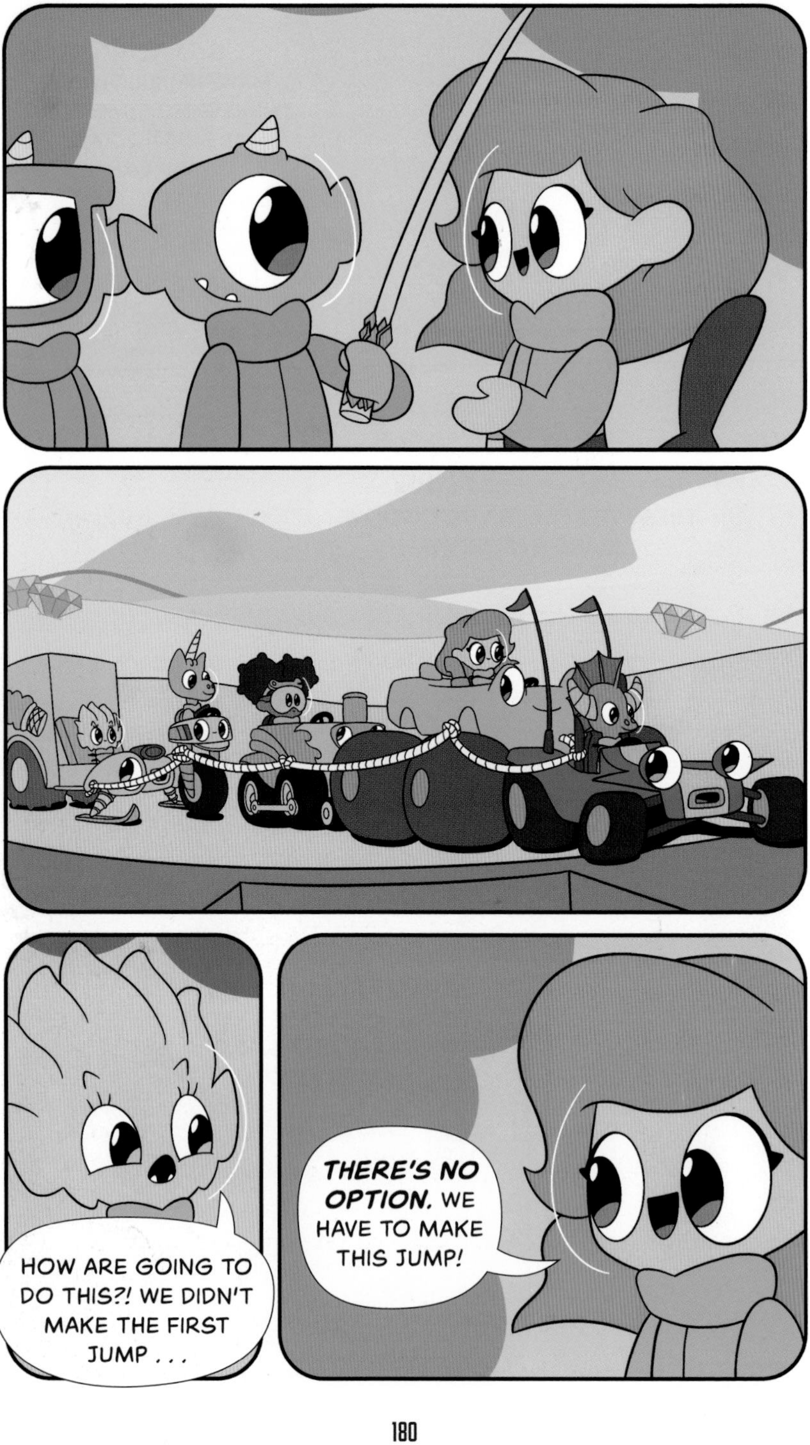
HOW ARE GOING TO DO THIS?! WE DIDN'T MAKE THE FIRST JUMP . . .
THERE'S NO OPTION. WE HAVE TO MAKE THIS JUMP!

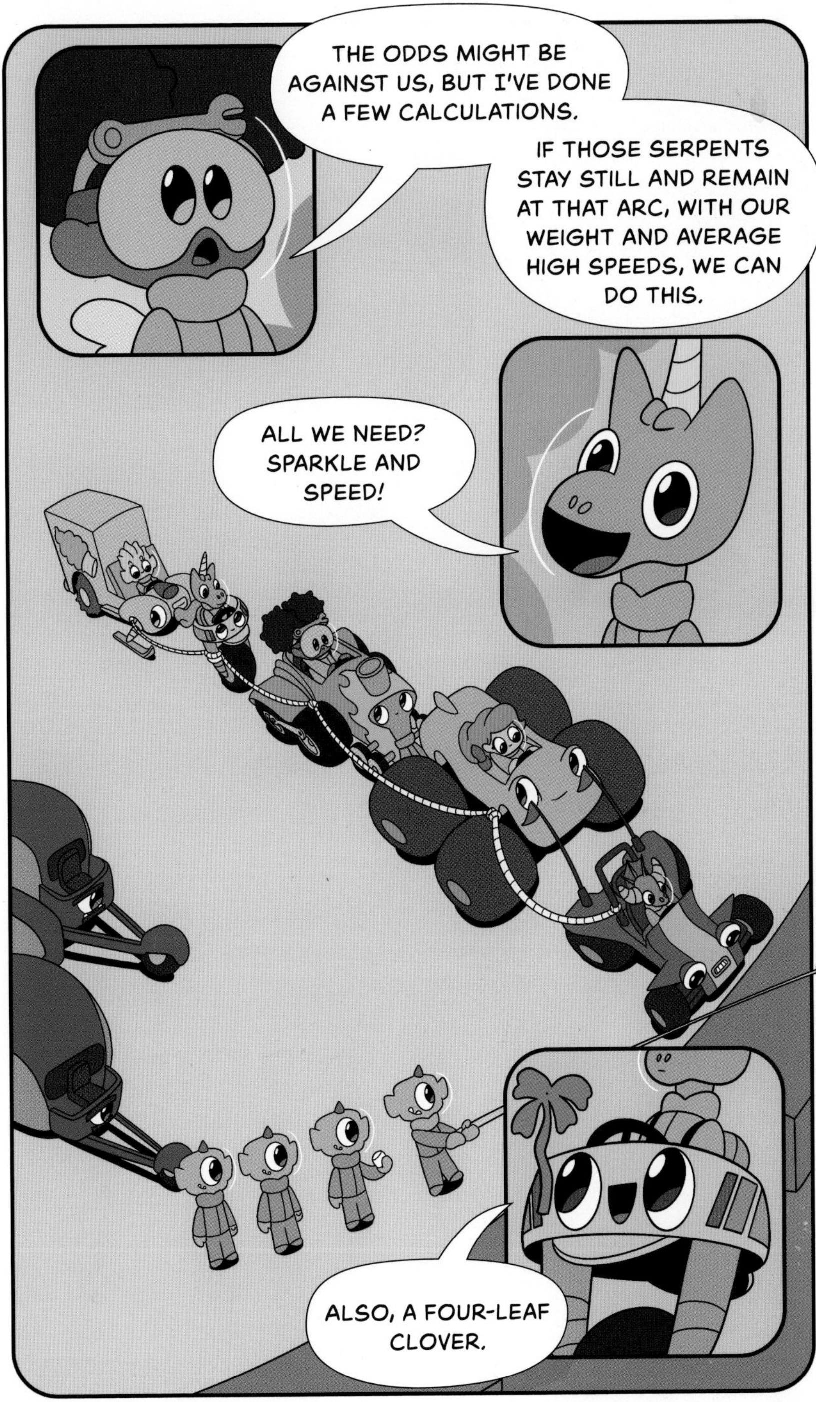
THE ODDS MIGHT BE AGAINST US, BUT I'VE DONE A FEW CALCULATIONS.
IF THOSE SERPENTS STAY STILL AND REMAIN AT THAT ARC, WITH OUR WEIGHT AND AVERAGE HIGH SPEEDS, WE CAN DO THIS.
ALL WE NEED? SPARKLE AND SPEED!
ALSO, A FOUR-LEAF CLOVER.

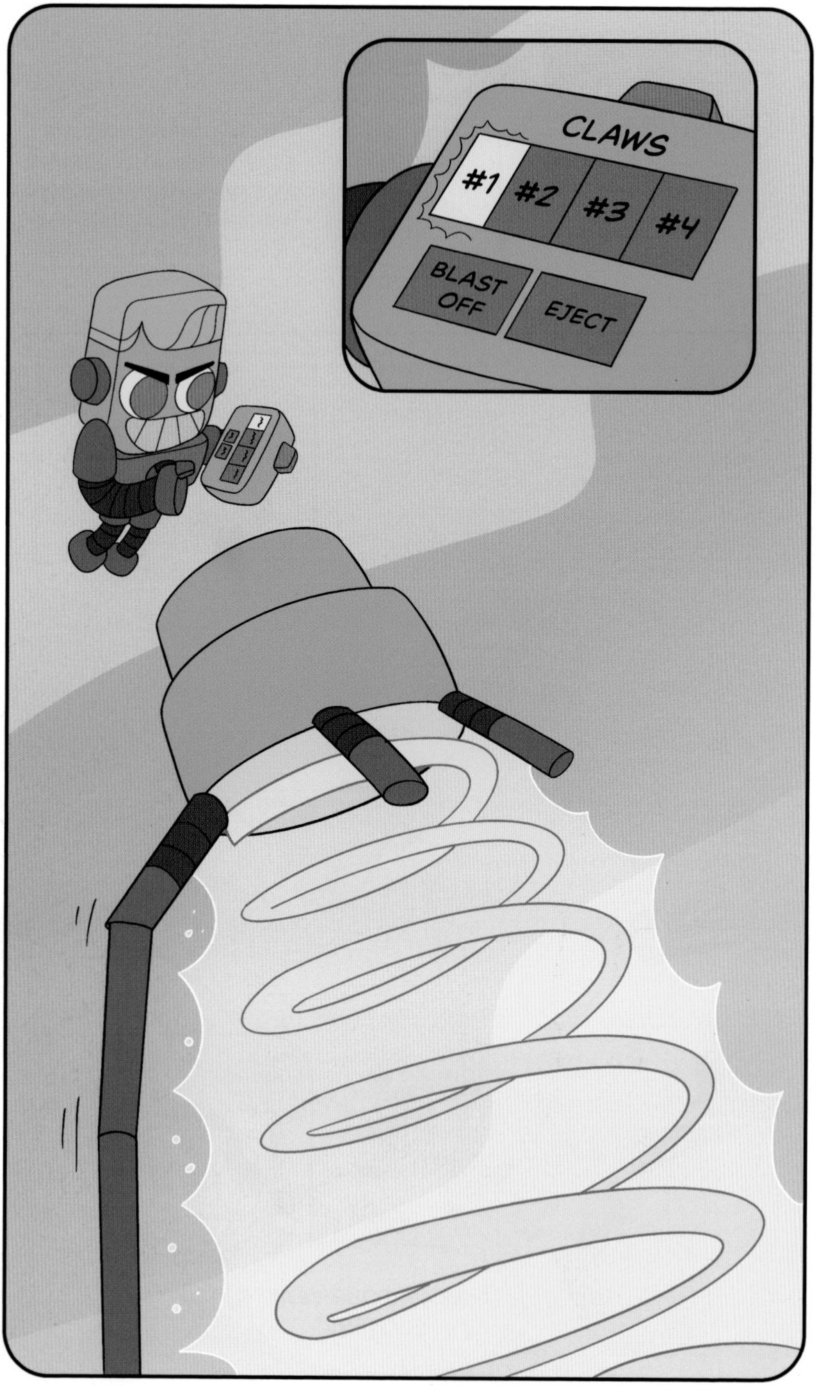
CLAWS
#1
#2
#3
#4
BLAST OFF
EJECT

CHAPTER 12:
BLAST OFF!

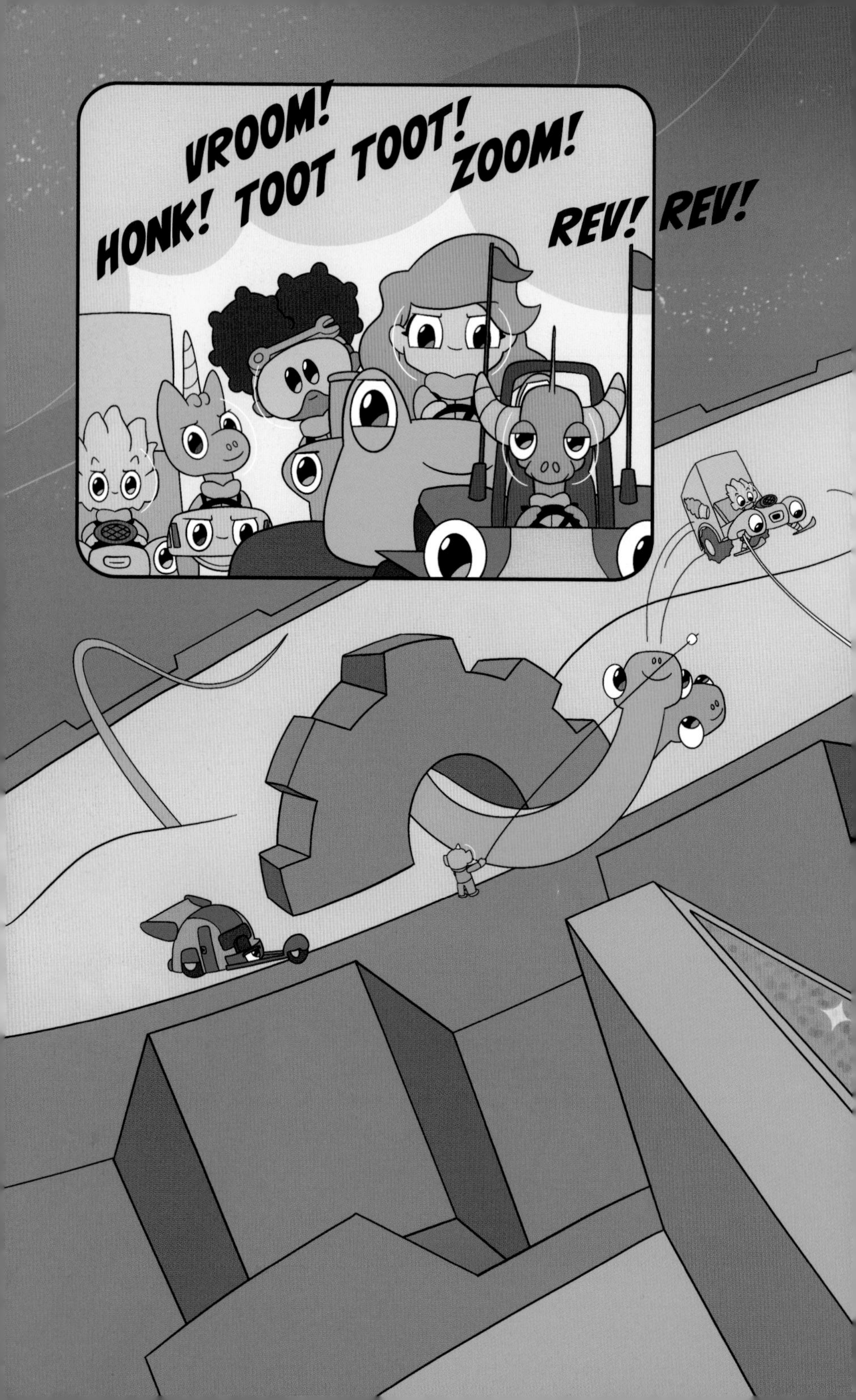
VROOM!
HONK! TOOT TOOT!
ZOOM!
REV! REV!

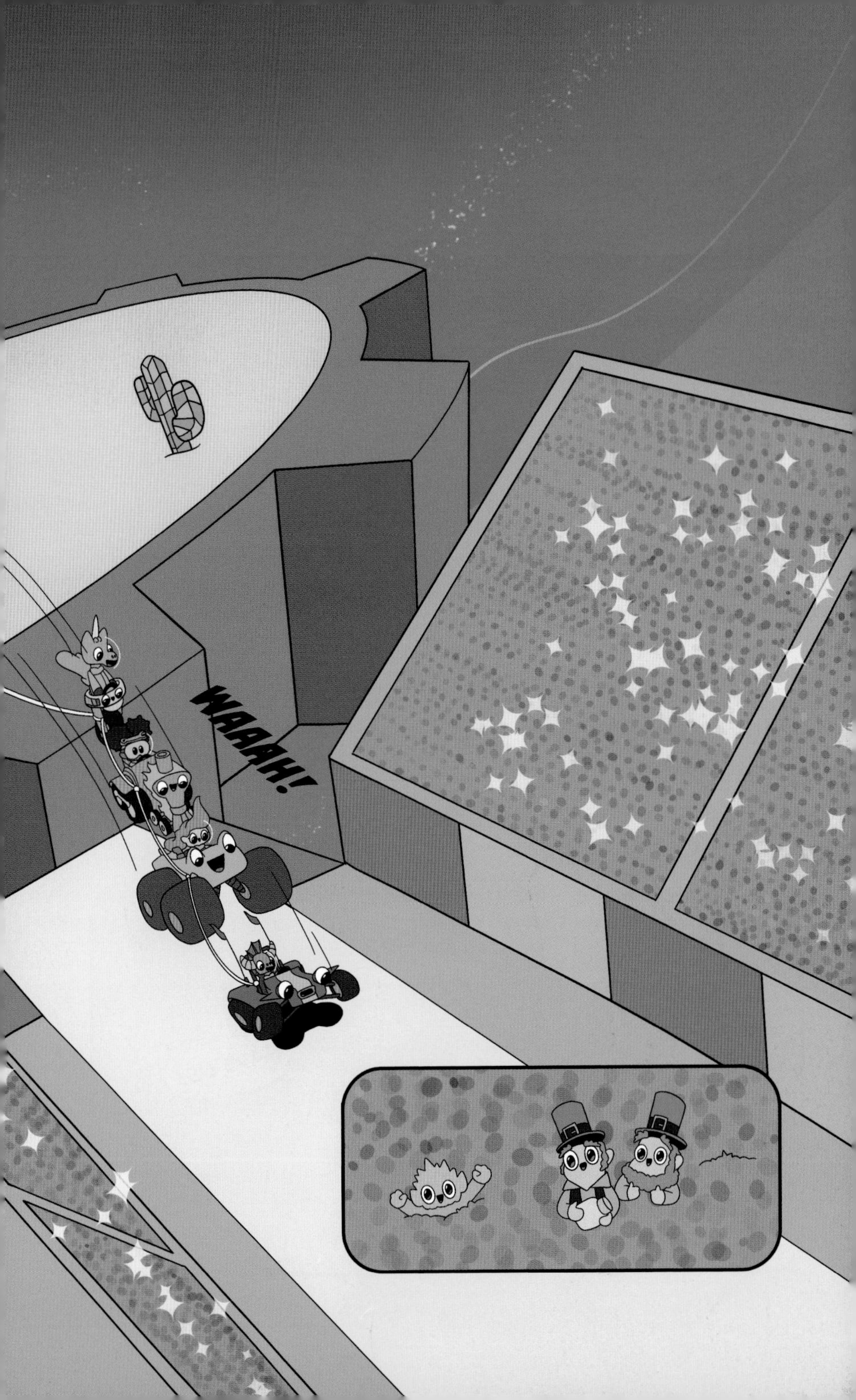
WAAAH!

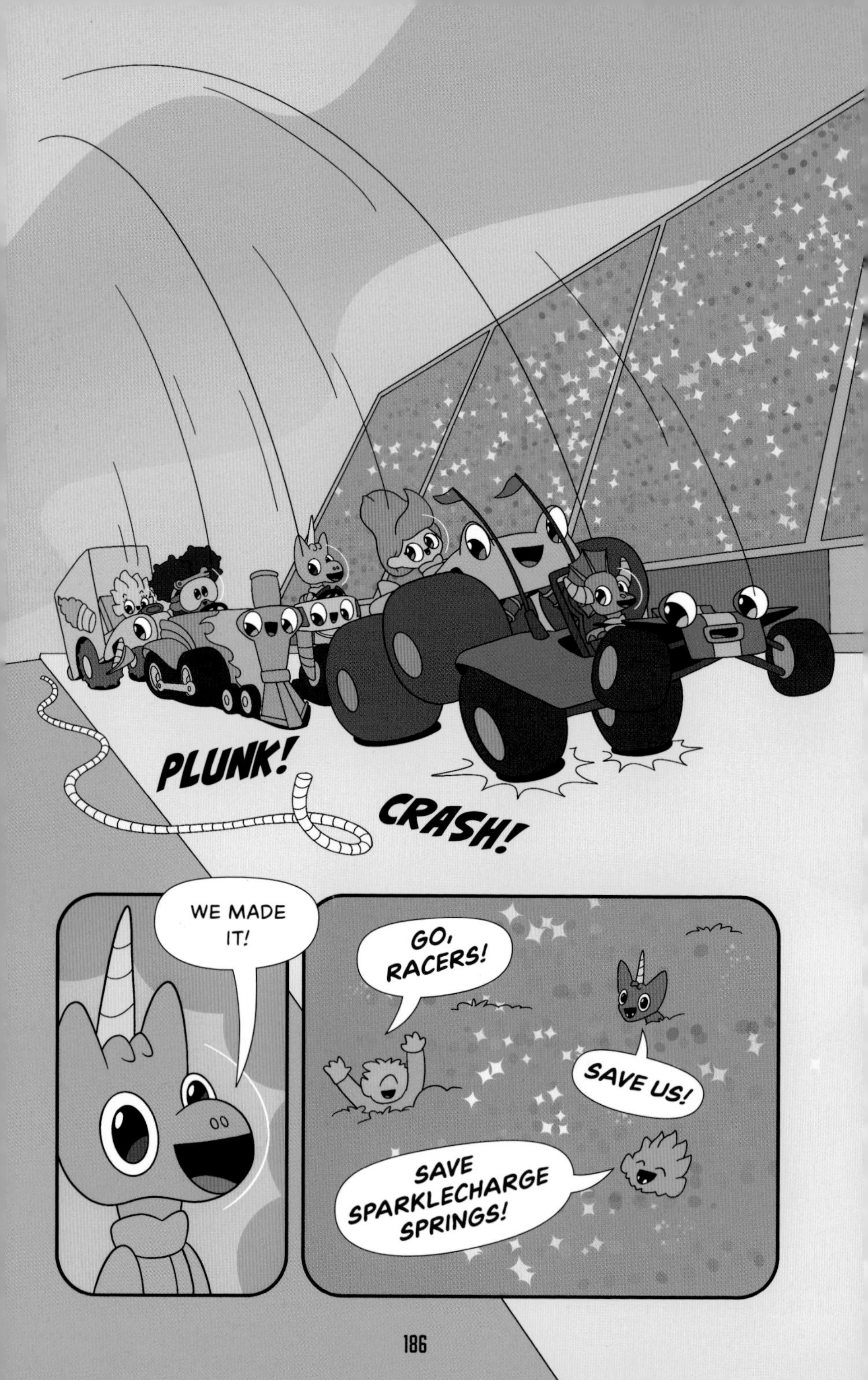
PLUNK!
CRASH!
WE MADE IT!
GO, RACERS!
SAVE US!
SAVE SPARKLECHARGE SPRINGS!

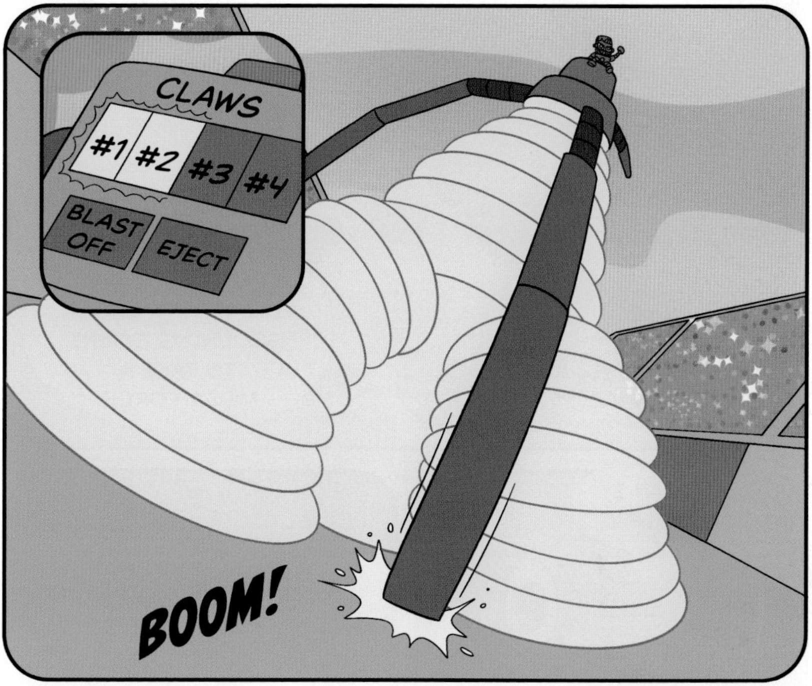
CLAWS
#1
#2
#3
#4
BLAST OFF
EJECT
BOOM!

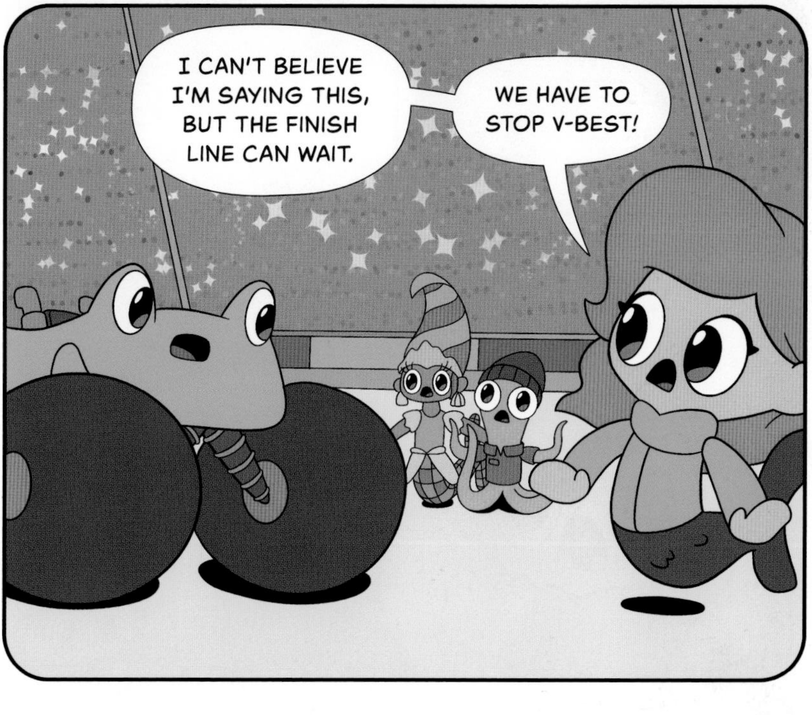
I CAN'T BELIEVE I'M SAYING THIS, BUT THE FINISH LINE CAN WAIT.
WE HAVE TO STOP V-BEST!

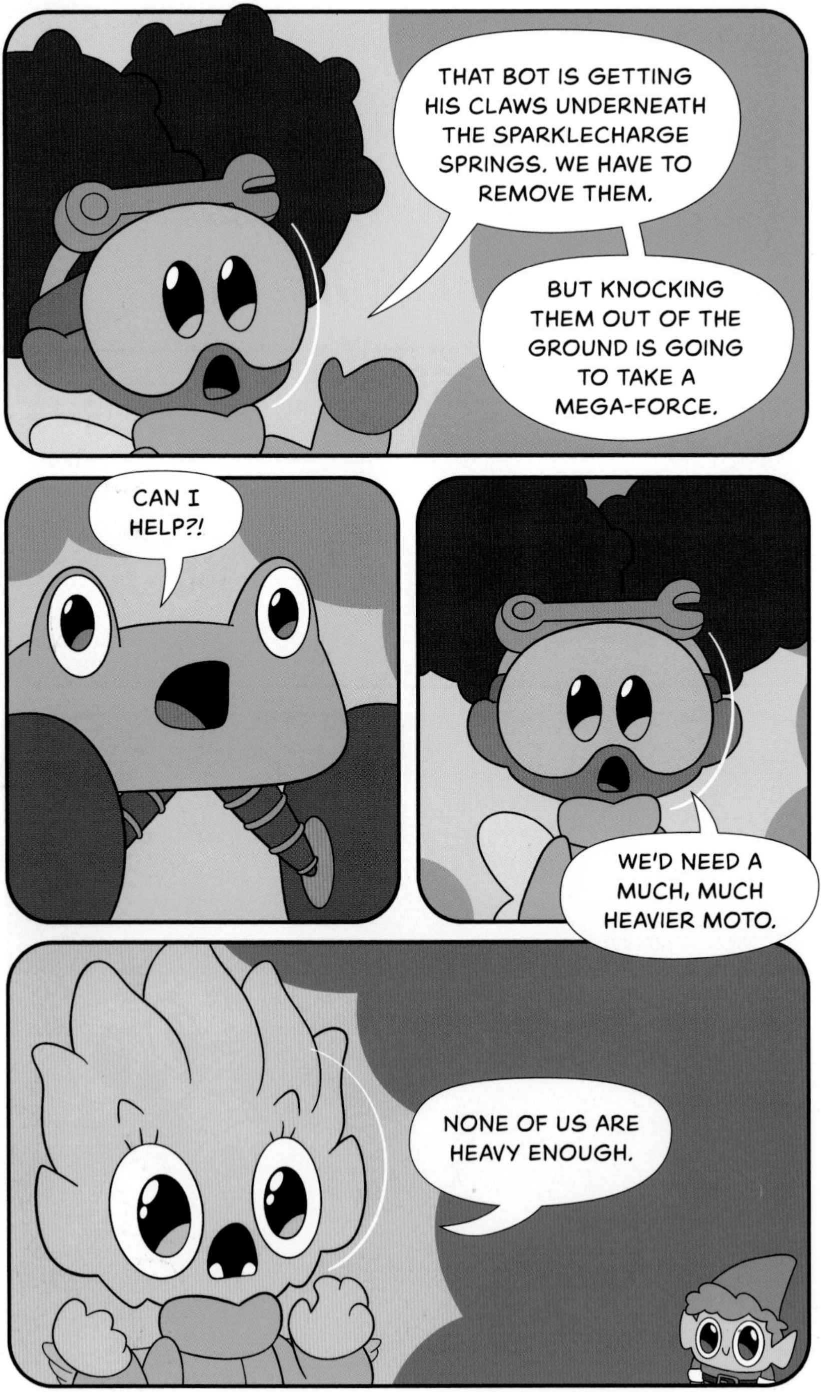
THAT BOT IS GETTING HIS CLAWS UNDERNEATH THE SPARKLECHARGE SPRINGS. WE HAVE TO REMOVE THEM.
BUT KNOCKING THEM OUT OF THE GROUND IS GOING TO TAKE A MEGA-FORCE.
CAN I HELP?!
WE'D NEED A MUCH, MUCH HEAVIER MOTO.
NONE OF US ARE HEAVY ENOUGH.

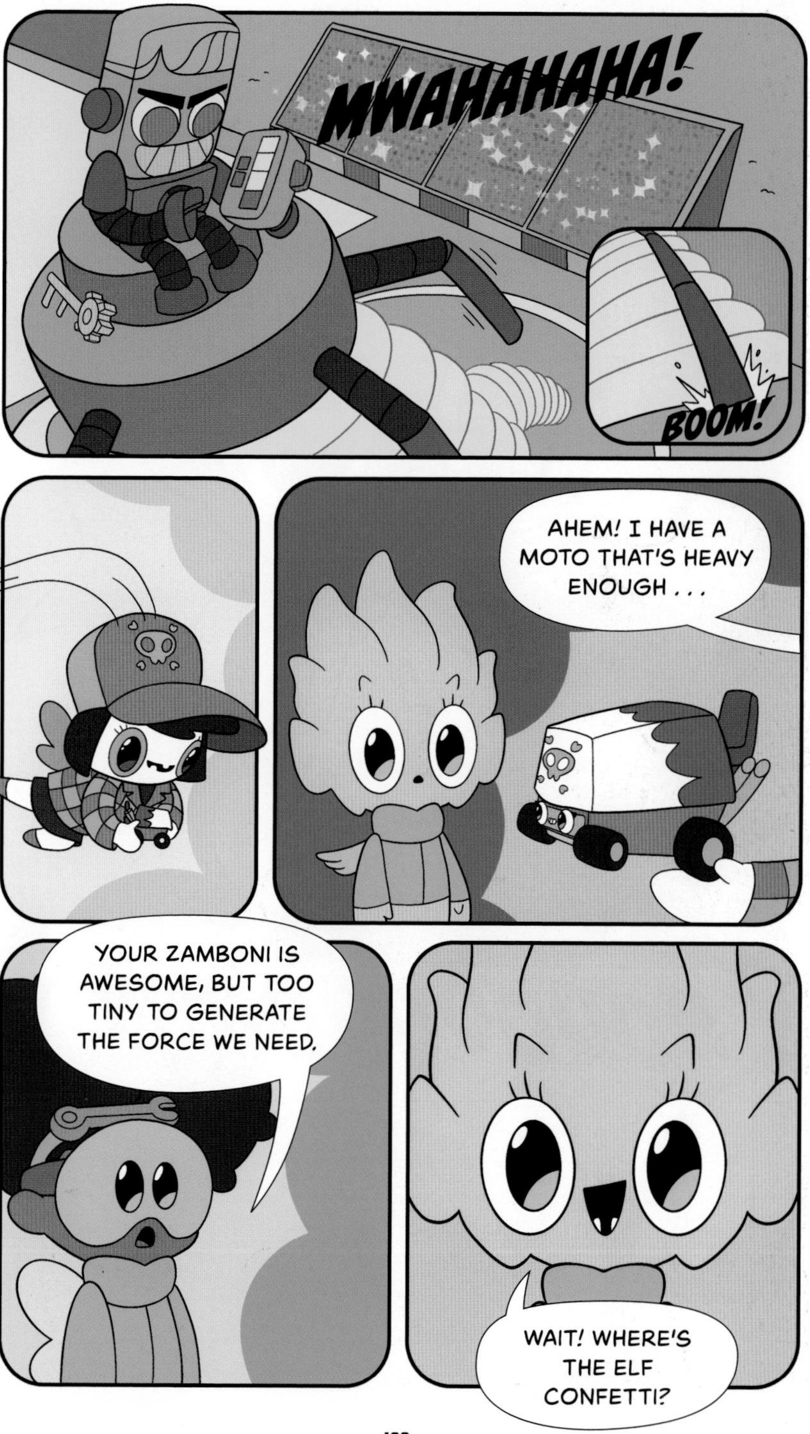
MWAHAHAHA!
BOOM!
AHEM! I HAVE A MOTO THAT'S HEAVY ENOUGH . . .
YOUR ZAMBONI IS AWESOME, BUT TOO TINY TO GENERATE THE FORCE WE NEED.
WAIT! WHERE'S THE ELF CONFETTI?

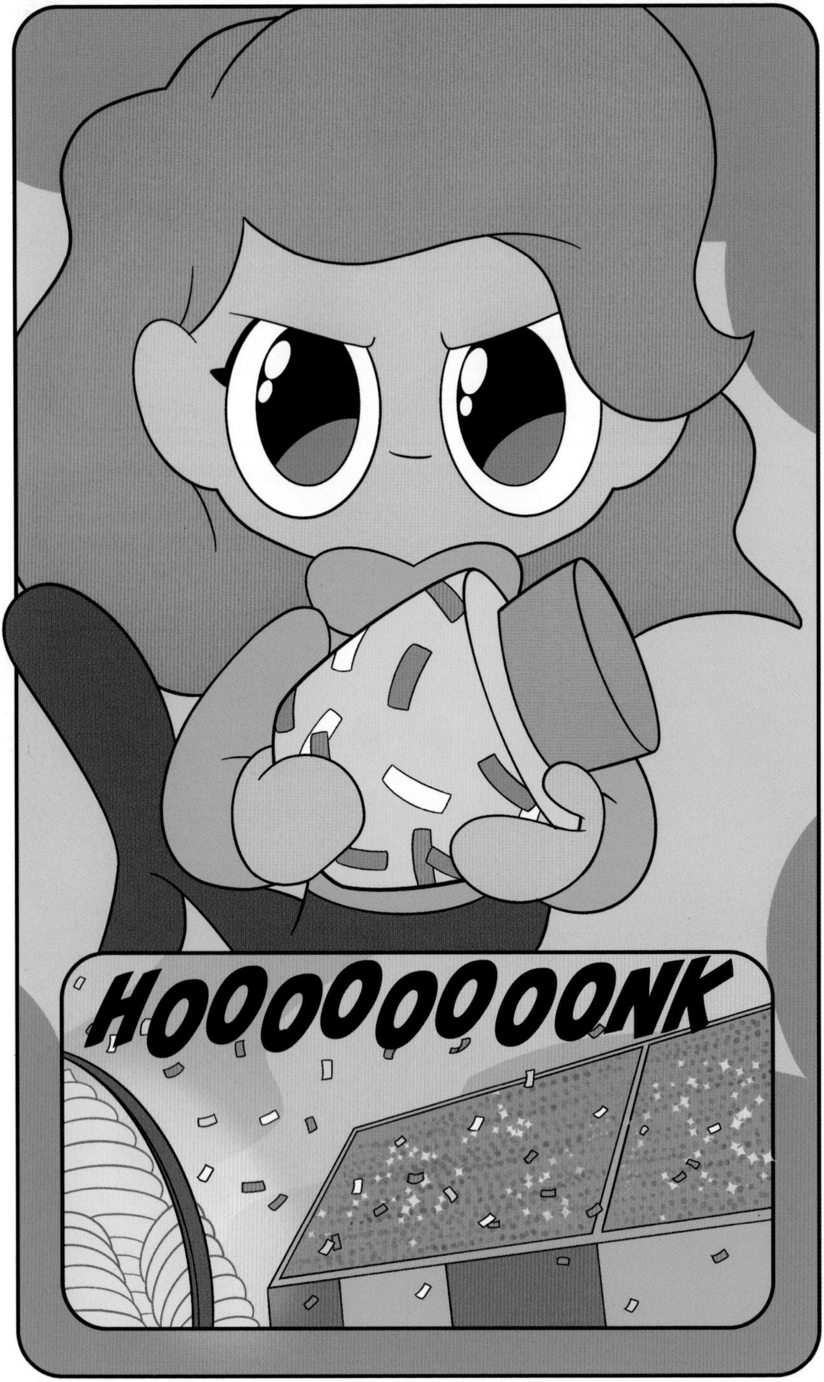
HOOOOOOOONK

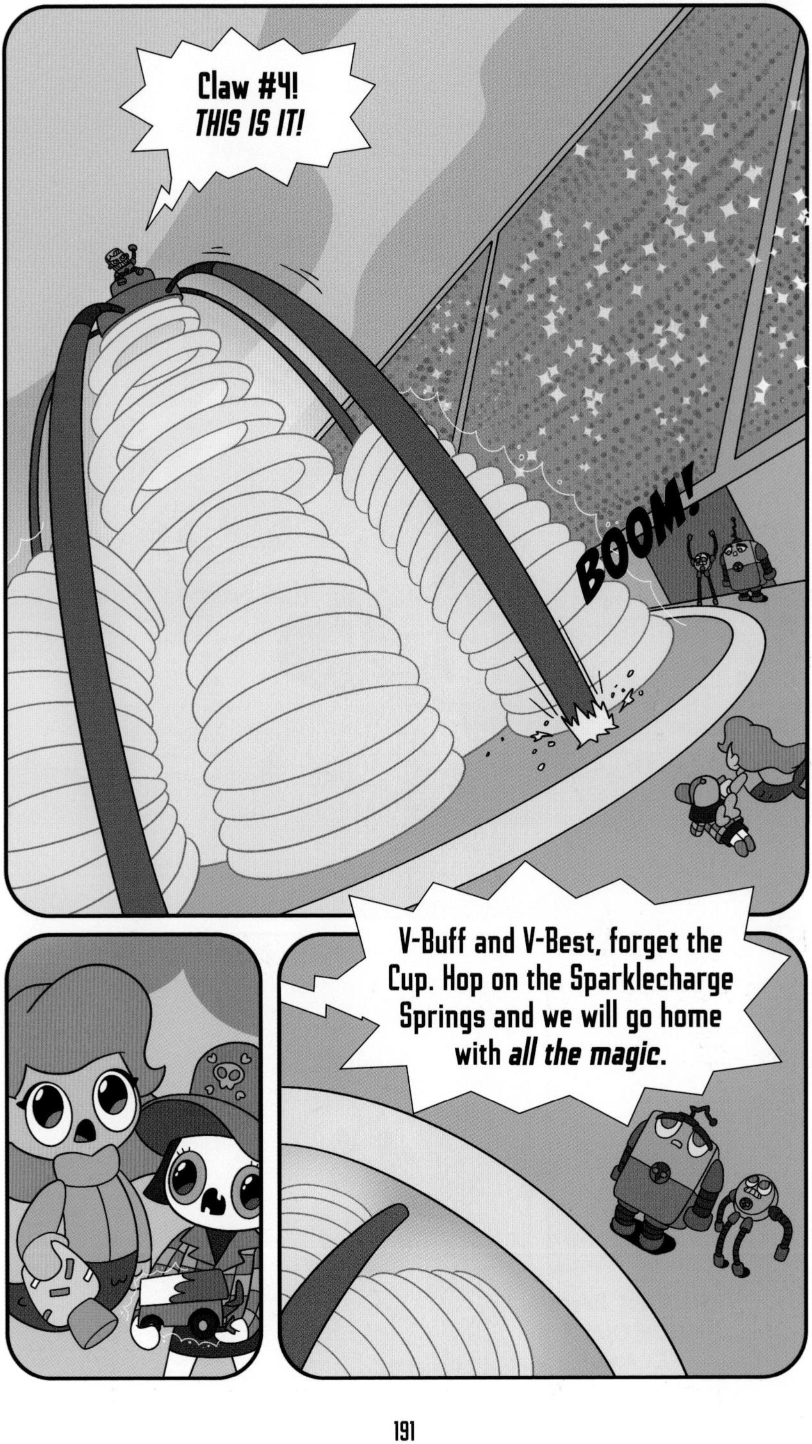
Claw #4!
THIS IS IT!
BOOM!
V-Buff and V-Best, forget the Cup. Hop on the Sparklecharge Springs and we will go home with all the magic.

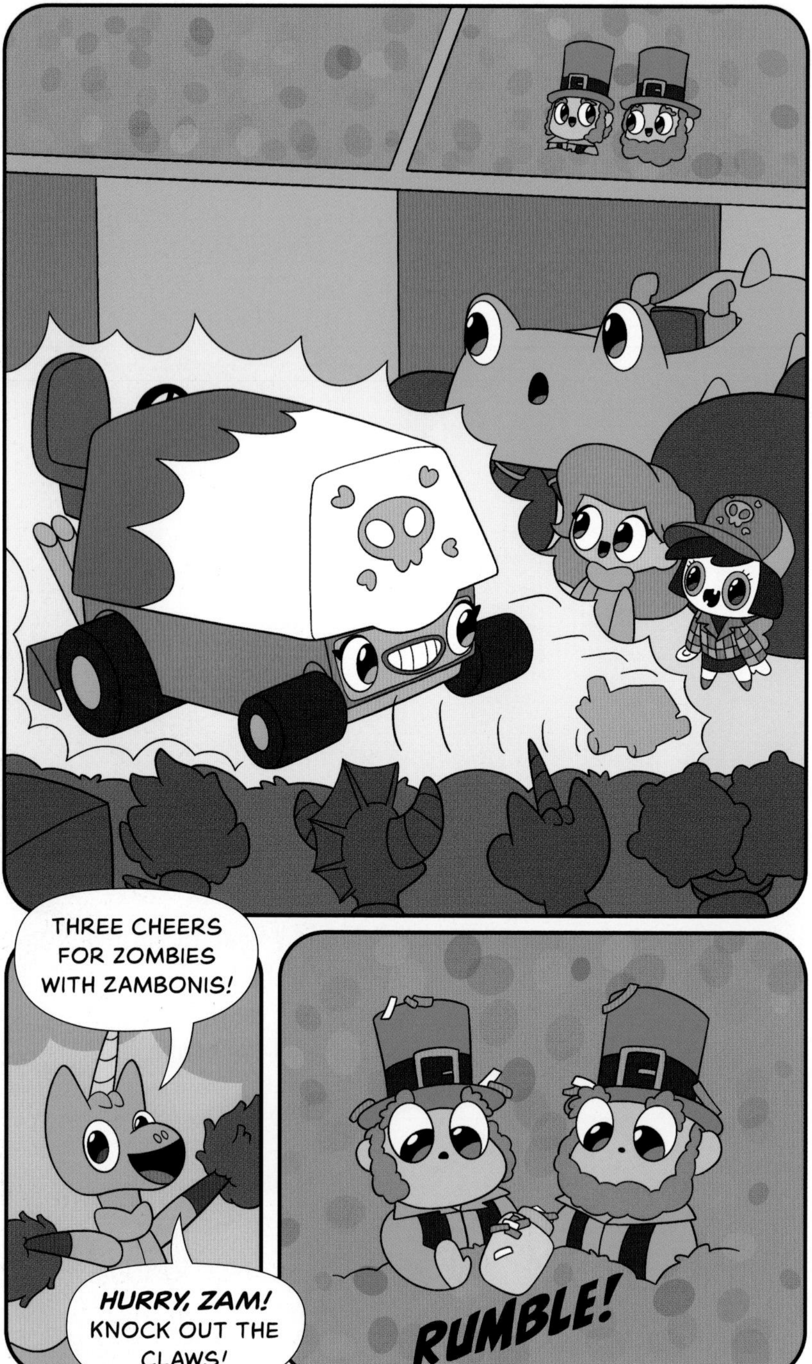
THREE CHEERS FOR ZOMBIES WITH ZAMBONIS!
HURRY, ZAM! KNOCK OUT THE CLAWS!
RUMBLE!

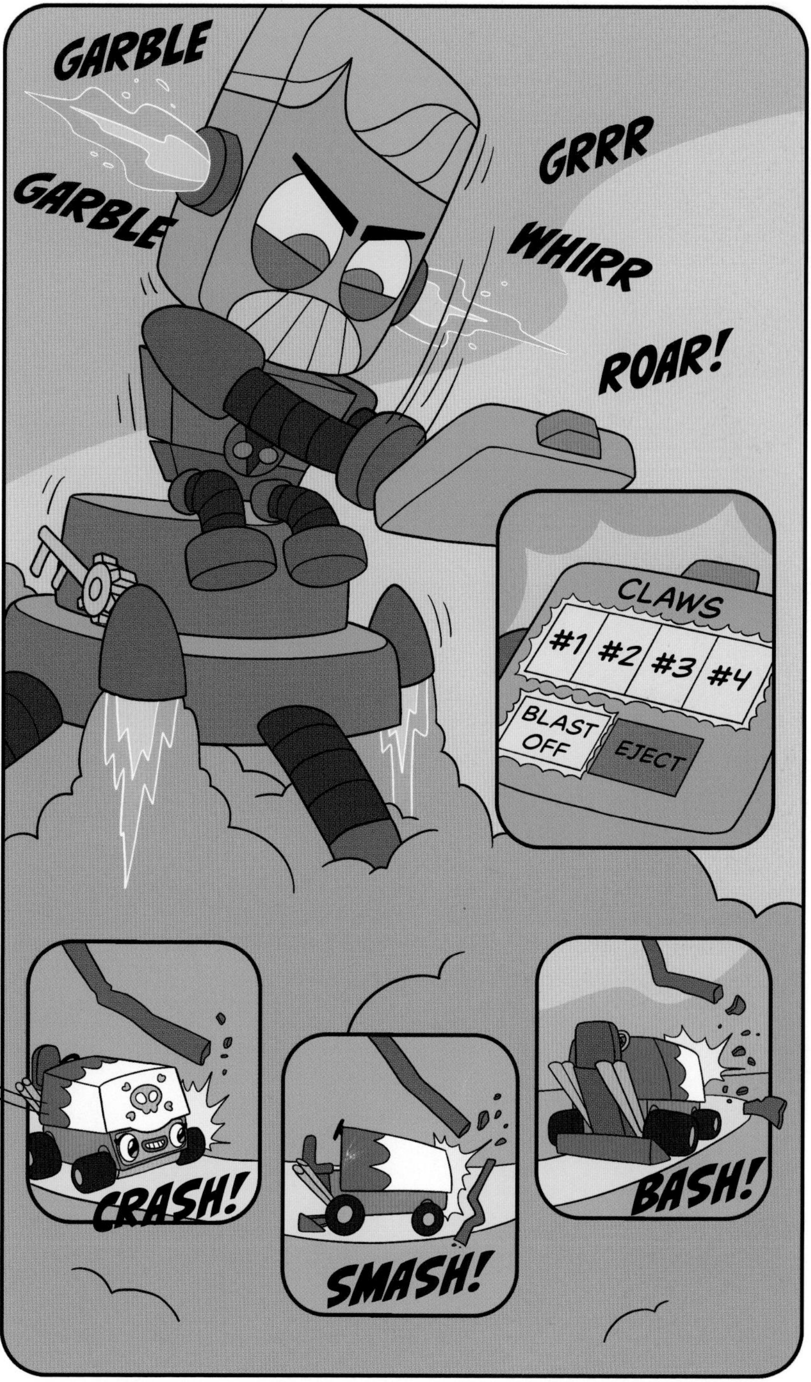
GARBLE
GARBLE
GRRR
WHIRR
ROAR!
CLAWS
#1
#2
#3
#4
BLAST OFF
EJECT
CRASH!
SMASH!
BASH!

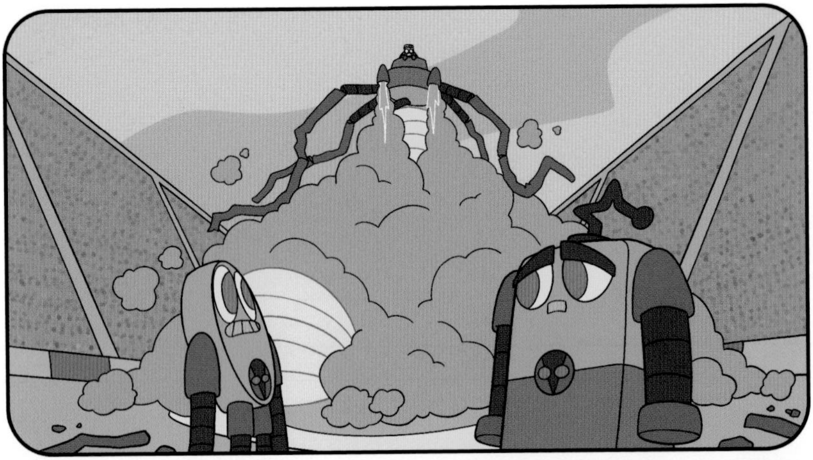

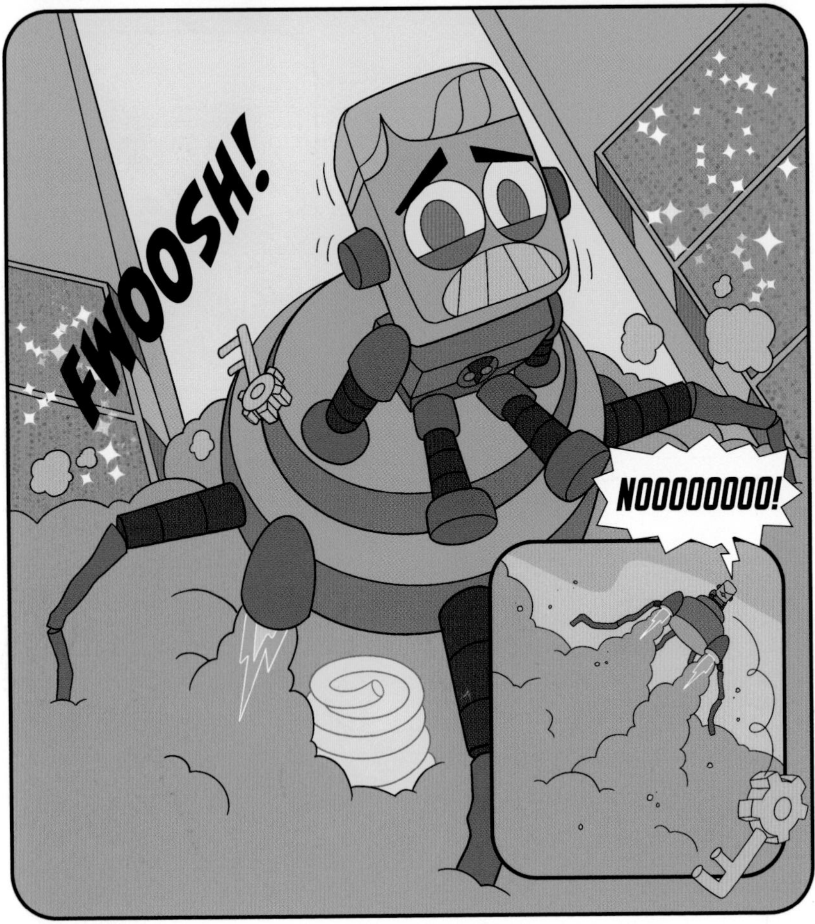
FWOOSH!
NOOOOOOOO!

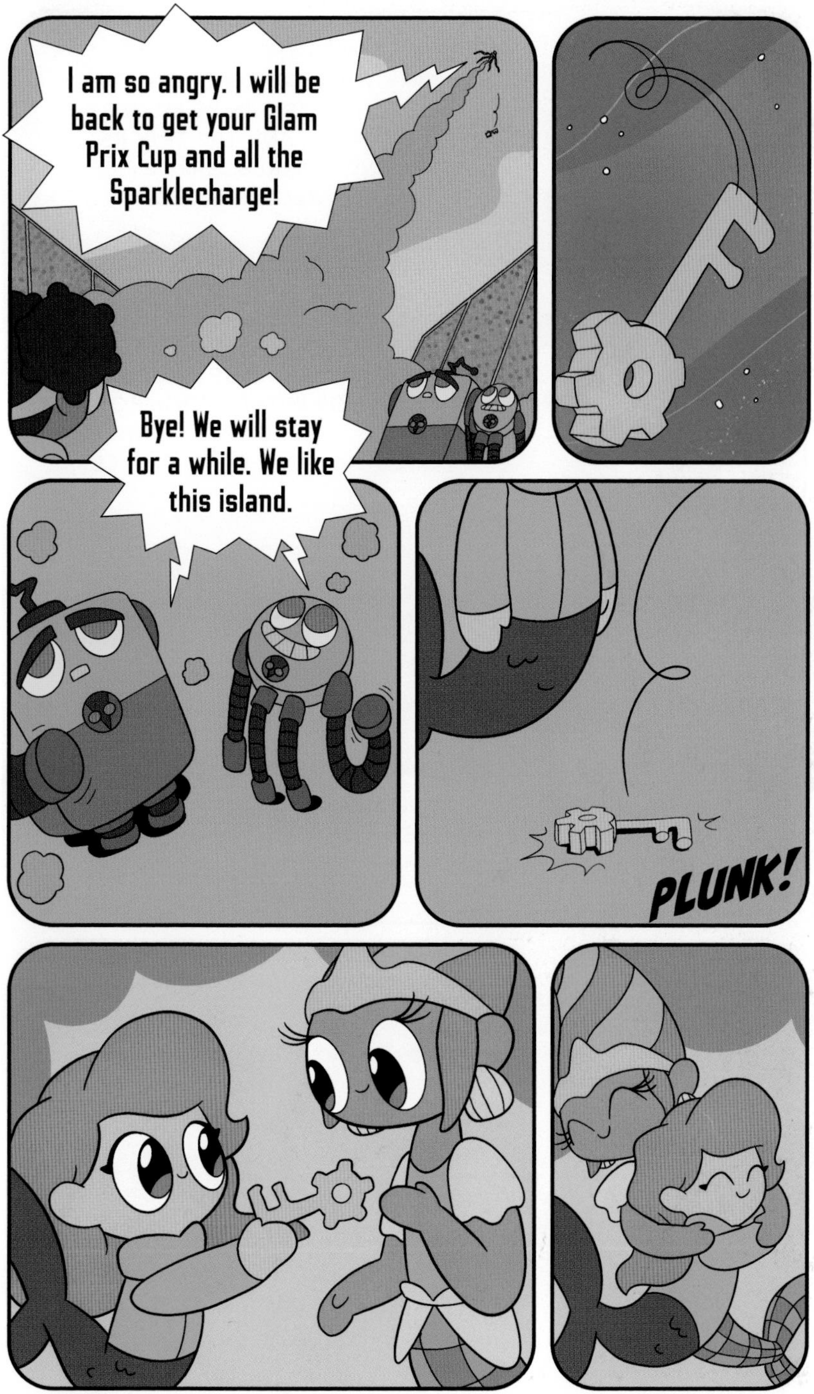
I am so angry. I will be back to get your Glam Prix Cup and all the Sparklecharge!
Bye! We will stay for a while. We like this island.
PLUNK!

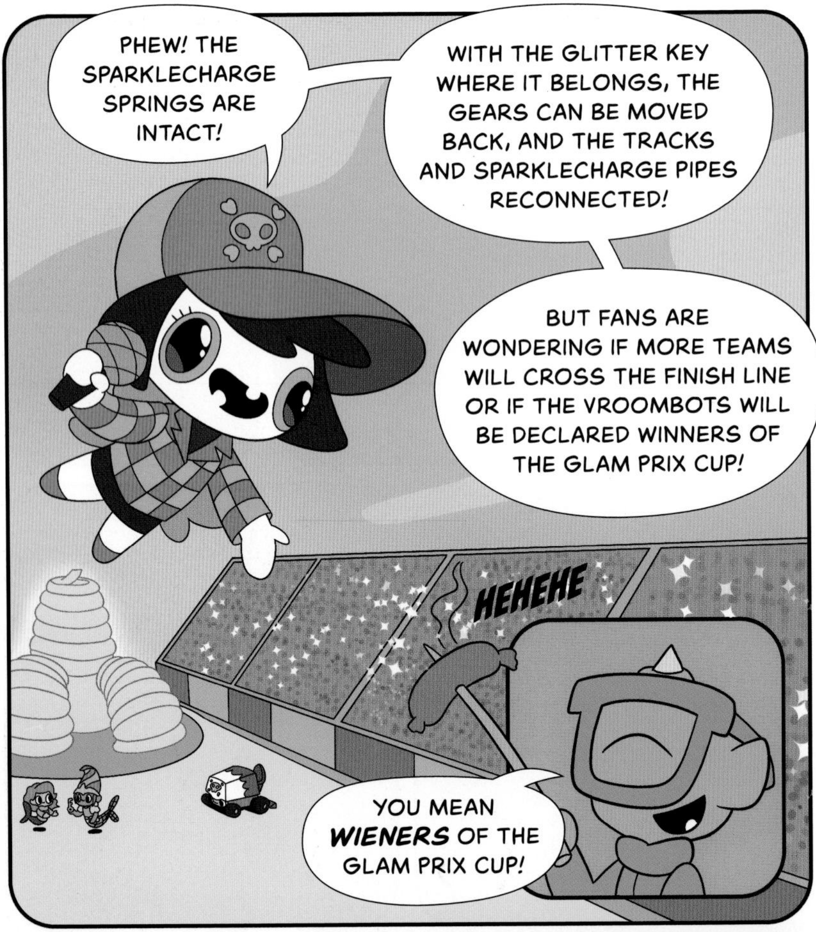
PHEW! THE SPARKLECHARGE SPRINGS ARE INTACT!
WITH THE GLITTER KEY WHERE IT BELONGS, THE GEARS CAN BE MOVED BACK, AND THE TRACKS AND SPARKLECHARGE PIPES RECONNECTED!
BUT FANS ARE WONDERING IF MORE TEAMS WILL CROSS THE FINISH LINE OR IF THE VROOMBOTS WILL BE DECLARED WINNERS OF THE GLAM PRIX CUP!
HEHEHE
YOU MEAN **WIENERS** OF THE GLAM PRIX CUP!

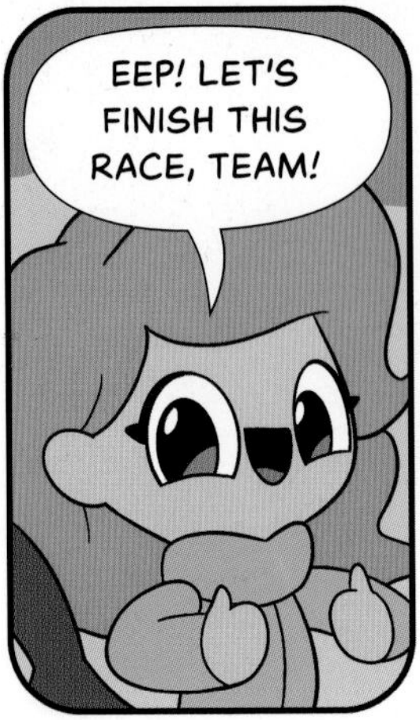
EEP! LET'S FINISH THIS RACE, TEAM!

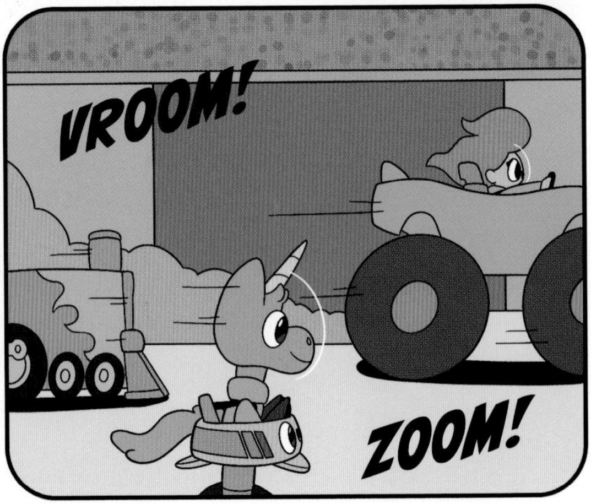
VROOM!
ZOOM!

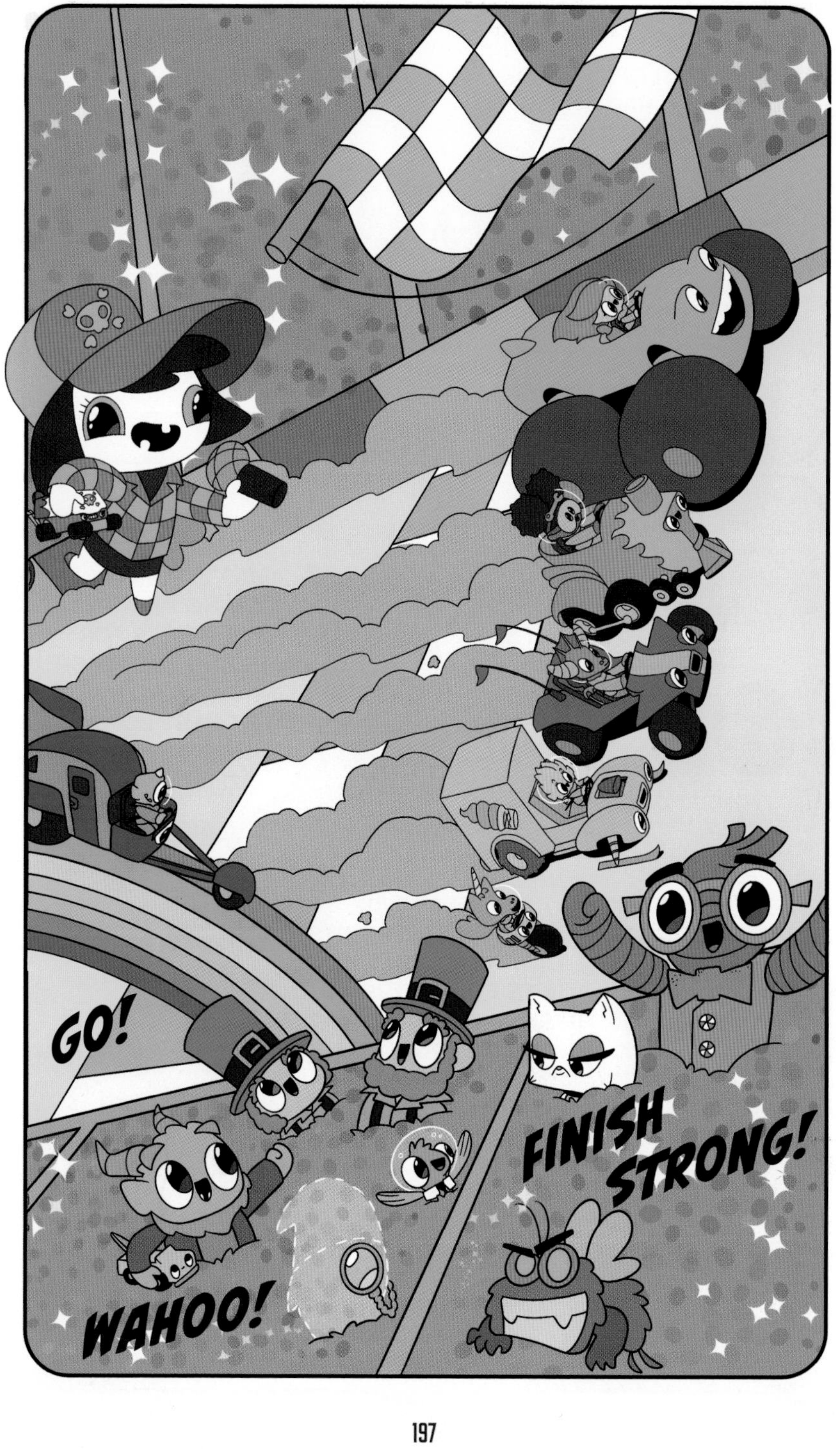
GO!
WAHOO!
FINISH STRONG!

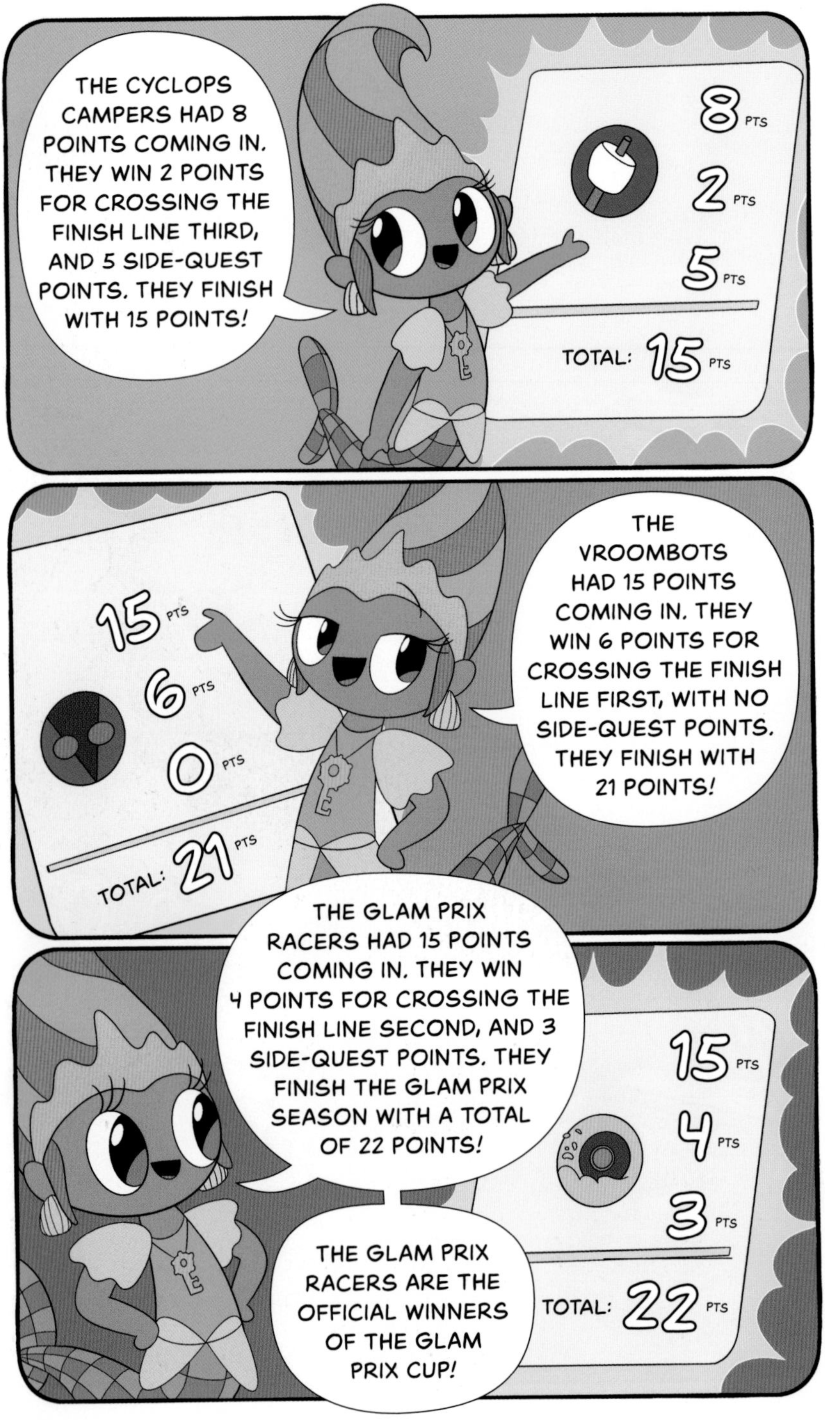
THE CYCLOPS CAMPERS HAD 8 POINTS COMING IN. THEY WIN 2 POINTS FOR CROSSING THE FINISH LINE THIRD, AND 5 SIDE-QUEST POINTS. THEY FINISH WITH 15 POINTS!
8 PTS
2 PTS
5 PTS
TOTAL: 15 PTS
THE VROOMBOTS HAD 15 POINTS COMING IN. THEY WIN 6 POINTS FOR CROSSING THE FINISH LINE FIRST, WITH NO SIDE-QUEST POINTS. THEY FINISH WITH 21 POINTS!
15 PTS
6 PTS
0 PTS
TOTAL: 21 PTS
THE GLAM PRIX RACERS HAD 15 POINTS COMING IN. THEY WIN 4 POINTS FOR CROSSING THE FINISH LINE SECOND, AND 3 SIDE-QUEST POINTS. THEY FINISH THE GLAM PRIX SEASON WITH A TOTAL OF 22 POINTS!
THE GLAM PRIX RACERS ARE THE OFFICIAL WINNERS OF THE GLAM PRIX CUP!
15 PTS
4 PTS
3 PTS
TOTAL: 22 PTS

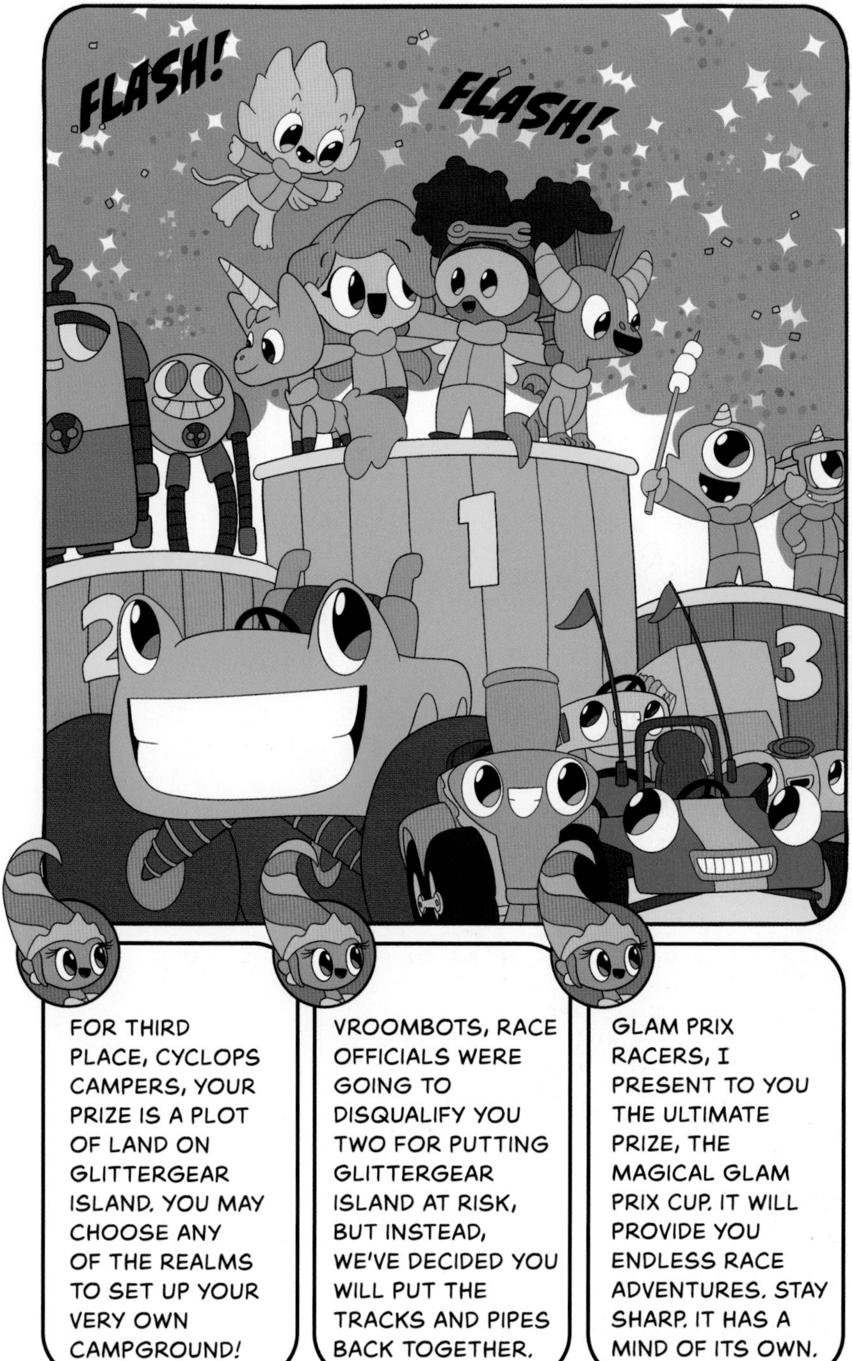
FLASH!
FLASH!
1
2
3
FOR THIRD PLACE, CYCLOPS CAMPERS, YOUR PRIZE IS A PLOT OF LAND ON GLITTERGEAR ISLAND. YOU MAY CHOOSE ANY OF THE REALMS TO SET UP YOUR VERY OWN CAMPGROUND!
VROOMBOTS, RACE OFFICIALS WERE GOING TO DISQUALIFY YOU TWO FOR PUTTING GLITTERGEAR ISLAND AT RISK, BUT INSTEAD, WE'VE DECIDED YOU WILL PUT THE TRACKS AND PIPES BACK TOGETHER.
GLAM PRIX RACERS, I PRESENT TO YOU THE ULTIMATE PRIZE, THE MAGICAL GLAM PRIX CUP. IT WILL PROVIDE YOU ENDLESS RACE ADVENTURES. STAY SHARP. IT HAS A MIND OF ITS OWN.

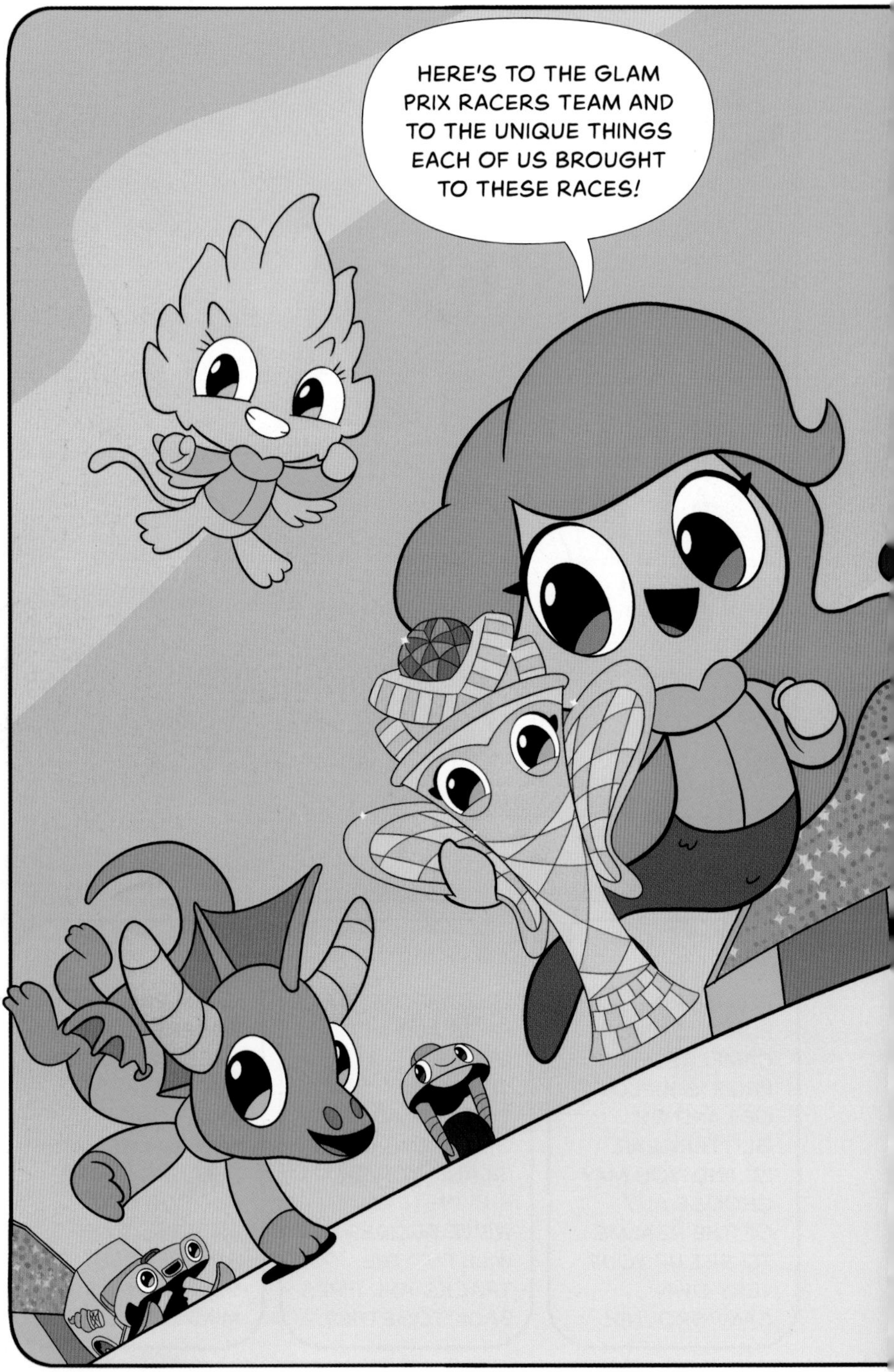
HERE'S TO THE GLAM PRIX RACERS TEAM AND TO THE UNIQUE THINGS EACH OF US BROUGHT TO THESE RACES!

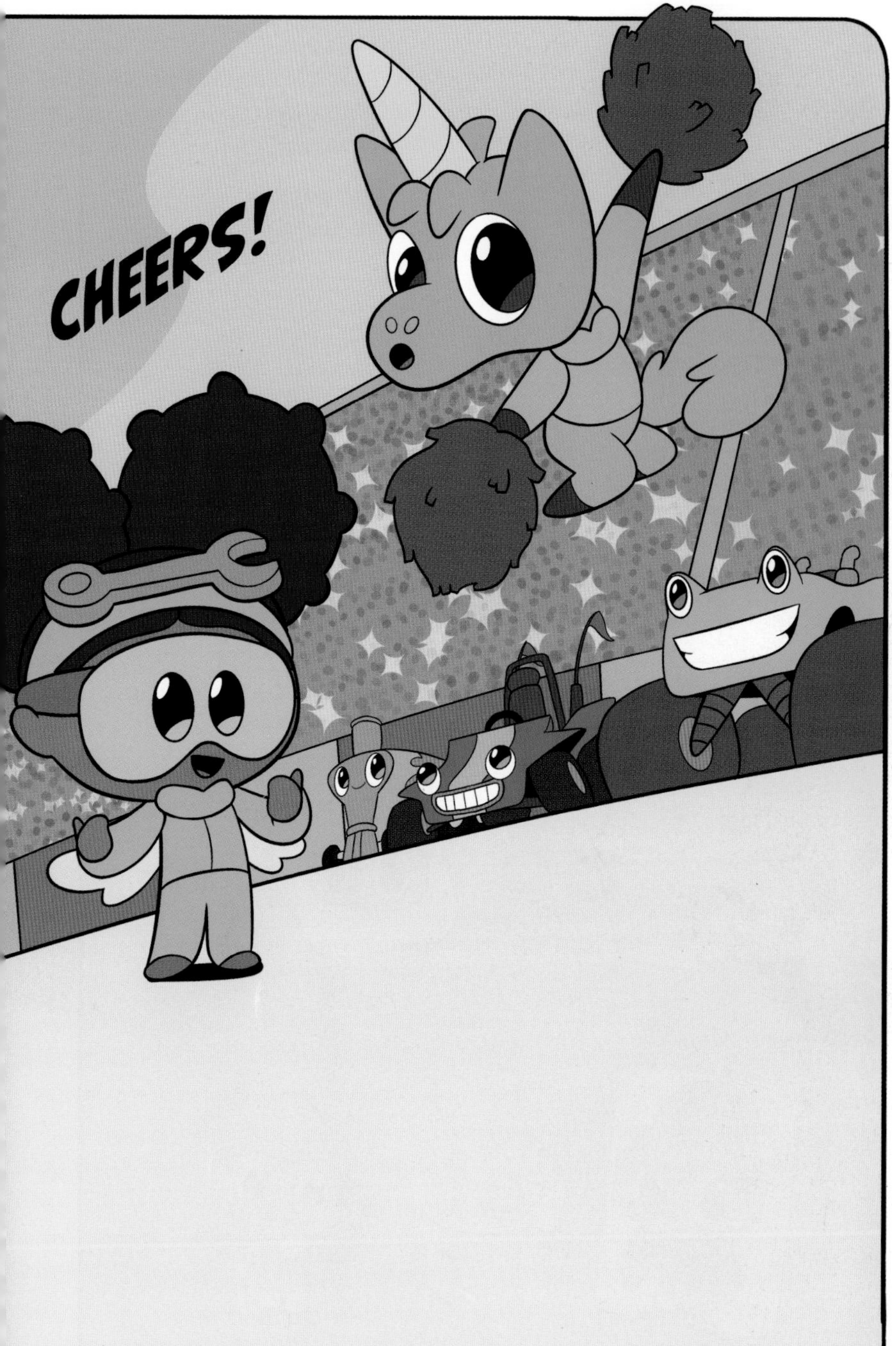
CHEERS!

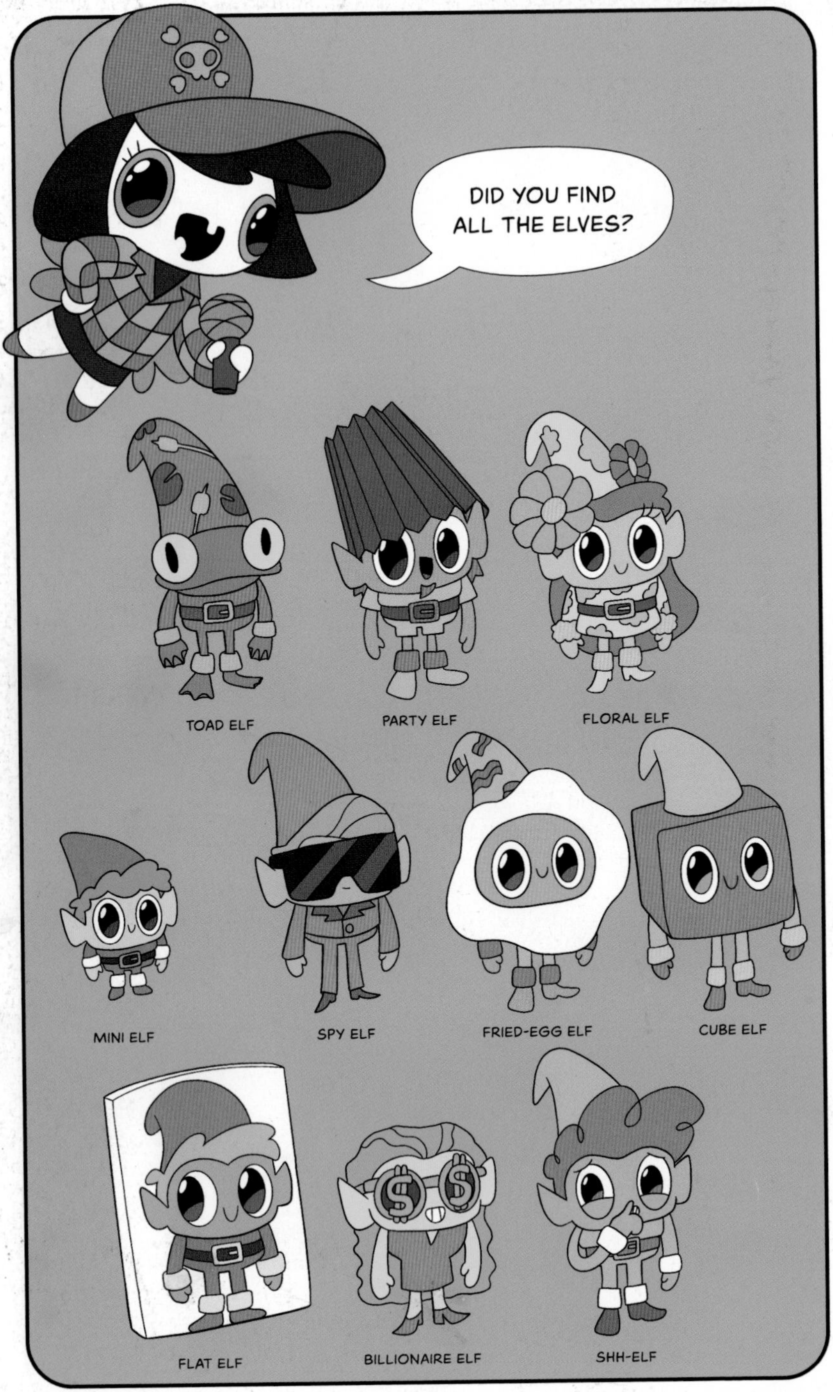
DID YOU FIND ALL THE ELVES?
TOAD ELF
PARTY ELF
FLORAL ELF
MINI ELF
SPY ELF
FRIED-EGG ELF
CUBE ELF
FLAT ELF
BILLIONAIRE ELF
SHH-ELF

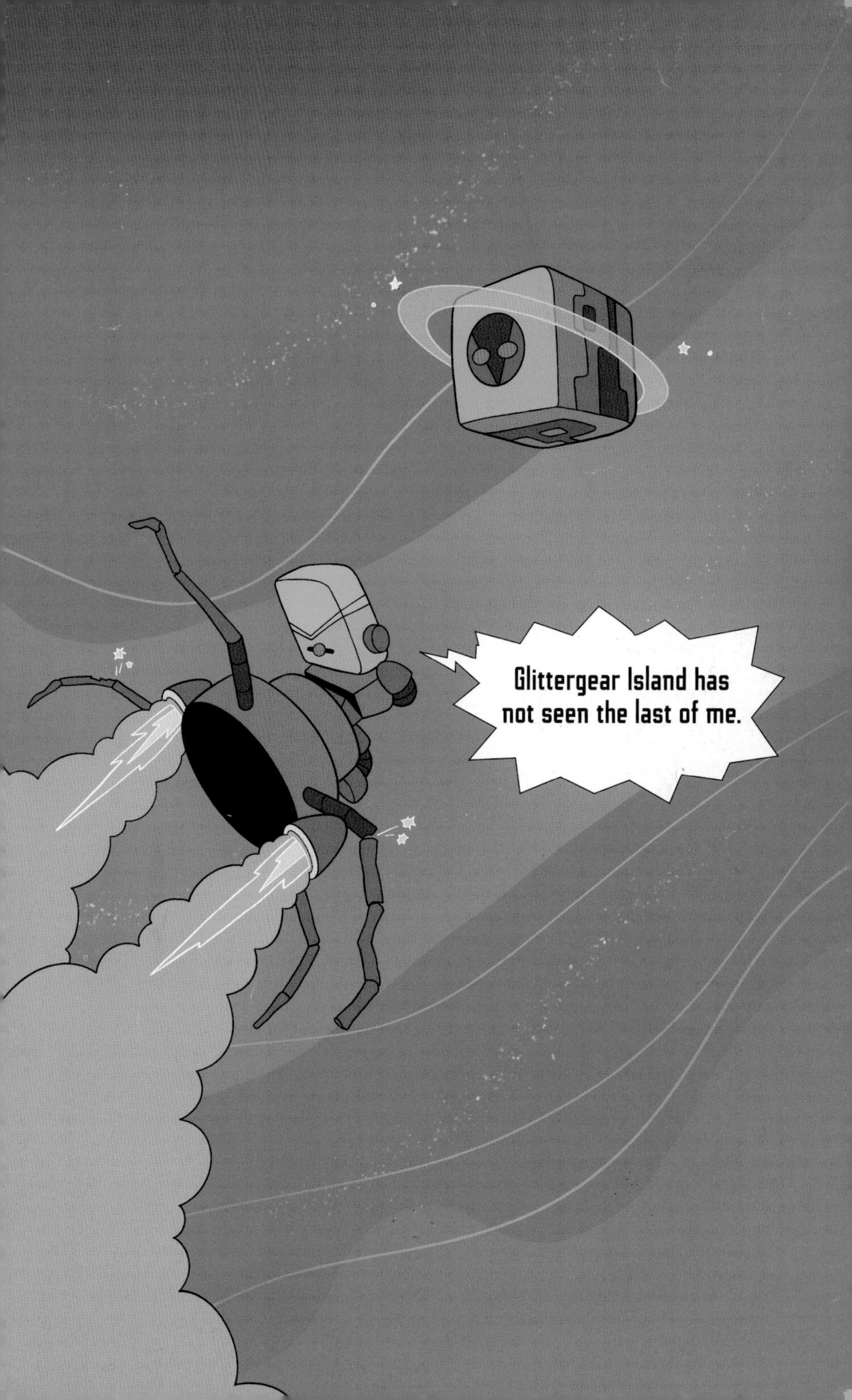
Glittergear Island has not seen the last of me.

ACKNOWLEDGMENTS

GRAPHIC NOVELS ARE A LOT OF WORK. WHEN WE EMBARKED ON THIS SERIES, WE KNEW WE HAD ***SO MUCH TO LEARN,*** AND WE WANT TO ACKNOWLEDGE AND GIVE GRATITUDE TO ALL THE TALENTED PEOPLE WHO HELPED US BUILD AND BRING THESE BOOKS TO LIFE. GLITTERY THANKS TO GEMMA COOPER, OUR AGENT EXTRAORDINAIRE, AND THE INCREDIBLE IMPRINT DREAM TEAM—ESPECIALLY ERIN STEIN, CAMILLE KELLOGG, WESLIE TURNER, AND NATALIE C. SOUSA—ALL GENEROUS WITH THEIR CREATIVITY AND EXPERIENCE. WE ALSO WANT TO THANK THE FEIWEL & FRIENDS TEAM, INCLUDING EMILY SETTLE, CAROLYN BULL, SHARISMAR RODRIGUEZ, ELYNN COHEN, HAYLEY JOZWIAK, ARIK HARDIN, DAWN RYAN, BRITTANY PEARLMAN, KENYA BAKER, ALLEGRA GREEN, ANNE HEAUSLER, AND SO MANY MORE. FINALLY, A SPARKLY NOD TO ALL OF THE WEIRD SPOTS WHERE WE WORKED ON THESE BOOKS: MAKESHIFT HOME OFFICES, THE FAMILY MINIVAN, VARIOUS COFFEE SHOPS AND PICNIC TABLES IN DIFFERENT B.C. CITIES AND TOWNS, OUR FRIENDS' CABIN (THANK YOU, KAREN AND DR. PAUL), AND LOCAL KELOWNA HAUNTS LIKE SPROUT, BRIGHT JENNY COFFEE, AND THE INNOVATION CENTRE ROOFTOP. THANKS FOR PROVIDING US SPACE TO CREATE.

ABOUT THE AUTHOR & ILLUSTRATOR

DEANNA KENT AND ***NEIL HOOSON*** HAVE WORKED ON BOOKS, BRAND AND MARKETING CAMPAIGNS, AND INTERACTIVE EXPERIENCES. DEANNA LOVES TWINKLE STRING LIGHTS, BLACK LICORICE, AND EDNA MODE, AND SHE MAY BE THE ONLY PERSON ON THE PLANET WHO SAYS "TEAMWORK MAKES THE DREAM WORK" WITHOUT A HINT OF SARCASM. NEIL IS KING OF A LES PAUL GUITAR, MAKES KILLER ENCHILADAS, AND REALLY WANTS ALIENS TO LAND IN HIS BACKYARD. BY FAR, THEIR GREATEST CREATIVE CHALLENGE IS RAISING FOUR (VERY BUSY, VERY AMAZING) BOYS. GLAM PRIX RACERS IS THEIR FIRST GRAPHIC NOVEL SERIES.

DON'T MISS THE FIRST TWO GLAM PRIX RACES!
GLAM PRIX RACERS
WRITTEN BY DEANNA KENT
ILLUSTRATED BY NEIL HOOSON
GLAM PRIX RACERS
BACK ON TRACK!
WRITTEN BY DEANNA KENT
ILLUSTRATED BY NEIL HOOSON

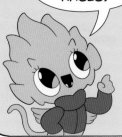

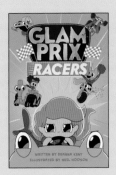

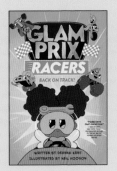